William Wells and Maconaquah White Rose of the Miamis

William Wells and

Maconaquah

White Rose of the Miamis

Julia Gilman

Jewel Publishing, Cincinnati, Ohio

Williams Wells and
Maconaquah, White Rose of the Miamis
A Historical Novel by Julia Gilman

Published by:
Jewel Publishing
165 Congress Run Road
Cincinnati, Ohio 45215, U.S.A.

First Printing 1985
Printed in the United States of America
Library of Congress Catalog Card Number: 85-60341
ISBN: 0-9614890-2-2

Second Printing 1992

Contents

Acknowledgments

This book is a work of fiction only by the words I placed in the mouths of people who really lived. I used actual letters and drafts of speeches wherever possible. I followed William Wells and Frances Slocum through the history books and have written their stories as accurately as I can, at the same time adding detail, through research, to make it interesting.

At the Filson Club in Louisville, Kentucky, there is a file filled with letters from people who have tried to learn the complete story of William Wells. I feel privileged to have lived in the right spot, for a few years, to fully research the life story of this fascinating man, and to perhaps set history right in his behalf.

My husband has been a corporation man throughout our marriage. We lived in all the cities included in the story, with the exception of Fort Wayne, Indiana. They are Pittsburgh, Pa; Cincinnati, Ohio; Louisville, Kentucky, Milwaukee, Wisconsin, and Muncie, Indiana.

As a child, I lived all over the state of Indiana. My parents owned a farm in Kosciusko County, near Fort Wayne. I was born and graduated from high school in Logansport, Indiana, but went to school in eight different schools over the state of Indiana, from top to bottom, and side to side, due to the vagaries of the school teaching profession. My parents both were teachers. Because of my summers living on a farm in Miami country, I know the names of trees, and other farm facts that I used in the story.

Northeast Indiana was the last part of the state to be settled, partly because the Indians owned it, and partly because its swampy, lake-filled terrain made it less favorable for farming. Because of this, it is wilder, or was when I was young, than other places. It was an area where it was fairly easy to visualize the days when hunting was a way of life for the Indians.

I had written freelance magazine articles for several years when we lived in Pittsburgh, Pa. Then James Michener brought out his book, Centennial, and I became obsessed with the idea of writing a similar book for the Midwest. However, the local libraries did not have books I needed to do midwestern historical research. About that time my husband was transferred to Louisville, Kentucky, just the right place to research this book.

The Louisville Filson Club, New Albany, Indiana, library's Indiana Room, and the Indiana University south Extension library had nearly everything I needed for the book. Thanks, all you backers of these libraries. Thanks also to Mr. Robert Whitsett of Logansport, Indiana, who has many years of research on the local Eel River Miami Indians to his credit, and who shared with me. Also, I'd like to thank Jo O'Rear, English teacher at Sellersburg, Indiana for her encouragement to continue this project when I was ready to quit.

My Mother, Ruth Snoke, and of course Ron Gilman, my husband, made this venture possible through their many ways of support. The cover photograph is by my daughter, Tamara S. Gilman. The picture was taken on the banks of the Eel River, across from the Eel River Miami village, Kenapacomaqua, raided by Wilkinson in 1791. The model in the picture is Sandra Davidson Shaw, who is part Shawnee.

Julia Gilman
Cincinnati, Ohio 1985

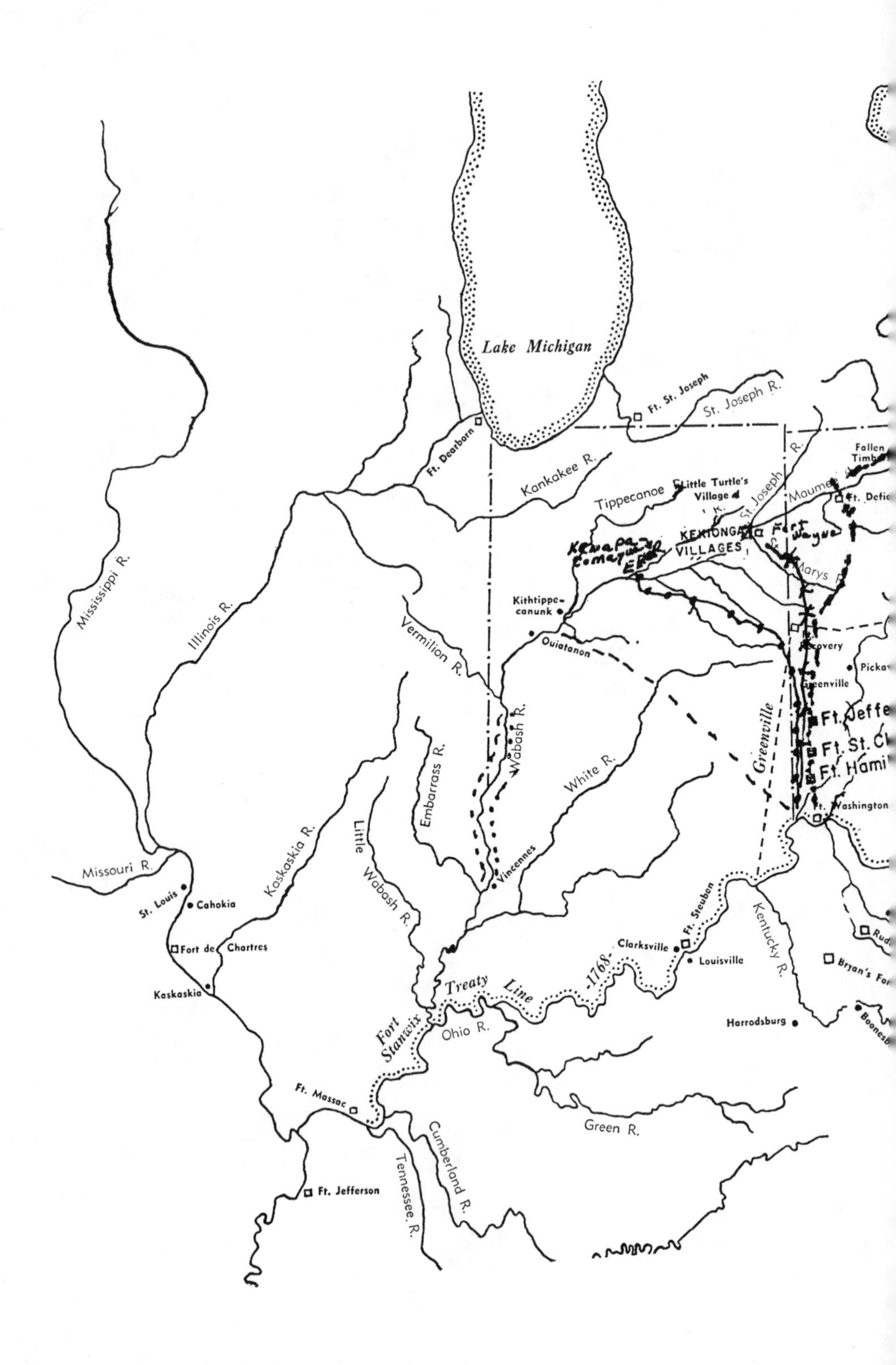

Lake Michigan
Ft. St. Joseph
St. Joseph R.
Ft. Dearborn
Kankakee R.
Tippecanoe
Little Turtle's Village
St. Joseph R.
Maumee
Fallen Timbers
KEKIONGA VILLAGES
Fort Wayne
Marys R.
Kithtippecanunk
Ouiatanon
Recovery
Greenville
Ft. Jefferson
Ft. St. Clair
Ft. Hamilton
Ft. Washington
Pickaway
Mississippi R.
Illinois R.
Vermilion R.
Wabash R.
Embarrass R.
White R.
Greenville
Missouri R.
St. Louis
Cahokia
Fort de Chartres
Kaskaskia
Kaskaskia R.
Little Wabash R.
Vincennes
Clarksville
Ft. Steuben
Louisville
Kentucky R.
Bryan's Fort
Harrodsburg
Treaty Line 1768
Fort Stanwix
Ohio R.
Ft. Massac
Green R.
Cumberland R.
Tennessee R.
Ft. Jefferson

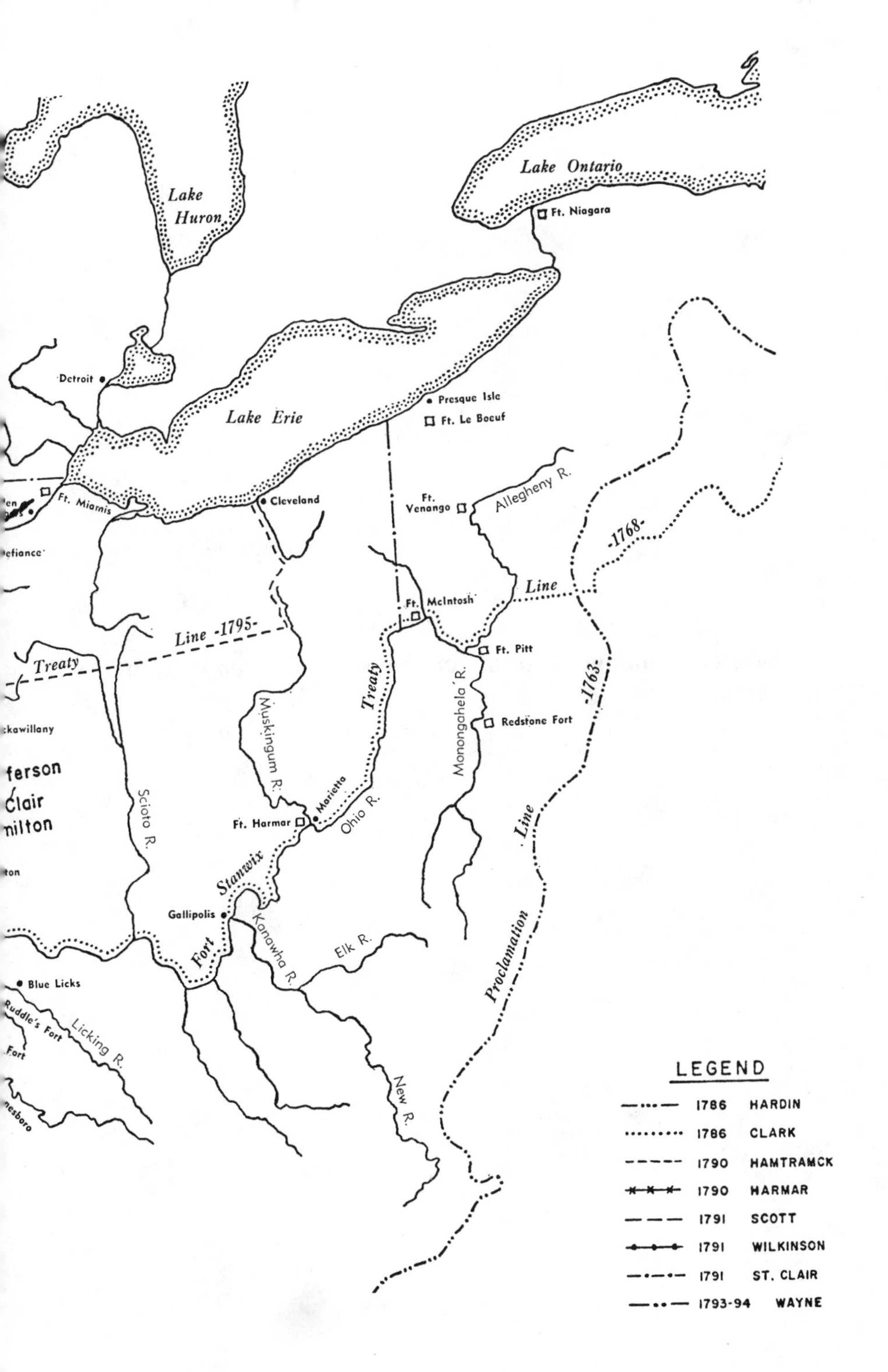

American campaigns against the Miami Confederacy, 1783–1794.

I am become a stranger unto my brethern and an alien unto my mother's children.

Psalms lxix-8

In the year of Frances Slocum's capture, the western frontier lay no further west than the middle of Pennsylvania. This was the point beyond which attack by Indians was inevitable. Adventurers and fur traders lived westward with their Indian squaws. But men of family and conscience did not venture far beyond the Susquehanna River. In fact it was risky indeed to settle and till the soil even here. For it was the frontier.

To the north lived the fierce Iroquois Indians known for their torture rituals. South were British Tories and to the east the Revolutionary War was underway. Life could end quickly and did for many settlers of Wilkes-Barre, Pennsylvania, the summer of 1778. Now, November, an uneasy calm rested over the country around the village.

The Susquehanna River made an easy route from New York and Canada for the Indians to strike the few remaining settlers that had stayed behind after the Indian and Tory massacre of the villagers during the previous summer. The Revolutionary war was well along and General Washington had no extra troops to spare for protection of the little wilderness settlement.

Chapter I

Wilkes-Barre, Pennsylvania, November 1778

Ruth Slocum carefully stirred the morning cornmeal mush. If you didn't pay attention it would lump. Through long experience with the process, her mind could wander as she slowly poured the cornmeal into the water while stirring with a long-handled spoon. The fire burning brightly on the hearth warmed her somewhat weatherbeaten face. Though she was a middle-aged woman and had indeed led a hard life, neighbor women often told her she looked young for her years. But the last one, had included many terrors. If she had owned a mirror, she would have known that a few new lines etched her face now, and before the year was finished, many more would be added.

It was five in the morning, a time of day that she liked best. Soon the children would have to get up and start morning chores. Still she had a few more minutes of quiet before the noisy throng of her offspring made thinking in the tiny cabin impossible. The starting of each new day in a normal way was just beginning to give her a sense of security. In the darkness and quiet of the early morning she daydreamed about the days of her youth when she still lived in the relatively safe East. Then if there were a moment of boredom, she had railed against it. She chuckled slightly as she thought that in her maturity she had learned to treasure moments of boredom, moments when no trouble or work threatened her ease.

Ever since the summer's massacre she'd imagined an Indian behind every tree each time she left the cabin for water. Each time she went to the garden or out to feed the animals there seemed a thousand of the murderous redskins in the shadows, waiting to strip the hair from her head before returning to the house to kill the work of her life, the children.

As time passed, there had been several more killings in more remote areas of lagging settlers who had not fled over the mountains, as the Slocums had not. But all along, Jonathan, her husband, had told her they were safe. There was no reason to worry. And in fact, it began to look as if it were true. As each fall day passed and winter neared, there was less and less chance of an Indian raid. Still, most of the neighbors had gone, and when Ruth had a moment to think about such things, and the moments were rare indeed, she wondered if they weren't making a mistake staying. But her many chores always stopped her in mid worry, and she had never really thought the problem through.

Looking up she saw the strong timbered door thump open as Jonathan entered the room with the milk bucket in one hand and an armload of wood in the other. He was rather short in stature but sturdily built. A curly blond beard hid a weak mouth and pale blue eyes often missed the true nature of a situation.

"Right smart cold this morning," he said as he glanced at his wife. The privacy of the moment brought a thought that it wouldn't be bad to be back in the warm bed. Ruth, though in her early forties, was a handsome woman, even after having ten children.

Ruth had other worries on her mind and no time for idling. A woman with as many children as she needed every second of time and ounce of strength just to get through the day. She was well aware of why the babies came and avoided the possibility of adding to her family whenever possible. But she wasn't too successful. The cradle near the fireplace filled with the newest Slocum, was testimony of that. Continuing with the consuming worry that never left her mind she said, "Jonathan, maybe we should sell the farm and leave. We could go back to Rhode Island and wait until the country is more civilized to come back here. All this killin'. A body never knows when you go to the out-back if you'll feel a tomahawk in your head on the way."

Jonathan frowned. "Now Ruth, the Indians won't be botherin' us. Haven't I been friends with those bucks who fish down on the Susquehanna? Anyway, my black Quaker hat will protect us. They know we don't believe in killin'."

"But so many been kilt. Over two hundred people. Just think on it! So many friends gone now. Those who ain't dead are goin' back to their old homes. The Thompsons went back to Connecticut last week. Maybe Paw and us should git while the gitten's good."

Jonathan, growing disgusted with the same old argument said, "Well, jest what would we live on? Nobody'd buy this place after the Indians kilt so many in Wilkes-Barre last summer. Anyway, the Indians are gone now and if they come back we kin go to the fort. Now I'm goin' to hitch up the horses. Tell Isaac to join me in the north forty after he gits his breakfast."

Jonathan left to begin the day's work and Ruth began setting wooden bowls and spoons out for the others. She turned as she heard a noise on the stairs. Her father, Isaac Tripp, was pulling up his suspenders. "Get the children up will you?" She said. "Breakfast's ready, but let Frances and the baby sleep awhile longer." The older man grunted returning up the stairs.

Giles, Ruth's oldest, came down with a quick step. At nineteen, he was thinking of finding a piece of property for his own. With ten children and his grandfather in the house, it was crowded and there was no privacy. He had done a sharp piece of work with the settlers in the fight last summer, narrowly escaping being killed himself. He'd hid in the river under rushes until the last of the Indians left the body-strewn field in front of the fort. In the mud of the Susquehanna he lost his childhood as he listened to the torture of a friend, captured by the Indians. Now he thought that the place for him might be General Washington's army.

Paw would have a fit, he thought. Last summer he almost threw me out when he found out I'd been with the defenders. "You'll have to leave the church," he'd railed. "We don't want no killers wearin' the broad-rimmed hat of the Quaker. You are a shame to me and the church!"

But how could a person be a man and stand by while neighbors were being killed? Giles had shouted back, "You don't give a damn about us. I'm not goin' to stand by while people are bein' killed. I'm different from you. I'm a man!" Since then tempers had cooled but there was still a strangeness between Giles and his father. Yes, it was time to make a life of his own. Taking a bowl of mush and sprinkling maple sugar on it he said, "Ma, I'm goin' over to the fort today."

Ruth was immediately on guard. "Why?"

"Some of the other fellers and me are thinkin' of joinin' up with General Washington. It's almost winter and you won't need me to work the fields. "'Sides, if I join the army, I'd get a land grant for a place of my own, when the war's over."

"You know what your father thinks of fightin', Giles. Still, it might be for the best. I won't tell him where you've gone 'til you decide for sure you're joinin'up."

"Jest tell him I took some corn to be ground today. I'll get it done while I'm at the fort."

Ruth returned to the many tasks of the pioneer wife necessary to run a large family. The baby was gotten up and dressed as was Frances, five, and Joseph, three. The other children had assigned chores themselves, so the morning fell into its usual routine.

The two Kingsley boys, neighbors whose father had gone to the war, and who were now staying with the Slocums, wanted to use the grinder to sharpen a knife. The older boy was wearing a soldier outfit which offered some diversion for the younger Slocum children.

Ruth enjoyed a moment of peace with everyone set to their morning endeavors. Chickens clucked, pursuing the remaining bugs not killed by the frost. Sun shone brightly on the Pennsylvania forest painted in brilliant fall colors from the frost. The riot of oranges and browns was enjoyed as one of the few things of beauty Ruth had. Even so, she gave a slight shiver as she thought of what usually happened at this time of year. It was one of the last good days before winter set in and Indians stayed by their campfires in their lodges. It was Indian summer.

They were taking a chance staying here in the Wyoming valley after the Indian massacre of over 200 men last summer. She knew that. But the land was so rich. The valley lay flat like a jewel along the Susquehanna River, hemmed in by mountains on the east and west. The 'Damn' Yankees of Connecticut had been struggling for possession of its rich soil for nearly twenty years. But they were constantly thwarted by the Delaware Indians from the north, who had previously owned the land, and now were forced to live with the Iroquois at Niagara Falls. The British Tories to the south, didn't like the independent Scotch-Irish moving in from Connecticut and other New England states. Yes, the settlers hold on the land was tenuous, and last summer, many had lost it, in death.

Thinking of how they'd so recently moved to Wilkes-Barre, Ruth could hardly stand the idea of moving again so soon. But her intuition told her they should. Jonathan Slocum first visited and bought the land seven years ago, in 1771, when he heard that the land was much richer than his farm in Rhode Island. He made periodic visits to the place, building a cabin and finally planting a corn crop before he and his family moved there in 1777. It was a terrible time to make the move. They were barely settled when Indians, led by a few Tories from Fort Niagara, descended on the settlers of the Wyoming valley, trying to regain their old lands.

But Jonathan Slocum felt confident that they'd be safe staying since he was a Quaker and friendly to Indians passing along the river. After all, they hadn't been harmed last summer. Anyway, if they left, they would have nothing and nowhere to go. Events were stabilized now with a few families living in the fort. Perhaps they would be safe staying.

Suddenly Ruth was roused from her revery as a shot rang out. Running to the door she was horrified to see three Indians coming toward the house. Her quick glance took in Nathan Kingsley lying on the ground by the grinder, blood running down the front of his soldier suit. Three Indians loped up and began cutting off his scalp.

Ruth was almost paralyzed with fright but collecting herself shouted, 'Indians! Everyone hide! Run, Mary! Take Joseph." Ruth grabbed the baby from the cradle and ran out the door with two children following quickly behind her. Fourteen-year-old Mary picked up Joseph and started for the fort. Mary was well on her way down the path when one of the Indians left his grisly task and made as if to follow her. Mary kept up her steady pace, head held high, with the child in her arms. The Indian laughed when the child started a kicking protest and decided to let her go.

The children remaining in the house had time to look for hiding places. As the Indians entered the house it was absolutely quiet. They moved stealthily among the rooms should there be other adults and found twelve-year-old Ebenezer.

"Help! Mother!" Ebenezer shrieked.

The Indian gripped his arm and dragged him downstairs to the kitchen. Ransacking the place, they poked into the cloth sacks of cornmeal on the wall, slung a bag over their shoulders and picked up some maple sugar pieces. After eating some mush from the pot in the fireplace, they were preparing to leave the house.

Little Frances, hiding under the stairway, had so far been unnoticed. It was a long time to be quiet but she'd practiced playing hide-and-seek with her brothers and sisters. Being only five, she thought that if she couldn't see the Indians, they couldn't see her. As she waited she got tired and straightened out her legs. Her bare feet, sticking out from under the stairs, were in plain view.

"Ha!" An Indian pulled her roughly from under the stairs. What a little beauty she was. Her skin was very white and she had auburn hair. A perfect captive.

Frances was not the type to howl and cry. This was one of the qualities which saved her life that moment. Her first glance at her captor was one of curiosity. He looked about the age of Giles and was very tan, with fierce brown eyes. His face was painted black with red stripes and he seemed to be having fun. These fleeting thoughts were quickly erased as the Indian tossed her over his shoulder and started down the path to the river. Suddenly alarm bells rang in her head. These were no friends. Her fear increasing, she wanted her Mother. Right now!

Another Indian was dragging the remaining Kingsley boy along, while the third pulled crippled Ebenezer, who stumbled because of his club foot. The boys' faces were ashen. They had the queer stricken look of those about to die. Little animal cries of fear escaped even as they tried to be silent. They knew what Indians did to people. Last summer they'd seen the battle ground with its broken bodies, each with the hair stripped from the head. A hideous example of what could instantly happen to them was Nathan, lying in a pool of blood by the grinder. His death twitches had stopped now, but the boys had seen the last of them.

Ruth, hiding in the bushes, couldn't stand just to sit by watching as part of her family was dragged away. Rushing from her hiding place, but staying a distance away, she shrieked, "Wait, wait! Don't take them!" Gesturing frantically and pointing at Ebenezer she said, "He can't walk. He's lame."

The Indian dragging Ebenezer looked at her questioningly. Ruth realized he didn't understand her. She nodded her head while pointing toward Ebenezer's feet. Suddenly, the Indian realized why Ebenezer was stumbling along and let him go. Being lame made him inferior material as a captive. He'd probably have to kill him later when he couldn't keep up. Ebenezer lost no time as he scrambled to his feet and hobbled into the bushes, out of sight.

The Indians turned, striding purposefully towards the river. Ruth saw they meant to keep Frances and Wareham Kingsley. Tears filled her eyes and a lump came to her throat. She stumbled toward them screaming, "No, no, no. Don't take my baby. Please God, no." One of the Indians turned, a menacing look on his face, and pointed his gun at her. Ruth shrank back falling into the dust of the path as she cried, "No, no, no."' She was a beaten woman. The worst fears of any mother were realized as her child was carried away. The Indians continued onward, knowing she would not follow.

Frances now knew what was happening. One hand held the beautiful red hair out of her eyes and she stretched the other toward her Mother as she was carried away. "Mama, Mama." She cried pitifully. "Mama, Mama." The sound echoed away into the woods until she could no longer be heard. This last view of Frances was to haunt Ruth through the remaining years of her life. But there was no time to stop and think. Quick action might still save the children.

Sharply she commanded, "Ebenezer, watch the baby. I'll go get the men in the field." Holding up her long skirts with one hand, Ruth ran down the path toward the north forty. Rocks cut at her feet, but she was a driven woman and ignored them. It seemed a much longer distance than usual. The woods were still dense along the sides of the fields. The thought that more Indians might have come and killed Jonathan and her father crossed her mind, but she didn't call out for them as she ran. What if more Indians were about to hear her? Then relief flooded over her as she heard the sound of the ax and the men came into view. They were working quite calmly cutting up firewood.

"Jonathan, Jonathan, Indians came and took Frances!" she shouted.

"God have mercy! Are they gone? How long've they been gone?" Ruth told him the details, and the men ran back up the trail to start searching for the children.

Meanwhile, Mary with her little brother reached the fort. After telling her story to the men living there, they immediately returned to the Slocum cabin with her. The space cleared in front of the small house held a group of milling people, uncertain of what to do. Crying mother and children, just now feeling the full strength of their reaction, huddled together. A concerned father and grandfather talked with neighbors who had recently seen the immense slaughter during the attack on the village that summer. It was all starting up again they said. It would be risky to go far into the forest with Indians on the warpath. They could be ambushed at any turn of the path.

A search party was organized. "Everybody stay in groups of at least five," ordered Jonathan. "Those Indians could be behind any tree ready to ambush us."

The obvious place for the Indians to escape was the river. The Susquehanna River snaked its way toward Canada, the British stronghold and headquarters for Indians who remained near the eastern seaboard. The British used the Indians whenever possible in this war against the colonists. Though difficult to control and work with, they were ferocious warriors in battle and made up for the lack of numbers and enthusiasm of the British soldiers.

When the Slocums reached the river banks, there was no sign of canoes. Parties were dispatched to follow the river and go along the paths through the woods. But as evening approached, all gathered together admitting failure of finding any trace of the children or Indians. Evening chores had to be done. There were cows to be milked, fires tended and food cooked.

Ruth tiredly worked, her eyes straying repeatedly to the new pair of shoes on the shelf that had been made for Frances just a few weeks before in anticipation of winter. If only she had her shoes, her poor little feet wouldn't get so sore and cold. The family moved in a daze. Nine children circulated in the small house but the absence of Frances made a void that could not be filled by the others.

As Ruth lay on her bed that night, a vision of her lost child came to her. She saw her feet, raw with frostbite, and she had no blanket to cover her. "Mama, Mama, where are you? I'm cold and so hungry. The owls are calling and I'm afraid. Mama, come and get me." Her little Frances; only five. How could she stand the hardships of living with the Indians, out in the cold November air, sleeping on the ground with no blankets? Frances cried all the harder, "Mama, Mama," holding out her hands towards Ruth. The Indian slapped her and raised his tomahawk. Then a scream pierced the quiet of the cabin bedroom.

"Ruth, wake up. You're dreamin'."

Ruth shuddered, still not quite awake. "Frances was being killed."

"It's only a dream. We'll look for her again tomorrow. Now go back to sleep."

Chapter II

Sullivan's Campaign, Summer 1779

The Delaware Indian, Grey Fox, had killed a rabbit which he roasted on the fire in the mouth of the cave. It had been an exciting and fruitful day. They had two captives which would be traded and a scalp that should bring a bounty. With his knife he divided the rabbit for his two companions and the white girl and boy captives. The children were very tired and quietly rested near the fire. Peconga and Waucoon returned from their lookout for the meal.

"No one comes," observed Peconga.

"It was a good raid today. We have good trades there." Grey Fox gestured toward the children with a rabbit leg. "I have friends who are in need of a young child. They will pay much for the girl."

"No, it was a bad raid. The false black hat was not home. He must be taught a lesson for letting his son kill Indians while he wears the black hat." Waucoon had lost a brother in the summer raids at Wilkes-Barre and was festering with grief and rage. "He will pay I tell you."

"The soldiers will be looking everywhere for us now. We can't go back to get the black hat this winter." Peconga said, ever the practical one. The three young friends had not come from the same village. Only this summer they had gone to Fort Niagara to fight with the British against the colonists. On their trip south the three had become fast friends. All were about the same age and belonged to the Delaware Nation. As in a marriage their various personality traits complimented and offset each other.

"It's the time of year to go home and sit before the long fires of winter," Grey Fox agreed. He didn't want to add that he was bored with fighting and now would pursue romantic interests.

Waucoon would not swerve from his dreams of revenge for the death of his brother. "The black hat must have been in the fields. Next time we will go there instead of the house."

Grey Fox took the rifle out and started loading it again. "I'm not going back. At least not before spring. Let's divide our captures and go our separate ways. We can go hunting together again next year."

Waucoon returned in a surly manner, "There are others who will go with me to gain revenge if you will not. I will not stop for the snows of winter. I will never stop until my brother is revenged."

Peconga was afraid Waucoon would work himself into another frenzy and kill their valuable captives. It would be wise to have a division of property now before some of it was lost. "I too would join my people for the winter. Grey Fox will take the girl as he has a buyer. I will take the boy and you can take the scalp which will not hinder you in your movements. You can trade it at the fort when you have finished getting your revenge.

"How will we travel? We have only the one canoe."

"We will go up to my village, Tioga. Waucoon can get others to go with him there if he wants. You can trade for a horse and travel overland to your village near Fort Niagara," Peconga reasoned for them all.

"That is a good plan. While we are traveling the soldiers will stop looking for us, and I will come upon the black hat later when he is not expecting it." Waucoon's brown eyes glinted with a light that was unnerving even to his red brothers. The anger he felt was a consuming thing, fed by the sight of the white man's riches he had seen at the house.

Quakers and Indians had been friends ever since William Penn and his followers had treated them kindly. Now Waucoon felt doubly betrayed that a Quaker allowed his son to kill Indians, especially after the man, Slocum, had been friendly to him and his brother. Waucoon was just another link in the chain started since the first shot was fired on Indians by the white man. Neither side would stop its relentless quest for revenge until one side had destroyed the other.

Agreeing on their plan, the Indians moved the captives into the cave and all retired for a relatively comfortable night's rest.

The dense forests of western New York were populated by villages of Seneca and other tribes of the Iroquois Nation in the year 1778. Few white settlers lived beyond the land adjacent to the British Fort Niagara. In point of fact, the land was technically owned by the Indians...not open for settlement.

It was toward this center of Indian activity that Grey Fox headed after leaving Peconga and Waucoon at Peconga's village, Tioga, on the Susquehanna. He and his captive, the little red-haired girl, traveled overland until they reached the Niagara River. Here they rejoined Grey Fox's people of the Delaware Tribe. The Iroquois only tolerated these people, whom they felt were stupid, because the Delaware allowed themselves to be forced from their home in the Wyoming valley.

Shouts of excitement went up from the village at Grey Fox's approach. Among the welcomers was a girl of sixteen, who was unmarried and admired Grey Fox. She viewed him as a mature proven warrior, victorious in the battle that summer at Wyoming valley. Her name was Red Leaf.

"You have been gone many moons, Grey Fox. You have been missed."

Grey Fox watched the captive, Frances, who was walking around nearby, followed by a curious group of Indian children who handled her hair and touched her skin to see how she was different from them. Indian moccasins covered her feet and she wore a blanket as a coat. These Grey Fox had traded for in Peconga's village. Her face was painted and her hair was dressed in a club, Indian style. She wore a string of wampum, and Frances felt herself quite beautiful. She had learned on the trip north that Grey Fox was impatient but not fearsome, so she was not afraid now in this strange Indian village. Near a lodge a woman cooked stew over a fire. The woman gave Frances a wooden bowl full of the food and she sat on a piece of firewood to eat it.

Grey Fox saw that his very young captive was not ready to run away and he turned his attention to the comely Red Leaf. Indeed, he was getting very tired of being a baby-sitter. On the long trip north it had seemed as if they stopped every fifteen minutes for the girl to make trips behind a bush. She was always hungry or thirsty. At times, if it hadn't been for the thought of the reward, he would have left her in the forest.

He said, "I have been on a long canoe trip to the south. All the way down the Susquehanna River. As you can see, I did not come away empty handed. The captive should bring a good price."

"Perhaps now you will be able to take a woman of your own. There is probably room for you and your new wife in my father's lodge." At sixteen Red Leaf was not without a certain subtlety. "The old Miami couple will be pleased to take the red-haired captive as their daughter."

"In which lodge do they live? I will be only too happy to find another caretaker for the squaw child."

Red Leaf pointed to a lodge on the far side of the clearing. Then, returning to a subject in which she had more interest, said, "I could speak to my mother and she could decide with your mother who might be a good woman for you."

"Red Leaf, you know they would not arrange for you to marry me. We are both of the Wolf clan so it would not be allowed."

"But your father was of the Bear clan and my father of the Turtle clan so where would be the harm?"

"It makes no difference about our fathers. Delaware tradition is that those whose mothers belong to the same clan may not marry, and our mothers are both of the Wolf clan. Your mother will probably arrange for you to marry a fine warrior whom you have never met and you will have many children and live many summers." As Grey Fox said these very true words they somehow made him sad. Because of this he left Red Leaf to find the buyers of the result of his long and tiring trip North with the red-haired girl. He crossed the clearing to the lodge in which the older Miami couple lived.

The Senecas of the Iroquois nation, with whom these Delaware were living since they were pushed north from Wyoming by the whites, had unusual bark houses, built fifty or sixty feet long and about fifteen or eighteen feet wide called long houses. No nails or pegs were used in framing. The frame poles were lashed together and carefully braced. Wide pieces of bark were lashed to the sides and roof. Holes were left in the roof at intervals in the hopeful idea that the smoke from cooking fires below would escape. Sometimes there were as many as thirteen or fourteen fires and corresponding holes to a house. But the smoke did not always go out.

The house was divided rather like an apartment house. The longhouses had an aisle down through the center and platforms were built on each side of the aisle where people could sleep, feet to the aisle. Some groups had double decker beds. People living in this arrangement had absolutely no privacy and the smells, smoke and other, were overpowering.

Grey Fox had met the Miami couple, who had traveled up the Maumee River from their home at Kekionga, now Fort Wayne, Indiana, before he left on the warpath that summer. They placed him on a sort of commission to get a captive child because they were now old and childless. The brave, Strong Bear, was a Delaware and enjoyed visiting his Delaware relatives, but having married a Miami woman, he was considered a Miami. The Iroquois and Delaware believed in matrimonial descent.

Strong Bear came to greet Grey Fox, leading him away from the noise and smells of the heavily populated lodge. "We are very glad to see you again. Were your travels fruitful?"

"I traveled many miles, enjoyed seeing new lands, and had many adventures. I return a warrior. Last summer the English and the warriors of many tribes fell upon white men at a place called the Wyoming Valley, old home of Delaware on the Susquehanna River. We killed many of the white men. I killed three myself. I now have friends from many other tribes and other clans. Two friends and I enjoyed many days of hunting together. One of my trophies I brought back for you." Grey Fox was proud of himself. In no time at all, he thought, he would be a great speaker like some of the chiefs.

"Is this trophy you speak of a child for my squaw and me?"

"Yes, a girl child of about five. She is very good and very little trouble," he lied. "She has perfect health and no flaws of bone. She is worth a high price."

Strong Bear raised his eyebrows. "I would see the child before I offered a trade for her. Go get her and I will call Meshinga to look at her."

Grey Fox soon found Frances watching several other toddlers who were making a village in the dirt with stones and sticks. "Come meet your new father," he said in the Delaware language.

Returning with his charge to the old couple, he watched Meshinga's face as he presented the child. As head of the household she would be the one to make the decision concerning the family. Meshinga was considered an old woman at forty five. She was not impulsive, but she had wanted a child for so long since her own daughter had died that it was difficult to maintain a severe expression so the trading position could be maintained. Lifting the child's dress, she looked at her arms and legs to see how plump and healthy she was. Frowning she rebuked Grey Fox, "You have not kept this child clean, though she looks to have had enough to eat." Musingly she said to herself, "The hair is the color of a rose, like the wild roses of the summer forest. The skin is like the white petals, edged with pink. Yes, she is a white rose." Smiling fondly at her husband she said, "I will call her Maconaquah, Little Bear Woman, after you."

"I will give you twenty hides for her," stated Strong Bear.

"I will need many blankets and kettles as I will soon have my own woman. Twenty-five beaver," countered Grey Fox.

Strong Bear realizing he had no position for bargaining after his wife's words said, "I will give you the necessary pelts to trade for these things.

But I warn you, let no white men know of this child as we mean to keep the white rose. She will be as our own blood. If white men or Indians come to steal her, I will treat it the same as if they took my only daughter."

"It is agreed," answered Grey Fox. He decided he should make a hasty retreat before they learned what trouble a five-year-old could be. "May you and your family enjoy many summers," and he left them to find Red Leaf to discuss his new wealth.

The grey December day began as usual for the Slocums. Mornings were cold, with frost warning of snows to come. But by noon, it was quite warm. Crops were in so farmers could turn to more leisurely pursuits of clearing land and cutting wood. Ruth Slocum busied herself spinning wool and knitting whenever a free hour was at hand. Christmas was coming. New stockings would make a fine, much-needed gift for the children. Unfortunately there was no time to dye the wool in lovely colors with natural dyes. With Mary's help she'd just get one pair knitted for everyone.

Thinking ahead to the day itself, she decided that a turkey, sweet potatoes, and mincemeat pies would do for the meal. Course, there'd have to be several other meats served as side dishes, as well as bread and milk. Maybe she could trade some eggs for apples to make pies. They'd planted a few trees but it would be years before they had apples of their own. Sitting at the spinning wheel was pleasant, giving her the opportunity to think as her hands worked automatically.

This year there'd be a sadness in the day. Usually because of a baby in the family, Christmas had special meaning. But with Frances gone, stolen and maybe dead, it wouldn't be the same. Wondering what it would be like to be in an Indian village at Christmas, Ruth thought, she probably won't even remember what day it is. If only....no! I won't think about her all the time. There are the others here still to think of. A tear slipped down her face, even as her fingers worked. Fine brave words they were, and truly meant. But the one lost child just couldn't be forgotten.

Far back of the house, Jonathan and his father-in-law were still working to clear a field. Today they and the second eldest, William, began cutting up the wood of a tree felled earlier in the year. The wood, somewhat dry now, would make tolerable firewood. They worked in only light shirts, no coats needed as sweat poured off them, even in the cool air.

A mule hitched to a small cart grazed on all grass blades he could find still unfrosted. Here in the valley the days were warmer than would be expected somewhere unprotected by the mountains on either side. The grand view of mountains in the distance went unappreciated by the trio. They were more interested in what moved in a view than the view itself, though they'd relaxed their vigilance now. Everyone knew Indians did not attack in winter.

William was a troublesome boy. The process of becoming a mature man was sorely trying for him and everyone around him. He couldn't seem to keep himself from teasing his parents or brothers and sisters until they gave him a well earned slap. Hoping for a moment of rest from the chore at hand he said, "Do you think General Washington will send troops after the Indians soon?"

The ruse worked as his father stopped sawing with the cross-cut saw to jaw awhile. "I jest don't know, son. They say Congress collected a million dollars to send them last summer before so many of our people was kilt, but nothin' come of it. After the fact, they must've decided it was a waste of money. Mr. Washington has his hands full fightin' the British, I guess, and can't be bothered with us."

"I'd sure like to go along with 'em if they's a group goes after 'em," William continued.

His father scowled, pointing a finger at him. "You got no business galavantin' off with all this work to be done here. 'Sides, you're too young."

Jonathan showed definite signs of taking up the saw again.William rushed on, hoping for a little more time away from the job. "Ma jest don't seem to stop carryin' on about Frances. With all us around you'd think she'd get over it quick. The baby to tend to and all. But she's always goin' on about Frances not havin' her shoes. Almost like she was goin' crazy."

"Shush your mouth, boy. We been mighty lucky. Most folk 'round here lost everythin' when the Injuns came." Forgetting his antagonizer as he remembered the scenes from the summer's massacre, he repeated to no one, "Everything." After a silent moment he came back to the present. "But our Giles came back without a scratch. You ain't got the brains to be so lucky."

William was not one to be squelched by such talk. "I heard tell of one widow that went back to Connecticut that fed her dead baby to the other younguns to keep them alive on the trail." He smiled to himself, enjoying the gruesome tale.

Jonathan straightened up, exasperated again by the boy. "Don't you be tellin' your Ma about that. She's bad enough off thinkin' what's happinin' to Frances without imaginin' things like that." He began sawing furiously. "You load the cart and take that load on up to the house, and don't let's have any more loose talk."

William picked up split logs and walked toward the cart. As he bent to place them in the wagon two shots rang out and a crease formed on the log he was holding. He jerked his eyes in the direction from which the shot came. On the edge of the field two Indians were reloading their guns. Glancing back, he saw his grandfather draped crazily over the log he had been chopping. William saw his father moving toward his gun propped against a tree. The Indians were ready to fire again. William turned and ran as fast as he ever had in his life, running across the small open space of the field until he reached the forest on the other side.

Again two shots rang out. A sharp pain came from his heel and he realized he had been shot. He ran all the faster never looking back. After awhile he knew he was not being followed, but he kept on jogging swiftly all the way to the fort, never doubting for a moment that his father was back there in the field, lying on the ground, without his scalp.

Jonathan Slocum and Isaac Tripp were buried by the remaining Slocum family who took the news with stoic patience. It did not seem surprising that this had happened. So many of the neighbors had lost their own fathers that there was little sympathy from them. Ruth, a strong pioneer woman, knew this was a usual end for a pioneer man. Not too many died of old age. Now she had to reassess her family goals so she brought the older of the nine remaining children together for a talk.

"Children, we have to decide what we'll do now, with our men gone. We could go back to Rhode Island, but we'd be very poor. We'd have nothin' at all."

Giles spoke up, "The land is rich, Ma. If we could jest stay on here, we'd all have plenty in the years ahead. We have a good start with the land cleared. I'm a man now and I can farm. William will help when his foot heals," Giles continued. "I will go to General Washington and make him see we have ta have some protection from the Indians and then we'll be all right."

Ebenezer chimed in, "He's right, Ma. We can do it. I'll milk the cow and work the garden."

"I think you're right. It's winter now and we can do without you Giles while you go to General Washington." Ruth's eyes strayed to the shelf where Frances' shoes still rested. "Besides, we can't leave little Frances here all alone if she should come back. She couldn't find us...her so little." The decision reached, Ruth got up and went to find the family bible to enter the names of the newly dead.

The following summer a July sun beat down relentlessly sending waves of heat into the boy's bare feet buried in the dirt. A row of corn stretched endlessly ahead, weeds needing to be hoed out waving tauntingly at William. He wiped the sweat from his face and then swiped listlessly at a deer fly that was buzzing around his head. Sure is temptin' to go swimmin', he thought. All them soldiers, jest sittin' there by the river, enjoyin' life fishin' or playin' fives. Looking at his hoe with dislike he thought, if I took off around the end of the farm, Ma'd never know I left. His conscience never had a chance. He quickly dropped the hoe and slipped away toward the Susquehanna River for the companionship of the gathered soldiers, boys of his own age.

Along the plain beside the river William could see the bush huts of the soldiers opposite the town. There were cooking fires where some were making dinner. Others sat talking in groups or playing in the handball like game called fives. Joining a group at the swimming hole he pulled off his clothes and dove into the cool clear water.

"Hey, Willy, how's about playin' Shiny or Fives?" A youth sitting on the bank addressed William, his recently found friend.

"Soon's I git some of this here sweat off me," William returned.

Jacob Roberts was a regular in Washington's army, but was assigned to this raid on the Indians under General Sullivan. He sat whittling a bowl while he waited for William to swim. Soon William stood dripping before him. William asked idly, "How long does General Sullivan think it will be before he gits all the supplies and you go after them Indians?"

"Who knows? Maybe a month. They say Sullivan and General Washington are at each other's throats, what with Washington wantin' Sullivan to take off now for up north. Travel light and do with less, I guess he said. Course Sullivan, bein' such a stickler for detail won't have none of it. You can bet we won't be movin' until there's plenty of shoeleather and beef for every man."

"Sounds right to me," William said knowingly. "You can't be too careful when fightin' them Indians. I know. I've got enough experience with 'em, Lord knows."

"You were here when the Injuns swooped down and kilt all them men weren't you?"

"Heck, I was almost kilt myself. See this scar on my foot? My Pa and Grandpa was kilt and they jest missed me. Sure wisht I could have a crack at 'em."

"Why don't you go north with us? You wouldn't have to be a regular soldier, jest go along on this raid. Then when the rest of us go back to fightin' the British, why, you kin go back to hoein' corn." Jacob laughed loudly.

William didn't want to go into the details of being a Quaker which meant no fighting so he changed the subject. "How's General Washington goin' to make it without a third of his army? We get a little news along, and it says he's in a right rough fight."

"He don't like it a little bit. That's why he keeps pushin' Sullivan to hurry up on this raid to get revenge on those Injuns, so's he'll have us all back for fightin' the Red Coats. We wouldn't be here at all if the settlers hadn't raised such a shout after the Injuns kilt them people. Not that it ain't nice to be here. Hell, I can use the vacation." Then he lowered his voice and said, "They was several young ladies that come last night to cheer up us poor soldier boys. You're really missin' out, Willy, stuck at home on that farm. "

William's mouth drooped at the corners. Since his father's death, he and Giles were required to do a man's work of being responsible for the family. But it was hard. With the army here waiting for the supplies before going into New York against the Indians, a carnival atmosphere pervaded the town. Townsfolk constantly entertained the men who they saw as saviors. William saw clearly that he was missing out on the excitement. "Not everybody thinks the army's such a good place to be," he retorted. "Like them German's that's sentenced to be shot for desertion."

"Hell, man, they won't be shot. They was jest ready to go back home to Lancaster for to work in their fields. They don't believe in settin' on their hands or in joinin' in on all the entertainments, so, they jest said their enlistment was up an' off they went. They even had a drummer and a fife to lead them. Don't that beat all?" Jacob shook his head. "Course we had ta go bring 'em back. Sullivan said five would hang, but we know he'll let 'em off in the end."

"I got to get back home 'fore Ma knows I'm gone." William looked sadly at the nearly one thousand men, all having the time of their life, it seemed to him.

"They're havin' a dance tonight in town. Think you could get away for it?"

"I'll see." William walked slowly home, knowing life was passing him by. Others were having all the fun.

The army gathered slowly at Wilkes Barre all June and July and waited while supplies were collected and shipped up the Susquehanna. Finally at the end of July, more than a hundred boats appeared on the Susquehanna, loaded with cannon, flour, and clothing. Farewell speeches were made saying goodby to the town that had entertained them so well. Then a brass band was loaded on some of the hundred and twenty river boats. It blared a march as the columns of men stepped northward. Loaded on the boats in the center of the river were ten cannon and two howitzers. Behind the men marching on the banks, herds of twelve hundred pack horses and eight hundred cattle moved slowly, prodded by the drivers who shouted and cursed in the dust behind them. All Sullivan's planning would pay off now as the army strode off on its mission of revenge.

Ruth Slocum was finishing up the last chores of the day. Supper was ready and the boys were in from the fields washing up. All except William. It wasn't like William to be late. Usually he was the first one in.

"Giles, was William on his way up when you stopped splittin' fence rails?"

"I ain't seen him since dinner time. He said somethin' about lookin' at the cattle in the pasture."

Ruth felt a touch of fear. It had been such a short time since Jonathan and her father were killed. Her voice rose as she called, "Ebenezer."

Ebenezer came inside as fast as his lame leg would allow. "Yeah Ma?"

"When was the last time you saw Willy?"

"Oh,I remember. At dinner he said to be sure ta look on the ledge above the door for a surprise at supper time." All eyes turned to look at the log above the door that made a natural shelf. One of the children's slates was propped up in plain view. Giles leaped forward to retrieve it. It said, "Gone to look for Frances, Willy."

Ruth sat down with a thump. He'd gone with the army of course. Her mind tried to sort through all the reasons he should not have gone, trying to come up with a logical good result. She finally said in resignation, "God go with him. Now, let's get some of those victuals et before they get cold."

At the same moment ten miles up the Susquehanna, William sat by his friend, Jacob, while Jacob wrote in his diary about the day's events. "What you sayin' there?" he asked as he peered over his shoulder while Jacob wrote with a quill.

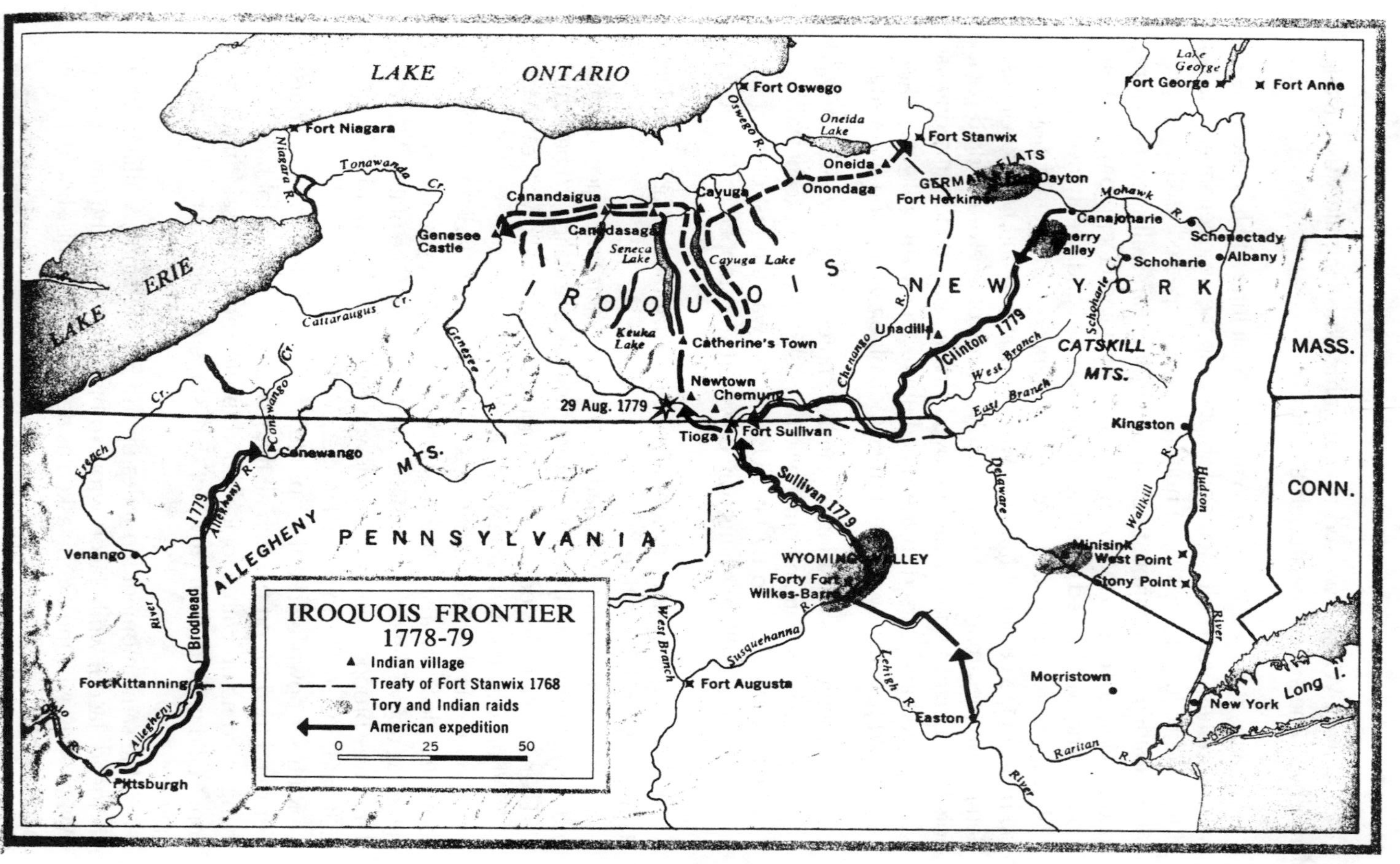

American Heritage Publishing Co., Inc.

"Jest markin' down this spot so's after I git out of the army I kin come back here. This land is mighty grand. See, I got it all wrote down." William read:

> 'the Land is the best that Ever I see...Timmothy as high as my head... the Warter is but poor, the Wild turkes very plenty the young ones yelping through te Woods as if it was inhabited Ever So thick.'

"It is a grand land," he agreed. "It's jest too bad we cain't shoot some of them gobblers, lest the Indians hear. Hey, maybe we should try ketchin' them by hand."

"By George Washington, you got somethin' there! Let's try 'er." The two young men shushed one another as they tiptoed into the forest. Soon others joined them. Stealthily they stalked a turkey. Those around the campfires suddenly heard a great squawking and gobbling in the forest. This was followed by a crash and much laughing by the participants of the hand turkey hunt.

After a lengthy period of crashing in the forest, hushed laughing and furious gobbling of the turkey, Sergeant Hanly decided to enforce some discipline. Walking manfully into the forest he said, "Boys, there'll be no more of that. Every Injun within five miles knows exactly where you're at with all that racket."

Jacob Roberts came out from behind a tree, a grin on his face, while he struggled to look repentant. "But Sergeant, we was jest hungry." He brought his hand from behind his back, holding up a half strangled turkey. The turkey struggled, wildly flapping its wings, while the others laughed uproariously, delighted with the comedy.

August, the best time of year for a little vacation. They would enjoy it to the fullest. As days passed, the trail along the river became difficult. Mountains or high hills had to be climbed along the river banks. At times pack horses slipped, falling into the river. Then men arduously climbed down the slippery banks to fish out goods, and the horse if it's legs were intact. The country was unbroken wilderness; waterfalls cascading over high cliffs into basins in shaded valleys silenced them with their beauty, and walnut trees four feet thick amazed them. Hazelnuts and little Indian apples made handy snacking along the northern reaches of Pennsylvania and then into New York.

Not everyone was enjoying the trip. Temperatures rising into the nineties helped cause two to die of fatigue. A young drummer boy slipped off one of the boats and drowned. But generally, the trip was extremely pleasant. Upon reaching the Tioga River, rushing current was a serious problem as the water came up to their armpits. But they laughed, holding hands as they crossed, while men on horseback tried to help. All made it across and they advanced onward toward the Indian village of Tioga.

A great plane surrounded the town, filled with tall grass, corn fields, and many fruit trees. Seems a shame to burn it all up, thought William. He saw some men digging up Indian burials in hopes of finding treasure. A pleasant breeze cooled his face while fleecy clouds sailed overhead. The beauty of the land made the act of cutting corn and fruit trees while burning huts and defiling graves seem all the more gross.

In the distance William heard General Sullivan upbraiding some troops. Sullivan had hoped to surprise the town and so was angry with the men who armed themselves with pumpkins and melons instead of guns. He sure is a fool, thought William, if he thinks this great army of men passin' through the forest kin be kept a secret. Our scouts know Indian spies are fallin' back jest a mile ahead of us as we move.

That night a detachment of the army moved to surprise a village called Chemung. The next morning they attacked. The Indians left so quickly that fires still burned and a dog slept. Here over fifty good log houses of split timber stood. Some even had glass windows. Indian homes and farms better than their own were put to the torch and the men hated doing it.

General Hand stood watching the men run from house to house setting each afire. On a hillside above the reflection of sunlight bouncing off metal caught his attention. Staring at the hill he commanded, "Captain Carberry, I want you to take a detachment of men up after those Indians on yonder hill."

Twenty-six men marched toward the forested hillside, glad to be seeing some action against the Indians at last. Later nineteen of the company struggled back, dragging their wounded. "We were ambushed," Carbarry stated lamely when confronted by his commander. He was wounded and carried by two men.

"How many were killed?"

"Seven didn't make it back. I guess we must presume them dead," Carbarry said stiffly.

General Hand kicked at the dirt, looking at the rolling wooded hills. "They sat there watchin' us. Watchin' us burn their houses." He was silent thinking about the scene of desolation as it must have appeared to the Indians, vowing not to underestimate them again.

The next day the entire army moved forward and came upon the ambush site. In a dark circle surrounded by towering trees the seven captured men were tortured before being killed. The soldiers crowded around, amazed at the sight of the bodies scarcely recognizable as once being men. Fingernails were torn off and eyes gouged out. Some were used as targets for tomahawk throwing. William couldn't stand the sight of two men who had their stomachs cut open before they were killed. His own stomach heaved at the gore. Their intestines were pinned to a tree and then they were driven around and around it until the tree was ringed with the viscera. There they lay before the grisley decorated tree, beheaded, blood covering everything.

William shrank back from the scene, as a terrible taste filled his mouth. His mind usually shucked off unpleasantness, just like water off a duck's back. But this was too awful. It brought back memories of his father and grandfather's deaths, and of himself running for his life. He left as quickly as he could, passing through the hundreds of soldiers until he found a quiet spot where he could privately throw up. This was no picnic he'd joined. After all, there could be any number of Indians, just waiting to kill him, but not until they'd removed his skin, piece by piece.

"Are you feelin' all right?" Jacob offered a tin cup of water to his friend.

"I guess so." William looked wildly at the forest. "I swear though, if I kin get out of this alive, I'll never complain about hoeing again."

During the following month General Clinton of New York joined Sullivan's army making a total of almost 5000 men, all dedicated to the destruction of the food supply of the Iroquois. The land was exquisite. Fields of corn, pumpkins, beans and squash were at the peak of harvest. Everyone was amazed that such land was here when their land was so poor back in New Jersey or New Hampshire. They filed away the information so that they could later return with families to farm it.

Near what would be Elmira, New York, the Indian chief, Joseph Brandt, made a stand behind an earthen brestworks on top of a wooded ridge. His little Indian army included English Tories. After Sullivan's scouts spotted the ambush the army had a chance to make a planned attack. Now all Sullivan's planning paid off. The soldiers had dragged the heavy artillery through the forest, cursing them at every step. But the six-pounders and howitzers were very effective weapons against the Indians, who had never seen what they could do. The bursting shot that landed behind their position led them to believe they were surrounded. As cannon and guns flamed and boomed, they thought the gates of hell had opened. Indians dropped in their positions as if by magic, and the others panicked and fled. The Battle of Newtown was won with the loss of only three Americans while enemy losses were said to be heavy. This was to be the only pitched battle of Sullivan's campaign.

The army continued into the fields and orchards of New York, the beautiful rolling land of the Finger Lakes. Every day it was the same job. Burn and cut crops, burn and cut corn. They wore themselves out with it. Although they were near the British Fort Niagara and could have defeated the British with their great force, they did not attack. Sullivan had been sick on the trip and though not yet forty, he was worn out from the campaign. Then too, he constantly worried about the army running out of provisions. He felt there wasn't enough food to go on to Niagara, so the sunburned, tired troops turned back. At September's end they were triumphant heros, returned to Wilkes-Barre.

The villagers gave a celebration for the troops who had liberated them from the savages. Although the Indians returned occasionally to harry the settlers, the army tour was indeed a success. Never again were the attacks on the settlers of the Susquahanna River valley to equal those before the army raid. Because the backbone of the Iroquois Nation was to be broken that winter. Not with bullets, but by starvation.

Chapter III

Near Fort Niagara, New York, October 1779

Strong Bear returned home from a tour of the invaded Iroquois lands. Jumping from his pony he entered the longhouse and called his squaw, Meshinga, for a conference. Finding her at her continual job of tanning hides, he said, "It looks very bad. The soldiers have laid waste the crops south of here. There will be much crying for food in the cold of winter."

Meshinga looked up from her hide scraping and asked with concern, "How many of our people were killed?"

"Only one brave from this village. Not many from others. But as far south as I traveled, there was not a stalk of corn left standing. Few fruit trees will live. It's as if a giant locust cloud had come down and eaten everything. I don't know why we were spared, but they have gone. The great spirit is looking out for us. But this winter many of the people here will die because the winter's food store is gone."

"We could go back to my people at Kekionga," Meshinga said thoughtfully. "We have been a long time away from the homeland of the Miamis. It would be best to leave before the others here know how bad it will be for them this winter. They might attack the Miamis again if they realized how bad things will be for them here. They have driven my people from their homelands on the Wahbashiki river in times past."

Strong Bear teased, "What? How could any tribe scare the fierce Miami? I thought your tribe was always invincible."

Meshinga's face grew solemn as she told the ancient story. "Many years ago my people left the Wahbashiki country, fleeing to Wisconsin to live. The Miamis still remember how the Iroquois came with guns from white men, before we had guns. They enjoyed their killing then. But we saw they were not such great warriors after my people traded for guns.

Then the Miamis pushed them from our country and we returned to our homeland along the Wahbashiki and Maumee rivers. We made peace with them but we always watch the Iroquois."

"They only tolerated we Delaware, it is true. Never trust an Iroquois, my father said. They like to kill too much. Yes, we will leave before any of them get ideas of going with us to Kekionga. Get Maconaquah's things ready and we will leave at first light."

Frost lay on the grass the following bright October morning in 1779. The canoe was heavily packed with household goods owned by Strong Bear and Meshinga. They had a good kettle for cooking, several blankets for each, many earrings and other trinkets, everyday clothing made chiefly of tanned deer skins, and some garments used mainly for ceremony, embroidered with feathers, quills, silk, and beads. Things easily remade, such as mats of cattails were left behind.

The couple was not a poor one'and owned numerous items purchased at the trading post. Strong Bear had a shirt of good cloth and there were woolen stockings for all three members of the family. Besides several bows and arrows and a good gun, Strong Bear possessed a rather peculiar item called a blow gun which he used at times to kill small game or birds. It was really more of a toy than anything else, but he enjoyed showing it to younger men on occasion. Fruit, vegetables and corn were still in great enough supply that they had adequate food for the trip they had in mind.

Meshinga told the women of their lodge that they were going on a fishing trip on Lake Erie, and so they were, but their voyage would take them all the way to the west end of the lake to the future site of Toledo and then down the Maumee river to Kekionga, later known as Fort Wayne.

Frances gathered her treasures to take on the trip. She had been given a string tied to form a circle by one of her new friends who taught her the basics of the game, Cat's Cradle. Frances could spend some of the long hours in the canoe weaving the string over her fingers to form figures of animals, tipi doors, and a design called fish spear and chicken's foot. For some of the designs, the string had to be held by her feet or stones. She would spend time making up her own special designs, some coming from her memories of her life with her white family. Sometimes when playing Cats Cradle with the string, she would think of her real mother sitting at the spinning wheel, spinning thread. At those times when she was sad, she would run to Meshinga and being duly comforted, soon would feel happy again.

Frances also had a little set of well matched sticks to play Whirl and Catch. The sticks were three inches long and about 1/4 inch in diameter. There were ten of them. She had been very careful to match them up so that she could catch them easily. This was a very popular game so she practiced as often as she could. These little sticks were to be thrown up in the air and caught by the flat open hand. When she was older she would try to catch the sticks on the back of her hand. The person who caught the most sticks won the game.

The Indians were very fond of games. Frances had learned a number of them to play with new friends wherever she traveled. She had lived with the Indians for almost a year now, speaking and living Indian fashion. Now she spent little time thinking of her native white family. Her new parents loved her and had all of their time to spend just on Frances. She didn't have to share them with nine other brothers and sisters, and she reveled in the attention. The lack of luxury, if living in a cabin in the 1770's could have been called such, was not noticed because being a very young child she gave little thought to the clothing she wore or the hardness of the ground on which she slept. Life was interesting. She had no lack of playmates, and she was content. She didn't like dirt and disorder, however. This was a major value she brought to her new life from civilization.

When Strong Bear's canoe left the Indian village there was little comment from the inhabitants. Indians enjoyed traveling and often left their village to go on hunting or visiting trips. Little drops of water fell from the paddle as each stroke pushed the canoe ahead on great Lake Erie. There was a crispness in the October air. Only the gentle waves breaking on the desolate shore and the cry of the gulls broke the quiet. Strong Bear gazed into the distance at the seemingly never ending waters to the north and thought, as many times as I see it, the great waters always amaze me. Meshinga trailed a line over the side catching fish for their evening meal. The water was so clear that Frances spent long hours watching the fish. Whenever she was thirsty, she cupped her hand, dipping the pure fresh water from the lake.

They felt no fear traveling alone on the great lake, though a person always took a chance when traveling on it. The weather could change with little warning, sudden storms being known to capsize canoes leaving no trace. Few white persons other than fur traders or missionaries traveled this far inland and no Indians were currently at war. It was a very pleasant trip. A little vacation before the cold winter weather.

That night as they cooked their food on the sandy shore, Strong Bear's heart was filled with the beauty that surrounded them. Stars twinkled over head. Gentle waves made a pleasant sound with their continuous lapping on the beach. Such comfort and quiet made him feel the power and love of the Great Spirit. He took out his pipe and after lighting it began this story.

"The Delaware know of the Great Spirit because of a little boy, maybe a little older than you, Maconaquah, who lived long, long ago. His parents did not love him and often beat him. One night he wandered into the forest very sad and hungry. After walking a long distance he began moaning and crying out to the Great Spirit. As he cried out, "Ooooo," he heard twelve voices repeat the sound, one after another. Then he fell asleep and a manitou appeared to him as a man, with one side of his face painted red and the other black. He told the boy all about the spirit world, and that the troubles of his people were due to their wickedness and their failure to worship the manitous for their goodness.

The boy asked who the twelve voices were and the manitou said, "Those are the voices of the manitous ruling in the twelve spheres of heaven, through which one must pass to reach the Great Spirit, and all prayers are passed in by them, from one to another, until the twelfth delivers them to the Great Spirit."

Then the manitou told the boy how the annual Thanksgiving feast should be held and how to build the temple for worship. The house would be divided into twelve parts, in each of which must be a post with a face carved on it, painted red on one side and black on the other, representing the twelve ruling manitous. In the center there must be a post with four faces carved on the four sides, representing the Great Spirit who sees and knows all things. The manitou told him the Indians must refrain from all gross sins, especially drunkenness.

Now my daughter, I will teach you a song of the Green Corn Ceremony. We have this ceremony when the corn is ready to harvest. All living things have power but the spirit that gives me the most power is the spirit of the green corn. In a dream your own personal spirit will be revealed to you. The spirits like to hear their songs and it is very important that you remember the words of the ceremony songs correctly. But you can sing songs of your own as they are revealed to you in your dreams.

When your spirit comes to you with songs you may not sing them to others until the spirit says you may. These songs will belong to you and no one else may sing them unless you say so or sell them to him.

Some songs have been so powerful that they were sold for as much as a herd of horses!

The corn spirit is the most important of the three life sustaining sisters; corn, beans and squash. Listen as I sing, and watch my dance steps. Then you try them." The leaping fire outlined Strong Bear's face against the sandy beach as he sang, "Nicely while it is raining, Corn plant, I am singing for you. Nicely while the water is streaming, Vine plant, I am singing for you."

Frances got up and sang the words and stepped the steps of the dance little girl fashion. Meshinga smiled with joy as she watched them dancing together and knew that indeed, the Great Spirit loved them all. After they were tired from dancing and singing, they rolled themselves in their blankets to dream songs of their own.

The family awoke to the sun sparkling like diamonds on the water of the great lake. As the day wore on, Meshing grew happier by the minute as each stroke of the paddle brought them closer to her old homeland that white men called Indiana. "Maconaquah, in a few days we will be in the land of tall corn and giant trees. The land of lakes full of fish and forests full of game. It is the most beautiful country in all the world. The soil is so rich that pumpkins and corn grow bigger than anywhere else. We do not starve in my homeland. Pigeons fly in such clouds that you need only a stick to strike them from the sky to fill the cooking pot."

"Will there be anyone for me to play with?"

Meshinga smiled gently. "Plenty of children! In my village at Kekionga are Miami children and there are many other villages nearby. Strong Bear's people, the Delaware, and Shawnee live a short walk away. Aye, it will be good to be back home again."

After several days of paddling across Lake Erie the canoe entered the wide river Maumee, and started its descent southwest to the town, Kekionga, capital of the Miami Nation. The Maumee River was the main highway between the Indians and the British fort at Detroit. Here the British bought Indian scalps and furs from all points in the Northwest Territory. Thus, the Maumee River banks were well populated with Indian villages in the year 1779.

The nine mile portage at Kekionga between the Wabashiki River, in the Miami language, or Oubache as the French called it, and the Maumee was the only break in a continuous waterway from Quebec or Montreal to New Orleans. To reach Chicago a canoer need only paddle up the St. Joseph River, carry his canoe the short portage and then on to St. Joseph, the trading post on Lake Michigan. Usually, though, Indians traveled the overland trail to visit hunting grounds and friendly Miami or Pottawattomi to the North. The British controlled the Indian trade now but many French remained as traders or settlers, many having taken Indian squaws as wives.

Each night the couple stayed in a different village on the Maumee. They traded news of events at Fort Niagara, and warned the Indians to be watchful for an invasion by the Iroquois. As the Maumee narrowed, Indian villages along it became more frequent, with just a few miles between them providing a buffer between the races.

Meshinga could hardly wait to see old friends and relatives and gave animated descriptions of the villages they passed. "Look Maconaquah." She pointed toward a number of bark leantos, a few circular, bent stick and reed mat covered wigwams, and some log cabins as the canoe passed. "There is the Shawnee village near ours. Soon we will come to where the Maumee splits. That is where Kekionga is."

"Shawnee." Frances tried out the difficult word. "Do they live with the Miami?"

"No. Their land is east of the Miamis, but this village has moved very near ours. There are more French and British traders at Kekionga where they can trade their furs. Then too, Kekionga is closer to the many lakes in the lake country north of Kekionga. That is where the people trap their furs to make trade."

The river became increasingly shallow and another village was passed. This time Strong Bear gave a description. "Those are some of my people, the Delaware. More and more of our people move to this land as the white people take our land in the East."

"Do you want to stop?" asked Meshinga.

"No," Strong Bear answered. "Most will be gone on fall hunt. I will join them after we set up our camp."

Vast black berry patches, for which Kekionga was named heralded the capital of the Miami Nation. These berries were an important food source and their location at the junction of the three rivers made this the ideal spot for the town. Frances saw wide fields of corn in every direction, mostly stubble now that it was picked. The vista here was one of field rather than of forest that had lined the river between Indian villages. As the Maumee ended, it split toward the north and south. The northern portion was called the St. Joseph by the French traders and the southern portion the St. Marys. South of Kekionga was a very shallow lake, with surrounding swampy ground that made attack from that direction difficult.

"What is that?" Asked Frances, pointing to what appeared to be a very large cabin in disrepair, enclosed by a palisade, some distance down the southern branch of the river.

Strong Bear answered, "Our French Fathers built that fort many years ago, in the days of my father. That was before the British came and said they would be our fathers and make our trades instead of the French. Now the British come and stay there from time to time. But usually they don't stay long. They say it is too damp and they get the shaking sickness."

"Where is the Wahbashiki you are always talking about?" asked Frances.

"You have to carry a canoe to get to it. It is a long carry. It is so far that you would get tired and I'd end up carrying you and the canoe." Strong Bear smiled at his little daughter who was looking up at him with an open mouth. "You will see it soon. It is the best way to travel south to other villages and to the big French trading posts Ouiatenon and Vincennes."

Smoke from the cooking fires gave a pleasant scent to the crisp fall air when the canoe quietly floated to a stop. In the distance beyond the fields, the forest wore its fall colors contrasting with a brilliant blue sky. A profound quiet existed outside the voices of Indians or sounds of dogs or horses. In the fall the silence seemed peculiar after the birds had flown south for the winter. Meshinga looked around happily thinking, the lighting of the sky here is different than anywhere else. I would know this place just because of that. Out loud she said, "Maconaquah, see the wigwams of my people? We are home."

Frances looked at the squalid cluster of cabins and wigwams. She was less than ecstatic, but glad the boat trip was at an end. Sitting cramped in a canoe day after day had been hard for the energetic little girl. Kekionga numbered about 400 people at this time, with the number increasing or decreasing depending on hunting or sugar making seasons. Villagers took their whole household and wigwam wherever they worked.

A group of Indians came down the bank and hauled the canoe onto higher ground. One brave with a tattooed face said, "Greetings, Strong Bear. It has been many moons since I saw you. Who is this little one?"

Strong Bear placed his arm with pride around his daughter whose red hair was of special significance for the Miami, implying fearlessness. "This is my daughter, Maconaquah."

The brave gingerly touched the red hair. "She is a white child. How did you get her?"

Strong Bear's face settled into more serious lines. "Indians living near Fort Niagara attacked white people, captured this girl and traded her to me. Then, a great army of white men came into Iroquois lands, burning all the corn fields and villages and cutting fruit trees. That is why we left. They will be starving this winter. But we are afraid they might come again to Miami lands, as in days of old, and attack us here."

The brave considered Strong Bear's words and then said, "The Great Lake Erie and Maumee River freeze in winter. Who of them would venture this far then? Even if they did, Little Turtle, our war chief, would never allow them to defeat us."

"That is probably right," reflected Strong Bear. "What is the news here?"

The brave scowled and said, "The Big Knives have not come to Kekionga but they took the British fort down the Wahbashiki at Vincennes. Only a year ago, our British fathers passed through here on the way down the Wahbashiki and took a number of our warriors with them. They gave us much flour and other provisions and we helped them carry over the nine mile portage.

The British took the Vincennes fort away from the Big Knives but then in sugar making time this year, the red bearded Big Knife, George Clark, took it back and has kept it ever since. Our warriors returned up the river, but the British did not. The Big Knives are ruining our trade route."

"Aye, the Yankees are a dangerous people," Strong Bear agreed. The army they sent into Niagara country was very large and they used something in battle that boomed and gave out fire."

Changing the subject Strong Bear asked, "Are there any cabins or wigwams that we could use until we have a place built for winter?"

The brave started, remembering his manners. "You can stay in the council house until you set up your own camp. Come. My son shot a turkey this morning from the wigwam door. It will be a good winter. The corn crop was very plentiful and the caterpillars do not have a wide dark band on their backs. It won't be as cold as usual. The Great Spirit smiles. We had the Thanksgiving ceremony over a moon ago."

Strong Bear relaxed, enjoying the familiar ways and hospitality of home. Smiling he replied, "The turkey sounds good as my stomach talks." His little party followed him loaded with their possessions toward their new home.

The word Miami meant cry of the crane, all beavers, all friends, or people who live on the peninsula. Originally, the French and British had called this people the Twightwees. The word may have come from the Miami word for themselves, cry of the crane, but more probably was from the Algonquian word meaning naked because during the summer months, the men wore only a simple breechclout and moccasins that made it possible to display the tattooing worked in the skin.

They were a people who enjoyed holding office and had an elaborate system of electing village chiefs, sending delegates to band councils and finally elected chiefs of the bands to the Grand Tribal Council. There were both a civil, or principal chief and a war chief of the entire band. In times of war, the war chief was the dominant figure. During the 1780's and '90's, LeGris was the principal chief and Little Turtle the war chief of all the Miamis.

Originally there were six Miami bands at earliest French contact. These combined to form the Weas, Piankeshas, and the Miamis. The area called Kekionga sometimes included as many as seven villages, some being those of Delaware or Shawnee. People moved often going from one place to another as the spirit moved them or the hunting and sugar making times came.

Chapter IV

Kekionga, 1780, Now Fort Wayne, Indiana

A year passed peacefully for those at Kekionga but the winds of change would not be escaped. In November, 1780 four young braves paddled swiftly up the Wabash to their village at Kekionga. They were returning from the Indian village and French trading post, Ouiatenon, just below the future city of Lafayette, Indiana, on the Wabash River. Springing from their canoes on reaching the portage, they ran with the famous Miami speed toward Kekionga. Arriving in their village, after running the nine mile distance, they hurried to the lodge of the principal chief, LeGris.

Panting, the brave among them thought to be the best speaker said, "We have news of Americans coming up the Wahbashiki. They are a large war party." The leader continued, "We were buying supplies at the trading post of Ouiatenon when a large group of Frenchmen, led by a man named LaBalm, coming from Vincennes stopped to camp overnight. They thought we were local Weas so they openly told the traders their plans. They said they were going to Detroit to attack the British, but we know we are in danger here at Kekionga because the British are our fathers. We paddled up the Wabashiki with great swiftness to give the alarm."

Concern etched the face of the dignified chief, LeGris. "How far ahead of them do you think you are, my son?"

"Half a day at most."

The chief reflected, "They are well armed but may pass on by. Still, we must be cautious. When they come, they will find an empty camp. Go spread the word, and tell the traders too. We will all go to Little Turtle's village a few miles from here on the Eel River so they will not pass near us."

As the noon sun streamed down the next day, a large number of canoes carried by French, newly Americans since George Clark had taken Vincennes from the British, arrived at Kekionga. The men were a jolly dirty bunch, dressed in the buckskins of the country, little different from the dress of their Indian counterparts. They had had a good time so far, though they were a little tired after the nine mile portage between the Little Wabash and Maumee Rivers.

Fortified with whisky from the traders at Ouiatenon, they looked forward to more of the same entertainment at Kekionga. Perhaps a few squaws would be willing too. They were supposed to raid the village first though, and raise the flag of the Americans. If all went well on this expedition they'd be heros like George Clark. If they cleared the British from Detroit the Revolutionary war would end all the sooner. The French leader, LaBalm, had clear visions of being a hero.

At Kekionga everything was strangely quiet. There were a few dogs about but no people. They obviously had left very recently. The men walked from one log cabin to the next, at first quietly, and then when they realized no one was about, they boisterously began ransacking the place. First, whisky supplies of the traders were brought out and all the clustered cabins and wigwams were denuded of their treasures. Songs rose above the trees as the day wore into evening, and the troops became more inebriated. Ever so often the crash of Indian pottery split the air like a shriek.

In the trees, the Indian wife of a Kekionga French trader, Beaubien, watched as her home was reduced to wreckage. "My brother, the Turtle, will agenge the ruin of my house! " She said to her husband. "Send a message to him to come later tonight, when the Big Knives are all drunk."

That night as the French commander and his men slept the deep sleep of the very intoxicated, the Indians, led by Little Turtle, stole upon them, killing the commander and thirty of his men. The rest, taken captive, would be traded for ransom through the British. Little Turtle sent a message along with the captives to Detroit of the proposed attack by the Americans. Consequently, the British sent rangers to occupy the Indian towns about Kekionga. Thus ended the first raid against the Miamis by the Americans.

"The best way to keep settlers away is to kill them," the British rangers said. This was welcome news for the young braves, as there had been no exciting wars among the nations for years. They left their towns in small groups to raid the cabins of Kentucky and the rising flood of Ohio river boats, which made easy pickings with a treasure load of goods, free for the taking. Then, the braves would fade away with their bounty and captives, returning over the rivers or overland trails to their distant villages in northern Indiana.

The years passed peacefully for for Frances at Kekionga. She had friends in the Miami village and also the Delaware village four miles up the Maumee. The young girls spent their days playing dolls and other games the Indians loved. In winter Fox and Geese was a favorite. A circle was tramped out in the snow with radiating spokes like a wheel. The fox chased the geese around the course until he caught one who in turn would be it. Snow boat was a favorite of the boys. They carved the canoes from wood, made race courses in the snow and spent hours on end racing the boats. Now, a budding young woman of thirteen, Frances spent more of her time scraping hides, grinding corn and tending crops.

The White Rose of the Miamis had become something of a celebrity in the Indian community. Her unusual red hair and white skin alone would be enough to single her out. But she was a high spirited tomboy who loved to show her strength and agility, especially if there were young braves about that could be beaten in a game or contest of horsemanship. She rode the meanest horses bareback and would break horses the boys couldn't. The Miamis were known for their swiftness when running the forest trails. Frances became one of the fleetest girls and there was no one who enjoyed the dances or games more than she. She had a devilish streak, that the Indians said was associated with her red hair, yet no child in the camps was more loving or appreciative of her parents than was Maconaquah.

There were some drawbacks to being a white girl, she had learned. Her skin was fragile, easily sun or wind burned. Often she needed to wear bear grease on her skin and upon occasion even had to wear mud smeared over her sunburned nose.

One fine day of early November, 1785 Frances stood watching a group of boys walking on stilts. She was planning her moves to get a pair away from them for herself when suddenly, she noticed that one of the boys had curly carrot colored hair and skin as white as hers. With her usual lack of restraint she ran up to him boisterously, bumping into the sticks so that he fell to the ground.

"White boy, white boy?" She pointed excitedly at his skin. Then, seeing he was older and handsome she blushed and retreated giggling nervously.

He was definitely not the type to be embarrassed by anyone, certainly not by a little girl. He got up and walked up to her. "You speak English?" He took a good look at her, peering into her brown eyes. Reaching out a rather grubby though fully grown hand, he touched the red curls that had escaped the usual clubbed hair style. There was no doubt that she was just as white as he. "Where'd you come from, Little Sister?"

"Long, far away. I lived on a river. A big river." Frances had not had occasion to use the English language for seven years and was having a little trouble remembering it. Contemplating the attractive boy with his blue eyes and appearance so similar to her own she asked, "Where are your Ma and Pa?"

"They're here doin' a little tradin'. I live with Chief Porcupine at Kenapacomaqua, down the Eel River." He puffed himself up a little with this remark. "Oh, you mean my real Ma and Pa? They're dead. I was stole from Kentuck, near the new town Louisville. Anyway, these Injuns are my real folks now. I could go home any day I wanted but I don't want to go. I'm an Injun myself now."

This was quite a bit for Frances to digest all at once. Looking at the attractive older boy and hoping for his respect she said, "I'm an Injun too. How long have you lived with The Porcupine?"

"Let's see, I was stole from the man my brother sent me to down in Kentuck after Pa was kilt. William Pope was his name. Three other boys an' me was out huntin' when up comes this Injun war party. Well, we didn't have no chance so we went along peaceful like. They didn't seem to be bad fellers anyway. We come all the way up the Wabash to Ouiatenon. Well, them other boys was homesick for their Mas, so they snuck off and left. They asked me to go too, but I had had enough of chores for the old man I lived with. You'da thought I was a black slave the way he treated me. Milk the cow, chop the wood. Work, work, work! So I stayed and traveled with The Porcupine. Now he's like my pa." He paused thinking. "My real ones are dead, you know. The Porcupine an' me go raidin' boats on the Ohio or huntin' and there ain't a dull day. What's your story, Little Sister?"

Now Frances grew flustered, not knowing how to reply. "I am not supposed to speak of it because the bad Americans might make me leave our people. Anyway, I do not remember very much, I was just a little girl then. I don't want to remember." Changing the subject she said, "What's your name, white boy?"

Laughing he said, "My real name is Man of the Earth, or Carrot-top, Apeconit in Miami, but my white name is William Wells. You can call me big brother if you want. Got to go now. You be a good girl and stay away from my stilts!"

Frances blushed at being so transparent and ran home to her mother. Meshinga was at her usual job of tanning the hides that were the chief item they could use for trade at the trading post. She had a special knife used to scrape the fat from the hide. Then the hide had to be softened with a mixture of deer brains. This was considered a "women's only" chore as was all of the cooking and tending of the extensive crops of corn, pumpkins, beans and squash. The mats used in wigwam construction were woven by the women. When permanent wood cabins were constructed, the men helped because of their superior strength.

The Indian male led an idyllic life doing only what he wanted to do. Hunting and raiding other tribes had been the traditional work. Now the raiding was accomplished against the white settlers of Kentucky. When treaties were signed to stop all aggression against the white man, the Indian brave would only have trapping and hunting or gaming to occupy his time. When trapping and hunting disappeared with the settlement of the country and the disappearance of the forests, there would be only gaming and drinking for him, as all other work was "squaw's work," unseemly for a masculine brave. With so little domestic work to be done by a young teenaged Indian brave, it is little wonder William Wells chose to remain an Indian, rather than return to a life of drudgery with a family to whom he was not related.

"Mother, mother, I saw a white boy, that looked just like me back there." Frances pointed in the direction of the river.

Meshinga straightened up, rubbing the middle of her back as she looked in the direction of the young braves play. "Yes, that is the white boy adopted by The Porcupine. He is strong, swift, and wilder than most Indian boys. Some call him Wild Potatoes."

"Oh Mother, that is not nice. His real white name is William Wells and he was picked to be the adopted son of a chief, so he is a brave of quality."

"No more quality than are you, my daughter. We picked you because we love you."

"I love you too, Mother." Frances knelt to hug Meshinga.

"I love you my Little White Rose." Meshinga smiled, her tiredness falling away.

The country was thinly populated. In all the Northwest Territory there were less than 20,000 Indians and these belonged to a number of nations and tribes. So Frances Slocum, the redhaired white skinned Indian stood out as a novelty among the few. The fact that she was becoming a beauty would draw attention in itself. But she seemed to seek out fame, on a small scale, as she competed with the braves at horse riding or running. As the years passed, the name Maconaquah, which meant Little Bear Woman, came to have new meaning as she developed her strength and became known as a squaw of great courage. Known as the White Rose of the Miamis, the fact that she was a white captive should have caused her name to be reported to the British, and hence her family to be located. But in fact, white captives were not uncommon as slaves among the Indians. During the years between 1785 and 1812, The Indians carried off as many as 2000 white captives from Kentucky and the Northwest Territory. Fewer than ten percent were ever heard from again.

Rough and loose would describe the social life of traders and French at Kekionga. Nights of freely flowing whisky and cards or more sprightly entertainments were usual. The French women loved to gossip rather than spending their time at housework. So the general look of the cluster of log cabins was one of disorder and outright garbage upon which pigs nibbled at the very doorsteps.

The day was hot with a dry heat, well suited for harvesting the vegetables before winter set in. But the corn would need to dry more on the stalk before picking so it would not mold, so Meshinga sent Maconaquah on an errand to the traders. Paths between the cabins had dried up from the sea of mud, their natural condition during spring. Now walking was difficult in thin soled moccasins because of deep holes left by hooves of many horses, when it was muddy. Frances picked her way around the piles of horse manure as she went to the trading house of one John Haye on this September day in 1790.

After entering the rough cabin she hesitated a minute for her eyes to adjust to the darkness. Looking around she saw a large front room, filled with goods shipped down the Maumee from Detroit. Hides trapped over the previous winter had already been sent up river so there was more space than usual along the walls. A smaller room for living quarters lay behind the large front room.

Haye, one of several French traders at Kekionga, was a paunchy man in his late forties. He enjoyed life here, free of any white man's law or constraints. He had no squaw of his own but rarely suffered because of this. Only yesterday, one of his acquaintances, a French woman, had been most accommodating.

Haye saw standing before him a seventeen-year-old girl, slightly freckled with lovely reddish hair, his favorite color. It was obvious she was white, even though she wore a calico blouse, buckskin skirt, and leggings. She was well developed he saw, certainly worthy of his investigation.

"You ain't really an Injun are you girl? Damn if you ain't a beauty!"

Nervously now because she had become increasingly aware of the kind of interest men seemed to have in her, she answered, "My father is Strong Bear of the Miamis. How much is the tea?"

"How's about you and me havin' a little drink on it first? Then we'll see how much its worth." He was edging around the counter now, toward the shrinking Frances.

"My father does not allow me to drink whisky. Just get my things." She looked around for the possibility of a quick exit. There were too many things piled on the floor for her to spring for the door. Her voice rose with fear as she said, "I must go now."

"Not so fast, we oughter get better acquainted." He grabbed her wrist, painfully twisting it behind her back. Pulling her to him he placed his ugly mouth on hers while his other hand reached under her calico blouse.

Frances was in a state of shock. No brave would dare do such things without the acceptance of his partner. The man's beard scratched her face and vomit rose in her throat at the stale smell of his breath, reeking of whisky. Quickly coming to her senses she gritted her teeth, shoving them against his to push him away. His hand slipped inside her skirt to her behind, squeezing it firmly. She began kicking his legs fighting desperately as he dragged her towards the back room. He was having no trouble, even as she fought with all her strength, because she weighed so little. He laughed as her determined fighting excited him all the more. "We'll just have a little party in my room, all by ourselves," he said.

"No, you won't, you sonofabitch." Someone had grabbed the back of the man's shirt swinging him away from Frances. A fist was placed squarely into the French-man's jaw. Haye crashed to the floor. The buckskinned man standing over him kicked him in the ribs and for good measure kicked him in the groin. "Pick on a gal that's willin' after this, you bastard," he growled.

Frances was shaking in fright. She edged away from the groaning man on the floor, as if he were a wounded rattle snake. The man who'd rescued her saw she couldn't move on her own. He put his arm around her shoulders and said, "Let's get outa this stinkin' hole."

Outside Frances was surprised to see the sun was still shining. Collecting herself a little she looked up at her benefactor and saw he was an old acquaintance. "It's you, William Wells." Then very softly as she was embarrassed she said, "Many thanks for your help." She dropped her eyes and began tucking the blouse back inside the skirt.

"It's nothin' little gal, but I can't say I blame the man. What's a good lookin' thing like you doin' running around by yourself? Where's your husband?"

As he stood there looking her over with obvious admiration, Frances flushed, flustered by the disarray of her clothing. "I am not married." She was silent for a moment, still trying to settle her emotions. Without thinking she added, "What of yourself?" She turned to look up at the young man of twenty standing before her. He didn't look much like any other Indian because he had a fine boned round face that showed his English descent. His white skin and curly red hair, slicked with bear grease and tied in a pigtail down his back, marked him as a white man, though the beading on his buckskins showed Miami workmanship. His face was free of facial hair, Indian style. It would have been difficult for anyone dressed Indian fashion as he was, to have looked more Caucasion. With his athletic build and classically perfect features, he was quite possibly the most handsome man, white or red, within five hundred miles in any direction.

Matter of factly he answered, "I been married for a year now. We live at Little Turtle's town about an hour ride from here on the Eel River."

Frances felt a pang of disappointment at this news. Though why this should be she wasn't certain. After all, he was a friend. The fact that he was married should make no difference.

Wells continued, completely oblivious of Frances' confusion concerning him, "It's high time you got a man of your own. It ain't safe for a young squaw alone in town with these French trappers and traders always lookin' for a ......who'd you say your pa was? I'll speak to him."

"Really, I don't wish to be married. My parents are old and have no one else. I should stay with them."

"Little sister, that just ain't the way of it, why me and Sweet Breeze are as happy as two larks." Almost as an after though he said, "My squaw is the daughter of Chief Little Turtle."

Wishing to keep him from talking with her father, she agreed with him. "Perhaps you are right. I will speak to my father." To put the embarrassing subject away she said, "I heard that your brother, a white man, came to take you away from your family here."

"That he did. Leastways, he claimed he was my brother. Come all the way up the Wahbashiki, past Vincennes, jest to see me. Must of been my kin to a done that. Him comin' into Miami country with as much hair as we lift makes me think he was my brother. It took a lot of guts to do that."

"How'd he know you were here?"

"Oh, I go as interpreter whenever the Miamis travel to Vincennes or Detroit. I've even been to Canada and I know several Algonquian languages and French. Anyhow, I was at the fort at Vincennes and the American Commandant there sent word to my brother in Kentucky that I was with the Miamis. When Carty, that's his name, came here, he tried to get me to go back with him. Course I'd never leave my family. So I said no. This here's my home. These, my people. Have your white relatives ever come for you?"

"No, I do not wish to leave my family here. Whenever the Miamis have white captives to be traded with the British, I stay out of sight." Feeling suddenly very tired and thinking it was time to go home, she said, "Again I thank you. I will always think of you as my friend."

The virile youth mounted his horse saying, "Don't forgit about findin' your own man to look out for you." He raised his hand in farewell turning down the road to gallop away bareback on the spirited horse.

As Frances watched she thought to herself, perhaps it wouldn't be a bad thing to be married after all. She left the road and walked the mile to the Indian village that was set apart from the cabins of the French.

Entering their cabin she saw her mother grinding corn for the day's bread. Using a stone shaped somewhat like a rolling pin, but shorter and thicker, she used all her weight to grind the corn in the pan. It was another stone, slightly hollow, that collected the corn meal. She watched her mother for a moment as Meshinga rocked forward and backward on her knees. This was a difficult subject Frances had to bring out. But what if she did nothing and Wells told her parents what had happened? No, she might as well tell them herself. Sitting on a mat by her Mother she said, "Mother, it may be time to find a husband for me."

Meshinga was startled. It really hadn't occurred to her that her daughter would one day leave. "Why do you say this?"

"Today at the trader's a man was rude to me, and now I think perhaps it is true, I should have a man of my own."

"Who was this man?" Meshinga asked outraged.

Frances suddenly saw the depth of the problem this could create. An Indian might rape another Indian with little punishment, but for a white man to do so meant probable death for the offender. "It was a trader going down the Wahbashiki to Vincennes," she lied. "He has probably left already. Anyway, no harm was done."

Meshinga looked at her daughter with new eyes noting her growing maturity. "For many years now, we have warned the Indians to say nothing to white men about you. There have been men who asked where you were. White men. Now, with your beauty, you will be noticed. We must be more careful. Maybe move to Little Turtle's camp farther from the traders of Kekionga."

"But Mother, now that I am grown, surely no one can make me leave our people."

Meshinga put aside her work and stared into the distance. "White men are very evil. Only a few years ago a group of Delaware lived on the Tuscarawas River in Ohio near Pennsylvania. There were white preachers who lived with them and taught the people not to fight or harm anyone. Some Indians from the Scioto River killed some white people. Then American soldiers went to the camp of these religious Delaware. They did not care that they were harmless, not guilty. They put everyone in a pen and then they smashed their heads, one by one, until over ninety of our people were dead. The people did not fight or protest because they had been taught by the preachers that it was wrong. So you see, you cannot trust white men, even when they appear to be good."

Frances sat stunned. The grossness of the act seemed impossible. Over the years of her captivity she had been treated as the petted only child of a prosperous Indian couple. Although young men of the village came with increasing frequency from hunts carrying scalps, dancing and whirling them on sticks, and she had seen a white man burned at the stake, she had never seen any mass killings. She knew her adopted people could be cruel and this story seemed to give a good reason for such cruelty. The story her mother told was one that would haunt her many nights and influenced her the rest of her life so that she worked hard to keep her true identity as a white woman hidden.

Meshinga decided there was no time to lose. She must talk to Strong Bear about the problem. Meshinga approached him when he returned with several pheasants that evening. "Strong Bear, Maconaquah's friend, Running Deer, went to the wigwam of her husband last week."

"Where is my tobacco?"

"In the small basket, there. The white traders look at the young Indian maidens with lust." That ought to get his attention she thought.

Strong Bear raised his eyebrows. "They do not look at you so, old woman." He laughed and pinched her thigh.

Irritated she burst out, "It is time for Maconaquah to be married."

Strong Bear paused in the process of lighting his pipe, startled. "She is only seventeen summers. There is still much time to consider marriage for the child. We have had her only a short time."

"Look at her. She is a grown woman. She has visited the menstrual hut now for four years. She has breasts, they should be used for something."

"Woman, woman, why all this talk of marriage all of a sudden?"

"Today I realized we are selfish old people. Our time left to us cannot be long. Who would look after Maconaquah when we are gone? She might be abused by the trappers and live in the loose way of those near the fort. Do you want that for our daughter?"

Grudgingly he agreed. "I suppose you are right. Who are the available braves she could marry?"

Meshinga reflected, "We must pick someone from another village than our own. Perhaps we should pick an older man as the Iroquois do. There are advantages to that for a young girl as bashful and naive as Maconaquah."

"I would like her to marry a man who is Delaware as I am...and not an old one. After all, I am no Iroquois. I do not follow their traditions. We will go to the Delaware village up river and see what braves are unmarried. We can go to the Thanksgiving dance and look over the young men. You speak with my cousins there and find out which braves are not promised to marry. Now, no more talk of breasts to be used." He rose and left the hut in a huff, thoroughly unsettled. As he walked to the banks of the river, he looked at the surrounding scenery with tired old eyes and a heavy heart. Things were changing. Aging. The sun did not shine as bright or the moon light the sky as in his younger days. Times would never seem so sweet or the land so beautiful as in the days of his youth.

The trees looked dusty, not shiny green and the dirt simply looked like dirt, not as a rich base for new growth as it once had. The ugliness of the town Kekionga appalled his eyes. It would be good to take a little trip to the lake country, still mostly unpopulated some forty miles to the northwest. A few days by myself would be good, he thought. He remembered a summer of his youth spending long days on one lake fishing and then moving to yet another. All was quiet, tranquil, and beautiful with no white trappers about making loud noise to mar the primeval beauty of the land. Game was abundant and he lacked nothing except companionship. How had the good times all gotten away? And now he must give up his most beloved possession, Maconaquah. He sighed and returned to the pine bough bed of his cabin.

The next morning Strong Bear told Meshinga he was going hunting to the west but first would stop at Little Turtle's town on the way.

"Churubusco?" she asked, but he only grunted.

Traveling the twenty miles comfortably on the wide trail, he came to the town on the Eel River to see if an old friend would be interested in joining him. Alighting from his horse, he was hailed by a brave he knew. "Strong Bear, you are just in time to join the war council." The man appeared very agitated so Strong Bear hastened to the council house. He was surprised at the large number of braves in attendance that included those from other villages. Little Turtle's son-in-law, William Wells, sat by his side.

Speaking to Little Turtle was a brave of twenty-eight or so saying, "and he has soldiers and men from Kentucky with him...thousands. They will advance on the Miami soon."

Little Turtle spoke with his customary calmness. "Does this white chief Harmar seem a strong warrior? What is the man like?"

"He drinks much whisky. He took soldiers to the Sciota River and killed Indians in a war party there for attacking flat boats on the Ohio River. He has built a fort on the Ohio and is collecting an army to attack us. Fort Washington it is called."

Little Turtle sat quietly reflecting, "We must be ready for them when they come. We will gather as many warriors as we can in this short time. I will send scouts to watch their approach and warn the Indian villages to leave when the army comes. We want no battles until we are ready. My son-in-law, Man of the Earth, will speak with the British to get more guns." He motioned toward William Wells who was also sometimes called Little Potato or Wild Potato, depending on who was doing the calling. "The Long Knife fools sent a message to the British telling them they were attacking us only and not the British. Of course our British fathers told us of this attack and will help us hold our land against them."

All agreed without question since Little Turtle was a man of such wisdom and integrity that he was known as one of the great chiefs of the times. He was highly intelligent, gregarious, and skilled in social graces. He had been recognized as a major Miami war chief since his massacre of LaBalm and his men ten years previously. In this year of 1790 Little Turtle was to begin his career as one of the greatest war chiefs of all time as this first campaign was launched by the Americans. The American army would try to rid Indiana and Ohio of the Indians who had brought settlement of the interior to a virtual halt with their constant raids on Ohio river boats and settlements in Kentucky.

As the meeting broke up, Strong Bear approached Little Turtle to learn what this talk of war could mean. "I was going to the Lake Country for fall hunt, but now I hear of war against the Long Knives. What has happened?"

"Scouts from the Ohio River report a force of over a thousand men advancing against us. They say that only 300 are trained soldiers, the others being old men and boys and others from Kentucky. Since many of the young braves are gone on fall hunt I will need every man available, even old grandfathers like you, Strong Bear." He smiled as he placed his hand on Strong Bear's shoulder.

"What would you have me to do to help?"

"I want you to return to the villages along the Maumee and Wahbashiki, taking all the women and children there north, deep into the Lake Country. Perhaps as far as the Elk River and from there Detroit. That is far from here and you won't be found for a long while. The swamps of the Lake Country are difficult to cross and if we are defeated, our people will live on through the children."

"We will not be defeated with you as war chief, Little Turtle. I will return to the villages and do as you ask." Turning away, Strong Bear felt a new, younger man, since he had been given an important task to accomplish. He leaped on his pony and returned down the path to Kekionga renewed in spirit.

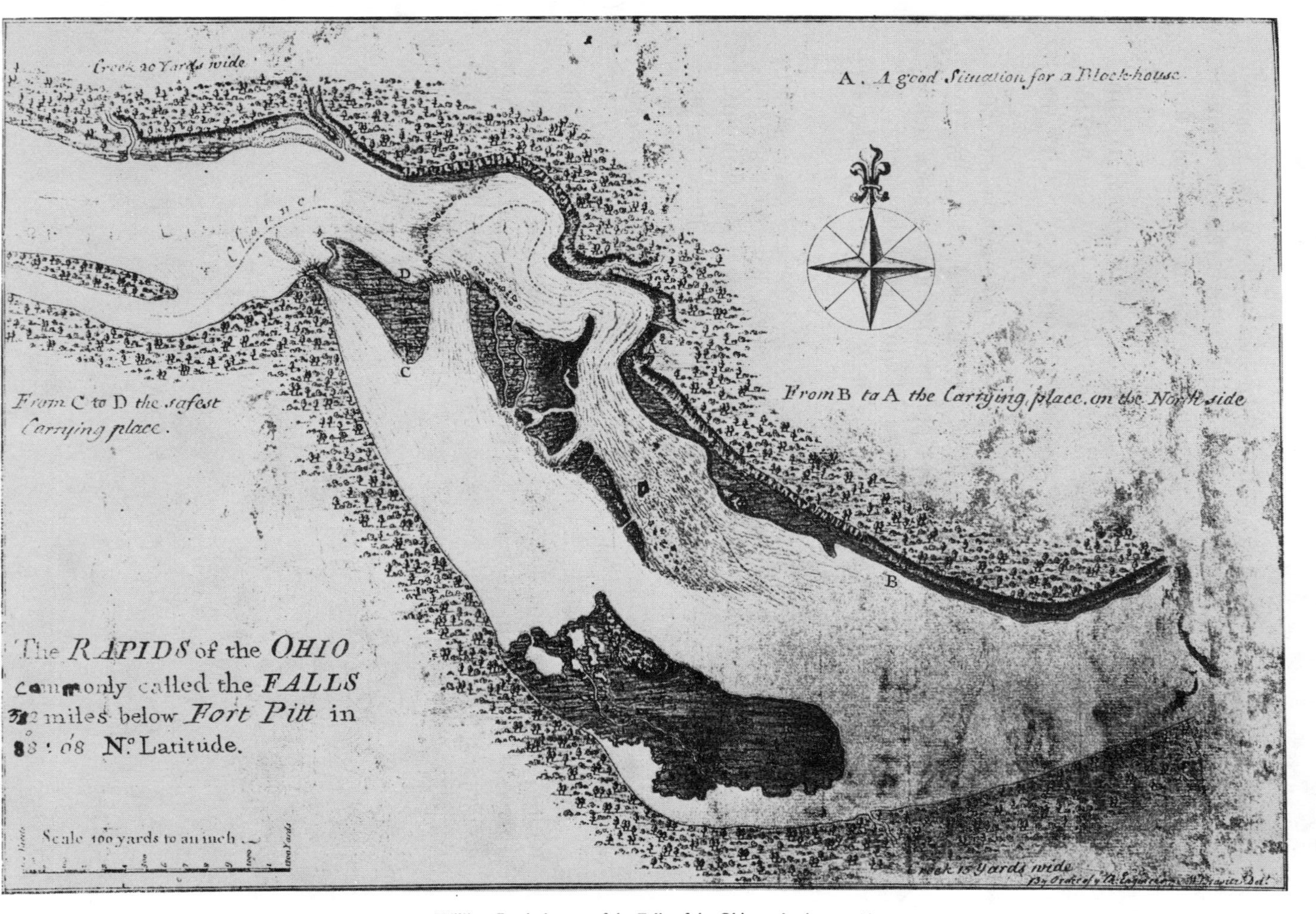

William Brasier's map of the Falls of the Ohio made about 1766.

Chapter V

Fort Washington 1790, Present Day Cincinnati, Ohio

Theoretically the Revolutionary War had been over seven years. Now, that a General was needed to lead an army against the Indians in the Northwest Territory, President Washington selected a man who had been a Colonel in the Revolutionary war, one Josiah Harmar.

General Harmar set the jug of good Pennsylvania whisky on the floor beside his chair. It would dilute the ink on all the paper used to get this new expedition against the Indians going. "Damn but it's takin' a long time to round up an army," he thought. "At this rate the fellers collected already'll eat up my supplies 'fore we even leave the fort." He wiped the sweat from his face. July along the Ohio River was hot. Then he took a swig of whisky, just to settle his nerves. He'd needed a lot of it this summer of 1790 while waiting for the troops to arrive at Fort Washington in Cincy town, or Losantiaville, in the Ohio Territory.

Maybe if he wrote out how many men there were, it would come clear in his mind. On the paper in front of him he wrote the figures, hoping somehow they had grown. "Let's see, there's the three hundred twenty regulars sent out from Fort Pitt." He leaned back in the chair. "Then there's the Kentuckians." He frowned thinking about them. "All them raids on the Kentucks by the Indians, hell, you'd think they'd be in here clamorin' to go rout out those Indians, 'stead of tricklin' in by twos and threes. They certainly screamed loud enough to Washington for an army to come here and fight and stop the raidin'."

Drumming the quill on the camp desk he used, he thought of the condition of the men he had. "I do believe half of those regular soldiers from Pittsburgh jest signed up to get a paid trip west. These soldiers jest aren't the men of quality and dedication that we had in the Revolutionary Army." He lifted the jug to his mouth and took another swig. "Then there's that bunch of farmers from Kentucky. Humph. Nothin' but a bunch of old men and young boys what wants six months of cash money for being soldiers." He spit toward a bucket used as a crude spitoon, missing. Sighing he placed the number six hundred on the paper behind Kentucky militia.

Outside the crude cabin that was his office, a loud clapping and cheering rose once again. He thought disgustedly, "Bet Colonial Hardin jest rode past ta set off his Kentuckians on that infernal racket. He's got their pride all pumped up. The pride of Kentucky he calls it. And they's jest a bunch of farmers! I swan, Hardin thinks he's still directin' the Revolutionary."

Hardin was a man from a proud Kentucky family who was a Colonel in the Kentucky Militia, a group of ever growing importance as an armed militia was increasingly needed to protect the settlers from the Indians. The Kentucky Militia was called up time and time again to fight against the Indians during the 1780-1812 period.

Harmar smiled somewhat crookedly as he thought of the little raid he'd led recently east to the Sciota River to keep the men from being bored while they waited for the others to arrive. Yes, he'd showed 'em then that he was the General. "It was almost like old times, fightin' under General Washington. Led them boys right up on the Indian raiders and singed their hides but good." Quite a nice little celebration they'd had after that too. Scowling he thought, "If we don't hit the road north soon, I'll have more desertions."

Giving up on doing any more secretarial work, Harmar envisioned the thick black forest facing him to the North. Stories of Indian abuses of river boaters were enough to make one's skin crawl. "It's them Miamis that's causin' all the trouble. Lord knows, they coulda signed treaties with us like those other tribes did. But no, they'd rather live the easy life of raidin' river boats and won't sell their land." As he continued to think blackly of the trouble the Miamis were causing him personally, the whisky began having its desired effect. Soon his head dropped forward onto his chest. Snores rumbled through the cabin as all his worries were forgotten.

Finally at the end of September, the army swelled to 1,453 men, started through the wilderness on the 150 mile trip toward the homeland of the Miami. The men were hard to manage. They were untrained and unsuited to the job. Away from chores of farm and home, they acted like undisciplined boys, and many were just that. The Turtle's scouts watched from the trees, taking army pack horses at every opportunity.

Seven days into the trip Hardin split off from the main army, taking six hundred men ahead in a forced march. Arriving at Kekionga before Harmar's army, Hardin's militia found the Indian villages desserted. Now the men began pillaging the towns as have countless armies throughout history.

Flames leaped into the air, licking up the funny round houses called wigwams in the village the guide said was Kekionga. The smell of burning animal skins gave off a stinking smell of things long dead. Colonial John Hardin watched the scene with satisfaction. "Let those thievin', murderin' Injuns worry about keepin' their younguns warm this winter," he thought. "Maybe it'll keep them out of Kentucky."

Looking beyond the Indian's houses he was amazed again at the good log houses and gardens of the village. Army men swarmed from one to another, taking anything of use. "If the Indians came on us now, it would be hopeless," he thought, "Hopeless. I could never get the men back in line for an attack." Smoke billowed up, warming the October 17th day to the heat of summer. Troops ran from wigwam to wigwam, setting all to flame. The corn crop must have been plentiful, judging from all that the men gathered from the houses before burning them. "Funny how no Indians are about," Hardin thought. "Knowing the savageness of the creatures, I'da thought they'd be here howlin' up a storm."

Finally Harmar's main army arrived. Hardin walked toward the tent of General Harmar, hoping to find him sober. The man seemed to have brought along enough whisky to pickle himself. Entering the tent he saluted his superior officer. "Sir, there don't seem to be any Indians about for us to attack. What plan do you suggest?"

"Oh, they're here all right. Watchin'. Don't you feel their eyes on you every move you make? Do you think all them pack horses we been losin' nights jest mosey off by themselves?" Harmar dug out a less than clean handkerchief to wipe his nose. "Damn this damp climate!"

"How many Indians do you think will attack, if they do attack that is?"

"Hamtramck, the commandant of the Fort at Vincennes, is supposed to set out against the Indian tribes on the lower Wabash. That should keep those Indians busy and cut down the numbers coming against us here. Fact is, we don't rightly know how many's in these parts. This town looks big enough to support as many as 1,500. But we'll jest have to wait and see."

"May I make a suggestion sir?"

"Go on."

"I'd like to lead out a party of men up that wide trail leading north from this town. I'll bet we can rout out some of those Indians up there. Though the men are so busy plundering the houses it will be hard to make them fall into line for duty."

Harmar looked at Hardin sourly. "This untrained bunch of yahoos are a tragedy of an army. You're riskin' your neck with them Kentuckians against any self respectin' war party of Injuns. But, we come this far. We'll run out of supplies soon enough so we got to make a stab at thinnin' out the Indians. I give my permission on it."

"Sir, my Kentuckians are men of pride. We won't let you down." Hardin raised his chin as he left the tent, feeling infinitely superior to the man he thought of as a drunken sot.

The Indians had set fires in the forest north of Kekionga. October 19, 1790, Colonial John Hardin set out with 180 of his Kentucky Militia and 30 of the regular army up the wide trail leading towards Little Turtle's town. The troops were silent, reluctant. They never intended to be in an actual battle, and now they were seeking one. As quietly as possible the horses passed three miles of ancient Indian trail. As they traveled, a third of the men slipped away from the group to return to the main army.

Mist rose eerily from the floor of the forest along the trail. It was easy to imagine Indians behind every tree. So far though, nothing. Perhaps the Indians had left the country in fear of the army. But there were the fires. Proof that they were still here. Weak sunlight filtered through the trees on the diminishing group of men. The smoke smell was getting closer.

Among the trees Little Turtle watched as the army passed his men. When they were strung out along the road well within shooting range of his men on either side, he gave the war whoop signaling them to fire. A hundred guns fired upon the American troops. As bullets found their marks, screams of pain split the air. Horses reared while inexperienced army men turned to flee back down the trail.

Hardin was aghast at what was happening. "Company fire! Kneel behind your horses!" Few listened. Indians reloaded and fired again. Hardin rode his horse among the men, imploring them to stand and fight, but many fled without firing a shot.

Most of the army disappeared but twenty-nine men stood against a hundred Indians firing, reloading, and firing again. Of these brave men the number that finally managed to return to camp was nine.

Back in the camp, Hardin dismounted from his sweating, lathered horse. Taking his time, he removed his hat, hitting it against his arm, making a cloud of dust fly from it. Rubbing his face with his hand he thought what a bitter pill it was to report his defeat to Harmar. He swallowed his pride, the pride of Kentucky, and entered the tent of his superior. Hardin stiffly saluted and said, "Sir, we were ambushed."

"How many casualties?"

"Sixty men."

There was a profound silence. Finally General Harmar said, "The men broke ranks and ran." Hardin made as if to protest, but Harmar rose his hand to stay his words. "I already received the captain's report. He just returned after sittin' in the river a couple hours listenin' to his men being tortured. It's enough to make you want to puke, hearin' him tell about listenin' to them screamin' while the Indians pealed off their skin."

Harmar took out a bottle of whisky offering it to Hardin. Hardin looked at the bottle, took it, drinking a long draft, then caughed. Harmar grimaced, shaking his head. "We never should have come up here with such an untrained army. Now we can hardly move our baggage with a third of the horses gone. Those left won't have anything to eat what with the frost. We'll be lucky to make it back to the fort."

Hardin, a younger healthier man than Harmar, was not ready to give up yet. His mind slowly worked through possible ways of attacking the Indians so that his men would recover their honor. "If it appeared that we were retreating the Indians might go back to their village. Then we could take a surprise force at night and attack them."

Harmar was very reluctant. "Hardin, you've seen what you Kentucky boys are capable of. They'd just leave you in the lurch again."

"Sir, if we don't search for them Red Dogs from Hell, this mission's goin' ta be a total waste. Tax money wasted, they'll say. And those Injuns will raid us more often in Kentucky 'cause they'll figure they beat us."

"I think it's a mistake, and I'll record it as such." Harmar thought sadly of the total ruin of his reputation if they returned now, having been beaten by the Indians. He should have retired to a little farm somewhere, after the revolution was over, but it was a difficult thing, changing careers in mid life. So now, here he was in the midst of bloodthirsty savages, leading an army of farmers. He left off his musings to say, "Perhaps it would be possible to surprise them. We will move the army back the way we came, to make it look like we're in retreat. Then I'll send a detachment back here to the site of these Indian villages where the three rivers come together. I believe the guide called it Kekionga."

The following day the army moved eight miles down the beaten path across which they had come, and set up a camp. The Indians seeing the army in retreat returned to their village. All was going as planned.

Stars twinkled overhead as the men silently moved through giant trees and then into Indian cornfields. The four hundred men were divided into two groups one to attack either side of the village. It was the early morning of October 22, 1790. The attack was to be a surprise, but they hadn't even reached their places when someone's rifle discharged alerting the Indians.

Little Turtle's men sprang into action sweeping over the men attempting to ford the Maumee. Panic ran through the horde of untrained Kentuckians as they saw friends scalped even before they fell from their horses. Indians seemed to be everywhere firing, loading and firing again into the herd of men thrashing about with no plan except for escape. The water of the Maumee ford ran red with blood.

Hardly pausing, the Indians chased the militia on the other end of the village; army men that as yet thought themselves the pursuers. Some of the Kentucky militia stood and fought but most fled as before.

Harmar heard the fight back in camp and ordered reinforcements to go help. Only about thirty would go.

When the air cleared of smoke from the rifles and the Indians had left the battle ground with their scalps, the American army had a total loss of 183 killed and missing with many wounded. Gathering their bedraggled forces, they returned to Fort Washington to send a message to the President of their defeat. Little Turtle had won the day. This was the result of the second American attack against the Miamis.

The sound of singing and drums marked a victory celebration in the Indian camps at Kekionga. Women and children had returned from their restful days at Lake Wawasee bringing squirrels and hind quarters of deer for the warrior's feast. Dancing and feasting would last over a week for they had won a great victory over the invaders. Joy and victory were the theme of the camps but in the council house the chiefs and elders met with Little Turtle on a more serious note.

As the tobacco mixed with dogwood and sumac inner bark called kinnikinnick was passed from chief to chief, a discussion of past and future strategy was engaged. The assemblage was distinguished. Shawnee chief, Blue Jacket, sat next to William Wells. The great Delaware war chief,

Buckongehelas, was present as well. Buckongehelas was a tall man with a handsomely planed face and well muscled body. He was known for his poise and thoughtful leadership.

Buckongehelas said, "Little Turtle has rid our lands of the Long Knives. Little Turtle is one of the great war chiefs of all times to whom we must give thanks."

Blue Jacket said, "Many of our Shawnee towns to the south are without food for the winter, but our braves will go to Kentucky raiding to replace food from the burned fields. The Kentuckians won't stand against us after Little Turtle's victory."

"We sure showed those yellow bellies how to fight," chimed in Wells, the only white man in the group except for Blue Jacket, also a captured white man and now a Shawnee chief.

Little Turtle quietly blew smoke rings into the air. "The British Agent says they will be back with an even bigger army."

A surprised quiet lasted a minute as the Indians felt some of their assurance slip away.

"We must be ready for them with a great party of braves," asserted Buckongahelas. "We must assemble braves of all nations to meet them. The Chippewa, Ottawa, Pottawattomi, Miami, Delaware, and Shawnee must all fight. All will fall and lose their lands if we are defeated."

Smoke from the pipes rose as they thought of the coming struggle. Blue Jacket spoke. "Buckongahelas has the most honor as war chief among all tribes. He should be war chief against the new Big Knife army."

Wells burst out, "Little Turtle jest beat over ten times as many enemy as we had braves. You shoulda seen our ambush. Why them butchers never knew which way to turn. There can be no other war chief than The Turtle."

Buckongahelas, well known to be as gallant as any knight of the Round Table deferred, "I am old and growing stiff in the joints. Little Turtle is still a young man and abler to lead such an army."

A short silence followed. Then Little Turtle said, "The days ahead will not be easy ones. I do not expect the Big Knives to attack during winter. They are not total fools. But the British have learned that they will form a new army against us. We will need every brave in all the nations. We will need every chief of the nations to keep the braves in line so they will be ready for the fight when the time is at hand. More arms will be available to us through the British and they will help us plan our attacks. We must be ready to push the whites out of our lands once and for all, south of the Ohio. Oherwise, they will keep taking our lands, piece by piece until there is no land for buffalo or deer to graze upon. Without game our people will die."

Delaware chief Buckongahelas spoke with the zeal of a missionary. "The Walam Olum is the record of the Delaware people since the beginning of time. These painted sticks tell how Manito created the earth and the Delaware people. They tell of our people when they lived by the sea and the East people came out of the sea to rob us of our lands. Starving wretches! They came with smiles, but soon became snakes. They were all received and fed with corn; but no land was ever sold to them; we never sold any land. They were allowed to dwell with us, to build houses and plant corn, as friends and allies, because they were hungry and we thought them children of the sun land, and not serpents." All of them sat back relaxing, enjoying the tale.

"They were traders, bringing fine new tools, and weapons, and cloth, and beads, for which we gave them skins, and shells, and corn. And we liked them and the things they brought, for we thought them good and made by the sun land. But they brought also fire-guns, and fire-waters, which burned and killed, also baubles and trinkets of no use, for we had better ones before.

After them came the sons of King George who said more land, more land we must have, and no limit could be put to their steps. And they took Canada from us. We moved west but they killed our chief at the Wyoming valley so we moved west again. Then they killed our brothers on the Tuscarawas. We went to the White River to be farther from them; but they follow us everywhere. We must stop them once and for all."

Little Turtle was deeply moved by the words of Buckongahelas, his old friend, Chief of the Delaware. "We will be ready to stop them when they come and I will lead a thousand braves so that there will be no smokes north of the Ohio River. This I so swear."

Loss of corn, bean, and pumpkin fields was severe. Food would be scarce in the coming winter. This seemed a small problem now, though, at the fullness of harvest time when plenty of food was still available, and they had enjoyed a great victory. A number of arms, clothing, and other goods had been taken from the fallen soldiers or stolen on the army's hasty retreat. Their fortunes had improved it seemed.

At the celebration in the village Strong Bear and Meshinga were enjoying the dancing though they were more restrained, because of their age, than younger tribe members. Taking a rest from the dancing,

Meshinga bent to her duty as that of matchmaker for her child, feeling the perfect opportunity was at hand with so many villages gathered together at once. Seeing an old friend from the Delaware village, she sat down on the ground beside her to discuss possible suitors. They watched the dancers singing and swaying around the fires for a moment.

"My friend, Little Otter, my daughter has come to the age of marriage. Strong Bear would like her to marry a Delaware, as he is of that Nation. What men of your village are available for marriage? I would prefer that she not be taken as a second wife. Times are hard and few men could support more than one wife now."

"There is Lawlewas. His wife died in childbirth last spring."

"He is too old. Isn't he in the late forties? The White Rose of the Miamis should have a strong young brave."

"That is true. Who would be the best choice? Tuck Horse did very well in the battle against the Big Knives. He is about nineteen and good looking. Perhaps he is too young."

"Which one is he? Is he dancing?"

"There by that fire. The one with the scar running down his arm. He once fought a bear with bare hands. He has always been a boy of great courage."

Meshinga, who was getting a little nearsighted, squinted as she looked at the young man. He wore a necklace of bear claws and silver earrings in his ears. As he danced stripped to the waist, the muscles of his back rippled while he swayed to the singing and drums. Looking at the others of the group, she saw that several young girls were watching him with great interest. He had the usual high cheekbones, but a rather weak chin. According to tradition he had plucked all the hair from his head except for a top knot left for the taking of his scalp, should he be killed by another.

"Who is his mother? I will speak to her of the matter."

"Singing Lark. They are camped east along the river. Come and I will take you to her." The two older women rose and walked a distance of about half a mile to the camp of the young brave's parents.

As they approached the wigwam that was the portable temporary home for this celebration, the two women saw that a meal was in progress. The turkey breast cooked with onions smelled most delicious. Little Otter called out to greet the woman. "Hello. We wish to talk with you but will wait until you are finished with the meal."

"Come, sit. There is plenty here and we will have some baked squash," Singing Lark replied. "It is a fine evening to visit with friends." The custom was to offer food to any visitors, regardless of how poor the household might be so it was usual to eat when visiting. The turkey, onions, and squash were eaten and declared perfect.

Meshinga opened the business at hand. "My daughter, The White Rose of the Miamis, has come to the time of marriage. You have a handsome son who is also a successful warrior I am told. Has he been promised to anyone?"

"Tuck Horse brought six scalps back from the fight with the Americans. He is a valuable warrior. Little Turtle said this himself. He is young still, but hunts well. He killed his first deer when only nine. Several girls like him and they are good to him. He is not inexperienced," she giggled. "But he is not promised."

"It would be a great honor to marry The White Rose. She is very rare. Also, I have watched her closely and she is a virgin. What could he afford as a bride price?" asked Meshinga.

"He has captured goods in the war and of course will receive money from the British for the scalps. They would live with us for a time until they gained more experience in their marriage."

"Maconaquah is a good cook. She was my only child and I have trained her well. She is kind to us, her old parents. We will miss her sorely, but wish her to be happily married. I have seen your son, a fine strong brave, and think he may be worthy of Maconaquah."

"Then it is settled. I will inform my son of his fortunate marriage when he returns," agreed Singing Lark.

As was the custom, the brave Tuck Horse was informed by his parents who his wife was to be. Marriage was not often a matter of romance among the Indians. Life was harsh and one had to be practical in matters such as this, regardless of the feelings of the directly affected parties. Because of wars and various pestilences there were not so many men of the right age to choose from, after all.

Maconaquah only knew Tuck Horse casually, but a dutiful daughter, she accepted her parents' choice. Tuck Horse was indeed very handsome. He lived in the Delaware village and and always played with children other than herself. Then when a grown warrior, he had been on many expeditions south raiding in Kentucky or pirating rafts and canoes that floated easy prey, on the Ohio. He was experienced in killing and cruelty.

Often prisoners were taken from the Ohio river boats with the intention of trading them at Detroit later, only to be burned at the stake or skinned virtually alive in one of their drunken debaucheries. Traders abounded in the forest ready to sell the Indians whisky, the liquid fire that drove them temporarily insane.

It appeared that they had some inbred flaw that caused a complete intolerance to the stuff. If a drop was tasted, they would not stop drinking until all was gone. When bottles were purchased from a woodland trader with the cargo of some unlucky boater on the Ohio, the Indians would have a party in the forest, drinking up the total bounty. Woe unto any prisoners they might hold at the time. If they were serious about keeping the hostages for trading, one or two Indians were charged to keep sober to guard them while the others drank themselves into insensibility.

These raids were sometimes led by Little Turtle himself. After all, was it not the only way to keep the settlers from infiltrating their lands, removing the forests, and killing the game? Such was the experience of the man Maconaquah was to marry.

In the days that followed, the ceremonial proceedings began that were due a virgin bride. The White Rose of the Miamis was held in great esteem by all the tribes of the area. She had great courage, could, in fact, run and ride horses like a brave. Then too, she was different and thought more beautiful with her red hair and white skin. Therefore, the gifts brought to her as a bride price were of great value, as the bride gifts were always given in accordance with the value placed on the bride.

According to Indian custom, the father of Tuck Horse gathered together a kettle, gun, some skins of beaver, a flat side of buffalo and a bolt of calico. These he had Singing Lark deliver to the cabin of Strong Bear.

Maconaquah instantly realized that these were gifts given to her by Tuck Horse, as it had been previously arranged. Going out of the cabin, she shyly greeted her future inlaws. Strong Bear went to talk with Tuck Horse 's father, as was the custom.

"Hello, Buck Feet. And what are all these gifts you bring to our cabin?"

"We come to seek moccasins." This standard reply indicated that they came for a woman who of course made the moccasins.

"What say you, Maconaquah? Do you like these presents?"

Shyly, for she knew this would be the moment of her acceptance of Tuck Horse, she answered, "They are very fine."

The next day Maconaquah was dressed in her most dazzling finery of calico and a silk embroidered shawl. On top of these she wore shoulder straps of glass beads, porcelain, and bells so that as she marched ahead of the small procession that included her parents bearing the gifts, she drew the attention of all the villagers. This noisy parade announced the marriage of Maconaquah. After arriving at the hut of her inlaws, she sat down in the center of it on a bear skin spread there for her by her parents. The parents returned to their home and Maconaquah held court all day in the home of her inlaws.

Then when evening approached, she was returned to her home by her father-in-law who carried with him a small gift of tobacco. The next morning the process was repeated as it was for four days. By the end of this time, there was not a soul in either of the Indian villages that did not know a marriage was taking place. In this process Maconaquah was given an opportunity to become acquainted with the family with whom she was to live. During this time the bridegroom was away on a hunting trip, but would be present the day she finally stayed in the home of her inlaws.

It was a cold January day when Maconaquah entered the life of a married woman. She spoke with her mother as they left her old home for the last time. "Mother, I shall miss you and will come soon to see you."

"Yes, perhaps we will move our wigwam to your village. It will be a sad life for us without you. If Tuck Horse is not good to you, you can always come back to live with us."

"I'm sure we will be very happy. Thank you for the pony. Now I will not have to carry such heavy packs when we move camp."

The trail to the Delaware village which earlier had seemed short, now seemed cold and long. Some of the excitement of being a bride had worn off and the actual facts of living with a strange man and family began to be real. The snow was softly powdered and the woods along the trail seemed bleak in the blowing wind. She looked at the trees along the trail as if it were the last time she would travel on it, which of course was rediculous, she told herself. "But the next time I come this way, I will not be returning to my home, but the home of my parents."

On entering the wigwam of her inlaws, Tuck Horse was there, home from the traditional hunting trip. Looking at the virile youth before her, Maconaquah did not regret her parent's choice, though Tuck Horse, as the day wore on, did not seek her out. In fact he seemed to ignore her. Finally, she took him outside for a walk so that they could talk in private, away from the noisy home.

"It seems strange to be a married woman," she opened.

Tuck Horse was not a man to waste breath on words and the silence lengthened.

"Will we have a wigwam of our own soon?" She asked timidly.

"There is no need of one. We will be very comfortable with my parents."

Maconaquah was silent as she digested this unwelcome piece of information. "What of your brothers and sisters? We will crowd them."

"They will keep you company when I am on raids to the South."

As the sun hung coldly in the western sky, they re-entered the Delaware camp, the smell heralding the Indian town before it could actually be seen. The Delaware were not known for their cleanliness as were the Miami. Tuck Horse's parents no longer had a log cabin as it had been burned in Harmar's campaign that fall. Instead, they had a typical wigwam of bent sapplings covered with woven cattail mats and bark. The floor was covered with these mats and the beds were of pine boughs. The quarters in the wigwam were cramped indeed. Tuck Horse had three brothers and sisters who were younger than he and the parents slept here also.

As night approached, Maconaquah watched the parents and brothers and sisters, wondering what they were thinking, knowing her marriage night would be in plain view of the others. That night, wrapped in their blankets, she did not expect a consumation of their marriage. But as the others dropped off in sleep, she felt a hand on her shoulder, turning her toward the waiting brave. Tuck Horse took his bride and as Maconaquah looked to one side, she could see a younger brother watching.

As the days grew into weeks, Maconaquah missed her own home and privacy sadly. Having grown up as an only child she had not had to share and she had been a petted favorite. Here there was the constant bickering of brothers and sisters and no one gave any consideration to her wishes. This winter food was scarce because so many crops had been burned that fall by Harmar's army. There was no privacy in which she and her new husband could get to know each other. Gradually she grew resentful, openly refusing his advances to the amusement of his family.

In the late days of February, snow storms grew soggy with wet snow clinging to every tree branch. The whole family moved the wigwam to a section of the forest they claimed as their own for sugaring off. Bark buckets were hung upon the Maple trees and collected sap was then placed in a large kettle that continually boiled. It took many buckets of sap to make a small amount of sugar so the chore was an arduous one. The women were kept busy cutting wood for the fire. During this time Maconaquah's monthly period came so she was required to retire to a hut by herself so as not to contaminate the others. Here, for the first time in over a month, she could spend time by herself thinking.

She sat quietly sewing the intricate silk applique the Miamis were so skilled in making. Tuck Horse and she were not getting on well together. It seemed he was unsatisfied in the choice of wife selected for him. "It isn't as if he hasn't sampled other girls," Maconaquah thought. "If only we could have a wigwam of our own, then we would have a chance. I will start making the cattail mats and there will be no reason for us to remain in his parents wigwam. If he just weren't so cold and indifferent to me, perhaps I would like him more. I never thought marriage would be like this. My own parents were always so happy. In fact, it is almost as if we were still children, living here with his parents."

At this she grew angry. "It is his job to be grown up and make a home for me. I will not continue to live like a child now that I am a married woman." Her resolve grew as the four days in the hut continued. When she emerged, she announced her decision to her mother-in-law.

"Tuck Horse and I will live in our own wigwam as soon as I can get the materials for it."

Singing Lark agreed. "That is as it should be. Though Tuck Horse has never been eager to leave our family. Perhaps he was too young to be married. Usually, our people wait until they are in their twenties and fully mature, to marry. But, I felt it would be such an honor for him to marry you. I will help you to make the mats and get the bark and poles for your wigwam."

By the time the spring winds of March had melted the ice in the Maumee, Maconaquah had constructed a wigwam for her new home. Moving day was simple as their private possessions were few. In fact, they owned no more than could be carried away easily to another campsite. This was convenient because the Indians moved frequently, even moving to the fields when they worked in them.

Tuck Horse was somewhat sullen at being thrust out of the family wigwam into the more adult status of his own home. He began to spend more time on hunting expeditions. On his return he quickly traded his furs at the trading post buying whisky. At the first break in the weather he announced to Maconaquah, "Several braves and I will be going to the Ohio to raid boats for goods."

"Who will help to plant our garden?"

"That is women's work. You can do it yourself. I have more important things to do."

"Yes, like getting goods to buy whisky!"

"You will not speak to me so woman!" He hit her several times, knocking her to the ground.

Maconaquah cradled her face in her hand and shrank away from him. She had never been treated this way before in her entire life.

"You, you are not worthy of the White Rose of the Miamis, Tuck Horse," she said tearfully. Tuck Horse stomped out of the wigwam and swung onto his horse. He caused it to rear then galloped away. It would be months before Maconaquah saw him again. Several other braves, also tired of winter in the village, went with him for the adventures of raids in Kentucky.

As spring opened its fresh beauty Maconaquah enjoyed her days of independence. She planted corn, beans, pumpkins, and squash, enjoying her status as head of the house without the irritation of an unloving husband. While visiting her parents she told them of the way her husband had struck her. They pleaded with her to stay with them, leaving her husband, but Maconaquah was not one to give up so easily.

Then the warm days of June brought the return of Tuck Horse and his friends. As they approached the village they gave the news of the numbers of scalps they had lifted in advance. They whooped eight times and Maconaquah knew her husband's foray was successful.

"Woman, see my trophies," Tuck Horse said gaily as he threw down a worn collection of scalps, clothing, a gun and a small sack of tea. "Come greet your brave."

Remembering full well their parting scene, Maconaquah said with reserve, "It is good you are back. Come, I will get you a dish of rabbit stew. My father-in-law has brought me meat while you were away," she added with some spite.

Grabbing her roughly Tuck Horse said, "Food will wait. I have been away from my woman a long time." Throwing her onto the bed of pine boughs, he roughly began to show her how he had missed her.

Trying to stall for time, she pushed him away saying, "Tuck Horse, I must take the kettle off the fire or our meal will burn." All her pushing and shoving was to no avail in the end as Tuck Horse, a six foot stretch of sinew and muscle had his way.

When he was finished, Maconaquah sat up and began combing the red ringlets that had escaped the smooth club at the back of her head. "Will you stay long?" she asked coolly.

Tuck Horse replied, "We heard from some Ottawa braves that the Big Knives came up from Kentucky and raided villages down the

Wabashiki killing twenty-two of our people. Five were chiefs. They burned their towns too. Little Turtle will surely send a raiding party for revenge. Of course I will go with him."

"Little Turtle is not allowing any braves to go raiding. He wants us to work in our fields raising food for the hard times ahead."

Frowning at the thought of doing unexciting farmwork he replied, "What is the point of breaking our backs in the fields when the whites only come and burn the crops." He punched the bed with his fist. "We must kill every one of those theiving land grabbers. Kill until there's no smokes above the Ohio."

"I'm just telling you what he has commanded. He spends much time in council with the British soldiers sent here from Detroit. He is sending runners to bring all tribes of the Miami Federation to Kekionga. He wants no braves away raiding now. Why don't you go to the council meetings and see what is happening. My own father is in charge of seeing that food stores are cached where we can use them in case of emergency."

"I'll just do that! Pack your goods and we'll go to Kekionga for a few days. I've several skins here I can trade at the trading post."

Maconaquah's eyes lighted at this. "Good. I need a hoe, some calico and salt. I have had nothing to trade for goods since you left."

Grabbing the skins he growled, "We'll see about that."

Sadly, as her hopes were dashed, Maconaquah could see that he hadn't changed for the better while he was gone.

Dawn saw them traveling single file west on the well worn trail. Smoke rose from many cooking fires at Kekionga. The town seemed to vibrate with activity. Dogs yapped and babies bawled. The population of the town was rising dramatically as Little Turtle called together the tribes of Miami, Delaware, Shawnee, Chippewa, Ottawa, and Pottawatomie to raise an army for the coming battle. Councils were held often with chiefs of the various tribes. The British had sent an army lieutenant and captain to instruct the Indians in the ways of white man's war.

Increasingly the British realized that a defeat of the Indians would endanger the forts they still held illegally in American territory. Because of this and the fact that if they did not help the Indians, the Indians might turn on them, they were obligated to supply ammunition and information to the Indians to stem the tide of American settlement.

While Maconaquah went to visit her parents, Tuck Horse proceeded directly to the council meeting place. There several braves, just coming in from other villages, gathered with William Wells to catch up on the news.

The red haired Wells was saying, "Our spies tell us the Big Knives have picked a new general, a man by the name of St. Clair, to lead an army against us since we beat Harmar's army so bad last year." There was general laughter and nudging of one another at this. Wells continued, "Don't let that give you the big head though. They learned something last year and we might have a hard time beating them back this time."

"We will show them the hard side of our battle axes. Let's go get them now." Tuck horse stood flourishing his weapon.

"No, Little Turtle says we got to plan this one so we'll win for sure. This ain't no little bitty fight we're in for. They say General St. Clair is collectin' upwards of two thousand men to send again' us. We're goin' to divide up into groups led by different chiefs just like the whites do. We'll have a battle plan, and with our skill as warriors we'll whop them good. They'll be plenty of scalps for all. In the meantime, just in case, we'll tend our crops and cache them in the lake country. We'll need lots of dried meat for our army. As you can see, more braves come here each day and it takes lots of meat to run a town this size."

A brave with a scar on his left shoulder suggested, "Wouldn't it be better to raid them now and thin their numbers?"

"No!" Wells said firmly. "Little Turtle wants every brave here trainin' for the fight. When it comes, we want as many warriors as possible. Would you weaken us because of your absence?"

Flattered, the brave answered negatively. Wells continued, "We train, we gather food, save our ammunition, and we wait. Now go to your wigwams and help your women ready themselves for the time when you are away in battle."

Wells returned to the wigwam used as his temporary living quarters that he shared with his squaw, Sweet Breeze and his baby daughter. That day Little Turtle came to lounge for a time during the heat of the day, as he often did. Wells and he had a curious relationship. They were closer than father and son, and more intimate than friends. They worked together as a team, the younger man admiring the elder's intelligence and bravery, tempered with patience that only time can bring. The elder, enjoyed these same traits in the younger man who still had the enormous energy of youth. Their bond was cemented by Sweet Breeze, The Turtle's daughter, and her baby.

Wells was dressed only in a breech clout, the dress of the Miami male for most of the year. "Bring me a bowl of that rabbit stew, Sweet Breeze. What your daddy has looks mighty tasty." Turning to sit on a pile of fur covered pine boughts, he said to The Turtle, "Those young bucks are very frisky. They're all for goin' south to Fort Washington and burning it down."

The Turtle answered, "We must keep them in line for the main battle. The army will be short of supplies and weak when it reaches our country. We must fight here so we have to keep our young men from scattering about the country, wasting our strength."

"It will be hard to do. That detachment of Americans that attacked Ouiatenon, under a fellow named Scott, down the Wabash a few weeks ago, burnin' Indian towns, made quite an impression on our Wea brothers. They might rise to fight on their own and take some of the Miami and Delaware with them."

The Turtle knocked the ash out of the pipe he was smoking while he considered the problem. "Perhaps you could move to your old home village, Kenapacomaqua, where the Eel and Wabash Rivers meet. You could keep the braves in that village and the others in the area calm until we need them. Kenapacomaqua is close enough for you to be summoned when our scouts tell us St. Clair's army has started to move. Then too, Sweet Breeze and the papoose would be safer there, away from Kekionga. With all the braves coming here for the battle bad things can happen. I told the French traders to stop selling them whisky but they're still selling it. The other day, a brave killed his own brother in the road in front of Haye's post. He was drunk, but it could have happened to my own grandchild. "

"You do have a point. The women and children will have to be moved north when St. Clair comes through anyway. Guess I'll jest go off and leave the handling of the new braves arrivin' to you. I'll do a little huntin' and fishin'." He laughed gently to himself at the prospect of such enjoyment.

"Remember, I'm not sending you there to have fun. You are to keep the braves busy doing other things than taking the war path or going south raiding. I want every brave available for the fight to come," cautioned Little Turtle.

And so Sweet Breeze was told the sad news that she was to move, just as many of her friends were gathering together in the town for the excitement of the war. Sweet Breeze was a quiet girl. She was like an Indiana sunset; peaceful and restful. Her rich black hair framed a face with high cheekbones, and almond shaped black eyes. Her skin was very light colored with its touch of walnut coloring. Being tall, her movements were graceful. The clothing she chose and made for herself showed unusual good taste. She and her young child had fine clear skin, because of her careful washing.

Wells, with his outgoing gregarious nature was drawn to her quiet reserve the first time they met. When his various deals, battles or social encounters became too complex, he rested at his home in the peaceful atmosphere that surrounded her. Being such a handsome man with a tremendously complex personality, he could have won any maiden he desired. But Sweet Breeze, quiet daughter of the highest chief in the land, was the perfect choice.

Her life was one of constant labor to keep her young family fed, happy, and dry. They owned no slaves or captives to help her with her chores. Now she took the baby to the wigwam of her mother to say goodby before she packed their belongings.

Sweet Breeze bowed her head to enter the temporary quarters of Little Turtle. "Mother, we are leaving to go to the village, Kenapacomaqua, until the American army comes. I brought the papoose for you to see before we go."

The older woman in her late thirties stretched her arms upward to take the baby strapped to its cradle board. Then she spoke to The Turtle's other wife, Little Bud, a girl of fourteen. "Get us some sassafras tea and maple sugar." Turning to her daughter she said, "Ah, so you go to beautiful Kenapacomaqua. I always wished we could live there, but The Turtle, having been born on the upper Eel would never hear of living in any other village. His father, Chief Aque-na-quah wanted The Turtle, Me-she-kin-no-quah, to follow in his footsteps as war chief of the Miamis, so, we never have lived in the Eel River Miami village. I do love the lakes that surround Little Turtle's town, but I would like to go with you, my daughter. If only to get away from the sounds of war here."

"You are certainly welcome to come mother. I could use the help and I'm sure Little Bud, would take care of The Turtle's needs very well."

Sweet Breeze's mother smiled archly at this. "I may be growing into an old tree, but the branches give forth fruit still. I do not leave my husband in times like these. Besides, if I left, there might be two young girls here when I came back, instead of just one. Give my greetings to my friends there, and do not be sad. You will be back with us in just a few months and we will all go to the Lake Country together when the army comes."

"But Mother, I will miss everything. Everybody is coming to Kekionga now. Nothing ever happens at Kenapacomaqua. Since it is just off the Wabash, on the Eel, no traders or Indians pass by, hardly ever anyway."

"I imagine with your husband being there with you things will not be dull. The Carrot shoots off sparks, lighting fires where ever he is. They come from his red hair. You are a lucky woman. Do not cry to me of having no friends. Many other young girls would love to have your life trail. Just look at Maconaquah, how her husband treats her. He does not stay with her one day in ten, it is said. It is an outrage, a woman with the spirit of a brave being knocked about as she is, an outrage."

"You are right of course. I will miss you Mother."

The Wells family were on their way down the Wabash the following morning bright and early as Wells was not one to waste time once a decision was made. He would paddle a canoe filled with their belongings while Sweet Breeze rode a horse on the trail along the river leading another laden with packs. The child was strapped on the cradle board on her back for easy care and feeding.

At first deer flies followed them with annoying persistence, so during a rest stop, Sweet Breeze swabbed all exposed skin on the baby and herself with bear grease.

As they continued Sweet Breeze enjoyed the tranquil surroundings of the warm July day. The sky overhead was an incredible blue as low fleecy clouds crossed overhead from the west. Crows cawed the news of their approach and occasionally a deer sprang across the path. They met no travelers and seemed totally alone in the midst of the forest. Only the trail along the bank showed any sign of men's previous passing. How pleasant life could be when no others were about to thrust their problems and their noise upon them, Sweet Breeze thought.

At times the trail led away from the river and Sweet Breeze was completely alone with the child. There were no distractions so she began to study the colors of the flowers as compared to the quantity of greens upon which they rested. The purples of thistles in giant clumps were flanked with beds of Black Eyed Susans, a riot of orange and yellow. She smiled to herself as she planned a garment embroidered with these colors. Suddenly, she realized she was really alone. It had been at least fifteen minutes since Apeconit's canoe vanished behind the stretch of trees between the path and the river. Alarmed, she kicked the horse, galloping ahead to where the river was in view again. But there, her relief became smiles as she saw her curly red haired husband, fixing a fishing line to trail behind the canoe. She bit her lip as she thought of the pain it would cause her if something happened to him. The forest did not frighten her. Only the loss of one of her people could do that.

After the sun set, the forest became too dark for travel. They made camp on a wide flood plane beside the water. A tour through the brush raised a Bobwhite to supplement their fish for the evening meal. Later a pile of dried grass under a buffalo robe made a pleasant bed for the two young people.

The long day of traveling had worn out the baby who immediately went to sleep in the sweet smelling grass. Sweet Breeze and The Carrot lay together quietly enjoying the stars in the black ceiling above. Crickets sang their night song, while the river softly lapped the bank near by. Sweet Breeze ran her fingers across the muscled chest of her husband. "It is so beautiful and peaceful here. I wish this night would never end."

Wells looked at the stars and thought of the complexity of his life with the Indians and thought of his white brothers in Louisville. He wondered what the whole thing meant after all. He stroked Sweet Breeze's long black hair, pulling her face down to his chest, holding her against him. "Sometimes I wonder who I really am, especially when I see how big the sky is."

Nuzzling his chin she answered, "You are mine. Mine and our children's." As they moved together in their love, they seemed to be one with the earth, the sky, and the forest that surrounded their bed.

General Henry Knox, Federal Secretary of War, approved an expedition against a few small Indian villages on the lower Wabash in preparing for the main attack against Kekionga, the principal fortress of the Miami confederation. He believed it would influence the Miamis if Kickapoo and Wea villages along the lower Wabash, near current day Lafayette, Indiana, were attacked and captives taken to American forts at Cincinnati and Louisville. These villages were of limited population so that an army of five hundred men could easily capture the residents.

In early June Brigadier-General Scott of Kentucky attacked and destroyed several villages around Ouiatenon with his army of eight hundred mounted men. They took many captives, leaving the remaining Indians with a written speech to the effect that they didn't wish to destroy the Indians but wouldn't put up with their continued warfare on the whites. Considering the Indians' lack of education, it is doubtful they understood the true meaning of the written speech.

St. Clair, preparing his army at Cincinnati for the attack on Kekionga, was so impressed with the results of Scott's expedition that he wrote to the Kentuckians, authorizing them to send another expedition to gather captives.

At Danville, Kentucky on July 5, 1791, the board of war invested Brigadier-General James Wilkinson, who had accompanied Scott on the first expedition, to take five hundred men, make a feint toward the Miami village at Kekionga, and then strike the Indian village six miles up the Eel from where it joins the Wabash River. The village was called Kenapacomaqua.

Chapter VI

Kenapacomaqua, August 7, 1791,
now near Logansport, Indiana

The day started out hot. It would probably be in the nineties before noon. Sweet Breeze looked out the cabin door toward the dance ring. A child walked around on top of the raised hump used for seating around the ring. It was a young girl child, who knew it was forbidden to dance in the war dance ring, but the girl thought no braves were looking. Sweet Breeze smiled at the little larceny of the child. Then taking a metal cooking pot, she walked to the river to get drinking water. This river, the Kenapacomaco, which meant Eel fish, was shallow. Trees grew like brush along the edges and in some places even in the center.

It was cool yet, here in the shade by the river. She glanced upriver and could see some of the neighboring cabins of Kenapacomaqua that stretched east a good three miles. To the left were extensive fields of the unique white corn cultivated by the Miamis. Sweet Breeze sighed as she thought of the work to be performed today. It was the beginning of the eight day Green Corn Ceremony of Thanksgiving, celebrating the new year. She would have to clean completely the cabin and the surrounding area. Also, tradition required the fire be extinguished and a new one started. Then there was the food to prepare for the feast. Songs and dances would honor the three life sustaining sisters, corn, beans and squash.

Were there any debts she had accumulated in the month they lived here? They'd have to be cleared if there were any. The family of The Porcupine had been so helpful setting up the cabin when they first came a month ago. But they were Apeconit's adopted parents from when he was first captured. That could hardly be considered a debt as the Porcupine was family. No, she thought, there are no debts to be cleared at least. She decided that the best way to start on the holiday work was to wash the blankets and other clothing.

The braves of the village had little to do now. They were waiting for the American army to start towards Kekionga. Little hunting was done at this time of year and anyway, it was too hot to do much. Probably most would spend the day gambling.

As the day grew hotter, the baby fussed in the heat and wouldn't take her nap. Finally giving up the idea of getting all her work done, Sweet Breeze took the baby down to the river to swim and play in the cooling water. Other children and parents were also enjoying a swim when a messenger from Kekionga arrived in the village. Everyone crowded around him to hear the news.

"Little Turtle sends word that the army is moving on Kekionga. The braves are to come at once."

Wells stepped forward as the War Chief. "We have been waiting for the word and are ready." To the others he said tersely, "All braves meet me here quickly with your weapons. We will travel up river on horseback rather than by canoe. That is faster and we'll need our horses in battle."

Back in their cabin he hastily gathered his needs for the war path. Sweet Breeze was disappointed. Now they would not enjoy the Green Corn Ceremony together. "How long will you be gone Apeconit?"

Wells paused in his gathering of arms, food and other supplies. He took the baby from Sweet Breeze's arms and placed his other arm around her. "We may be back within a week. It just depends on St. Clair's army. How close they are to Kekionga. You go on with the ceremony. It will give the women something to do other than to worry about us. I'll leave a few braves here to protect the camp."

"May the Great Spirit watch over you, my husband. Please try to be careful. Don't come out from cover in battle just to prove bravery. Everyone knows you are brave enough now."

"Woman, woman!" He didn't know what to say in the face of her concern. He gave her a hug and left the cabin.

Sixty braves met in a field on horses already sweating in the heat. On the signal they mounted, going single file along the Eel River towards Kekionga to battle the American Army threatening their people. The women watched dejectedly for a time. Then the civil chief of the town, an old man, said, "Come, we will continue preparing the ceremony. Perhaps the braves will return in time to share in it. I want all the captives to go with me to dig roots to roast for the feast." They went into the forest to dig the wild root similar to potatoes and Sweet Breeze went to check on the clothing and blankets drying on low bushes.

Several children played on top of the cabin next to hers. She called to one to come watch her baby while she picked corn for the evening meal. She would remember what happened next as if it were done in slow motion for the rest of her life. As the child clambered down the side of the cabin, a great splashing and neighing of many horses came from the west side of town. Her first thought was, how could the braves be returning from the west when they left on the east. The remaining braves, guards of the village, hearing the sound ran from the cabins, guns in hand.

Muskets cracked and the sounds of many horses and guns became deafening. Close by a woman screamed and a child cried out. Sweet Breeze stood as if frozen watching a great army of white soldiers that was almost upon them. Coming to her senses she realized there was no time to waste. She grabbed her child and looked about wildly to see which way was best for escape. The horses were so near she couldn't run across the field into the corn, especially while carrying the baby. More gun shots. She had to take cover. The cabin was the only place she could reach in a short time. She practically dove into the hut and there cowered on the floor. Outside the thunder of a great number of horses mixed with gun shots and screams continued. Soon it was all over. Now there was the sound of men speaking a strange language.

A soldier burst into her cabin, grabbed her arm roughly and thrust her outside. Looking around with the eyes of a trapped animal she saw an enormous number of white soldiers and her quick glance took in the bloodied bodies of the braves who had been left to guard them. Soldiers were removing their scalps, though some of the braves appeared not quite dead. It was gratifying to see two white men lying dead among the braves. The few villagers were gathered together along with the old chief and his group of root digging captives. Dazedly they looked silently at one another. Sweet Breeze could see that some of the women and children were missing, having escaped into the forest. In her mind she prayed, Manito, go with them, and protect us too.

An imposing man on a large stallion rode forward to the center of the village. The other soldiers fell back, giving him center stage. Lt. Col. James Wilkinson, one of the most powerful army men on the frontier with the greatest drive for his own self interest led this foray into Indian territory. This was a man who would stop at nothing to further his army career or to increase his wealth. If it were possible to gain the credit for another man's work, he'd do it. If it meant making a side deal as secret agent for a foreign country he'd do that too. He was smart and would never do anything that would endanger his own person. Certainly, he'd never lead a raid on the main Indian capital, Kekionga. But this smaller village of Kenapecomaqua would offer no resistance, and he could claim a great victory.

Now he dismounted his horse, removed his hat and began fanning himself. He was sweating from every pore in the hot uniform. "Gather up the captives, men, and count the casualties," he commanded. He walked through the village inspecting the casualties. There were six braves killed. Pausing, he looked with dismay at an older woman, face down in the dirt, but somehow obviously pushing a younger squaw and child ahead of her. Now they were sprawled grotesquely, dead too. He returned to the center of the village, a ring perhaps used for dancing. The captives were brought up and when counted they amounted to thirty-four women, children and old men. Wilkinson looked at them pensively. They didn't appear to be a dangerous bunch, but their sullen stares returned enormous hate.

"Begin burning the cabins and cutting the corn," he commanded his men. Then pointing to an old squaw he asked through the interpreter, "Ask her where the braves are."

"They have gone to a trading post up river to buy ammunition," was the reply.

Wilkenson considered this for a moment and said, "Caldwell, take your men up the river to search for the warriors. We'll camp here tonight while we destroy the village." Then he asked again, "Where are the others of the village?"

"This is all we have. No one escaped."

Looking at the few people he felt she was probably lying, but what could be done about it. Out loud he said, "Begin the burning, and be sure not to leave anything of value!"

Wilkinson sat on the ledge around the dance circle watching the men work, burning the village. What a stroke of genius it had been to make a feint toward the Indian's capitol and then turn west to attack these smaller villages. The surprise here had been complete and there was no resistence. "Get some of that corn yonder for roasting," he ordered.

Watching the smoke curl up from a cabin set afire, he could see that his mission to collect Indian captives would be a success, adding to his military laurels. The idea was to distract the Indians' attention before St. Clair's main thrust into Indian territory. If the Indians saw that American armies could take their people successfully, they'd be ready to parley for peace, maybe. St. Clair was so impressed with Scott's attack and capture of captives at Ouiatenon in June that he'd sent Wilkinson with five hundred troops for this short foray into Indian territory to take more captives.

Appraising the sullen Indians Wilkinson thought, "Seems a damn shame to drag all my Kentucky boys away from their farm work for such a motley bunch as these here. But St. Clair said go. Guess it don't hurt none to learn the lay of the land." Smiling to himself he thought, "It won't hurt my career none either."

Planning the next phase of the expedition he mused, "Probably the best thing to do was to go on west, where they'd raided in June. There was supposed to be a large Kickapoo town there that they'd missed. Hunh. They sure wouldn't be expectin' us again so soon. We'll jest give them a little surprise."

Sweet Breeze gathered a few items of clothing before the cabin they lived in was set afire. She watched tiredly as the corn she had labored on with the other squaws was cut down. Thank Manito my husband is gone, she thought. She could envision the bloodshed that would have occurred had the warriors remained in the camp. Their few warriors could not have killed these hundreds of soldiers. She placed her baby to her breast as she watched the soldiers setting up their camp, wondering what the life of a captive would mean for her and her child.

The troops had returned from a tour up the Eel River not having glimpsed a single Indian. On the morning of August 8, Wilkinson brought before him several squaws to inquire the direction of the Kickapoo towns he knew were somewhere to the west, as he planned to raid them also.

One of the squaws said, "Kickapoo are our enemy. I will show you the direction of their camps."

And so, the thirty-four captives were mounted as well as possible, many two on a horse, since the horses had not fared well on the long trip north and were scarce indeed now. The old squaw directed them across a wide plain and then onto a trail across a marsh that she said led directly to the villages. The marsh became a swamp in which the horses floundered and finally the men had to walk through the mud and water, leading them.

After floundering in the mud for hours it dawned on Wilkinson that he had been tricked. The order was given to retreat and the worn out men and horses finally regained solid ground. They had been directed into swamps Indians did not transverse because of their enormity. Legends said a man could enter and not reappear. They made camp on the edge of the Tippecanoe River and next day Kithtippecanuk and Ouiatenon, two Indian towns that had been destroyed in the spring by Scott's raiders, were again attacked. Here the replanted crops were cut before the worn out army began the return trip south to Fort Washington.

On the way home to Kentucky, the farmers, only temporary soldiers, looked at miles of beautiful country through which they passed. There were no Indians as they preferred the rivers and lakes of northern Indiana for their settlements. Kentuckians looked at the country, planning their return, but next time, with their families and plows.

The excursion had been a success in that the winter food supply of several Indian villages had been reduced. Now the Indians would know the whites could strike a blow against them in their own country, and these villages would sue for peace to regain their captured families.

A runner raced down the Indian trails eastward along the Wabash, relying on all his years of training. For centuries the Miamis were known as the greatest of runners. He had escaped notice in Wilkinson's raid and slipped away into the forest, running to tell the war party that the women and children had been stolen. Following the trail toward Kekionga he stopped only to take water from the river for his thirst. It was two days before he arrived at Kekionga to deliver his message. Running up to the wigwam, of William Wells he collapsed on the ground in front of it, panting. When he caught his breath a little he gasped to the surprised Apeconit, "Man of the Earth, the Long Knives came and raided Kenapacomaqua."

"How can this be? The messenger said the army was coming to Kekionga."

The tired Indian answered, "I do not know. You had only gone from the village an hour when the army burst upon us, firing their guns. We had no warning. They killed the braves left as guards and took the women and children with them. Then they burned the village."

Fear gripped Well's heart. "I'll get the warriors who came with me and we'll return at once." Then a thought occurred to him. "Did the army head toward Kekionga after they raided the village?"

"No, they headed West."

Strange, thought Wells. The country directly west of Kenapacomaqua held a vast impassable swamp.

A day later, when the warriors finally returned to their silent village, the smoke of the burned cabins had died away. A rain had washed away the marks of the horses, and the blood. Charred timbers of cabins stuck up at intervals from the earth, roofs caved in, in total ruin. Here and there lay bloating bodies. Wells was shocked as he passed the remains of an old friend, eyes already plucked out by birds and the flesh chewed by wolves. He kicked his horse to urge it to the cabin site where his young family had spent a tranquil month. Now it was a heap of ash. Dismounting, he forced himself to rake through the ashes with a stick. Greatly relieved, he found no bones. Seeing a flash of light, he bent to pick up a silver earring. Lifting it in his hand, he gazed at it for a moment, then placed it in the band of his breech cloth, his face a study of both pain and anger. The men who did this would pay, he vowed. From the far side of the village the eerie sound of the death wail rose and he hurried to see what other dead had been found.

He turned his face from the sight of a brave grieving over his dead mother, wife and child. "How many were killed in all?" he asked one of the others.

"Nine, including the two squaws and child there." He named off the dead, none being personally related to Wells.

"There must be others about who were not captured, who could tell us what happened."

Sure enough, out of the forest from the east waddled a very old wrinkled grandmother. The braves surrounded her to learn the story of what had happened here.

"Where did the army go, old Mother, and who was taken with them?"

The old woman eased herself to the ground. "The chief man left me here to give you a speech as I was too old to go with them. We were preparing for the Green Corn Ceremony, as you know, when you left. The chief and some others were gathering the roots to be baked with the corn. Then, without warning the army sprang upon us from the west. There were only women and children left in the village and a few warriors. After they killed the braves, we did not resist. What would be gained? There were so many men, all on horses. So many men! All shooting and galloping among us. Then when they saw there were no others, they burned our village and cut down the corn fields. The next morning they rode away to the west with our people, leaving me here to tell you that they will not tolerate any more warring against the whites."

A red sheet of anger filled Wells' eyes. War against the whites? What about these outrages against the Indians? His family was gone and he would get them back, no matter how many Long Knives there were. "Come brothers, we will find our families and we will revenge our brothers whose bodies lie here in the dust!" The indians sprang onto their already tired horses to follow the trail west made by the retreating army.

Even though it had rained and several days passed, the marks of five hundred horses were clearly visible. They followed the trail twenty-five miles west to arrive at the edge of the great swamps surrounding the Tippecanoe river. The place was feared, taboo for the Indians. Their horses were tired and would not make it in the swamps so a rest was essential. Camp would have to be made for the night before anything further could be accomplished.

The hour was late as the Indians prepared for a fitfull night harried by the mosquitos, ever present menace of the swamps. Finally a fire was started, even in the heat of the August night, so that the smoke would keep them away. A discussion began concerning what should be done. Apparently the army had plunged straight into the swamp, unaware of the quick-sands and mire that could exhaust or swallow up a horse and unmindful of the snakes or the fact that they could get lost. The Indians held great fear of this place and were not really interested in entering it. They spoke of ghosts known to live in its interior and began telling the traditional ghost stories of the Miamis.

Fleet Foot opened, "Have any of you seen the ghosts of the three Miami on Sycamore Island in the Wabashiki?"

They answered no and he continued, 'It was the spring of the year when I saw them. I was canoeing home from the trading post at Vincennes, trying to make good time so it was very late at night. Nothing could be heard but the occasional shrieks of an owl or scream of a panther. The water lapped the shore quietly and there was a full moon. Then, as I approached Sycamore Island I saw a group of strange lights. They lifted into the air and separated so that I could see they were only lightening bugs.

It was so late I decided to land my canoe on the island to make camp for the night. I was very quiet and I wasn't surprised to see in the clearing two braves dressed in war paint and wearing feathered headresses, but nothing else. They were naked. Sitting on a log watching the two was a strange sight. It was a young squaw, also completely nude. The braves began fighting, first wrestling and then using knives. But the strange thing about it was that there wasn't a sound. Usually there'd be quite a racket in such a fight, even at the distance I was standing. But you couldn't hear a single leaf rustle.

All of a sudden they both reached into the air and grabbed war clubs. They were fighting to the death, you could see as their faces twisted with the strain of the battle. The squaw would jump up and clap her hands together ever so often, hollering at them and cheering them on. Finally, one Indian got his arm free and came down on the other's head with the club, splitting it like a ripe watermellon. He stood over the dead man, flexing his muscles and making a speech to the squaw, and all the while I couldn't hear a sound. She listened intently and then ran into his arms. Well, he picked her up and carried her away into the forest. I just sat there, until finally, I rose to get a better look at the dead man." Fleet Foot stopped for a moment thinking on it. The crickets of the swamp called out for mates and frogs croaked into the late night sky.

"Go on, go on," urged the others.

"I looked at the spot on which the dead man should have been and there was nothing there. Nothing except a cloud of lightening bugs, hovering on the place as if they were his soul. And it wasn't even the time of the year for lightening bugs!"

The Indians were silent, reflecting on the story. Soon, others were told until all went to sleep about the fire. By morning the Indians had talked themselves out of entering the great swamp. Only Wells, a white man, had the courage to enter the forbidden place and he was understandably disgusted with his red brothers. Here were these men, fearless when facing a known enemy, but cowards before the unknown swamp.

"You yellow bellies stay here and wait a day for me," he said. "Then go on back because I may come out of here somewheres else."

The grasses of the marsh often rose above his head as he rode into the swamp, muck sucking at the feet of his horse. At first it was easy to tell where the army had gone because of the matted cattails and grasses. The ground had received a through mixing job and was very soft from the passing of so many horses. It made Wells' travel even more difficult. For hours he struggled from one hammock to another, soon going on foot, leading the horse. He was covered with sticky mud and carried a rock to break the backs of any snakes that got in his way.

The banks of the actual river itself were very low, leading to endless swamps on either side. A heavy growth of timber, mostly ash with some elm, maple, oak and birch grew very tall and were under grown with swamp alder and wild rose making an almost impenetratable forest. The soil, a loose yellow sand, was so soft that Well's feet could hardly be drawn from it as it gave great sucking noises with every step he took.

Once a sudden rush of fur leaped from a tree. A panther screamed shrilly at Wells but having recently fed on a prairie chicken, it slunk off, leaving the horse and rider shaken, but unmarked.

Wells lost the trail as a space in the marshes, became open river. Gazing across it he saw endless marshes, here and there broken by a clump of trees. The army horses had gone across, up, or down, but it was impossible to guess their direction.

Admitting defeat after eight hours in the swamp, he retraced his steps, returning to the waiting men several hours later, totally exhausted. He sat down resignedly and began smearing mud on his body that was a mass of scratches and bug bites. The others looked up from their card games that passed the day for them. "You didn't find them," one said.

"Is that a fact?" returned Wells wearily. "That swamp could swallow up ten armies big as that and we probably wouldn't find none of them, no thanks to none of you neither."

"We might as well return to Kekionga. The army may have headed back there for a fight," said Fleet Foot.

"Now that jest don't make sense. Why would they travel west if they wanted to attack us at Kekionga? I don't know what they thought they was doin! This path here don't lead anyplace. Crazy. That's what it is. They're long gone now. There's no sign of them anywhere so I guess there's nothing for it but to go back."

On the long trip back to Kekionga, they vowed they would have revenge. "Those white dogs will be raided until they'll wish they never heard of Kenapacomaqua. We will kill every white man who sets foot on this side of the Ohio," they said, trying to raise their spirits with big talk. But it was no use. Their families were gone and their homes burned.

Kekionga was still booming with activity, which surprised the returning braves. They thought the awaited army having struck Kenapacomaqua was gone and would not now be a threat to Kekionga. Wells proceeded immediately to the council house to speak with Little Turtle. Pacing up and down, he told the sad tale of the raid on Kenapacomaqua. "The whites left an old woman in the village to give us a message, so we know what happened. We had only been gone an hour when the village was attacked." Wells began pacing again. He was almost beside himself with nervous anxiety, made worse because he could do nothing.

"We hightailed it back there but the army was long gone. So we trailed it to the big swamp and lost it there. Where they went with our people, I can't say. I found no trace of Sweet Breeze and the child, but at least I didn't find their bodies. All I can do is hope they won't be abused." He struck his palm with his fist. "And to think we thought it would be safer there!"

Little Turtle was aghast at the capture of his daughter and grandchild. "Did the old woman know how many were in the army?"

Wells stopped pacing for a moment. He didn't really care how many there were, just that they had taken his family. "She didn't say. Just that there were many."

"We will have our revenge, my son. We know from our spies that the two raids on the lower Wabash villages this summer were not the main army. It is still being readied by a chief called St. Clair at Fort Washington. Our spies are watching the army closely and will tell us when it begins to move. we will show the land grabbers that we will defend our land and our people to the last man. But we must be patient. If we moved against them on their own ground we would surely be defeated. We must wait until they are far from their forts in our own territory. Try to be patient my son, and you will see a day of victory."

"Where could they have taken them? I go over and over it in my mind. They seem to have vanished into thin air. I just can't rest until I have them back safe." The Carrot seemed to be talking to himself.

It was obvious to Little Turtle that Wells would have to be kept busy so he would not do anything to spoil the carefully laid plans, by going off on some unplanned mission of his own. "I am going to give you a group of two hundred Miamis over which you will be the chief. You should begin working with them and the British agent to train them for battle. See to their arms and food supplies. You will be totally responsible for them, so begin training today. That will be something you can do to revenge your family."

Wells brought himself back to the present. "Yes, father. I will begin today." With his energy directed to doing something constructive, it was possible for him to withstand the two months between the loss of his family and the Miami Confederation's battle with St. Clair.

All that summer Little Turtle had restrained the young braves and counciled with the proud chiefs of the other tribes. After waiting so long they were eager to do battle when word finally came that General St. Clair's poorly paid and trained army was ready to move.

As news of the army's movement came to the Miami town the Indian's prepared for battle with a night of dancing. Tuck Horse and several others gathered to dance the Miami Dog Dance.

Killing two dogs they took the hearts and livers from each, cut them into strips and placed them upon a pole as tall as their heads. The pieces of liver and heart hung down from the pole. Only the braves who had been in a war and could boast of their proud deeds were allowed to enter into the dance.

A large crowd including Maconaquah watched as Tuck Horse and another stepped into the circle. Each told in turn with deafening yells, how many they had killed. Then, as they yelled and sang, dancing, they came to the pole trying to bite off and swallow a piece of the meat. Drums beat the rhythm of the dance as the braves whirled singing. Tuck Horse's face was flushed and Maconaquah knew he had been drinking. As he approached the pole he missed a step. The watching chief, LeGris, declared him out of the game.

Maconaquah laughed at Tuck Horse's defeat. Tuck Horse turned angrily, and seeing who laughed sprang at her. "You would laugh at me would you, you bitch?" He drew his knife and cut her on the face. The crowd watching the dance gasped and became silent with shock. From back of the group a man stepped out and gave a hand to the girl who cringed in misery, holding her face while it dripped blood. He led her away through the crowd, away from the quieted circle. No one would dare to touch him, or stop him from interfering in the domestic strife for he was Little Turtle's son-in-law, William Wells.

Taking Maconaquah to the river he pressed a wet cloth to her face as he cleaned the wound. "I guess marriage didn't turn out too good for you Little Sister. I shoulda kept my mouth shut when I told you to get married."

"It is not your fault. I did not know Tuck Horse well when we married. He has not been good to me and he's always drinking whisky and hitting me."

"It ain't no problem. You ain't got no kids so just set his things outside your wigwam, or take your goods back to your parent's wigwam. There's lots of other braves that would want you. Not all men are like him and you don't have to take that kind of treatment. Anyway, maybe he'll be killed in the fight with the Long Knives."

"No, he is never hurt. He is the one who kills. I will just leave him. The others have seen how he treats me so there will be no dishonor in divorcing him. I wish you were not going to this fight. You are....a friend. I would not want to see you hurt."

"Yes, well, ah, I'm headin' up a whole division of braves. They got my wife and baby as captives and we're goin' to show them what we do to men that take our women like thieves in the night. We got to keep the settler's back, because they want all of the land. They don't want to leave any for us. And they'd just as soon kill women and children who are Injuns as spit. Just you remember this though Little Sister, if the worst happens and we lose the fight, always remember you are white. Claim your rights as a white if the Indians get beat. Now I want you to stay with your folks tonight. It ain't safe in your wigwam." He left her and returned to the dances, while Maconaquah sadly went to her childhood home, a place of safety.

Chapter VII

Cincinnati, Ohio, October 1791, St. Clair's Campaign

St. Clair's army moved north in October 1791 from Cincinnati, Ohio. He had a force of fourteen hundred men and two hundred women to do the cooking, because an army moves on it's stomach. As with Harmar's army the previous year, many soldiers were recruited Kentucky farmers, present to serve a period of only six months. When their time ran out they would take their pay and leave.

The General took his time on the way to Kekionga. After moving twenty miles north the army built a fort on the Great Miami River. Forty-two miles north of that they built another one. All of this took a good deal of time and labor, wresting forts from trees. Some of the recruits were getting bored with rationed food and the slow development of events and so deserted. St. Clair had his own problems being a man of fifty-seven, plagued by gout. He couldn't get on or off a horse without help.

It was clear that the Indians knew the movements of the army. If a man wandered off alone into the woods, he was mutilated and scalped. Horses disappeared at night. Those who planned to desert did not leave alone but in groups large enough for a safe return to Cincy Town.

As the army slowly advanced into northern Ohio, the enlistment time was almost up and the men wanted to return to their homes. A frost had ruined the grazing for the horses and supplies for the humans were running low. St. Clair knew it was time to make their move if they were to do it before winter.

The night of November 3, 1791 was cold. The army had marched eight miles that day and now camped by a stream about sixty miles below Kekionga in Ohio along the present day Ohio, Indiana line. General St. Clair's gout was very painful so he left the disposition of the camp to the commander of the troops. They were camped on a treeless plateau that had once been the site of an Indian village in a valley through which ran a stream. The guns were placed in two lines in front of the camps. The general felt that actually there would be no danger here now as Indians never attacked an armed camp. Women went about the usual chores of getting water, firewood, and cooking.

Above the camp William Wells looked down at the assembled sixteen hundred whites with curiosity. It had been many years since he lived with a white family. He was only a boy of thirteen when kidnapped by the Indians. A woman with red hair was stirring a kettle with a long spoon over a fire. Men were tending the horses and arranging their beds under wagons or under hastily constructed lean-tos of tree boughs. They were a ragtag bunch. Not much better, if as well, clothed as the Indians. Some had army uniforms but most were poor farmers. Thinking of his past he wondered if he knew any of them. Then, remembering his captured family and the burned village a feeling of intense hatred began to fill him so that he nearly choked on it. He swore he would get revenge for the evil the whites had worked on his family and home village. Retreating from his lookout he rejoined the Indian camp a safe mile and a half from the army.

No fires were allowed in the Indian camp this night before the attack. It was to be a surprise ambush. Little Turtle had a last conference with the leaders of the battle wings of which William Wells was one. With a stick the layout of the American camp was drawn on the ground. Little Turtle spoke saying, "The British captain told me the Big Knives usually expect Indians to attack at dawn. That's when they will be most ready for attack. So we will wait until later in the morning when they are breaking camp. We will hit them from all sides, dividing ourselves into groups of twelve by tribes. Now we will sing the song of war once more to Manito to ask for his help in ridding our lands of the white scourge."

A Delaware warrior sang the ancient words for all so that their presence would not be detected by the none-too-distant American army.

Oh poor me! Whom am going out to fight the enemy, and know not whether I shall return again, to enjoy the embraces of my children and my wife! Oh poor creature whose life is not in his own hands, who has no power over his own body, but tries to do his duty for the welfare of his nation! O, thou Great Spirit above, take pity on my children and on my wife! Grant that I may be successful in this attempt, that I may slay my enemy, and bring home the trophies of war to my dear family and friends that we may rejoice together. O take pity on me."

When the song was finished, the Indians were quietly reflective as they lay down on the ground for the swiftly passing night.

Five A.M. saw the entire American army alert in their lines, weapons at ready. They paraded in their regiments peering into the early morning fog for the first sign of Indian attack. The hour of caution passed with the coming of broad daylight. The men were dismissed for the breakfast women were cooking over the mess fires. As the men loaded pack horses and attended to personal needs, Little Turtle attacked.

In the distance at a camp somewhat detached from the main army, shots were first heard. These men quickly came running to the main body of the army for protection. Confusion was everywhere as deadly musket fire from the Indians poured in, dropping running men in their tracks. Artillery men found it difficult to commence firing cannons as men ran across in front, obstructing the line of fire.

It took two men to get General St. Clair up on his horse, the pain of his gout was so severe that morning. Others were already on duty, though, trying to regain some order from the chaos of the battle ground. Horses reared and plunged trampling fallen men. Women fell dead about the cooking pots. Ever so slowly, the Americans formed a firing line and the Indians were forced to take more concealed positions. The battle settled into a steady pace of firing muskets with the artillery falling silent, gun by gun, as the Indians concentrated their fire on them. For three hours the battle continued. St. Clair, who was sitting his third horse as the others were shot under him, realized the battle was lost when half his men were dead or wounded. As a last resort he organized the remaining men for a charge through a section of the surrounding Indians which appeared weaker than the other sides.

Charging with the fury of condemned men, they broke through the encircling Indians and ran down the road with all the speed they could muster. The red haired cook led them all, her red hair streaming as she ran down the road toward the fort they had built twenty-nine miles south. Howling Indians jumped onto the battle field scalping the wounded and dispatching any unfortunate stragglers.

William Wells hacked white men with his war hatchet until his arm was so tired he could no longer lift it. With every downward stroke he vented his rage on the very men who stole his family. The Indians packed mud and sand into the mouths and eyes of the land lusting whites. "You want land, take this!" they said in their vengeance. Thus ended the fourth army attack by Americans against the Miami confederation. Six hundred of the original army did not make it back to the fort. Three hundred of those who did were wounded. General St. Clair asked for a court martial, the usual fate of a defeated general, but he was retained as governor of Ohio, stationed at Cincinnati. The remaining Kentuckian farmers went home while the three hundred regulars of the army stood alone on the frontier, awaiting the raids of the victorious Little Turtle.

The cut on Maconaquah's face was healing nicely as the braves returned, victorious from the battle with St. Clair's Americans. Scalp whoops were so numerous as they entered Kekionga that the very air seemed to expand with the din. Plunder from the battle field weighed down the horses. Meat from slaughtered army cattle graced the cooking pots of every wigwam. Captives entertained some of the villagers as they were slowly burned at the stake. Maconaquah was sickened with disgust by this display and did not join other Indian women in their torment of the captives. In times like this she remembered that she too was white, and really Frances Slocum, and she remained inside, out of view.

Tuck Horse returned to an empty wigwam in the Delaware camp on the Maumee River. Its emptiness was surprising to him. He had forgotten his fight with his wife as soon as he was on the road to war. Now he returned, the victorious warrior, and he wanted his just rewards. He went to the wigwam of his parents and demanded, "Where is Maconaquah?" His mother looked at him with impatience, "Why, she left you and went to the cabin of her parents. That was the night you cut her face, don't you remember?"

"Why didn't you drag her back to her home? She should have her nose cut off, like any other whore." He was striding back and forth now, an animal ready to attack.

"She did not commit adultery and you have no right to cut her nose. Everyone saw how you treated her when she left. No one will contest her divorce of you."

"But she is my squaw!"

His mother sighed. "Not any more my son. You will be held in contempt for mistreating the White Rose of the Miamis. It will not be a happy place for you here now. The Miami can be a dangerous people when they feel insulted by another tribe. They do not forget you are a Delaware. Maybe you should travel west to join the tribe of Delaware that left here because of the Miamis two years ago."

Tuck Horse stamped his foot. "Yes, what is she to me anyway. I will leave now and people will know I no longer care for her. You tell them this. "He gathered together the most valuable of his belongings and threw them on his horse.

"My son, have a care. The Western Indians are fearsome indeed, though not as fierce as the Miamis. Send word of any good lands you may find and we may follow at a later time." With these words, the old woman sadly waved goodby to her oldest child, one who had always brought problems, but was never the less loved.

Another brave also came back to the village to an empty wigwam. The flush of victory did not soothe the ache in William Well's heart from the loss of his family. The Indians had performed as desperate men. The army raids the previous summer against their people had given them the reason and will to fight with great courage and zeal. They were protecting their land and their families. As the army had taken its hasty retreat, the Indians worked out their anger on the dead and wounded, driving stakes into bodies of men and women alike, tearing off limbs, and scalping until they were exhausted.

Now after all the excitement had died away, Wells had only his empty wigwam to comfort him, and long days of winter in which to reflect on his loss. What had he done anyway to deserve such treatment he wondered. Lying down on his bed a vision of himself swam into view. Looking at himself, he was disconcerted to see that he was a white man with red hair. He was not used to viewing himself as a white man. Then, thinking on it further, he remembered seeing the red haired cook in St. Clair's army. Suddenly it occurred to him that she might be a kinswoman. The way she ran down the path ahead of all the soldiers it was highly possible. He giggled then caught himself. All those soldiers he'd hacked up. What if some were relatives? Men whose blood was the same as his. Men like Carty Wells who had come all the way to Kekionga because he said The Carrot was his brother.

No,no he hadn't seen Carty among the army. But what of his other brothers. He didn't even know what they looked like as grown men. Had he taken one of his own brother's scalp? Thoroughly shaken, he began to take stock of all the white men he could remember killing, trying to match faces of the dead soldiers with the memories. There were the boys with whom he'd played and then been kidnapped from Mr. Pope's pond in Kentucky. How would he feel if he had killed one of them? He ran through the various emotions possible concerning the whites he knew and came up with enormous guilt. Now he knew why the Great Spirit had taken his family. He was guilty and perhaps had the blood of relatives on his hands. His face twisted into an unusual position of sadness. He felt utter hopelessness and couldn't think of anything he could do. With these thoughts he sank into a depression that was to last several months.

Wells removed himself to Little Turtle's town on the Eel River, where he and his little family had lived before the battles with the whites. There he fell into a state that approached hibernation, like that of the animals in winter. Once he rode his horse the six miles north to Blue Lake. This gave him some small amount of comfort as he trapped a few muskrat and beaver for trade. The gray winter days spent at the forest surrounded lake suited his mood. Then, as he gazed into the cold water faces of his family swam into view and then those of men he had butchered. He fled from the place, back to his empty cabin, a tormented man, eating little and often sleeping away whole days.

Little Turtle returned to his town on the Eel, a general who had earned his rest. During winter months no new attacks were likely to be mounted from the south. Then seeing the state his son-in-law had fallen into, he determined to do something about it.

The Turtle entered the lodge with fresh meat for the young twenty-one year old who had become something of an invalid. "Where is your fire, Carrot? It is cold here. My daughter would be disgraced to see the mess you've made. The sun is high. You should be up and out hunting while the weather is still warm."

Wells slowly threw off the robes from his bed and began putting sticks in the fireplace. "I just ain't felt like doin' nothin' lately. I don't know what I can do. Nothin' seems worth while since I don't know where.....they are. Maybe the spirits are punishing me.

Sometimes when I was sittin' by this little blue lake, I could remember things from when I was just a little tot. I had an older brother. Him and me, we used to sneak pinches out of hot bread my mother baked. She used to smack our britches if she caught us. Then there were parties when neighbors would come and a man would play a fiddle. Apple cider was passed around for all. Then I wonder, did I kill some of them people, ones I knew as little children who are now grown up like me? I tell you, I just can't stand that. It makes me want to throw up. And then I can't eat right, can't sleep. I watched the young bucks burn some of the whites they brought back to camp after the battle. My family is now held captive. What will happen to them?" He looked wildly at the Turtle. "I think I'm goin' crazy!"

"Perhaps you should look for them."

"Look where?"

"At Blue Jacket's Shawnee village there is an old woman, a medicine woman, who is known as a gifted seer. She sees things others cannot and can tell the future. Perhaps she could help you find Sweet Breeze."

"What is the woman's name?"

"Queen Cooh-Coo-Chech. You only need paddle a canoe up the Maumee River to where it meets the Grand Glaize, a day's journey. And if she can do nothing for you, there will be nothing lost, and you will have tried everything."

"Hell, I don't believe in that mumbo jumbo." He reflected a moment and then said, "But I'm ready to try anything. She's probably just an old bag tryin' to earn her meat." He paused then continued, "But, guess it's better than sittin' here doin' nothin'. I'll go see her.

Wells gathered his gun, a few blankets, and fishing gigs for the trip. It wouldn't hurt to pay the old girl well. With that thought, he threw the few furs he had collected into the bottom of the canoe, not forgetting to tuck Sweet Breeze's silver earring into a pouch he carried. The weather was warm for December. A few light snowflakes fell, but the river was not frozen. The muscle action needed to paddle the canoe was a tonic, healing the depression he'd endured over the past months. Stroke after stroke brought back his zest for life. Once again he felt he was equal to any challenge life might hold for him, and that he would find his little family.

Blue Jacket's Shawnee village lay some sixty miles northeast of Kekionga up the Maumee River at its junction with the Auglaize River. Surrounding the town of many log cabins was an extensive plain of corn fields. A short distance north on a high bank of the Maumee at a spot called The Point, were the posts of several traders clustered together. On the opposite side of the Maumee was a small stockade enclosing two hewed log houses, those of James Girty, brother of the infamous Simon Girty, and one occasionally occupied by McKee or Elliot, British Indian agents from Detroit. Several other English and French families lived in cabins along the river.

Gaining the village in a light snow, Wells went directly to Blue Jacket's large cabin to pay respect as a visiting Miami. He was shown into the large room by an unusually good looking woman with lighter skin than the average Indian. Blue Jacket, said to be a white man captured in his late teens by Shawnee, was younger than Little Turtle, perhaps in his late thirties. He had two sons about eighteen and twenty who were educated by the British and his daughters were now pretty teenagers.

Blue Jacket was highly respected as war chief, ranking only behind Little Turtle and Buckongahelas. He was about six feet tall with a solidly built muscular body. Large piercing bright eyes expressed intelligence, firmness and decisiveness. The forehead was high and broad and the nose straight. A wide mouth gave a somewhat sensual note to his face. Having heard that Wells was on the way, he was dressed in his finery to impress the Miami visitor. He wore a scarlet frock coat, richly laced with gold, held tight to his waist with a party sash, red leggings and moccasins, ornamented in the highest style of Indian fashion. On his shoulders were a pair of gold epaulettes and on his arms broad silver bracelets, while from his neck hung a massive silver gorget, and a large medalion of His Majesty George III.

"Apeconit. What brings you away from your fireside in the chill of winter? Surely, there are no Long Knives coming against us so soon. Our braves see that no white man ventures up the paths toward our villages. In fact, they carry scalp poles and booty away from the Long Knife forts almost every day."

Wells looked around the lodge hung with rifles, war clubs, bows and arrows and sat down on a deer skin pointed out for him. "Little Turtle sends his greetings. But I come for myself, to see the medicine woman that lives near here. I have not heard anything from my captured family and thought she might be able to tell me where they are."

"Ah, old Queen Cooh-coo-cheeh. She gives answers to many. Sometimes she is even right. She does seem to have a certain power. Perhaps an answer will come to her for you. But that will be on the morrow. We will have a little gaming and a good meal tonight."

"Who is this woman,Cooh-coo-cheeh?"

"She is said to be a princess of the Wolf clan of the Iroquois. Her husband was a great Mohawk war chief but moved here with Cooh-coo-cheeh and their four children when the Long Knives defeated the Mohawks. He was killed in the war with Harmar last year. The old squaw would have nothing else than he be dug up where he was buried down river and brought up here. Then she built herself a new cabin beside the war trail and had him buried beside it, sittin' mind you, so's he could have the satisfaction of watchin' the braves return with their white men's scalps. You'll see it when you go up there. As a marker its got a red post with a face carved on the top and notches carved on the side for the number of scalps he took. She's quite a seer. I hate to admit it, but I ask her myself if its wise to go before leavin' on a raid."

Wells said, "I don't believe in witch-craft normally. But this business of the missing captives has me stumped. I thought maybe she could give me advice, or at least say where they are."

"Oh, she'll give you some kind of answer. It just may not be what you're lookin' for. Now, let's have a little game and I swear to leave you enough furs to pay the medicine woman."

The Old Queen, as she called herself, had her house about a mile from the town. It was a bark cabin covering an area fourteen by twenty-eight. Poles planted upright in the ground and laced together with hickory strips supported large pieces of elm bark, seven or eight feet long and three or four feet wide that had been pressed flat and fastened to the poles by thongs of bark. The six foot high narrow doorway faced the East and when necessary was closed by a piece of bark placed beside it and fastened by a brace. Inside, a bark partition separated the room into two parts, the back one was entered only by the old squaw as it was where she performed most of her incantations.

In the main room a low bark frame on either side served as beds or seats. On the ground, in the center was the fire with a corresponding hole in the roof above it.

Indians who wanted only a small favor, and not an audience, would leave gifts of venison or other food tied to the door. These gifts were not poor things, but the best they could afford. Wells was a little awed as he stepped to the door of the place to meet the mysterious woman.

The door opened before he knocked upon it. Facing him was a heavyset old person, her face painted oddly. Covering her body was an extravagant costume decorated with beads, silver broaches, and feathers. Around her neck was a necklace of bear claws and from her ears hung five earrings from each lobe.

"The spirits told me you would visit this morning. Enter Man of the Earth, that we may serve you."

A chill ran down Weli s back as he passed the strange woman to enter the room. It seemd an evil wind whirled into the room with him as he entered. Drying herbs hung in a row against the walls. The old woman lifted her arms letting the costume move tinkling loudly as the silver on it banged together. "Now then, tell the spirits the question you have travelled so far to learn. Wait! I see your mind. It touches me. I hear the wail of a child. It is far, far away. I can see the face of the child. Yes, it is a squaw child. A little girl. Her face is almost white. No, she is not a white child. Now she calls. What does she say? She says Father, where are you? I want my father!"

Wells exclaimed, "That would be my daughter! Can you see where she is? My family was captured last summer by the raiding Long Knives and I don't know where they are."

"It will be a hard thing to get the spirits to tell me where they are. The voice of the child comes from such a long distance."

"I have a bundle of furs to give you."

"Wait outside for the answer. I am not sure the spirits will tell me, but I will ask them for the answer. Sometimes they will help and other times not."

Wells went outside, seating himself away from the blowing wind. The old Queen started twirling and dancing in the lodge. At times she sang in strange words, at other times it sounded like gibberish. The hours passed slowly. It was cold and Wells had to walk up and down to keep warm. Still the old Queen chanted. The sun was beginning to set when she finally came forth, looking very tired. She looked at Wells without seeing him, as if she were in a trance. Slowly she lifted her arm and pointed dramatically with one finger to the southwest. Without a word she returned to her cabin. Now all was quiet. Wells was stunned. Was that it? What could she have meant by pointing like that? Then it came to him. Of course, the only settlement in that direction was the American held village of Vincennes. He was irritated with himself for not thinking of it sooner. Where else would the Americans have taken the captives but to

Vincennes? In the morning he would return down the Maumee to the Wabashiki and would follow it all the way to his family who surely were held in the old French village.

The next morning the weather was unfit for travel. Snow storms had come in the night bringing high drifts. The Maumee River was frozen halting all canoeing until the spring thaw. It was February before Wells finally returned to the Miami village on the Eel, Little Turtle's town.

Little Turtle rejoiced to see the return of his adopted son. The countryside was bleak at this time of year and he was bored by the chatter of his women. Any traveler was welcomed as a break in the monotonous winter weather. News traveled slowly now so a visitor was like a new book to be read. "Welcome, welcome my son. Did you receive an answer to the riddle?"

"In a way I did. The Old Queen pointed the direction and I supplied my own answer. They have to be at Vincennes."

Little Turtle stroked his face as he knitted his brows. "Of course. That must be right. But Vincennes is held by the Americans. You can't just walk in there, you, a Miami brave. They would probably shoot you before you reached the gate. It would be best to go as interpreter for a party of Indians seeking peace."

Wells reflected for a moment. "I could visit the Wea villages at Ouiatenon. They will want their captives back that were taken by the Long Knife raiders too."

"Yes, that is a perfect answer. As soon as the weather breaks and the Wabash is free of ice, you must go and find my daughter. You, a white man who speaks the white man's tongue, are the only one who can free her or any of the other captives. I will give you belts of wampum to parley with the Long Knives to seal any treaties that should be made. The Ouiatenons will be poor since their villages were distroyed last summer. We will send corn with you, too, as a gift for their village. The usefulness of the Miami Confederation is not over yet."

Chapter VIII

Vincennes, April 1792

Cold winds blew through the thriving French village as the small party of Wea and Eel River Indians left their canoe on the bank of the Wabash before approaching the fort. Vincennes was picturesque for a frontier town. White washed houses stood close to the street behind high picket fences. Most of them were built of logs set upright in the ground, but some were more ambitious with puncheon walls and shingle roofs and piazzas running round all four sides. Some were even built of stone. All were clean and white, surrounded by hollyhocks in summer and fruit trees with long gardens stretching behind them. There were over three hundred houses or cabins and a barn church, presided over by a French priest.

Friendly Piankeshaw Indians lived in Vincennes and they spoke French as did the native inhabitants. This town was one of the first trading posts settled in the Northwest territory, originally by the French, so that now, in 1792, it was an established town, having been a French mission as early as 1702. The Americans under George Rodgers Clark had taken the fort from the British in 1779. The current officer in charge was Major John Hamtramck who took care of its defense and minor treaties with the Indians.

Hamtramck was a career military man. He was placed in his current position five years earlier by Colonel Harmar, to replace the "lawless" troops of George Rodgers Clark. His job had been well done and he had brought some degree of law and order to the village as well as carrying on his military duties. He had a good relationship with the Indians but he could not stop them from raiding into Kentucky or stop the Kentuckians from making unapproved raids against the Indians.

He knew the Wells brothers of Kentucky intimately, since they were active military men, especially Carty and Samuel. He had already talked with William Wells when he acted as interpreter for the Indians several years previously. Then he had given Carty Wells the word that his brother was with the Miami and Carty had made his unsuccessful trip to Kekionga, trying to obtain William's return. Hamtramck now knew that the Indians had been successful, totally integrating the young Wells captive into their culture.

Seven Weas from Ouiatenon and two of the Eel River Miami Chiefs from the destroyed Kenapacomaqua accompanied Wells to discuss the trade of the captives in return for peace from the Indians. Inside the solid walls of the fort they were directed to the office of Major Hamtramck. Hamtramck looked up from the letter he was writing at his rough hewn table used as a desk. Before him were a group of shave headed Weas, bald except for the scalp lock. They were a typical group of Indians except for the redheaded young man that stepped before him as their interpreter. Wells was in the prime of manhood. Muscles bulged under the deerskin tunic. The face was strong, chin jutting fiercely at the moment. The eyes were dangerous and flashing. Hamtramck had the same feeling that he had when in his barnyard facing a strong young bull, pawing the earth. "Ah, William Wells, isn't it?"

"I am called Apeconit in my home village at Kekionga," Wells said stiffly.

Hamtramck continued, "You have grown some since I saw you last, a few years back. I sent word to your brother that you had been here as interpreter then. A pity you didn't return to Kentucky to live with your kin."

"I come here to free my wife and child and those of my brothers the Wea and Eel River Miami, stole by the Long Knives last summer," returned Wells in the stiff reserve of a true Miami.

"I'd surely like to oblige you," Hamtramck grinned slyly, "but all the captives are at Fort Washington, at Cincinnati. About the only way to get them back is for Little Turtle himself to sign a peace treaty."

This was surprising news to the Indians who thought they would quickly have their friends and families returned to them. They talked quietly among themselves discussing what could be done. Then through Wells they answered, "We can not speak for our eldest brothers, the Miamis at Kekionga, but we, the Weas and Eel River Miamis, would sign a peace treaty to regain the captives."

Hamtramck sat a few minutes looking at the group before him, considering the possibilities. He was an unprejudiced man who had a great deal of empathy and felt the pain of these men whose families were captured. Finally he said, "I do not have sole authority to sign a treaty with you to return your families, but I will send a message to Fort Washington with your offer. We will also have important news for Little Turtle."

He looked pointedly at Wells. "In the meantime, I offer the hospitality of our town until a reply comes."

As soon as the group left, Hamtramck sent a messenger with two letters down the road following the old buffalo trace to Fort Nelson at Louisville, Kentucky. One letter would be sent on to General St. Clair at Fort Washington in Cincinnati. The other was addressed to Mr. Samuel Wells, Hoglands Station, near Louisville, Kentucky.

There was little the Indians could do but stay until they had other news. They made their camp on the banks of the Wabash somewhat distant from Vincennes in the Piankeshaw village. The time was spent pleasantly, visiting with the Piankeshaw and exploring the pleasures of civilization. One of the first places they toured was the sugar loaf mounds left by a race of Indians long gone from the earth. After climbing to the top of one, they could see a good long distance in all directions. Farmers were beginning to plow the ground in the balmy spring weather. Great work horses, oxen, and in one case a mule struggled to pull the plows through the ground, as the farmers walked behind offering encouragement. On the outskirts of the cleared ground men or women drove carts the mile to the forest to cut wood. Perogues, split logs carved out in the center, traveled the river, one of the best modes of travel for hunting trips or carrying trade goods to and from the town.

At week's end a church ceremony was called in a barn. Wells and the Indian delegation went out of curiosity and a lack of anything else more pressing to occupy their time. Rows of log seats had soon filled so they sat on the floor in the back, not feeling truly a part of the group. People of the town were not at all surprised to see Indians in church. The French had long lived, almost as brothers, with the Indians. A black robed priest began the sermon in French, the universal language understood by French and Indians alike. Temperance was the subject of the sermon. The priest looked over the assembled crowd and decided a tone of high drama would be suitable.

"Brothers, everywhere our eyes are insulted by the damage that liquor does to our men and our Indian brothers. The streets are loud with the sounds of strife as brother kills brother, a husband strikes down his wife, or damage is done to property. The Indian race is disappearing before our very eyes because of the toll taken by whisky. What can be done to stop this carnage in our town so that a lady might walk the street in safety?"

In the middle of the congregation sat a well padded farmer, his balding head drooping dangerously low on his chest. The unaccustomed few minutes of rest were too much and loud snores rumbled from his throat. His wife, horrified, gave him a sharp elbow in the ribs whereupon his head snapped up, the snore ending with a snort. Wells seeing this laughed out loud. Half a dozen people turned to stare, loudly shushing him. The congregation rustled on their seats, then settled to listen further.

Continuing, the priest said, "We live in troubled times when it is easy to say an eye for an eye and a tooth for a tooth. But our Lord showed us this is not the way. We are to turn the other cheek when someone strikes us. Remember the commandment to love our neighbors as ourselves. But who is my neighbor you might ask? We have the scriptures which tell the story of the good Samaritan in which we see that even traditional enemies may be our neighbor. Take this thought with you and ponder upon the question of who, indeed, is your neighbor. See with new eyes those whom you might not think of as a neighbor and treat them accordingly."

The assemblage left the barn and stood outside to talk with one another; the pleasantries would continue over an hour. This was the only break they were to receive during the week and they wanted to enjoy it fully.

The Indians filed out of the barn in their accustomed silence walking with their extreme straight posture, and the last to leave was the red headed Wells. One of the Frenchmen placed a hand on Well's arm saying, "Say, you're a white man. Why do you hang around with those Injuns there?"

Wells looked at him in some confusion. He did not think of himself as being white. Finally he shook off the man's hand without answering and left the grounds with the Indians.

During the weeks they waited for the return of the messenger, Wells watched the white settlers of Vincennes, an occupation that brought back old memories from his life before captivity. He watched their manners with their women, and with other men. Their life though harsh was not as difficult as the one experienced by those at Kekionga. They had more trade goods available to them than did the Indians whose goods of civilization came entirely from the British. The village of Kekionga was burned by Harmar's troops only two years ago. This town had such a look of permanance, apparently never ravaged by war. What would it be like not being constantly on the move? It appeared that a man could collect a great number of possessions when they were not destroyed every few years.

On the fifth week of their stay, a messenger came to the camp summoning Wells to Hamtramck. Wells had been cleaning his gun. Putting it aside he leaped to his feet, hastening to the fort. At last he would see Sweet Breeze he thought. Once again he entered the small army office. Inside, instead of his petite wife, a handsome man in his thirties stood casually leaning against the fireplace mantel. He was dressed in a linen shirt, black trousers and on his feet were black leather boots. His brown hair, accented with red high lights hung in a neatly tied pigtail down his back. Over his arm was a black morning coat decorated with two rows of brass buttons. There was not a single doubt in William's mind that this was his brother, Samuel Wells.

The man stepped forward, a benign expression on his face, extending his hand. "William, I'd know you anywhere, even after all this time."

William ignored the hand and turned to Hamtramck saying with barely supressed rage, "Is this the messenger I have waited for with news of my family? I've been tricked!"

"So you do remember me," Samuel Wells said with a grin. "After the way you claimed you didn't remember Carty when he went all the way to Kekionga, I knew you'd claim you didn't know me neither."

William's face flushed. "Where are the captives stole by the Big Knives? Why did you come here? I'm not interested in you, only in the captives."

"Now just simmer down, little brother. Gol durn if you wasn't always a hotheaded little devil! We aim to get your wife and baby back, but it ain't all that easy. It's the government that has them, not me after all. I come all the way from Kentucky for to help you."

"Why didn't someone come from the fort at Louisville?"

"Well, you see, the captives are all at Fort Washington at Cincy town. So we at Fort Nelson in Louisville have no control over what happens to them. If you could speak directly to someone at Fort Washington, mayhap you could get them released. But, you'll have to return with me to Kentucky so that we can get this thing arranged. You see, brother, your little family is in the hands of the United States Government. It ain't goin' to be easy to get them back." He paused noting the stricken look on his brother's face. "General Putnam, special envoy from President Washington, is comin' out west ta make peace with the Indians. If you wait for him ta arrive and then convince him to release the captives, you'll have your object."

William paced the floor not wanting to return to Kentucky for he felt he was placing himself in captivity by doing so. But there seemed no alternative. Without his family he had been miserable. It seemed he would have to accompany his brother back to Louisville. "I'll go with you, but you remember, Kentucky ain't my home anymore. Soon as my family is returned ta me, I'll go back to Kekionga."

Samuel came forward clapping his arm around his wayward brother. "That's the way, little brother. Now go get your gear so's you can come stay at the inn with me tonight."

William drew back. "I'll tell the chiefs of my camp the news that they must wait for the release of the captives. I'll stay in my own camp tonight and meet you in the morning."

Samuel looked at his brother and thought, he really thinks he is a savage. Out loud he said, "As you wish. Until mornin' then."

The land was abloom that late May morning. Flowering crab apple, dogwood, and redbud made bright spots in the greeness of the forest. The ground was covered with beds of blooming violets and trillium. Bees buzzed happily and William thought if he had more time he'd find one of their trees for a little sweet honey.

The road they followed from Vincennes was once traveled by buffalo to the salt licks in Southern Indiana. It was a poor thing; trees had been cut off just low enough so that wagons could pass over the stumps. Now in springtime, it was a muddy morass. If a wagon were to pass here now the occupants would spend most of their time pushing. It was because of this road that the cost of living was more expensive in Vincennes than Louisville. Usually trade goods were transported there the long way, down the Ohio and up the Wabash by boat. Going back to Louisville was easier across country, rather than trying to fight the Ohio River current upriver.

Because Samuel knew horses were very expensive in Vincennes, he had brought an extra one along for William, expecting in advance that his brother would return with him. The horse was a spirited black stallion, a forerunner of famous Kentucky racing horses and one which he felt would suit his brother. When William was presented with the horse, he had run his hands over it, smiling to himself as it quivered with nervousness under his touch. But he said nothing in the way of thanks to Samuel.

The country through which they traveled was not settled, even thinly. Raiding of any lone cabins by the Miami and Shawnee had seen to that. They would not see any houses until they came to the Falls of the Ohio and the village of Clarksville. Here were only ten or twelve houses protected by a small stockade. The people lived there nervously because the larger Fort Nelson was on the other side of the river at Louisville. Those living on the Indian side made an easier target for raiding parties.

It took six days to make the trip. Relations were strained between the two men. William gave only the briefest of answers to Samuel's questions concerning his life with the Indians. As the two men rode through the great forests over the high hills of southern Indiana, Samuel felt a certain amount of fear, expecting Indians to appear ready to lift his hair. His brother, William enjoyed the trip, completely at his ease, since he personally knew the majority of tribesmen in the country. In order to raid the settlements of Kentucky, Indians traveled long distances from their villages at Piqua, Ohio, Kekionga or other villages of the North. Wells knew that targets were more likely to be east of this road, where there was traffic on the river: profitable and easy pickings for the Indians.

Samuel said, "I took quite a risk traveling over this road to get you. Although the raids aren't as bad as when they stole you back in 1784, we still see plenty of bloodshed in Kentucky."

William returned flatly, "There won't be any raids in these parts now."

"How do you know?" Samuel asked, incredulously.

"Why would they waste their time on this seldom traveled road when they's boats comin' down the Ohio loaded with goods to attack? They don't attack you jest for the thrill of it. They got to feed themselves like ya'll do. They've got used to havin' cloth shirts, flour, ammunition, and other geegaws, so where can they get it without working their butts off trappin'? Right off that there river!"

"Do you really know them so well?"

William was silent for a long time. Finally he said in a low voice, "Little Turtle's been my father-in-law for four years now. Give me whatever I wanted, even his daughter."

The horses traveled in a steady gait. After a time Samuel said, "It won't last you know. The Indians will be defeated and tamed. You'd best throw in your lot with the winning side."

"Appears to me I am. Were you or any of my brothers with St. Clair?"

"Yes, I was. Why?" Samuel replied.

William felt a chill at this answer, like that from an open tomb. He said, "Oh, ah....there's so many of them, I just thought some might have been there."

"Was you there boy?" Samuel asked almost in a whisper.

"Yes."

"My God!" Samuel bellered. "Our family raised a butcher! Wilkinson went back to the battle ground last winter and saw how the savages stuffed dirt in the mouths and eyes of men, driving stakes through their bodies, and them probably not even dead yet! Tell me, I want to know! By God, how could you have stood by while that was done?"

"I didn't stand by, I helped do it." William stated calmly.

"What? By all that's holy, how could you, a white man, join in such butchery? If you wasn't so big I'd horseship you myself. You ought to be hanged!"

"You forget, the army came on our land. They was comin' to kill us, take our land, and burn our homes. Why, this very minute, my wife, baby and adopted mother are held captive in some stinkin' hole by you whites that think you're so holy. I saw the village after Wilkinson's raiders left last summer. They killed women and children, as well as braves. I helped bury them myself. The only thing left when I got there was this, everything else was burnt up." He brought forth the silver earring, flourishing it at his brother. Continuing in his maddened tirade he said, "Hell, yes, we stuffed dirt in them soldier's mouths. Take this dirt you filthy land grabbers, we said. You want our ground so damn bad, take this. I hacked up those soldiers until I couldn't lift my arm no more. And we'll do it again, to any other army that comes lookin' for us."

Samuel rode quietly for some time sorting things out. How could it be that his own brother was guilty of such killing? Then, thinking on it, trying to see his brother's viewpoint, he realized that the Indians would think of him too as a murderer since he had fought with the Kentucky militia. The Kentuckians were defending their land from the Indians, of course. But the Indians probably didn't look at it as being their land. It was a new way to look at it. The settlers didn't think of the forest as belonging to ayone but as empty land, waiting to be claimed by them. And they were dismayed and furious when attacked by the Indians who in turn felt the land belonged to them.

Breaking the silence Sam said, "Let's forget about the past and work for the future. As I said before, you ought to be on the winnin' side. And that side ain't goin' to be with the Indians. The government is raisin' and trainin' a new army right now to go up to Kekionga to clean out the Indian resistance. This will be a trained army, not a bunch of farmers hired for six months like Harmar and St. Clair had. Your friends won't have a chance. Your best bet would be to act as a go between and convince The Turtle to give up the fight." Reflecting a moment he reiterated, "In fact, that would be the perfect job for you. There's not another man on the frontier that could go in there now to talk with the Miamis and keep his hair."

William Wells, Apeconit, thought angrily, the Miamis defeated, never! I am Miami, and will not betray my brothers. Then he looked at his blood brother riding beside him. Who was he, really, but a man with many names? His very soul was sickened with his confusion.

Chapter IX

Louisville, Kentucky, May 1792

The falls of the Ohio were as awesome as ever. Water boiled over the limestone outcrop a distance of over three miles while the mighty river dropped more than twenty-five feet. Samuel watched the frothing water while waiting for a flat boat to ferry them across. He imagined himself attempting to shoot the rapids as some men did. The vision showed him being thrown from his canoe, pushed under the water and dashed against the rocks for an endless time. He jerked his eyes away to the smooth water down river that they were to cross. Even below the falls it was a long distance across the Ohio to Louisville and Kentucky. The town grew up at this spot because of the falls. Men had to stop here and carry their goods around. So the town, the taverns, and the trading posts prospered and grew.

He smiled to himself as he watched the care his brother used in settling the black stallion on the flatboat for the crossing. Sam had been too young when his father died to really care for the boy. At the time he was newly married and had a sickly pregnant wife. He'd felt it necessary to place William with his inlaws, the Popes. It had been a disasterous decision when the boy was captured by Indians. Perhaps now he could correct the past mistake.

Since that time Samuel and his brothers had been busy building up plantations and careers of their own. Their father, Samuel, and his brother, Haden Wells, had left their home on the Monongahela River in Pennsylvania about 1775 to found Wells Station in the lush bluegrass country of Kentucky. They were among the very first settlers of Kentucky and were constantly harried by the Miami and Shawnee from the north. Being a veteran of the French and Indian war of 1756 the senior Wells had little fear of the Indians. He'd misjudged them. He was killed in battle with them in 1782 in which his young son Samuel also fought. His wife died soon after, leaving William, a boy of 12 still needing care. The other children, Carty, Haden, Samuel, Yelverton Peyton, and Elizabeth were old enough to be on their own.

The horses clanked off the boat, ready to climb the slight incline to the town sitting on the limestone table above the river. William was amazed at how Louisville had advanced during the eight years he'd lived with the Indians. At the time of his capture, Indians were raiding settlers who dared to live a few miles outside the town or even outside the fort established by George Rodgers Clark in 1778. He himself was stolen about six miles south of the fort at Roberts ' Pond while fishing with three friends.

He stared at the numbers of people as they rode toward the fort. Though most were dressed in buckskins, there was a new breed who wore silk stockings and frockcoats. Louisville was no longer just a raw settlement on the frontier. Soldiers, wagons, horses, people, many speaking foreign languages, filled the unpaved streets. William thought to himself, with every battle and bottle of whisky the Indians decrease in numbers, whereas the country is filling up with white men.

Dismounting at Fort Nelson, Samuel went to ask if news of General Putnam's arrival upriver at Cincy town had come. No word yet was the answer. Samuel said that he had urgent business with the man, and an interpreter available for him. He should be sent for as soon as word came that he had arrived.

While Samuel talked with the officer in charge William looked over the fortifications, tentatively wondering if the Miami could take the fort. Though it was little more than piles of dirt against the walls of the cabins, surrounded by a log fence, the population of the town was great enough that he doubted the Indians would have a chance here.

The soldier on duty looked Wells over and William returned the man's stare. Soldiers here were uniformed, wearing tight fitting pants, white buttoned vests, and a coat over all, similar to a tuxedo coat, hanging down to the knee in the back. Long rows of shiny buttons decorated the front and shoulder while a large bushy hat including a feather completed the outfit. The uniform would be more suitable at a ball than for working in and about the dusty, dirty fort. Never the less, William wished he had one.

The brothers left the fort for the comforts of a tavern, a hot meal and real bed, shared. Many years had passed since William had such luxury as a feather bed. Even the fact that the room they rented was shared by others who slept on the floor did not diminish the wonder of it.

Fresh baked bread, bacon, and eggs started the next day. Samuel said, "I'd like to buy some linen and cotton for new clothes for you before we leave town. Also, I have a few necessaries to get for the farm. You're welcome to come with me or walk about by yourself if you'd rather."

The two went their own ways agreeing to meet at the tavern for the noon meal. William walked along the street looking at the local people doing their business. He felt a complete stranger in this civilized town. Here there were no brawling Indians in the street and women went about quite calmly shopping. Stopping at a trading post he marveled at the variety of goods available for trade. Linen was a dollar a yard. It would be good to have a new shirt he thought. There was a small looking glass in front of a group of ladies hats. He peered curiously into its depths at himself.

He saw a young man of twenty-two, very white skinned with freckles, brown eyed, and beardless, with lots of red hair tied in a pigtail with a piece of leather that fell down his back. He could clearly see he did not look exactly Indian but the Buckskin shirt was obviously made by a squaw. In fact, he appeared to be a back country trapper who didn't have any money. The idea was somehow unappealing.

Returning to the street he ran his hand over the flank of the beautiful horse. It was not his, and he had never had such a fine horse, nor did he have the money to buy it. A new and completely foreign idea came to him that he was an insignificant person here. But I'm the great chief Little Turtle's son-in-law, he thought. Several farmers walked by. Looking at them he knew this would mean nothing to them. They would probably run for cover if they knew that in his heart he was an Indian. Everywhere the fact was apparent that to have any power in the white man's world one had to have money. Still a voice drummed in his head, you are Indian, my son. Slowly the thought came to him, maybe I could find some way to get money for me and the Indians. But as he gazed across the river at the wilderness on the Indian side of the Ohio, he wondered, how ever in the world was he to do it?

At noon the brothers met at the tavern to eat a well cooked meal of stew before mounting the horses for the trip nine miles south along Beargrass Creek to Hoglands Station. This was one of the many small settlements in Kentucky called stations. Here Samuel had a flourishing plantation. The road crossed slightly rolling country, the forest largely cleared for the new farms surrounding the growing town, Louisville. The land here on the south side of the river had a more southern atmosphere than on the north side. Somehow the grass was lusher, and here and there Magnolia trees bloomed. The Ohio River seemed to be the line between the northern and southern climates.

Samuel kept up a running conversation as they rode. "This here country's to be made a state this summer. The state of Kentucky. We sure as hell've worked for it long enough. Virginia don't want to lose this land, but it ain't right, us bein' ruled by laws made by men hundreds of miles away. Why, it takes a man several days jest to ride to their courts of law, up and over the Cumberland Gap. Now we can make our own laws ta suit us. I've a mind ta stand as representative myself when our State Congress gets organized. Being a major in the Kentucky militia gives me a certain amount of pull." He gave his brother a meaningful glance that was completely wasted, as his brother really didn't understand what he was talking about. William was silent. This was a totally foreign subject.

Samuel continued, "They've collected money from a good many settlers to build a road back to Virginia. It's to be called the Wilderness Road. Maybe you'd want to work on that. The pay ain't too bad I hear."

Wells looked at him for a time, wondering why Sam thought he was here to stay and then said, "I won't be here long. As soon as my family is freed I'll be goin' home."

This reply surprised Samuel. He'd completely forgotten about the savage world for a moment. Now he realized again that his brother would need to learn many things about the politics of the world and that the free life of the Indians was a doomed thing.

"Boy, the Injuns get their guns from the British don't they?"

William said, "Yes."

"Have your British friends told you that they are at war with France and won't have guns to spare for you?"

This news caught William totally off guard. The Indians' guns were always needing repairs. Without a continued supply of new ones, they'd soon be in trouble. They had become so dependant on them that it was unthinkable to go back to the days of only the bow and arrow. "We haven't heard anythin' of such a war."

Samuel's words started William thinking along new lines. The Indian culture depended upon the warrior system in which going to war was the major work available to the male. It didn't occur to them that they were being used. That their deaths were not an exalted thing, but merely a convenience to another country. But how could they live without the British? They had become as dependant children on the trade goods they received from them. William wasn't sure he could trust his brother enough to discuss the problem openly, at least not yet.

Samuel noted that his brother was seriously considering the things he'd said. Looking at the beautiful country through which they passed he began, "It ain't been too many years since Dad and his brother Haden come out with a few other men to survey this country. I believe it was 1775. It was wild, really wild then." He looked at his brother, "Probably much like it is up north in Indian country now. Anyways, they built a camp called Indian Camp near Kenton's Station east o' here. All these men set out their own cabins some half to three quarters of a mile apart. Eventually, Dad and Haden laid out Wells Station for themselves before goin' back to Pennsylvania to git Ma and us kids."

He laughed to himself as he remembered an old story. "You know, your Uncle Haden never married. Well, they was this fellow, name ot John Rusts, in the group of surveyors. He called Hayden some name. They was in their camp the night that this happened. Well, sir, thev had such a desperate fight that the others thought one would surely kill the other. People later called it a damnation fight and named the place Battle Creek. Now its got our name. Wells Creek. I've got a pretty good idea of what he called him." Looking sideways at his brother he winked. "Do they have any of that type of men among the Indians, you know, kind of female like?"

Wells smiled. "Yes. But they don't look down on them. In fact, they're sorta prized. I guess as a curiosity. Those braves doll themselves up in beads or whatever they fancy, and I guess everyone else gets a kick out of watchin' what they do." The two felt closer somehow, for having shared the bawdy story.

William began growing curious about the other members of his family. "What are my brother Carty and the others doin' to earn their livin'?"

"Carty lives at Cox's station. He runs a company called the Wabash and Ohio River Boat Service. It runs boats back and forth twinxt Vincennes and Louisville. I rode out to Vincennes to get you on one of his boats. Yelverton Peyton surveys everything between here and Shelbyville. Then there's Elizabeth." He didn't say anything more but just sat on his horse as it trotted down the dusty road.

"What about Elizabeth?"

"She threw in her lot with the Catholics and is a nun."

William sat back in surprise. "A Nun? But there ain't any catholics in our family." William began laughing. He laughed and laughed, seeming not able to stop.

Sam grew flustered and then angry. "I don't see what's so all-fired funny."

William struggled to regain control and finally said, "Its jest that, well, you in the army killin' the Indians: me. killin' whites and all; well, a religious jest don't seem to fit in our family."

Samuel scowled. "It's probably my fault. When Ma and Pa died, Carty had a young family of his own to care for. I was jest newly married and had all kinds of problems, what with Rebecca always sick and then dyin'. I jest didn't see any way to keep you and Elizabeth so I had to farm you out for your care. Then Elizabeth started goin' round with the catholic set and I jest didn't pay any attention. I don't know if I can ever make things right for her....or you."

The two rode along silently. It was a new experience for William, having someone care this much for him. He stole a sideways look at his brother as the silence lengthened. Finally he said, "You can't be blamed for anything that has happened. Elizabeth picked her road. I have a different life now but maybe you can help me by fillin' me in on the American's plans for the Indian territory. As you said, we only get half the news...the British half. The Indians are my people now and maybe I can learn ways to help them live through these times."

Samuel smiled, cheered up. "That's the ticket little brother. With Haydon, Yelverton and my help, you'll come out of this on top. Now the thing you want to do is work in the military for the U.S. Government. That way you can get a grant of land to start your own farm. Like I did. I'll give you some slaves to help you out. So when word comes that Putnam wants you as an interpreter, you'll be on your way. As interpreter, I'm sure you can see ways you can help the Injuns." A light flashed in Samuel's brain and he said, "You'll be the bridge between the Indians and whites, boy. By God, I believe you'll be famous."

William thought this over and the idea appealed to him. He would be someone after all, someone of importance. All he had to do was to play the game on both sides, white and Indian, and he'd come out on top. He would wear silks and uniforms, have money to buy any trade goods he wished, and own his own land. It was all a matter of walking the line between the two cultures. And he would do it. He would learn from this caring brother how to make it in the world of white men.

The land was mostly cleared now as they entered Hoglands Station. Several cabins were clustered together, built close for mutual protection from Indians. Set away from the others was the large cabin of Samuel Wells. Behind it were a number of smaller cabins and several barns. The walls of what appeared to be a huge house were being built from a pile of bricks. This was set at some distance from the log house. A black man came forward as the two brothers drew up near the barn. "Moses, take good care of these horses. They seen a lot o' miles."

"Yessair." The man led the horses away and the brothers walked up onto the porch of the cabin and on into the house.

"Mary?" Sam called. A black haired woman of thirty-two came quietly from the back room. She ran forward to give him a quick hug. "I brought an Indian home for you, Sweetheart. This here's my little brother, William. He'll be stayin' here awhile."

Mary smiled, holding out her rough hand. "I'd know you anywhere, you're so like Sam here. Bet ya'll got the appetite of a bear. I'll get some supper stew and biscuits right smart quick."

William smiled back, feeling at ease. This woman would not be hard to like. She was rounded, sure of herself, and obviously kind. He would learn that she was very feminine but had the strength necessary for survival on the frontier.

"How many acres did the boys get cleared while I was gone," asked Sam mischieviously.

"Acres? The men been workin' on the west. They're havin' a smart bit of trouble with that field they cleared last winter. Moses broke a plow handle on a big tree root in there last week. The Jersey cow dropped a calf Friday. Nice little heifer. And course, I've kept the younguns busy hoein' in the garden. Keeps them from fightin' leastways."

"You've been real busy I can see. Another good crop year and I'll buy you another kitchen woman to help out."

"If I get any older, I know I'll need her. When you're gone it's 'bout more 'en I can handle 'round here."

"Well didn't I bring back another hand to work the place?" He winked broadly at William. "I'm goin' to turn this here Injun into a first class farmer, see if I don't."

William made a token protest, "Remember, I'm not stayin' here forever."

"Son who knows how long it'll take Putnam to come west down the Ohio from Washington. Why, your red brothers may lift his hair and we never see him. In the meantime, it won't hurt you to learn how to make a livin' from the soil. You'll want to know how to run a farm of your own one day. Now, let me show you 'round the place before supper." Leaving the comfortable cabin, the two walked to the place where the new brick house was being built. "Gittin' prosperous enough that we got to build a new house. I had a carpenter out from Louisville to lay it out. Now, the boys are makin' bricks and we even got a few walls started."

William was very impressed with the size of the future home. It was the most amazing house he'd ever seen, and to think that his own brother would possess it. He became more determined than ever to become successful on white man's terms. Next the slave quarters were toured. Samuel owned a large number. He introduced William to them, while telling his brother the strong points of the various men. "You'll need slaves of your own to clear your land. When you do, come to me and I'll give you a share, as your inheritance from Pa. Let's take a look at the crops before we go in. I raise hemp, corn, a little tobacco and I been tryin' out cotton but so far it don't do too well. Not a long enough growin' season here it seems. The thing that grows best in this country is grass. I may go to raisin' cattle and horses only. Now, if the Indian raids would jest stop altogether, we'd be sure o' gettin' real prosperous. What kind of crops did you raise up north?"

"The squaws raised corn, squash, beans, melons and such. Braves don't work in the fields much."

"Well I'll be jiggered. I'll have to tell Mary that one." He laughed loudly with raucous ha, has. "Wouldn't that be a sight? Her with her belly out to here with a youngun, hangin' on to a plow." He laughed again.

"Our women don't use plows, they use hoes."

"But, ya'll was jest a bunch of savages so that's not surprisin'. While you're at our place I'll learn you to use a plow all righty." He laughed again while William frowned helplessly. But, he knew he would have to go along with his brother if he were to reach his dream of success.

And so William Wells, Indian, spent the next month learning the fine points of farming. He became intimately acquainted with the business end of a cow, plow, and saw. Extra minutes were not to be wasted on a pioneer farm. Ceaseless toil was needed to accomplish all the work, even with the help of slaves. but these people did not starve in winter. They worked tirelessly collecting and preserving enough food to last through the cold months.

Constantly William compared his old life with the new. The women dressed well, but were required to work long hours. Their life was hard even though they owned slaves. They had more possessions and greater comfort than did the Indians. Also, they had greater security. He could see that his Indian family would have a better life if they lived this way.

In the evenings William sat on the porch watching the slow summer sunset, thinking of the family he had missed for so long. It was almost a year since they were captured. Sam's youngest, Rebecca, soon learned it was pleasant to play by the silent man. Rebecca was named for Samuel's first wife, who died having his first child, Sam, in 1784. Little Rebecca was a charmer with golden reddish hair and bright blue eyes, framed in an innocent face of baby sweetness. She was just four years old.

She had learned that he was another person who did not fit in entirely with the adults. She adopted William as her best friend to whom she brought all manner of shiny rocks or sticks. Whenever he sat down for a few minutes of whittling, she came to sit beside him and in no time was riding his shoulders or sitting on his knee. The void in William's heart caused by his own missing daughter was filled with her company. Complications of life disappeared when viewed through the eyes of a four year old.

Mary often brought her sewing out onto the porch these evenings. She was making several shirts and a suit for William. It wouldn't do for a Wells to appear clothed as a savage. They had their standing in the community to think of, after all. Then there was the matter of William's manners. He had many...Mary searched her mind for the right word... unusual habits learned from the Indians. She would be cooking something in the iron kettle and he would casually walk up, take a handful out, and eat it. These evenings on the porch Mary gently talked of manners and the way one did things to be thought a gentleman.

One Saturday they all went to Louisville to a large brick house where Samuel introduced William to his friends of society. With his virile good looks, dressed in a new suit, William was the center of attention. Everyone wanted to hear about the Indians and about his adventures. He began to change his way of thinking and began to portray the Indian's life style somewhat derisively.

The young women vied with each other to teach him dancing. They did not smell of beargrease and were very beautiful. Since he was married to an Indian princess, the flirtations were safe, the women thought. It never occurred to them that had they been Indians he would expect more from them. William was finding this way of life more and more to his liking.

The morning of July 10, 1792, the family started the business of farming as usual. They were well into the day's work when a rider from Fort Nelson came in mid morning. It was the long awaited messenger from General Putnam, seeking William Wells, the Miami interpreter.

Samuel pressed the man for information as his brother hurriedly gathered his belongings. "Sit down for a cup of milk and piece of rhubarb pie," Sam said. "What's Putnam plannin' to do with my little brother? He ain't goin' smack into war is he?"

"Putnam's been sent out to parley with the Miami Confederation to make a peace treaty. I don't think he'll do'er though. The Indians are attackin' the boats on the Ohio now like they was tryin' to foil the peace meetin' in advance. Two days ago they attacked a boat jest two miles up river from Cincy town. Kilt a man, injured one and captured a boy. A woman was thrown in the water, floated downstream and escaped. She were damn lucky!

The northern Indians are havin' some sort of Grand Council up on the Maumee River that Putnam was to go to, but I don't think he'll go now, the Indian situation is jest too tense. They was four messengers sent from Cincinnati with speeches to the Grand Council to ask for this peace meetin' with Putnam, but none has showed up again at Fort Washington. I bet they're dead. You might know one who went. Colonial Hardin of the Kentucky militia."

Sam was shocked to hear this. "We was with St. Clair together and I was with him several other times as I'm in the Kentucky Militia myself." Sam sat thinking of the battle less than a year ago. "Hardin was always so sure he was right. To the point of being foolhardy. Is there any news from Washington as to who he's picked to lead another army if Putnam fails to make peace?"

"Yep. It's old Mad Anthony Wayne. The news is he's already pickin' an army and layin' out a camp south of Pittsburgh. Putnam sends him a stream of letters about what's goin' on here."

Sam mused, "Anthony Wayne was a stickler for detail in the Revolutionary. But he's gettin' on in years. It'll be a wonder if he's up to a trip into the wilderness. But hell! He couldn't do worse than we did last year with St. Clair. Maybe it'll take someone who's a crank on detail and drillin' as he is to win a war against The Turtle." He paused, then nodded toward Wells. "My little brother here's been tellin' me all the achievements of the great Turtle himself." With some pride he continued, "He's Little Turtle's son-in-law and his wife and child are captives there at Fort Washington."

The messenger jerked his head in surprise. "I probably outhten to say this, but I'd keep that under my hat at the Fort. Who's to say if they'd let her go know'en she were the daughter of the chief."

Listening, William was forewarned that he would need to have his wits about him to get all the Indians freed.

Outside as the two men made final adjustments to their saddles and gear, Sam said, "William, stop if you take the Indians home by way of the Ohio and Wabash. Let us meet your wife. Stop and tell us what your plans are." The two men shook hands, looking each other in the eyes, silently recognizing their bond. Then Sam watched as his brother traveled down the dusty road, troubled by thoughts of the difficulties facing him.

Chapter X

Fort Washington, Cincinnati Ohio, July 10, 1792

General Rufus Putnam looked out over the burgeoning town of Cincinnati below his rough fort office. Set on a two mile plain along the river, the town extended some seven miles northward along the road. There was a lower town along the river, protected by the fort set on the cliff about forty feet above. To serve the fort and the armies that had already been raised and billeted here, the town was growing at a fantastic rate. Merchants crowded in to supply the fort and the needs of the heavy flow of river travelers. Lots originally selling for four to six dollars now were going for thirty to sixty dollars. Two hundred houses already were built and the air was filled with the sound of saws and hammers.

Putnam thought the townfolk were overly optimistic. He was very uneasy because of the recent Indian attacks. It seemed they'd increased their raiding since he'd come to make peace and it appeared this was their negative answer to peace overtures. Originally he was going north to the Miami villages to talk with the chiefs, but the recent raid on Fort Jefferson, just north of Cincinnati, proved the Indians were unwilling to make peace.

As Putnam looked at the colorful cultivated gardens outside the fort walls, and the bustling town, he tried to quell his fears. He'd seen plenty of travel throughout the wilderness, but now he had a terrible case of nerves. The proceedings were not going at all well, and there had been no news from the messengers sent north to the Indian tribes.

Secretary of War, Knox, made an excellent choice in Putnam as the United States Indian ambassador. He was a man of wisdom gained from great experience. For years he was a judge in the Northwest Territory and was newly appointed Brigadier General, in the United States Army, by Knox. With his experience, wisdom, and kindness, the project should be a success, if it hinged on the quality of the man doing the job. Unfortunately, the mood of the Indians was more important, and those that operated from the towns north around Kekionga showed every indication of being extremely hostile.

Putnam returned to his office to fulfill his duty of keeping General Wayne informed of the proceedings here. Wayne was raising a new army back in Pennsylvania. It was Putnam's mission to make peace, but if he failed, President Washington would send this new army against the Indians. The west would be settled, one way or the other. It took him a long time to compose the following letter.

Fort Washington July 10, 1792

Dear General Wayne,

I am instructed by the Secretary of War to keep you constantly Informed of my progress and prospects relative to the treaty which I am Indevoring to bring about. I presume that you are fully acquainted the Capt Hendrick of the Stockbridge tribe left Philadelphia in the month of May with the design to repair to the grand Council of Indians Supposed to be then Setting or about to convean on the Oma, or Tawa River (Maumee), and from thence was to come to Fort Jefferson to conduct me to the Indian council provided they Should agree to the measure.

I wrote you from Marietta the 23 of June. I left that place the 26th and arrived here the 2nd of July, when I learned that on the 25th a party of over 100 Indians attacked a party of haymakers neer Fort Jefferson. When they killed & took 16, foure dead Bodies only were afterward found. On the 7th. Insident one man was killed one wounded and a lad takin prisoner bout three mile from this place as they were ascending the Ohio. These events are by no means flattering to my hopes, and besides, we have a report Indians had killed 4 men going from one of our Forts with a Flag which if true, it is Supposed must be Major Truman and Col. Hardin, however this report wants conservation. and Some Wabash Indians tell us the War Club left by the party who did the Mischef at Fort Jefferson belongs to the Charokees, a Banditte of outCasts that live on the Oma River but not admited into the National Councils; but are fit Instruments for British Emmerseris to make use of if posiable to prevent a treaty—I propose to remain here for the present and Shall write you by every oppertunity and Should the wished for Capt

Hendrick arrive I will by express give you notice as soon as posiable.

Rufus Putnam

Putnam sealed the letter to be sent the perilous trip upriver to Pittsburgh. Letters to Secretary Knox he'd been sending overland to Lexington, Kentucky and then on to Philadelphia. He called out to the soldier on duty, "Is Mr. Heckewelder about?"

"Just returnin' there, sir." The soldier pointed toward the warehouses on the river side of the fort. In these buildings mechanics worked on all the trappings of war. Also supplies for the fort were stored here. Putnam walked down to join his friend, a Moravian minister from Bethlehem, Pennsylvania, who had accompanied him west in hopes of helping on this treaty. Heckwelder had worked with the Delaware Indians in Pennsylvania and eastern Ohio, converting many to Christianity. Since many Delaware had moved west, it was thought he might be of some help in this venture, as a translater.

Heckwelder said, "The rains yesterday raised the river enough that a boat just came through from Pittsburgh. I was just down there talking to the crew."

"Did they see any hostile Indians?"

"As they passed the Sciota River they were fired on. The devils had taken their canoes to overtake the boat when three other well armed barges came up from behind and fired cannon at the Indians. One of the boats took twelve shots from the Indians but no one was hurt."

Putnam answered, "We were lucky there was a fog when we passed the Sciota on the way out. If there is a parley with the Indians, at least we'll have some supplies now to hand out since these boats came. It appears more and more likely that we should pass on down the Ohio and go up the Wabash to Vincennes to make a treaty with the western Indians. They are the ones whose people are our captives, so they're more likely to be interested in cooperating. From the tone of the news from the north, it looks as if we'd be killed if we make a move in that direction."

"It sure looks like it. Are you going to wait to see if any messengers got through to the Miami Council before moving down river?"

Putnam said, "Yes. Soon as the interpreter gets here we can talk to those five Indian chiefs that came to see the captives the other day from Vincennes. They probably know the minds of the Northern Miami better than anyone just now. Then too, I'll have to wait for a letter from Knox giving permission to make a treaty with the Western Indians. Frankly, that appears to be the only thing we can do. I'd want a good army escort if I take the captives down the Ohio. There don't seem to be any secrets from the Indians of army movements. It'll take time to get enough food rations to give out to the Indians when we do have a council meeting. I tell you, Heckwelder, I feel very discouraged about this whole mission. Somehow I know those messengers we sent north are dead, and that's our message from the Indians of what they think about makin' a peace treaty."

Heckwelder placed his hand on Putnam's arm. "Sir, I have worked with the Delaware for many years. they are a noble people who have been pushed west continually by the white man. I can't say I truly blame them for not wanting to sell their lands and move west again."

The two men stared out across the Ohio River as it continually flowed toward the Mississippi River and then on to the ocean. Finally Putnam said, "There is nothing that can be done to stop the flow of settlers west. You might just as soon try stoppin' that river. We'll just have to do the best we can to keep the settlers and Indians from killin' each other off. This peace treaty is the only way I can help. Maybe it will give all the people a little more time to live."

The evening of July 12 the interpreter, William Wells, arrived at the fort where a guard ushered him into Putnam's office. "Sir, it's William Wells, the Miami interpreter you sent for."

"Come in. Come in, young man. I've been eagerly awaiting your arrival as there is no one here who can speak to our captives. Tell me a little about yourself." Putnam smiled, well satisfied with the appearance of the clean-cut young man. He wore new well-made clothes, was young, and looked very strong and healthy. By all reports he was of a good Kentucky family.

William looked at Putnam somewhat hesitantly. He wasn't used to telling his life story to anyone; certainly not to an army man. But the man had something about him that made him want to trust him. In fact, he immediately liked him as he had a somewhat fatherly appearance. He began, "Eight years ago I was stole from Kentucky by the Eel River Miamis. I was adopted into the family of the Sachem, Gawiahaetle. There I learnt the language and was a good brave to them." He paused thinking, then said, "My adopted father gave me my freedom in the Spring and so I went to Post Vincennes and then on to visit with my brother in Kentucky."

Putnam was charmed by the story and beamed at Wells. Here was a man who really knew the Indians and could help him know how to deal with them. This young man could be a savior in this conflict with which he was so poorly equipped to deal. "Son, what does your father's name mean. Gawahae...."

"It means hedgehog or porcupine."

Putnam looked at the young man for a minute and then asked, "Were you with the Indians when St. Clair took an army against them?"

The ground was getting dangerous, but Wells didn't care. Defiantly he said, "Yes sir. The white men raided my home village and stole my adopted mother and sisters. They burned my house. And hell yes, I was with the Indians when they took their revenge agin' St. Clair."

The two men took measure of each other silently. Finally Putnam asked very calmly with some pity, "Give me your account of the battle. Do you know where the cannon were hidden by the Indians? I'm told they were not there when the battle ground was visited last winter."

William gave his account of the war with St. Clair and said he knew where the cannon were buried. "Now, I'd like to see my mother and sisters, sir. It has been almost a year since they were captured."

"Yes. I'll pay you a dollar a day as my interpreter and if all goes well, you'll be kept on in that capacity. Now you go on and see about your kin." Putnam watched the redhaired young man leave, wishing he were twenty again. There was a very likable quality about Wells. And with his background, he could very well save this whole mission for him. Smiling, he thought this had been a profitable day indeed.

William ran down the hill on which the fort stood to the stockade where the fifty-seven captives lived. The soldier on guard opened the heavy wooden gate and Wells walked into the enclosure. The sound of coughing came from many places in the camp. Smoke from several cook fires filled the air and the stench of the place was strong. His eyes moved from face to face, looking more closely at those women with children. Finally his eyes came to rest on Sweet Breeze, his squaw.

"Wangopath?"

She looked up startled and gasped, "Apeconit!" The two laughed throwing their arms around each other and then she began crying. He wrapped her in his arms, rocking her, trying to comfort the sobs she'd saved for a year. A little girl stood watching this, very surprised at her grownup mother crying. The joyous word spread that it was Apeconit. Instantly he was the center of the crowd that included his adopted mother. The din of loud wailing and crying rose above the stockade. With tears rolling down their faces they bewailed the waiting and hardships they had endured for almost a year.

Finally, when they had settled down a little, they had many questions for him. Not knowing English, they'd had little news and didn't know what was going to happen to them. Wells motioned for them all to sit down so they could all hear. "Mother, my friends, very much has happened since the white men stole you from our villages a year ago. After you were gone, we had a great victory against the Long Knives for revenge.

We killed so many white men we couldn't raise our battle axes any more. We should have been happy but we were not, for you were gone. The chiefs and I went to Vincennes to find you but you were not there, so I went to Kentucky with my brother. He is a white man and he knew the way to get your freedom. So I came here as interpreter for the Long Knives to help make a peace treaty.

Our people said they would make peace for your return. In a few days the soldiers will take you all downriver on boats back to Vincennes for the treaty talks. My friends, the times are not the same. We will have to work with the white men to stay alive."

An old chief asked, "What does Little Turtle say of this?"

"The Turtle did not go to Vincennes. I can't answer for him. It was just the chiefs of the raided villages that went there." Having answered their major questions, he returned to Sweet Breeze and their daughter to continue their reunion. "I told Mr. Putnam you were my sister. My brother in Kentucky thought they might not release you if they knew you were Little Turtle's daughter."

"This brother, what did he have to say to you?"

William looked down at their intertwined hands. "He wanted you to come and live in Kentucky. He wanted all of us there."

She searched his face. "You said?"

"That I am an Indian and will stay with the Indians."

Relieved, Sweet Breeze gave him a hug. William continued, "It may not be true. We may have to live with the whites because my brother showed me how the Indians will be defeated if there are any more wars. And I want us to live a better life. Our cabins burned all the time, people killed, it jest ain't the way to live." He looked at his little girl. "I want a better life for us"

Sweet Breeze began crying again. "The year has been so terrible, so bad. So many are sick here."

He tipped up her chin. "But you had enough to eat didn't you? Warm blankets, a cabin to live in? Would it have been different if I had just gone on the war path?"

She couldn't believe it, but he didn't understand. She had been locked up, away from her people, in a strange land for a whole year. She began crying again for all the days of sadness and hardship. The small family went into a cabin to cling together, beginning to mend the heartbreaks of the past year.

Five chiefs and a squaw had come from Vincennes earlier in the week to talk with Putnam. One of them, a favorite chief, promptly died bringing much sorrow to everyone. Putnam arranged a funeral with full army honors for him and had him buried in the local Cincinnati cemetary, raising a white flag on a pole above the grave so the Great Spirit could find it, according to Miami custom. This was highly unpopular with town residents. Their own people were being killed almost daily by Indians. It seemed to them that a murderer was being honored.

A week passed. The captives were impatient to be released so a chief sent Wells to ask Putnam for a talk. Putnam agreed, walking to the enclosure with William. There the old brave stood in the customary attitude of one making a speech. Wells stayed to one side between the men, translating.

> The Wea said:
>
> Companion or confident friend, I call you so because brothers may sometimes differ but companions never do.
>
> I am no chief; nor do I know well how to speak. This man (pointing to one setting by) is a chief but not a great chief nor can he speak; the man who is dead was a Chief, but not the greatest Chief, and could speak well.
>
> I fear these women and children will all die if they remain here much longer. I pray you will take us all, along to the Ouiatenon post as soon as possible. I fear very few of our chiefs, if any will come to this place but a great many chiefs will meet you there, who can speak well. I pray therefore that you will go along with us to the Ouiatenon Post as soon as possible.
>
> A string of wampum was given to seal the speech.

"Tell him I'll give him the answer tomorrow. Right now I've got my hands full. The chief that died was dug up and drug through the streets. We buried him again, put the white flag up and all, like your people wanted. But I've had to put a guard on his grave." Putnam turned away, carrying the speech of the Indian written out on paper.

The next day he had his answer, even with the customary opening greeting that the Indians expected. It said:

> July 20th 1792
>
> Brother!
>
> You call me confident friend, which name is very expressive.(good) But I wish us to retain the name of brother, since we were born on one island, and are of one family. 'Tis true, brothers may sometimes differ, yet they soon unite again.
>
> Brother,I feel sorry for the loss of your chief who was a great man and a good speaker, and who was to trans-

> act the business between you and me. You spoke to me yesterday with tears in your eyes; yet I understood you. I can't say all to you this time what I wish to say, but when our mourning shall have ceased a little I shall be able to speak cheerfully.
>
> Brother, I wish to make you happy in every respect. Your women and children are under my care and protection and I am making the necessary arrangements for our journey to the O. Post where I hope and expect to see all your chiefs and great men. There to consult on and make a lasting peace between the Indian tribes inhabiting the Wabash country and the people of the United States (or the 13 great Fires). In 30, days I shall be ready to set out with you.

Having answered the Indians most urgent questions Putnam returned with Wells to his office to take up once more his education about the Indians. "Do you think the Miami will come to the treaty meetings at Vincennes?" he asked.

Wells answered, "The Wea and Eel River Indians will agree to sign a treaty, but that is only because you have their captives. They are great liars and I cain't say for sure they won't turn around and make war again. When I left, the highest chiefs of the Miami had gone to council to see the Shawnee and Delaware to find out whether they wanted to go to war. They won't be goin' to the treaty council at Vincennes."

Putnam answered, "That doesn't surprise me. We received word that the four messengers sent north with peace overtures were all killed. It appears that making a treaty with the Indians of the western quarter is the only alternative open to us now. Since their chiefs came here it is like an open invitation to hold it. We'll send them back to gather their people for it. We'll get supplies and then start on the trip."

Wells said, "You'll have ta have lots of provisions ready 'cause the chiefs will bring their whole tribes with 'em. There'll be hundreds of Indians there, all expectin' to be fed. Oh, and bring lots of strings of wampum. Speakin' to an Indian without wampum is like talkin' to a lawyer without money."

Putnam laughed thinking once again what an amazing find this young man was.

The following days were filled with activity for General Putnam. Letters of his intent were sent to President Washington including the speech sent to the western Indian tribes asking them to meet at Vincennes for a council meeting. With every such speech, the proper strings of wampum, a string of carved shells, was sent. These strings of wampum had come to mean the same as the signature on a contract. Certain Indians were charged with the job of remembering what the various strings were for.

A letter to Hamtramck at Vincennes asked that soldiers be at the mouth of the Wabash to escort them through the more dangerous territory up the Wabash. Then too, cattle herds needed to be bought and taken overland from Louisville for the council. Bacon, silver broaches and earrings, bolts of calico, and blankets all had to be purchased to take as gifts for the Indians. Finally boats were bought and all was ready for the great trip down the Ohio River then up to Fort Sackville at Vincennes.

Boats filled with captives and an army guard of sixty men started down the river August 15, l792. Putnam and Heckwelder waited two days before following in order to get last letters sent from Secretary Knox. If it weren't for the Indian threat the two men would have thoroughly enjoyed the trip down the river. West of Cincinnati the land was completely wild. Buffalo, wild turkeys, brown and yellow bears, and flocks of geese could be seen grazing on the shore. Some were shot when needed for food, right from the boat. During the night they floated with the current rather than risking a camp on shore.

By August 20, Fort Stuben at Clarksville on the Indian Side of the Ohio came into view. Built on land given to George Rodgers Clark, a few houses had grown up around the fort at the Falls of the Ohio, or Lewekeomi, in Miami. Rejoining the others, they enjoyed a few nights sleeping in tents, guarded by sentinels. The interpreter, William Wells, had gone ashore in Louisville to visit his brother while the boat's goods were hauled around the falls by wagon.

The arduous job of getting the boats down the falls was begun the next day. The water was low, so that getting the barges, two being forty by sixteen feet over the falls, would be difficult indeed. Putnam hired special pilots at a guinea a day to navigate the falls.

Heckwelder had time on his hands while the goods were being transported around the falls. He had been keeping a detailed report of the trip describing the countryside as best he could. Making a thorough investigation of these falls, he found the change in "the wild stream" very surprising. In his diary he wrote,

> The falls are indeed remarkable as they have three different channels, each of which distinguishes itself. The one channel on the south side consists of many steps of smooth and pointed rocks, the middle one shoots down, more like a mill dam, while the one on the north side, is a very rapid, tearing stream, full of large stones. Trouble-

> some and dangerous as it is, to pass over them in low water, when the water is high the passage is made very easily, and without the least danger. The falls themselves consist of a deposit or bed of smooth rocks, that are high and low in spots. In the falls, at low water large and dry rocky banks may be seen, upon which everything which lodges on them is caught and petrified. Walnuts, hickory-nuts, acorns and shells of the same, branches, deer and buffalo horns, roots, fish skeletons, snails etc. are frequently seen lying on the flat stones, but if an attempt is made to lift them up they are found to be immovable and petrified. Near the falls on both sides of the shore there are beautiful Lombardy poplars which they here call cottonwood trees. Below the falls, in deep water, large quantities of rockfish are caught. In the summer the falls feed thousands of wild geese, and also the pigs which always find dead fish and the like there.

He was distracted from his writing by a mob of townspeople on the opposite shore at the town of Louisville. It appeared they were threatening to shoot the Indians gathered there waiting for the boats to be taken safely over the falls. Hurriedly he gathered his things and called for a perogue to take him across. The sound of the mob and sobbing Indians made quite a din by the time he arrived. He marched up the slope of the bank and said with all the authority he could muster, "These people are wards of the United States Government. I order you to disperse."

"These filthy Injuns ought to be strung up for all the killin' they done." The speaker was a heavy set woman with dirty hair tied up in a knot. Picking up a rock, she pitched it, hitting a four year old Indian boy who set up a loud wailing.

"Woman, if you care to look, you'll see these are helpless women and children."

"Get them redskins offen our land," a farmer joined in. The whole crowd began jeering then, while throwing sticks and stones. Heckwelder could see it was best to get everyone to the other side of the river where they could be protected from the townsfolk by Fort Stuben's cannon. And he began ferrying them back to the Indian side of the river.

So far one of the boats had been safely taken over the falls. The next one, carrying two sick squaws and two soldiers ground to a sickening, screeching halt on the rock. Water poured relentlessly past it, spraying the two soldiers as they tried to pry it off the rock, but they were hopelessly stuck. Other boats couldn't approach this spot to help for fear of being grounded themselves. Soldiers from the fort came with ropes to try dragging the boat off the rock. Finally they said the job was hopeless. "We'll be back tomorrow," they called to the four trapped on the boat.

At the crack of dawn the fort commandant again sent his men out with their ropes. Coming to the river their shock was complete when they saw the boat had sunk. Coming closer, they saw the people who appeared to be riding the tops of the waves. They were sitting on the roof of the boat. Men threw them long ropes and finally all four were rescued. Smaller boats loaded with the provisions passed safely over the falls, as did the boats for the troops. All then made a camp below the falls, safely away from the townsfolk. Here they remained several days while a rudder on Putnam's boat was fixed and arrangements were made to buy cattle and send them overland to Vincennes.

While these things took place, William Wells took his little family to his brother's home at Hogland's Station. At the sound of arriving horses, Mary came out on the porch. Before greeting them she appraised the slim dark haired beauty riding beside William. The girl looked very young to have a toddler strapped to her back. She looked clean in the calico blouse and long skirt, but she rode astride the horse and her hair was bound up in an unusual clubbed knot at the back of her head. "You must be Sweet Breeze. You are so lovely, it's no wonder William picked you for his wife." While William translated this, Mary took the toddler from Sweet breeze, giving the child a kiss.

Sweet Breeze had never met a white woman who seemed so warm. The Indians had received nothing but abuse from the townfolk of Cincinnati. With a rare smile she said in Miami, "We are honored to be guests of your house."

Rebecca came running when she learned Uncle William was here. Flinging herself on him she said, "Uncle William, we've got new kitties!"

William swung her up over his head saying, "How's my big girl?"

Coyly Rebecca said, "I missed you ever so much, Uncle William."

Mary laughed at her young daughter, the southern belle at the age of four. "Ya'll come in and we'll have some dinner. You, Rebecca, go get some toys for your cousin to play with." Later when the children were settled for naps, the adults retired to the parlor.

Samuel opened, "Now that the captives are freed, why don't you stay here and set yourself up in business or farm?"

William answered, "I only have a few dollars I earned as interpreter. Not enough to buy land. "Sides, there's nobody to go along to interpret for the treaty but me. Nobody ta see the Indians get a fair shake on the deal."

Sam argued, "Sweet Breeze ain't in the best of health, William. She's got quite a cough there. Bein' in jail for a year didn't do her no good.

I think you ought ta leave her and the youngun here while you go up ta Vincennes with Putnam."

William gave his wife who didn't understand the words a searching look. He knew she was not well, but he just couldn't be parted from her again so soon. She wouldn't like it anyway. "Sweet Breeze, my brother here says you should live with them while I go north with the Indians."

Sweet Breeze started in alarm at these words. "No, no, my husband. I want to go home. all year I have waited, hoping I would not die before once again I could see my homeland. You can't make me stay here now." Tears started down her face. Mary instantly went to her, placing her arms about the young girl.

William looked back at his brother. "You can see how it is. We jest don't fit in here. Our life is with the Indians. Putnam says I can keep on workin' as an interpreter for the U.S. Government if all goes right."

"If you go back to the villages in the North, promise me you'll come back here and bring your family if the Indians decide to make war. You know full well, it jest don't do, your bein' in a fight against white men, William. You're a white man, like it or not."

William stared back belligerently, not liking to be told what he should do, then erased his dangerous thoughts. His brother had been nothing but kind. Silently he turned away.

"William, I want your promise. Do you want your own wife and child murdered in war by a white man? That would be a stinking tragedy–all on your own head if it happened."

Giving in, William finally answered, "I will bring them here and not fight with the Indians if there is a war. But that land up there is jest about as important to me as it is to Sweet Breeze. I guess 'cause I spent so much of my young days there. It's jest my home, now." His face crumpled for an instant, then the years of training as an Indian brave took over and he regained his composure.

"While I was at Cincy town I spent a lota time lookin' an' watchin'. All them people that's there now, an' they jest keep on comin', while the Indians get fewer all the time. The wars, whisky, and then small pox and white men's sickness. They's been two big wars in the last two years. We kilt lots of whites, but they jest keep comin'. Ride down the Ohio and they's lots of game, but it don't grow so fast as what people's killin' it from boats. I jest don't know what to do. All I really want is to go back to Kekionga away from all these people, but like you say, my skin is white."

Samuel felt compassion for his strange brother. He was a mixture of ruthlessness, and tremendous energy, yet at the same time he had a curious feeling of responsibility for the Indians and even for the whites. It appeared he had a growing ambition too, probably because of his new family responsibilities. The boy, William was fast becoming a man. "I will help you whenever you need it. There will be ways I can help you deal with the whites who will take Indian lands if they can. If I sit as a State Representative I will know better what the government's intentions are for the land up north. But, if the Indians go to war, send Sweet Breeze here to me."

William translated this to Sweet Breeze. Just then the children romped into the room. "Mama, we woked up," Rebecca said leaning on Mary's lap.

Mary put her arms around her and around Sweet Breeze's daughter who came to peer up at her with liquid almond shaped brown eyes. "Your girl's name is Ahpezz...."

"Ahpezzahquah." Answered William.

Sam said, "Why don't you call her Ann for her Christian name. That's easy ain't it?"

Sweet Breeze thought it was a good name. So Ann it was whenever she was in Louisville.

When the Wells returned to the river camp, Putnam's boat was repaired and the cattle and other goods ready for the treaty council. September was ideal for the trip. Food was in abundance and it was warm. As they traveled down the Ohio, the captives grew more cheerful daily as they neared their people who would meet them at Vincennes.

John Heckwelder, the Moravian minister and interpreter, had considerable interest in Indian cultures having spent many years as a Delaware Missionary. He studied Wells in curiosity. Wells was a white man but had many Miami mannerisms. Yet he could explain in white men's words why he did these things.

It was the job of the guides to provide the company with meat. Buffalo grazing along the shore provided most of it. One night, camped along the river, a yellow bear came to investigate the cook pots. As the hapless creature ambled closer, Wells raised his gun, resting its long barrel against a tree to steady it. the gun roared and the animal fell, loudly crying in pain. Heckwelder watched amused as Wells ran up to the animal giving it a serious speech in Miami, ever so often hitting it on the nose with the ramrod of his gun. Finally, he killed the poor beast with a knife, his attitude showing something of disgust. Heckwelder walked over to watch him prepare the meat.

"What were you saying to that animal there?"

"I was jest tellin' him what an awful coward he was actin', him a bear an' all. After all says I, he knew the fortune of war. One or the other of us was to fall. It was his fate to be killed, and he shoulda died like a man, like a hero, and not like an old squaw. I told him if the case was reversed and I had fallen into the power of the enemy, I would not have disgraced my nation yelling like him, but woulda died with firmness and courage, as becomes a true warrior." Wells, returned to the job of cutting up the meat while Heckwelder pondered what he'd said. apparently that was the way the Miami braves thought. It explained why they showed such bravery in battle. Certainly it was worthy of recording so he brought out his diary and wrote down the speech.

By September the third, the boats reached the mouth of the Wabash, or Wabashiki according to the Indians. Where the two rivers met the Wabash was almost as wide as the Ohio. Troops sent down by Hamtramck from Vincennes hailed them from an island in the center.

"What a wonderful country," enthused Putnam as the boats grounded on the island. "It reminds me of my home, Marietta, Ohio. This would be as good a spot for a town as that."

A soldier said, "After you've listened to these damn paroquets for awhile you won't think so. Their racket like to drove us out of our minds."

Putnam gazed at the colorful red parrot-like birds marveling at how many there were. "Maybe that's what brings my hometown to mind. Really sir, they're quite a lovely bird." Smiling he added, "Its been so long since we sat at a table. Have your men bring up some planks from the boats. We won't be able to take these big boats upriver anyway. Yes, we'll sit down to a regular table and have us a feast, serenaded by the cardinals."

Not everyone was charmed with the tables. As the boats were wrenched apart Heckwelder was overcome with a great wave of homesickness. His beloved Bethlehem, Pennsylvania, was such a long distance away and he had to go even further into the wilderness. It seemed to him that the means for his return home from this vast wilderness was disappearing along with the boats.

The feast prepared by the squaws was very good indeed. Buffalo, bear, deer and pork, a turkey, two ducks, pike and turtlesoup, besides various vegetables comprised the meal for the group of about a hundred. The table and benches were added luxury and novelty after days of sitting on the ground for meals.

The next day a small fort was made on the island from the boat timbers. Some goods sent for the treaty council were left here, guarded by twenty-five of Hamtramck's men to be brought upriver later. Six pirogues, hollowed log boats, loaded with the captives and soldiers who rowed the boats, started a pleasant trip up the Wabash. Each day was still quite hot. Often mosquitoes hung in clouds around them. In early fall, they were in their greatest numbers.

September 6th, John Heckwelder began feeling feverish. Riding in the boat, crowded among the people, he soon felt he could no longer stand the rocking or smells, so he was put ashore to walk. In the distance the boats full of laughing chattering women and children made a pleasant sound as John walked along the river bank. He thought, in any other circumstance I would love walking through these noble woodlands. There was little brush so it was easy to keep up with the boats battling against the river's current.

But the malaria attack soon engulfed him. He called to the boat to take him back on board as he was too sick to walk. The next four days the fevers, chills, and headaches were so severe he knew little of the continued journey. Arriving at Vincennes September the 12th, Heckwelder was taken to a house and nursed to the best of their ability, but it was over a month before he would be fully recovered. Malaria carried by mosquitoes, was a continual problem for midwest settlers.

As the perogues landed at Vincennes, groups of Indians already arrived for the council joyously surrounded the boats, firing guns into the air and singing songs of happiness to their friends. Putnam called them together, delivered a speech and then released the captives into the hands of friends and relatives. Vincennes streets vibrated with the noise of celebrating Indians.

After seeing that Heckwelder would be cared for, Putnam went with General Hamtramck to the fort to discuss the cattle that were sent overland. "At long last we meet, General Hamtramck, though I feel I almost know you through letters we've exchanged. Thanks for the men you sent me and all the help and advice."

Hamtramck rung the hand of the pleasant looking older statesman before him. "You're goin' to need more help yet. Let's hope the Indians don't get too drunk and behave themselves. When they all arrive there'll be near on six hundred. I've only got ninety men to keep order, and usually about twenty are sick."

Putnam agreed with the harrassed Vincennes commander. He could see the thickset little man meant well, but was overworked and under staffed. "My friend, Mr. Heckwelder has been very sick during the trip up the Wabash. I can see that the reports that this country is unhealthy are true. But you always have trouble with river towns and bad health."

Changing the subject Hamtramck asked, "Did William Wells join you as interpreter?"

"Yes. A very personable lad he is, too. He has been an invaluable aide to me, teaching me the habits of the Indians, so I won't make any mistakes in my etiquette. I must say I've grown fond of him."

Hamtramck smiled covertly. "You don't want to believe everything you see on the surface there. That's an unusual mix of Indian and white man and I'll bet he's ninety percent Indian in his head. He wasn't the least interested in goin' back with his brother to Louisville 'cept that his

Indian Ma, squaw and child were bein' held captive. That was the only way to get them back, I told him. Otherwise, I do believe he'da lived and died an Indian."

"Well I'll be damned!" Putnam laughed delightedly. "You know, one of the first things he said to me was that the Indians were great liars. All along he led me to believe it was his sister and her papoose that was captive." Putnam laughed harder and finally had to bring out a handkerchief to wipe his eyes. "I kinda wondered why it was he insisted on sleeping out in the stockade with the Indians." Putnam laughed again. "Ah me. You really have to admire the young buck. And he has been a great help to me. The reason I'm wearing civilian clothes instead of an army uniform is that he said the chiefs wouldn't talk peace with a war captain."

Hamtramck agreed. "That's right. That's why we needed someone sent from "The Great Father, Washington" to make peace. The big chiefs wouldn't speak ta me 'cause they think I'm only a war captain. Old Gaweahaetle, the Eel River Chief, did send his brother down, who was also a war captain, but he wouldn't come himself. You have ta know Indian manners and Wells can be a real help to us there. For instance, when you speak with the Indians, there are certain formalities you use, like, I am here to wipe away all tears for the dead, but rejoice for the living. You have ta be a right smart speaker with them 'cause many are real good at it. To get their respect you have to give good speeches."

"Speaking of great liars, that fellow, Wilkinson of the Kentucky Militia. Is he a respected man in these parts? "

Hamtramck rubbed his neck pensively. "He keeps an eye on his own interests."

Putnam continued, "I thought so. He made a curious request just before I left Fort Washington. He wanted me to ask the Indians for the return of several negro slaves that belong to some Kentucky judge in his parts. Now that certainly smacks of looking out for his own interests." Putnam paused, "Of course I will try to get all captured people returned when we make the treaty."

Hamtramck said, "One more thing before you go. The French here are sellin' liquor to the Indians. Now there's a law agin' it, but I'd appreciate it if you'd give a speech to the town folk so I don't have to throw a bunch in jail for sellin' it. They might pay more attention to you, bein' an army man sent out by Washington. We could have a lot of real trouble with liquored-up Indians."

"I'll do it sir, first thing tomorrow."

In these times of slow travel and communications, a council took weeks for the arrival of the participants. This one was no different but summer was disappearing and the time for fall hunt was fast approaching. Then Indians trapped furs to make the bulk of their trading goods. Those already gathered became anxious for the beginning of the talks.

Cook fires for over six hundred Indians filled the Wabash river valley with smoke. Members of all the tribes in western Indiana and eastern Illinois had come, hearing of the food and gifts to be given out. It would be a great entertainment, meeting with Indian brothers and the white men sent by the thirteen fires in the east. Eel River Miamis and Weas were most anxious to make peace since their people had been captured, while neighboring nations came along for the enjoyment of the event. These others were Pottawattomi from the land above the Eel River on to Lake Michigan, Piankashaws from between the Wabash and Illinois rivers, the Kickapoos from Kahokia, Illinois, and the Kaskaskias and Mascoutens, also of Illinois. It was a great convention. Wives and children that for various reasons had to remain in their home camps expected gifts brought back by their men. Most able bodied women and children came along.

Putnam watched the crowds, relieved that he had taken care to bring adequate food and gifts for the Indians. He thought to himself, if they were offended, the whole town of Vincennes could become a blood bath. When he told Wells of his misgivings, Wells said he had nothing to fear since the Indians brought their women and children. There had already been a few deaths. Drunken Indians killed a few of their brothers.

Sunday, September 23, a group of Indian chiefs came to the fort to talk with Putnam. The interpreter was called for the speech made by an Eel River Miami chief. The chieftan, naked except for a belt and breech cloth, wore a necklace of bear claws and large hoop silver earrings. His hair was decorated with some five feathers and his posture was such that there was no doubt that here was a person of stature, a chief. He said:

"My friend. The wind grows cold, and the leaves turn many colors. The animals are waiting for us with winter coats. We want to begin the talks so that our people can go on fall hunt. All important chiefs are here so there is no need to wait for others."

Putnam demurred, "I had hoped that the Miami and Delaware chiefs would come to these talks."

The chief answered, "We can not speak for our elder brothers, the Miamis. But we do not expect them to come to this meeting."

Putnam answered, "Today is the Sabbath but beginning tomorrow a cannon will be fired at ten every morning as a signal to call together the meeting. The United States desires to live in peace with all Indians and to that end I am sent here to discuss with you all the things that have happened so that we can wipe away all tears, and cleanse all blood from the war clubs to begin a new treaty."

Another chief stepped forward, shook hands with Putnam saying, "You, Major Hamtramck, told me there would be a treaty. Now it is come to pass and we are met for that purpose. At such important meetings deliberation and time are necessary. Let us not then be in too great a hurry. We will consider your desire for peace and return an answer to your speech tomorrow."

At ten the next morning the cannon sounded and chiefs of various nations arrived at the council house for negotiations. The meetings that followed were held with great pomp. The first chief that spoke was picked unanimously by the tribes to make the major speech. Then each chief took his turn giving a short message. Four interpreters, including William Wells worked with the tribesmen. The speeches that follow are as given, though in some cases condensed.

Ceremoniously the first chief, a very young man, came forward presenting Putnam with a large pipe then turned holding up a fine wide belt of wampum with thirteen diamond designs worked in shell for the thirteen states. Speaking to the Indians he said, "You my brothers of all nations present: I am glad you are assembled here. I call upon you to hearken to what I say to our Brother of the United States. I should have been glad if matters had remained as they were in the days of the French. Then, all the country was clear and open." For emphasis he repeated the words. "Then all was clear and open." Turning, he shook hands again with Putnam.

"My Older Brother, the French, English and Spaniards never took any lands from us. We expect the same of you. These are the sentiments of the Indian tribes. We would regret the loss of our beds. The author of life created us on these lands, and we wish to live and die on them. No person can take them from us but he who gave them to us. Were the French, English, or Spaniards to attack us, what would become of us? We request of you never to usurp our lands, neither to destroy our game. I tell you the plain truth. Our lands have been stained with blood, which grieves us. But now we are glad. You are come for the purpose of peace.

My older brother, do not blame us for striking you. It was the English that gave us the tomahawk to strike you. You cannot be ignorant of the cause of the war. This war has destroyed many of our people who would otherwise be here, but I am convinced you will wipe off the stains that have been made on our lands. This is the wish of all of us.

My older brother, you are many and so are we. Were we on the same land we might quarrel. It is best that the white people live in their own country and we in ours. Formerly our lands were extensive. Now they are but small. Therefore we wish to keep what we have. We desire of you to remain on the other side of the river Ohio. These are the sentiments of all the chiefs and warriors." The Chief then raised his hand and continued.

"Observe how clear the sky is today. It is a good omen. It has been clear since we began to speak. It promised that our negotiation will succeed. Which is the ardent wish and desire of all the tribes here present.

My older brother, the English and Spaniards by giving us goods, endeavor to keep us strangers to you. It is this cause that there are no more of us here. We desire you to consider our poverty, and to send us something every spring to make us comfortable. You have it in your power to render us all happy and to rejoice our women and children. We desire you to send traders among us."

Turning back to the Indians he told them to listen to Putnam and to leave off stealing horses from the Americans who they reduced to using the hoe instead of plowing. Several smiled at this and the young man sat down.

Following this speech were a succession of speeches, all saying the same thing in different words except for one Piankashaw chief who rose and said, "The great chief, who has spoken to us wants peace, and I want a wife. If he will give me a wife I will give him peace." He turned to shake hands vigorously with Putnam while the others laughed uproariously. Then he continued, "Our ancestors were buried here and this is the proper place for us to speak in." Putnam knew he was referring to the ancient Indian mounds in and about the town.

"You have called us from afar and since we came you have rejoiced our hearts. We hope you will consider the want of our women and children before you leave us, for we are all very poor. I agree that the whites should remain on the other side of the Ohio." With this he delivered two white strings of wampum and retired.

General Putnam was impressed by the eloquent speeches given by those some called savages. Now he rose saying, "Brothers, I have listened to all you said. I have treasured it up in my heart. Tomorrow I shall give you an answer but now we will drink a glass and retire until morning."

That night Putnam worked long hours to prepare a speech that would in some measure equal those the Indians delivered. Sitting back thinking about the events of the day, he thought, the beauty of these speeches is amazing, considering that none of them have been schooled. These are men who care for their people and could hardly be called savage. Thinking on it further he thought, it is we who are taking their lands. The dishonesty of it was repugnant. But there seemed nothing he could do. White settlers would continue to move west and unless he could get the Indians to agree on peace there would be more bloodshed. The candle was almost completely gone when he finally lay down to a fretful sleep.

Again the cannon roared and the meeting was called to order. Some of the Indians had further thoughts on the proceedings of the day before and wanted to elaborate. A chief of the Pottawattomies gave the first speech. He said, "When I received the message that a great chief would arrive here from the United States and that he wished to speak to us, I expected the business would be of another nature, not what I find it to be. I did not expect that we would spend our time in speaking of land, as I find is the case. I have often been asked by the British to sell them land, but merchandise never tempted me. I never yet have listened to those who came to speak of buying lands. I foresaw that if I parted with my land, I should reduce the women and children to weeping, "If your land was dear to you, why did you give it away." He shook hands with Putnam then turned to speak to the tribesmen.

You know I have no complaints to make to the United States for lost women and children as you have. Whenever I went to war, it was against my own color. Alter your conduct. Let the tomahawk remain forever buried. Have pity on your women and children. Chiefs encourage your young men to peace. Young men, listen to your chiefs. Hearken to each other, and assist one another in that which is good." He then presented two strings of wampum to seal the speech.

Finally when all the speeches of the Indians were finished, Putnam rose to present the position of the United States. After the customary opening phrases, he got to the meat of the message.

"When we first met together the sky was indeed very clear as you had observed to me. But in the course of our council, I discovered a cloud had arisen in some obscure part of the sky, which prevented my understanding what you meant by part of what you had said to me.

Brothers, let us understand one another right. You told me it was best for the white people to remain in their country, and you in yours. You said, as the whites were a powerful people they ought to live at a distance from you. You said, that the Americans had best remain on the other side of the Ohio.

Brothers speak plain that I may understand you, and there be no mistake made. Do you mean that we shall get up from this place and other settlements on the Mississippi and go back over the Ohio? Do you mean that this garrison which is built for the protection of the settlement and trade shall be evacuated?

I have often heard that you had permitted your Father the French to sit down on the Wabash River a great many years ago and had given him lands to raise corn on and a range for his cattle. I have since heard that when your Father's family had increased and you saw them so much crowded, that you then extended their limits so that they might have land enough to raise corn and range enough for their cattle. I also heard that the case was nearly the same with the other settlements on the Mississippi.

Let me inform you that the United States are bound to protect all its subjects and since their alliance with France, are become as one people. They live not only here in this place together, but are so throughout the United States.

The United States do not want to take away your lands. When you become their true friends, they will become your protectors. They will protect you in your lands and in your hunting. They will never take any of your lands away from you against your consent. But if at any time you should wish to sell any of them, they will buy them of you honestly. Brothers when the white people give away a thing, they never ask for it back again, and what they have once sold, they never any more look upon it as theirs. I now desire you to inform me how far your lands extend up and down the Ohio. I wish also to know how much land you have given to the French at this place. I wish to know the grants and sales you have made to the settlements on the Mississippi. Give me a plain answer this afternoon."

In the afternoon a chief named Ducoigne rose, presented the wampum and shook hands before beginning. "My older brother, it is not our intention that any persons settled on this side of the Ohio should move away. Our request is that no other settlement shall be made.

Consider, were we to sell the graves of our ancestors would not he who gave us life, and placed us on these lands be displeased? I believe there is no son so unworthy of his ancestors as to sell the graves they are buried in. Were we to sell our lands, we must sell their graves; and the game which affords us daily susbsistence. We therefore wish you never to take our lands by force. There is nothing will prevent a lasting peace and friendship between us but your attempting to take our land from us. Fulfill what you have said. Why would I make a new handle for the axe? I know it would be impossible for us to overcome you in the end. And we believe you have no intention of destroying us.

The whole, you see, is that by leaving us our lands you secure to yourselves our friendship. We do not wish you to be strangers to us. We wish to be your good neighbors and you to send traders among us, to furnish us for our wants as the French, English and Spaniards have done. The white people clothe their women and children. Ours are running naked. Take pity on them and send something every spring to make them glad."

Finally a chief of the Weaughtenows or Weas stood saying, "Our wampum is almost expended and it seems the business is near to close. I am indeed happy that we have met and have made an acquaintance together. We have said a great deal but it all tends to peace. We hope you and the French are as one as we wish it to be so." The council broke up with its usual drinking of a glass together, agreeing to meet the next day to sign the treaty.

September 27, 1792 the treaty was signed which contained seven articles. It said that there would be peace between the tribes of Indians and the States, and that they placed themselves under the United States protection. Also, all white or negro prisoners would be freed, that the Indians would stop stealing negros and horses and would not commit any more hostilities against Kentucky and that they would tell of plans of attack that they knew neighboring tribes planned. In case of any violence that occured to either party, they agreed not to retaliate unless the aggressor refused satisfaction.

The Fourth Article stated:

> The United States solemnly guarantee to the Wabash and Illinois Nations or Tribes of Indians all the lands to which they have a just claim, and no part shall ever be taken from them but by a fair purchase and to their satisfaction. That the lands originally belong to the Indians, it is theirs and theirs only. That they have a right to sell and a right to refuse to sell and the United States will protect them in their said just rights.

The treaty was read to and signed by thirty one chiefs.

Putnam delivered a farewell speech delivering the seal of seven belts of wampum to the most prominent chiefs. Outside the fort, Putnam lit a cannon and the seven who received the belts also fired off the cannon. Then he gave them four oxen, bread and brandy to have a festival.

The shaking fevers finally overtook Putnam, though he had been resisting them during the week of negotiations. Now, he gave in to them, taking to his bed, so ill that the others thought he would die.

Outside the walls of his cabin he heard the merry making of the celebrating Indians. The Vincennes Streets were filled with painted Indians, costumed in their best finery wearing green garlands around their necks as they marched singing to drums, to the dance at the City Hall. Each Nation painted themselves differently, seeming to compete with one another in the designs. Once in the hall they danced, relating their warlike achievements through figures and motions of the dance, all the while brandishing tomahawks in the air. Around their legs anklets of dried deer hoofs rattled in time to the music. The festival lasted far into the night, and it cost two Indians their lives in fights due to the liquor given them.

In the following days Putnam's life hovered on the line between the living and dead. John Heckwelder had recovered from the malaria bout and oversaw the passing out of gifts. Blankets, corn hoes, old hats, bridles, lengths of calico and lindsey, tobacco and silver ornaments, powder and shot were divided among them.

Sixteen chiefs and one squaw agreed to accompany Putnam to Philadelphia and another group was to go with a speech to the hostile Indians at Kekionga, accompanied by William Wells. But because Putnam was so ill, he sent the chiefs and Heckwelder ahead on the overland trail to Louisville, asking that they wait for him at Marietta, Ohio.

By October 7th Putnam could sit up and work a little. He sent for William Wells to discuss the trip to Kekionga and the message he was to take there. The quill scratched across the paper as Putnam strained to gather his thoughts for the letter to the hostile tribes. Wells entered the room, dressed in his buckskins, a typical trapper except for the gleaming red hair. The sight of the handsome young man never failed to bring a smile to Putnam's face.

"Ah, William, so you'll be taking your Indian Mother....and wife back to their old village."

William blushed at being found out by this superior man he admired. "Yes sir."

"I have here a message for the Delaware and other hostile tribes that I wish you to carry to them. Because of the danger of the trip, I'll pay you three hundred dollars to take it to them. The letter asks that they meet me at the mouth of the Muskingum river in Ohio to have peace talks. If you can actually get them to come, I'll pay you two hundred more."

"How will I let you know if they won't talk peace?"

"If it isn't safe for you to travel overland to the Muskingum, then I would expect you to travel to Fort Washington, or some other fort on the Ohio where I will make provision for you to be taken to Marietta by boat."

"Sir, you know it'll take a couple months travel time by boat to do this. Winter's comin' on fast. I don't see how I kin make the trip to Kekionga in time by boat. If you was ta give me a horse, I could probably make it to the tribes and get a message to you in say, two months, afore winter hits hard."

"That's a good idea. But I'm prepared to wait through the winter months for a reply if you can't get one to me faster, since Marietta is my home. If you can't get the Indians to come there, its very important to get word to me what their intentions are. That is, whether they mean to make peace eventually or to continue with their raiding on white settlers. I've got your instructions all written out here, along with a speech for the Indians." Putnam paused as a new worry came to him. "You do read don't you?"

A quick flash of anger crossed Wells' face but was just as quickly gone. "Of course," he said curtly. He reached for the speech, carefully placing it in the carry pouch. "I hope you get feelin' better double quick, sir. It's been real pleasurable workin' with you. A man of action, he was up and gone before Putnam was ready to release him.

Putnam felt a great sadness at being separated from the young man of whom he'd grown so fond during the past three months. As he watched Wells speak to his squaw in a boat leaving upriver before he went to buy his horse, he thought, I'll be surprised if I ever see him again. He felt a certain guilt, sending him into the jaws of the enemy where four other messengers were so recently killed. But it can't be helped, he reasoned. He is the only hope we have of getting a peace message to the hostiles, and besides, that country seems to be his real homeland. Never-the less, Putnam felt the sadness of a parent sending his young son into war as he walked back into the fort.

After Rufus Putnam returned to Marietta, he sent a copy of the signed treaty to Philadelphia. He continued to wait there for William Wells until mid January when he finally gave up hope of the Indians' arrival, having heard nothing from them or Wells. In February he resigned his army commission, due to the ill health caused by malaria contracted on the trip west.

In Philadelphia the treaty of peace and friendship was rejected by the United States Senate. They objected to article IV that said the land belonged to the Indians and that they had the exclusive right to sell or not to sell, but did not include wording to the effect that the United States had the exclusive right of purchase. The Senate voted January 9, 1794 not to ratify it.

Though the United States did not ratify the treaty, they still received the benefits as if they had. In the war to come, the Indians who attended the treaty council at Vincennes did not fight, in large numbers, with the Miami Confederation against the United States.

Of the seventeen Indians that went to Philadelphia to talk with President Washington, nine died of small pox enroute. The remainder asked President Washington not to allow white settlers to take their lands.

Chapter XI

Kekionga, Fort Wayne Indiana, November 1792

After purchasing a fine horse for seventy dollars, paid for by General Putnam with army money, William bought another horse, a gentle blond mare for Sweet Breeze. Gawaihatle, William's adoptive Indian father, had not waited for Apeconit, but was paddling swiftly up the Wabash with his squaw and their daughter-in-law, Sweet Breeze and baby Ann. Originally Wells had thought to send them to stay with his adopted parents. But later, thinking how much more enjoyable the trip overland would be with Sweet Breeze along, he rode along the river after them, catching them about noon.

For once Sweet Breeze was completely surprised. The gift of a horse was a great one, not to be easily passed off. William made light of it, explaining that they could make the trip to Kekionga overland in six or seven days by horse, rather than the twenty-five or so it took by river.

Leaving his adopted parents to continue their journey, they followed a trail along the White River in a northeasterly path. This river was the province of the Delaware Indians in the northern part of its reaches. The most prominent Delaware towns on the White were Anderson's town and one of a Delaware subgroup, the Muncee. William planned to give his message asking for the peace talks to the chiefs as they passed their villages.

The idea of being alone with his little family, away from the various Indian relatives was a romantic one for Wells. They hadn't been really alone since before Sweet Breeze's capture, more than a year before. Hard lessons were learned during the year of separation and hardship. Sweet Breeze would never again know the security of being able to take for granted her life in the village, surrounded by relatives and friends. She would never forget that it could all be whisked away in the space of an hour. William learned that the whole way of life he had adopted and come to love was on the brink of disappearing, erased forever by the expanding settlement of white men. This was to be only a brief visit at Kekionga. He was to take Putnam's message to the chiefs and then return to the American posts with the Indians, or their negative answer.

Sweet Breeze chattered happily, speaking of her plans for her life back home again. "We'll be staying at Kekionga now, won't we, Apeconit? With the village burned at Kenapacomaqua, there will be no place to live and no corn to eat."

"You forget, it's been over a year since you were there. They probably got a crop raised and harvested this summer. Probably even got cabins built again. Though it's stupid to rebuild a village where the Big Knives know one stands."

Sweet Breeze was a little shocked at the tone of disdain for her people she heard in his voice. "The ground is cleared there. Where would you have the people go? North to the land of the Pottawattomie?"

"There's other places to build villages, like down on the Mississinewa. This is a big land with lots of lakes and rivers white men ain't seen or heard tell of yet. If you think the armies won't come again, you're wrong. The people will have to live where it's safe from the armies or they'll have to make peace and let the white settlers come in. If they don't make peace, the armies will come again and again killin' and burnin' jest like they did a year ago." The two rode on in silence, Sweet Breeze's exuberance at coming home considerably dampened.

Rounding a curve in the trail, the river came into view again, a stiff breeze making it sparkle like diamonds in the pale winter sun. The horses surprised a flock of migrating geese, settled for a moment's rest. Honking and flapping, they rose into the air, but not quickly enough. Wells fired into the center of the flock, neatly dropping two birds. Ann, startled, began a loud wailing at which Wells nervously told her to hush up. At this she cried all the harder. Sweet Breeze looked at her husband accusingly as she tried to comfort the child.

Galloping his horse into the shallow river, he collected the birds. On shore, Sweet Breeze soon had wood burning to cook them. While she prepared the birds, Wells felt sorry for his nervous outburst. After all, the child wasn't used to him and hadn't learned that quiet was important in the forest. He took the little girl by the hand and said, "Do you know that a beaver can talk?"

"Beaver?"

"Beaver is the animal that makes wood piles in the river, daming it up. Do you see the wood piles there?"

"Unhuh."

"One time there was a hunting brave that came to a river like this. It was flooded and he couldn't get across. He waited and waited, and was so hungry 'cause there was nothin' to eat, except for the beaver in the river. Course the old beaver didn't want him to eat him." Ann laughed. "The beaver came out on the log and sang a little song to the hunter, hopin' he wouldn't eat him. The song said soon the water from the flood would all go away, and the hunter would find plenty of game on the other side. It went like this.

Sawwattee sawwatty,
Sawwattee sawwatty,
Kooquay nippee ta tsa;
Waugh waw waugh whaw,
Waugh waw waugh whaw."

Anne chuckled and clapped her fat little hands together. She toddled down to the river, straining her eyes in hopes of seeing a beaver. William sat back against a tree, looking out past the river at the flat bottom lands while the savory smell of roasting birds filled the air. Along this river were flood planes that extended on either side about a mile until low hills began. It was rich soil and would have been heavily wooded except it was often flooded. He thought, what good farmland it could be if the flooding could some way be controlled. As one of the first white men in the country, he could pick the best land. He could see himself giving directions to a number of slaves on how to cut down the trees, as he had on his brother's plantation. Then his vision of broad fields, edged by the river disappeared as Sweet Breeze called him to the meal.

Forgetting her former pique, she began talking excitedly again. "Since we were not home to raise a crop this year, how will we get enough food for the winter?"

"I was paid a dollar a day while I interpreted for Putnam. Course I spent most of that on the horse and supplies." Shrugging he continued, "When I take the Indian's answer to a fort I will get more money."

"Aren't you going to stay at Kekionga? I don't want to go back where white men throw things at me and call me bad names." It was becoming more and more clear that Apeconit did not mean to stay permanently to live their life as they'd done before, but she didn't want to face the fact that things would never be the same.

"Sweet Breeze." William pulled her down on his lap. "I can't stay with the tribe all the time anymore. If we're to have a good life like Sam, I'll have to be a messenger for the Big Knives. They pay me good money that can buy us all those things Mary has. Do you want to live in fear from day to day and have your cabin and all your goods burned up every year? If I don't do this, that's what will happen. All the Miamis will be hurt more if I don't work for the white men. They kilt all the other messengers, and like it or not, the Miami need to know what the American army is up to."

She began crying softly, her tears wetting the front of his buckskin shirt. "I don't want to live with those strange people. I want to stay home."

He began rocking her like a baby. "Those strange people are my people you're talkin' about. But, maybe, if The Turtle agrees to make a peace treaty we can live in the Wabash country and I would just travel back and forth taking messages between the Indians and the forts. If he won't make peace, there'll sure be another war. And this one the Big Knives will win. I'll want you and Ann to be safe with Sam's family then." William sighed as he looked across the river to the trees, the bright blue sky, and the tranquility of the place. How pleasant it would be just to live here now, not having to deal with wars, Indian or American politics, or the changes of the times. But that was only a pipe dream, and he had to go on with the struggle of life. Putting out the fire, he gathered his family to continue the long ride to Kekionga.

An older woman straightened from her wood gathering work, shading her eyes to better see the newcomers riding into town. Suddenly, she dropped the wood to run, even with the stiffness of her years, towards the horses bearing the redhaired brave and his family. Gasping, as she reached them she asked in disbelief, "Wangopath?" Tears came to her eyes as she turned her hands skyward. "My prayers to the Great Spirit have been answered. My daughter is returned to me!"

"Mother! Oh Mother!" Sweet Breeze jumped from the horse to embrace her mother and the two began loudly, tearfully to rejoice, while at the same time bemoaning their long separation. Wells looked at them, half smiling crookedly, then turned awkwardly away to unload the horse. Word passed quickly among the villagers that the Carrot had returned, bringing back his captured squaw.

Hearing the excited villagers, Little Turtle came from his cabin, going with all the speed he could without a loss of dignity, to join the group. At the sight of his family he'd not seen in such a long time, he had difficulty maintaining a severe expression as a great lump had come to his throat. Without a word, he bent to pick up his grand-daughter. She'd been just a baby when he'd last seen her and now was a wide eyed toddler. Looking gratefully at the watching Apeconit he said, "I thank you for the return of my daughter. There are no others who could have rescued her from the white dogs."

"The path I took was long and hard. Now I am happy to be here with the people again." answered Apeconit.

The formalities over, Little Turtle proclaimed to the watching villagers, "I will give a celebration feast for all who would come to dance, sing and eat."

The others gave a shout of approval, dispersing to ready themselves for the feast the Turtle would provide. As head chief he was given extra food so that visitors could be entertained or other occasions celebrated.

The men left the chattering women for the council house, a sort of club house for braves. The council house was a building twenty by forty feet, made of split logs with a door at either end and ten foot high walls. Center poles supported a gabled, tree bark roof with three smoke holes. Three fires were kept kindled and pots of food simmered for guests of the village or anyone that needed it. Along the longer sides of the cabin were benches or bunks, covered with grass used as seating for Indians in council or for bunking visitors.

After getting a bowl of food, pipes were brought out and they began the exchange of news. As the soothing smoke of kinnickinik from their pipes circled overhead, Wells began, "This summer I stayed for a time with my brother in Kentucky. Then I worked for the American army as an interpreter when they made a treaty with the Wea's and other Western tribes. They, and your brothers, the Eel River Miami of Kenapacomaqua, signed a treaty promising not to war against the white men anymore in exchange for the captives. The white chief of the thirteen fires sent a message with me for the Delaware, Miami, and Shawnee, asking for a meeting with him at the mouth of the Muskingum to make peace talks."

The Turtle asked, "How can we speak to him of peace when even now war parties of Delaware have gone to attack a fort south of here? At the end of summer, Blue Jacket, Buckongahelas and others went with me to meet with the Iroquois, the Six Nations. Our many tribesmen met at the Rapids of the Maumee while the Western Tribes met at Tschubhicking. (Post Vincennes). The chiefs of the Six Nations brought messages of peace from the white war chief of the thirteen fires, Knox. But the Miami Confederation voted against peace. We voted that there should be no smokes above the Ohio River and that we would fight strong and well, as we did against the army last year."

"Father, I have seen the forts on the Ohio River. I have seen the white people coming day after day down the river. They are many and will never stop coming. Even now, they are training a new army to come against us if we will not make peace. They will never stop sending armies against the Indians until we make treaties with them."

Little Turtle continued pompously, "Did we not destroy the armies that came before? We will do the same again, and fill all the mouths with dirt that would take our lands."

Wells looked at the strong proud chief, and frowned. "You saw how many white men I killed when the army came against us. You know I would not tell you that the Miami Confederation cannot win unless I knew it was true. But, I have a white family, just as I have a red one. They don't speak with forked tongues, but tell me a true thing. The British are at war with the French across the ocean and won't be able to keep the Indians in guns and ammunition because of it. Without the trade goods and backing of the British, how will you win another war against the Big Knives?"

The Turtle sat smoking considering what Wells told him. "This news you bring could mean we should make a different plan. We will council with the Shawnee and Delaware chiefs at Blue Jacket's town so that we can decide what should be done together. You read the message to all and tell them what you told me so that all may decide what should be done."

Several days later, the chiefs came to the council house of the Shawnee town on the Auglaize River, near Old Queen Cooh-coo-cheeh's house that Wells visited the previous year. After Little Turtle explained the reason for the visit, Wells stood before the group and began, "Brothers, I have been sent here by the Big Knife chief, Putnam, to give you a message asking you to make peace so that your women and children may not live in fear."

Blue Jacket interjected, "It is the white chief who lives in fear. Our last raid on the fort south of here, Fort St. Clair, showed them that we do not stop in our demands that all whites stay south of the Ohio. The white dogs ran like frightened children from our guns, back inside the walls of their fort. It is they who were imprisoned in a prison of their own making."

Wells asked casually, "How many of your own dead did you carry away?"

The Shawnee scowled and looked away.

"How many guns are broken and how much ammunition do you have? The British will not continue sending guns and ammunition to the Indians. They are busy fighting their own war with the French across the great salt water. Who will help the Indian now against the Americans? The ghosts of our dead? Listen brothers to what I say. The man Putnam is a good man. He tries to do what is best for all peoples. He is not a war captain and he waits at the mouth of the Muskingum for you to come to talk of peace. If you do not make peace with him, a new army will be sent against you. This time you will get no support from the Eel River Miami or the other Western tribes. You say the Six Nations to the East already made peace with the Americans, so you cannot count on any help from them. Can you hope to win as ever more tribes decide not to join with you and more of your guns are broken?"

Blue Jacket waved his hand to show disgust with Wells words. "You speak like an old woman grown stiff in the joints. See our braves with their scalp sticks? We would keep the whites away, even if we only used bow and arrows or war clubs."

Wells said, "Let me read you the message Putnam sent and see if you don't hear the man as a good one."

> Brothers, the great chief of the United States, General Washington has sent since early in the spring messages to you of peace. And I who have come from this great chief and his council more than 4 months ago, have also sent a speech to you for that purpose.
>
> After waiting a long time for your answer and not receiving any; I was encouraged to speak to the Nations on the Wabash and Illinois Rivers and finding their ears open, I held a Treaty with them at Tschubhicking where we have buried the hatchet, wiped off all the stains of blood and concluded a firm and everlasting peace.
>
> Brothers, I believe were you but once agreed to hear what I have to say to you, and should meet and hear me you would find that it would be for your good. As long as we don't see and hear one another, but listen to the singing birds which fly to and fro; we are carried away with every story and not only remain strangers to one another, but enemies also.
>
> Open your ears to the truth–I speak from my heart, not with my lips only. I wish to see you happy–I wish a peace established between you and the United States–I wish to see your women and children go to rest without fear, and your young men become industrious hunters, so that you all young and old may live comfortably.
>
> Brothers, all this can be the case if you chose it. The United States don't mean to wrong you out of your lands–They don't want to take away your lands by force–They want to do you justice.
>
> Now Brothers, I send you this my speech by some of those who have been here at this great treaty–they have seen and heard me, and are witnesses to all what has passed between us, and they will tell you the truth.
>
> Brothers, when you have heard my speech, and all what my messengers have to say to you, I desire your

> wise men to consider it well. The great and good spirit will then convince them of the good intentions of the United States, and the Road is yet open to them to become a happy people.
>
> Brothers, I desire you to send some of your wise men with my messengers to meet me at the Mouth of Muskingum, that we may see one another and speak together before I return again to our great chief General Washington. I shall direct every thing so, that you will have nothing to fear. Arise then, come and see me, and let us shake hands with one another.

"He sent this wampum belt." Wells held it up for them to see. The Indians sat silently smoking their pipes, considering the speech. Finally Buckongahelas said, "The White Chief speaks well. He sounds like a man who could be trusted. His words have a ring of truth. Perhaps we should go to the Muskingum to talk with him."

Blue Jacket said in alarm, "It will be a trap! They could take us all captive and hang us." Blue Jacket's alarm was not unfounded. As a white man who had turned Indian, and a murderous one at that, he had reason to fear the army.

After listening to the various speeches against making peace, Little Turtle gave the final message. "Brothers, we have just returned from a council of all tribesmen at which we agreed not to make peace unless the Americans agreed to stay south of the Ohio. This is not the time to make a treaty with the chief Putnam. Another Grand Council would have to decide this, even if we ourselves decided we should make peace. Winter is coming. It is not a good time to make a long journey. When the leaves put out, we can call the Nations together for another council to decide what we should do. But Apeconit has told me that if we decide against peace, another army will be sent against us. Ready your people for war so they will not be surprised. Send messengers to all tribes about the new council for when the leaves put out."

When the Miamis returned to Kekionga, Wells spoke privately with Little Turtle. "I will take word back to Vincennes that the Indians will not go to the Muskingum now for a council, but there will be a Grand Council to consider peace when the leaves put out. The Big Knives will probably wait before sending a new army against us, in hopes that the Indians will make a peace treaty."

Little Turtle considered his words carefully, as he always did before speaking. "It is important that we have more time to ready ourselves before we have another battle with the Americans. We need time to trade for more guns from the British. I hope that you are not right in saying they won't have arms to give us."

Wells shook his head. "While I was at my brother's in Kentucky, I learned that the British don't always speak the truth. If the Indians are to stay alive and keep their lands, I'll have to keep a foot in both camps, the white and the red, so we'll know what the truth is. So, I'll take this message down to Tschubhicking and see if there's any news of the army that is to be raised at Fort Washington."

The trip down the Wabash was made as speedily as possible. White Loon and Apeconit paddled silently down the cooling stretch of water, each day expecting a snow storm, but luckily, none came. Never the-less, they wasted no time visiting in the villages along the Wabashiki. Sweet Breeze had no interest in making the trip in cold weather that would take over a month to go and get back. She didn't want to leave her people so soon after her release from captivity.

Vincennes looked little different than it had less than two months before. Wells studied the fort, as it was somewhat optimistically called. Its walls were but six feet high with a shallow trench dug around the outside. A determined effort by Indians or others could no doubt take it, he thought.

Inside, Hamtramck was more jovial than usual as he greeted the younger man. "Back so soon? I wouldn't have thunk it if it weren't for the fact that I still have that three hundred dollars Putnam left you."

Wells gritted his teeth, then remembering it was to his benefit to be civil, he reached forward to shake hands, giving Hamtramck a somewhat wary look. "With winter settin' in I come as soon as I got an answer from the Confederation."

"Since you're here 'stead of at Marietta, they answered no to a peace meetin'."

"That's right. I talked with Blue Jacket, Little Turtle and the others. They said they'd meet when the leaves put out with the Six Nations of the Iroquois and the Cherokee down south and any others that has an interest in whether peace is made or not."

Hamtramck rubbed his chin thoughtfully. "Another Grand Council huh. sounds like a stall tactic to me. They're tryin' to delay the army from attackin."

"Maybe, but none of the chiefs individually has the right to make a treaty or say what the others will do. If he did, the others would say he didn't have a right and they wouldn't honor the words of the treaty."

"Where'll they be havin' this new council?"

"I'd guess the Maumee Rapids, but if the Americans wanted in on it, they could probably send their messages through the Six Nations, as they have some sort of treaty with them now."

"I'll send word of what you said to secretary of War, Knox, and General Wayne who's gettin' up a new army. If they want you to go to the council to find out what's goin' on, will you do it?"

"If the pay is good enough."

"I'll get a message to you if that's what's wanted."

Wells was already on his way out the door, then paused, remembering something. "Oh, by the way, when I was up at Blue Jacket's town I saw a young boy, say eleven or twelve, name of Oliver Spencer. 'Bout the time I was in Cincy town last July, he was taken by Shawnee from a boat on the Ohio. A woman on that boat floated on her back down to Cincy town and told his folks he was captured. It was all the talk when I was there. I jest wanted them to know he's safe with an old Shawnee squaw called Queen Cooh-coo-cheeh."

"Somethin' like that happened to you, didn't it?"

Wells started, since the thought hadn't crossed his mind. A parent himself, he knew the pain of losing a child, and not knowing its whereabouts. But he wasn't about to say it to Hamtramck. "Jest let his parents know he's safe. They kin git him back by sendin' money to the British who'll buy him and send him back 'way of Niagara and New York." With this final word, Wells left to return up the Wabash, with his money.

Hamtramck followed him saying, "Appreciate it Wells. Bring down any more news we should know." Pausing he added, "We'll pay for it."

The winter of 1792-93 passed peacefully for the Indians. Now brisk winds blew through the dreary forest, raising a smell of damp and decay. The hunt had been successful but the deer was a poor thin thing, since it was so near the end of winter and it had used up its body fat. Little Turtle and The Carrot cleared the entrails from the body but saved the skinning job until they were at their cabin. Later, skillfully separating the hide from the meat, The Turtle said, "Why not stay and live forever with the Miami. It may be the council will decide for peace and there will be no war with the whites. You and Sweet Breeze could live here as you have always done, with your children."

Apeconit tied the legs of the deer together to raise the carcass high in a tree for safekeeping. "I have no wish to live with the white men, even if they are my blood brothers. If it is true that the Indians decide to make peace with the Americans, I could stay. But I won't go to war against the Long Knives again. Too many of them are my old neighbors or kin. I'll go to the council to see what the other tribes say. But if they plan war, I'll have to leave and live with the whites."

Little Turtle looked sadly into the distance at the gray sky and the barren corn fields. How involved life could be that he might have to go to war against his own son-in-law whom he loved. "If your heart tells you that you must leave us, you must. But, there should be some way you and I can work for the best results between our two peoples. Though I have long been war chief and despise the thought of white men on our soil. I am weary of burned villages and women and children crying for food after armies come. I am tired of our blood spilled on our own land." He paused before saying something totally unexpected. "I will vote for peace at the council."

Cattle grazed contentedly in the fields, though most stood under trees in the mid June heat. On the Wabash two pirogues filled with the naked brown bodies of Indian braves passed silently on their way to the growing town, Vincennes. On the bank below the trading post, braves unloaded the hides they'd brought along to trade for goods while here. William Wells proceeded to Hamtramck's office to collect the message for which they'd made the trip.

Hamtramck was startled at the sight of the redheaded Indian before him, unclad except for a breech clout. "Ah, Wells, I see your inlaws didn't boil you alive during the winter. Believe me, I kin tell you it's a mite bit surprisin' seein' a redheaded buck, decked out like that." He pointed his finger up and down Well s' body.

Wells frowned, unhappy to have to contend with this thick set little man once again. He was always so provoking. "What you want?"

"I got a message from General Wayne. He wants someone who speaks Indian to go up to the council. The government's sendin' some of their people to it from the East, but they'd like some trapper or other to go from here. Do the Indians know that General Wayne moved the army down river from Pittsburgh to Cincy town?"

"We-er, the Indians been watchin' the road bein' built up past the last fort, Fort Jefferson. They seen all the signs of war with the forts bein' built and road put through. It hurts the possibilities of a peace treaty bein' made. How much are you payin' for me ta risk my neck 'mongst all them savages?" A wicked glint of humor lit Well's' eyes.

"Well, I couldn't say for sure, but it should be a goodly amount. I won't be here much longer but will be stationed with the army somewheres above Cincinnati as Wayne don't like the boozin' and carousin' the men do in town there. The place he's at is called Hobsin's Choice. Damn fool name ain't it?"

Wells hesitated uncharacteristically before answering. "I'll go to the council for you and then come to collect my money at Hobson's Choice. I will be riskin' my neck. The Indians don't like it that I'm takin' messages to you–'specially the Shawnee. When I go to the white's side, I'll be bringin' my wife and maybe some others, so leave word that the Indians with me are to be safe when we come through."

Hamtramck now realized this was a big, painful decision Wells was making, leaving the Indians for good. In a more serious tone he said, "Very well, I'll send a message to Wayne tellin' him to get his troops to let you through the country, but if I were you, I'd dress like a white man goin' in there." Smirking rudely he continued, "And get rid of those feathers!"

Later Hamtramck sent this dispatch to General Wayne.

> To His Excellency General Wayne, Camp Hobson's Choice
>
> July 16,1793
>
> Sir,
>
> Agreeably to your excellency sir actions of the 25th of May last,
>
> I have procured an emmissary to go to Sandusky in order to attend the treaty and as he is to return by the way of Fort Jefferson, he has requested that the different garrisons on the road should be informed that he will have with him few Indian's and have for a sign a white flag.
>
> This emmissary name is William Wells: I have made no bargain with him. But only promised that he should have a liberal reward as also that the Indians who should accompany him should have each of them a trifle.
>
> I have the honor to be with every sentiment of Respect your Excellency most obedient and very humble servent.
>
> J.F. Hamtramck

Chapter XII

Beginning of Wayne's Campaign, July 1793

The Indian Council of 1793 was a time of great frustration for the emissaries of the United States government. In March President Washington had contacted three men asking that they study the treaties the United States already held with the Indians in preparation for making a new peace treaty. These men were to be accompanied by John Heckewelder, the Moravian teacher, who was to help them understand Indian etiquette and methods of speaking.

The commissioners left Philadelphia April 30th, arriving at Fort Niagara in May. Here they remained until June 30, waiting for the Indian Council to send word that they would meet with them. Indian representatives finally came to Fort Niagara, sent by the Council meeting at the Maumee Rapids. They told the three men that the Council would not meet with them face to face because of the war preparations being made against them by General Wayne at Cincinnati.

Not giving up so easily, the Americans sailed anyway for the British settlement at the mouth of the Detroit River, arriving July 21st. From there they sent a letter to British Indian Agent, Alexander McKee, who was with the Council at the Maumee River Rapids, asking when they might meet with the Indians.

McKee's answer was that he'd let them know when he knew what the Indian's plans were.

Finally July 30th, a deputation of about twenty Indians met with the Americans. Delaware chief, Buckongahelas and the Renegade white man, Simon Girty, were among them. Simon, a firm enemy of the United States, translated the speech given by the Indians to the commissioners. The Indians wanted to know if the Commissioners had authority to make the boundary line between the whites and Indians the Ohio River. This was what they demanded as being the boundary

The Commissioner's answer was that they were empowered to declare for the United States but could not make the Ohio River the boundary. Previous treaties had already ceded some land above it to the United States and they could not move off.

They waited for one more letter from the Indians but the impasse was complete. They could not come to any agreement. Arriving back at Fort Erie August 23, 1793, they sent this letter to General Wayne at Fort Washington.

> Sir:
>
> We are on our return home from the mouth of Detroit River, where we lay four weeks waiting for the Indians to close their private councils at the rapids of the Maumee, that we might all remove to Sandusky and open the treaty. But, after sending repeated deputations to us, to obtain answers to particular questions, they finally determined not to treat at all. This final answer was received on the 16th instant, when we immediately began to embark to recross Lake Erie.
>
> Although we did not effect a peace, yet we hope that good may hereafter arise from the mission. The tranquillity of the country northwest of the Ohio, during the (supposed) continuance of the treaty, evinced your care of our safety; and we could not leave this quarter without returning you our unfeigned thanks.
>
> We are, sir, yours, etc.
>
> Benjamin Lincoln, Beverley Randolph, Timothy Pickering

The enjoyable days of the Council were gone. The food was eaten, the last jug of English whisky drunk and final war dances danced. Now the tribes took down their wigwams and gathered their women and children for the return trip to their homes. It would be several weeks before the braves regrouped to make war.

Gifts of British ammunition and guns assured them that a war with the Big Knives could be successful, so most felt well satisfied with the result of the meeting. Little Turtle voted against war and consequently was passed over as principal war chief. The Shawnee, Blue Jacket, would lead them in battle.

As Little Turtle and The Carrot returned to Kekionga, they knew they would soon part, perhaps forever. Riding single file along the Maumee made conversation difficult. At a point where the river banks were low they paused for water and a short rest. Little Turtle led the horse up the bank after its drink. Quietly he studied the younger man who was removing a pebble from his horse's hoof. At last he spoke. "I will be sad when you leave our people."

Wells didn't want to discuss his feelings and didn't look his father-in-law in the eye. Leaving the Indians was something he hadn't dealt with emotionally, yet.

The Turtle continued, "Perhaps it will be safer for Sweet Breeze if you take her south to Kentucky to stay with your brother. Even though the British promise to supply us with arms, I believe you are right when you say the new army may destroy the Confederation. I wanted our people to make peace. But, as you saw, Blue Jacket, the Shawnee and the Delaware are for war. Even our own Miami braves are for it. They only listen to me when I speak of war because I am a war captain. They think speaking of peace is foreign on my lips."

It would have been impolite for The Carrot to show disinterest while his father-in-law bared his soul. He came and sat on a rock near the older man, for a moment quietly listening to the late summer songs of the crickets. The sun beat down warmly. Finally he broke the silence. "I can no longer live as an Indian, though this land is like a piece of my body. Sometimes I think I could melt into it. But I won't kill white men anymore. I like stayin' sane in my mind. After the fight with St. Clair I couldn't see nothin' but blood and blind, dead, starin' eyes for days.

In fairness to all my Indian brothers, I will let all know I am no more a red man. We'll have a ceremony separatin' us, so I can leave an honest man, and they'll know, if we meet in battle that I'll have to kill them."

A look of pain came into Little Turtle's eyes. He gazed out across the Maumee River. Here in the bright sunshine death seemed far away, but it could come anytime, perhaps soon. "When do you think the chief who never sleeps will attack?" He asked.

"I don't know. Hamtramck said he drills his men and whips deserters. You heard what them two deserters told the Council about the General's tactics. But for all their down mouthin' of the man, from what Hamtramck said, he must be a very good war chief." Wells sat thinking about what a large army might do to the villages when it came. Quietly he said, "It'd be best to send the women and children far away, up near the British Fort Detroit, when the army comes."

Now the hot day began to have an ominous, waiting sort of quality as the two men thought of death and distruction. Little Turtle said, "Yes. I will do what I can to keep the Miami out of the fight, but it is my duty to lead them, if I must. Tomorrow, before you go, we will have a ceremony so everyone will know you are white."

At Kekionga, Wells returned to his cabin where Sweet Breeze had remained with Ann. "Apeconit?" Sweet Breeze came joyfully to embrace her husband.

He moved his hands down her backbone, enjoying the comfort of being with a woman who was so familiar. "We must pack our goods for the trip to Fort Washington."

In alarm she jerked away from him, "But I don't want to leave my people. Why don't you go to them alone, and leave me here as you did this summer."

Wells pulled her back and said possessively, "Because you're mine, and you won't be safe here. The white men are goin' to swoop into the villages and they're goin' to burn all the houses, cut down the corn, and they're goin' to take any women they find runnin' around loose just like this." Laughing he pulled her down on the couch of furs, stripping her blouse roughly away to bury his nose into her breasts.

Sweet Breeze's arguments were momentarily pushed off as the two playfully completed their reunion. "Tell me you didn't miss me." He nipped her ear gently with his teeth.

"I miss you when you're gone, but it is lonely, away from the people. I might die of it." She looked at him with this threat to see if it had any effect.

He grabbed her around the waist and brought her over on top of him. "You won't die because I will keep you company. And I don't intend to share you with any soldiers." Night closed down softly on the cabin in the peaceful village. Owls called out and occasionally a dog barked. The rivers lapped the banks of the ancient town. It was a good night for sleep.

The next day, word passed around Kekionga that a ceremony would take place at noon. Miamis particularly loved plays and ceremonies so as the time neared, a large group gathered on the Maumee, talking and laughing as they waited for the central characters.

Sweet Breeze loaded all their belongings on the horses and went down the trail with Ann, to wait. The Carrot had dressed in his newest buckskins. He joined Little Turtle who was also in full ceremonial dress that included the feathered headress, silver earrings, and bear claw necklace. Silently they walked to the Maumee. They were followed by the tribesmen to a spot on the river called Big Elm for the enormous tree spreading shade for many people. Villagers gathered around in the shade as the two men stood somewhat apart to give their speeches.

When all were quiet Wells looked at Little Turtle for a moment, thinking of all this man meant to him. This could be the last time they ever saw one another, alive, again. But for the good of all, he must leave. The Indians were waiting, so he sighed, and said theatrically, "Father, we have long been friends. I now leave you to go to my own people.

We will be friends until the sun reaches the midday height. From that time we will be enemies. If you want to kill me, then you may. If I want to kill you, I may."

Little Turtle stepped forward saying, "You have been as dear as my own son, but fortune has caused us to part. I send you back to your own people." He gave his son-in-law a final embrace, and then Wells walked down to the canoe to cross the river.

For a moment longer he looked up at his friends standing in the shade of the mammoth tree, watching them until the sun stood directly overhead. Then crossed the river in the almost audible silence and walked down the trail to Sweet Breeze waiting with the horses. His face was set in such grim lines that she didn't raise any argument or speak as he kicked his horse in the side heading toward the forts far to the south.

The galloping horses arrived with a flourish at Hobson's Choice, General Wayne's armed camp just above Cincinnati. The riders from the northern wilderness dismounted and went down to the river watering the horses and refreshing themselves. Having ridden long and hard they smelled of sweat and horse. This far south, the days were hot in September. Their buckskins reeked of body odor, but horse flies couldn't bite through it so they endured the uncomfortable clothing on the trail. Wells removed his trail clothes enjoyed a swim and changed to a linen shirt before presenting himself to the tent of General Anthony Wayne.

Mad Anthony Wayne, as his Revolutinary soldiers had called him, was a fanatic about war from his very early youth. As a Pennsylvania school boy, he'd preferred playing war to study. A good spot to study his favorite subject was found only a mile from his father's farm, at the Blue Ball Tavern on the Lancaster Road. He wasn't old enough to drink or join up with the army, but it didn't stop him from listening to the soldiers talk in the bar. Here he learned that army life was not all fighting. Bridge and road building, discipline, keeping track of supplies and drill were all important parts of making war. And so, he decided he would go to the academy as his father wanted him to do. Engineering, science, and mathematics seemed to be essential knowledge for waging war.

When he graduated the country was at peace and there were no calls for soldiers. He took a job as a surveyor and later returned to his father's farm to take up the tanning industry. During the Revolutionary war he gave good service. Then in 1792, Washington called him from his retirement as a farmer on his Pennsylvania farm to perform his favorite role, that of General of a large army. His health was poor, but it was not something he would allow to interfere with his job.

Wayne looked up from his plans, laying the quill aside when the tall redhead was presented to him. He had received enough information about the translater, William Wells, from Putnam and Hamtramck that he felt he almost knew him. His face did not relax into a smile when the young man was presented, but his mouth moved into a line suggesting one.

Wells was glad he'd taken the time to wash and don clean clothing before this meeting. The General before him was in full uniform, clean and polished down to his boot-tops. He was an Eastern dandy, something which in itself was a thing of awe to the youth who had spent most of his life in the back woods.

"Ah, Wells, how did you find the road the men cut through the forest?"

"Very fine, sir. Wide enough to get an army into the woods easy, looks like."

"It's sixty foot wide Mr. Wells. Wide enough that the Indians can't just reach in from the woods snatching our horses. Now then, I want a full report of the proceedings at the Indian Council. Jones, come write this down," he called to his Aide De Camp.

"Well sir, we arrived there July 10th at the Rapids of the Miami of the Lake, or Maumee as the Miamis call it."

"Did they have any suspicions about why you were there?"

"Hell, I'm a Miami as fur as they know. Why would they have any suspicion?"

"You must understand son, I have little experience with Indians and don't know what they'd think. That's why I'm hirin' you. How many were there when you arrived?"

"Round 'bout 1400. Then they kept stragglin' in until July 20th to come to a total of 2400 Indians of which I'd guess 1800 were warriors."

Wayne let out a long whistle. Then he told Wells," The Commissioners sent by Washington never got to speak directly with the chiefs except through a go-between. They just sat at Fort Maldon at the Detroit River with the British, waiting for news from the council. You were the only white man there that wasn't British. What actually happened at the Council?"

"Well sir, they counciled every day and Simon Girty, he's a British turncoat, set with them at all the councils. The Governor Simcoe's Aid De Camp and a Lieutenant Silvy of the 5th British Regiment and one other British Officer an' Colonial McKee stayed in McKee's house only 'bout fifty-sixty yards away from the council meetings. Ever' night some of the head chiefs of the Shawnee and Delaware met with them in the house, drinkin'."

"Did you find out what they said in that house?"

"It was jest the same old song and dance. The British promisin' that the King, their father, would protect them and offerin' them everything they wanted in case they went to war-arms, ammunition and provisions. But they told the Indians they must come to them there at the British fort for the goods 'cause they couldn't carry it no further. Also, they said they shouldn't make peace on any terms other than that the Ohio was the boundary line. They should defend their lands and the King would not allow them to be imposed on.

Most of the Indians were for peace. Three times they decided to send for the commissioners to come parley, but that British Indian Agent, McKee, always made them rescind next day, with his promises to those chiefs I was talkin' 'bout in his house at night. He'd get them liquored up so's they'd see his side on it. All the Indians wanted peace 'cept the Shawnee, Delaware, and Wyandott. Hell, if the British wasn't there, we'd have us a peace treaty."

Wayne rose to begin walking nervously back and forth. All his preparations for war would be realized now, and he would be allowed by the Secretary of War in Philadelphia, to attack. But the season was too advanced. He didn't want to make the same mistakes as Harmar and St. Clair, attacking when grass was gone for the horses and men were stiffened by cold weather. "Damn those foxes! They stalled us with this council so we couldn't attack this year. They did make plans for war didn't they?"

Wells stepped back, intimidated. It didn't do to stir up Wayne's anger. Behind his back the soldiers called him Mad Anthony because of his incessant drilling of the soldiers, and his whipping and shooting of deserters. They learned to fear him more than they did the Indians. "Whilse I was there, the Indians spent ten days plannin' their war after they sent word to the commissioners to go home, 'cause the commissioners wouldn't agree to name the Ohio as the boundary line twinxt Indians and whites."

"Give me their plans for the war," Wayne demanded.

"All Nations are to join for a war on the whites to kill everybody who lives on the frontier. The Creeks and Cherokees south of Kentucky never did want peace, ya know. They said the best thing ta do was ta join up with the Western Nations at the Falls of the Ohio, 'crost from Louisville. Then, they'd have no trouble gettin' provisions 'cause the Kentuckians had plenty of cattle and corn so's they could supply themselves. Then from there they's plannin' to plunder all the settlers into Kentucky.

This winter, the western Nations will fall upon and distroy the army whilse the southern nations fall upon the frontier of Georgia. McKee, the British Agent, was ta furnish the Indians with arms, ammunition, scalping knives and tomahawks as soon as the council was over, and promised clothing, too, when they wanted it."

Wayne glanced up sharply, "Just how much ammunition were they to get?"

"Oh, much more than they could use this winter. It was partly rifles and partly fusils (flint lock muskets). Also, they got horseman swords and pistols."

"And what is their fighting man power, as you guess it?"

Wells gave the following numbers as available braves for war:

Shawnee	300	Chippewas	150
Delaware	350	A few from the	
Miami	100	Six nations	35
Wyandott	200	Cherokees and other	
Tawas (Ottawa:)	150	Indians including those	
Muncies	30	on Lake Michigan	112
Pottawattomie	100		
Total	1230	Total	290

This is the number of braves currently ready for action. If the army advances as slowly as it did in '91 they could have two thousand warriors to send against you.

After the council was done with business, there was a general war dance, at which the British come out and attended. You shoulda seen Governor Simcoe's Aide-de-camp who painted hisself like an Indian and danced right along with the others."

Wayne allowed himself a small smile, then continued with his thorough questioning. "Did they make any more definite plans for attack against the army?"

"Yes sir. After the Indians separated about the 28th of August, they was to gather at the Auglaise River in twenty-five days to watch the army and wait fer a good time ta strike. They'll attack the convoys of pack horses and fire on the army at night ta wear it out if they think your numbers are too many. If your men pass the previous battle ground and they think their numbers are strong enough, they'll attack. They keep a good watch on the forts sir. It only takes a runner a day to go from here to Fort Jefferson, and then a day more to reach the Auglaize, so they pretty well know what you're doin'."

"What about the British. Would those at the Detroit Fort advance against us if we traveled that far?"

"If the army was ta git as far as the Rapids of the Maumee I believe the British would attack. They've about fifteen hundred soldiers, accordin' to McKee. Course, it could be lies, comin' from him. If they've got fewer than that, they certainly wouldn't be tellin' the Indians, you can bet on it.

The Eel River Miami, Weas, and Kickapoo didn't even go to the council. Jest sent messages. So I doubt they'd join in a war, 'specially since they jest signed the peace treaty with Putnam. Then the Creeks and Chickasaws were at each other's throats so much that they probably will be at war with each other, and not a threat to the South of Kentucky, though the Creeks come ta the council meetin' with a Britisher. He's tryin' ta get them ta fight agin' Americans, 'stead of wastin' war on each other."

Wayne pondered all that had been said. Finally he answered, "Then I should write Knox that you believe a general confederacy is formed among the Indian Nations against America except the Wabash and Illinois Kickapoos and the Six Nations of the Iroquois."

"That's it sir. Ain't no way 'round it. Since they beat St. Clair in '91, they think they can whip any army sent against 'em 'ceptin' maybe the Miami. Little Turtle is beginnin' to see the light, since I've told him many times that he ain't goin' to win this war. That hot head, Blue Jacket, always was jealous of The Turtle, though, and he wouldn't go along for peace."

Wayne spent some time reflecting on the situation before saying, "You've done an admirable job, son. I'm going to be depending on you and a small group of scouts to tell me of Indian movements. You'll be a commissioned captain and draw pay accordingly. I'll expect you all to dress and act as Indians, keeping us constantly informed as to what their intentions are so there'll be no more ambushes."

This appealed to Wells. "Will I get to pick the scouts? I'd only want fellers who knew Indian ways."

"Yes. I'll leave it up to you." With this final word, Wells was dismissed and Wayne sent his report to Secretary Knox.

The wigwam Sweet Breeze was making for their camp was almost completed when William returned from his talk with General Wayne. William whistled tunelessly as he drew the horse up beside a large burr oak tree. Throwing the reins over a branch, he leaped from the horse. At the cook fire, he reached into the swinging kettle for a handful of food.

Surprised at his good mood, Sweet Breeze said, "You spoke to the white chief, Kitcho Shemangan?"

"You'd better not call him that here. General Wayne ain't the type to like bein' called The Big Wind from the East. 'Sides he jest made me a captain."

"Captain, what does that mean?"

William lay back against a buffalo robe with his hands behind his head. "It means I'll get better pay than most of them men out there. Facts are, I'll be the boss over a bunch of spies who I get ta pick."

Sweet Breeze was silent a moment and then frowned. In an accusing tone she asked, "You would spy on my people?"

William jumped up angrily, clenching his hands, then turned away from her. "These are my people now. Yours too and you'd jest better get used to it. I fought with the Indians agin' the white men. But I made it clear to them that I'm a white man now. I'm workin' for me. For us."

Sweet Breeze returned sadly to her work saying no more. After a few moments of thinking, William said, "We'll be headin' north in a couple weeks to go to war with the Confederation. I want you and Ann safe with Sam in Kentucky. I'll be sendin' you down there with a messenger goin' to Louisville. I got to get my men picked who'll be my scouts. We'll be spendin' our time in the forest so the Indians don't give the army no surprises."

Sweet Breeze began quietly crying, saying nothing. Wells continued. "This place won't be safe for Indians. 'Specially a squaw, pretty like you. Too many's been kilt by Indians and they might take their revenge on you or kill Ann. Would you want that?"

Sweet Breeze was now openly sobbing, "I'll never see my people again. What will happen to us if you are killed and we are with your brother? My father may be killed. Maybe even by you. Maybe my brothers will be killed too, while I, daughter of Little Turtle, am here in the heart of his enemy."

"Now you hush that bawlin'. Here you are, a princess, daughter of the strongest chief in the land and bawlin' like a baby. Hah! You're daddy'd kick you good if he saw you carryin' on like that. Now you stand tall and proud, like a princess should, 'cause you're wife of Captain William Wells."

Sweet Breeze thinking about it slowly straightened her drooping shoulders, then wiped her eyes on her skirt. William looked at her somewhat more gently and added, "I want my daughter to learn white men's ways. Now she can do that. Later, when the war is over, we'll all go back to Kekionga."

In the following days Wells began picking men for scouts who knew Algonquian dialects and could pass as Indians. There weren't many suited for the job. The regular army had been drilling at Hobson's Choice since April when it moved from its camp south of Pittsburgh. Recently 366 men with the Kentucky Militia arrived under Charles Scott. Samuel Wells was in this group and sent Sweet Breeze to his Kentucky home at Louisville with a servant.

By the end of the first week, William had picked several men, among them a Mr. Heckman, Mr. Thorp, and John McDonald. One cool September afternoon he stood watching soldiers in the distant drill field, amusing themselves with footraces. Wayne encouraged these as they provided exercise and diversion. Wells could tell men were placing bets on their favorites. a group lined up and then, as he watched amazed, one man passed the whole field of others, outdistancing them by a wide margin. The crowds cheered and then, apparently he told them he could do some other feat. The others fell back while a canvas covered wagon was pulled onto the field. From the distance it was hard to tell what new sport he planned.

The race winner was a very tall, muscular man who began stripping off his trousers. This disclosed a physique like those of ancient Greek athletes. Now the others became silent as he retraced his steps a good distance back from the wagon. Then with the grace of a deer he ran toward the eight foot high wagon. William stood up as the man neared the wagon at full speed. Suddenly he jumped. Time seemed to stop as he soared over the top. The silence was broken as watching soldiers cheered and whistled.

Wells approached the group surrounding the young athlete, curious about the man. Stretching his hand toward him he said, "Captain Wells at your service. Could I have a few words with you? In private."

Merry blue eyes appraised him from the face coursed by rivulets of sweat. "Sure, Captain. Let's go down by the river. I could use a drink of water." Kneeling, he slapped the cooling water on his face. Finally he had caught his breath and said, "McLelland's the name. Robert McLelland. What's on ye're mind?"

"I'm settin' up a group of Indian scouts. Men who are in good shape to escape from Indians in a hurry. You sure looked like a goodun ta me. You had any experience with Indians?"

"I was with St. Clair in '91. I was one of the few who got away 'cause I kin run so good. Jumped clean over them savages thata liked ta kill me. You shoulda seen their faces."

"I thought you looked familiar."

"Was you there? I don't remember you. Were you with the Kentucky Militia?"

"I'll tell you the whole story sometime. But if you're interested, I'd like to have you as one of my scouts. We kin have any horses we want at any time, and there will be special pay. I can guarantee it'll be more interestin' than bein' jest a regular."

"Sounds good ta me. When do we start?"

"Right away. The Indians have already attacked Major Adair's camp and run off a bunch of his pack horses. Wayne woulda been right on their tail if it wasn't for so many men sick with the flue."

McLelland agreed, "Aye, and then that bunch of braves that attacked the Station near Fort Hamilton and kilt that man and two children. It sure wouldn't hurt none for some of us to try and find out what they're up ta next. Say, I know another feller that would be right fer the job. Man by name of Henry Miller. He and his brother was captured by Indians when they was jest kids. But then when they was growed up, Henry left the Indians ta go back to his kin in Kentucky. Ya know, his brother, Christopher, didn't go with him. He stayed with the Indians. Can ya fathom that?"

"Henry sounds like a good man for this job. Is he here now? I'd like ta talk with him."

"He jest come up with the Kentucky Militia. I'll get him for ya if he 'pears interested." The man rose stretching a muscled limb forward to shake hands and then departed. William shook his head in wonderment that such a swift runner existed. The Miamis were well known for their swiftness but never had he seen the equal of Robert McClellan.

Later, Henry Miller came to Well's camp, sent as promised by McClelland. He was an unlikely looking soldier past his mid twenties. Dressed in ragged clothing, he appeared to be from the poorest Kentucky farm. His pale blond hair and sallow complexion made him look undistinguished; in fact inferior. He was thin and stringy looking. The only distinguishing feature was the rifle he carried. It was thoroughly cleaned, expensive, and had seen much use. Tied to the barrel were a few little round balls that on closer inspection proved to be human hair. When the lanky youth appeared silently at Well's campfire, Wells said, "Miller, you devil. Didn't know you'd left the Shawnee 'til I talked to McClellan today. I didn't let on I knew you. Less said 'bout our Indian life the better."

"Apeconit, you son-of-a-gun. I wouldn't a believed it if I hain't seen you in the flesh. How you gittin' away with this anyways?"

"Got friends in high places, relatives that is. When my squaw was captured by that son-of-a-bitch, Wilkinson, I had to get my Kentucky brothers help to get her and the others released. One thing led to another and here I am, captain of the spies agin' the Indians. Don't that beat all?" The two laughed at life's strange twists.

"How'd you happen ta leave the Shawnee?" Asked Wells.

"I never did make a good Indian. Always meant to go back to the folks in Kentucky. Then, when I kilt a young buck, name of Partridge, I left, sudden like. My brother, Christopher, is still with the Shawnee, fur as I know."

"Interested in bein' one of my scouts?"

"Long as it don't mean long hours of drill or marchin'."

Wells clapped him on the shoulder. "We'll seal it with a glass of Kentucky's finest whiskey."

October 7, 1793 Wayne's army of 2600 set out for the North, prepared to attack the Indians. Captain Wells scouts went ahead to see that no Indian ambushes awaited them. But no Indians were to be seen. The wide army built road made travel fast. In six days they passed the forts already built and used principally as supply depots, arriving at Fort Jefferson and the end of the good road. It was too late in the season to attack, Wayne decided. Then too, he'd had so much trouble with the suppliers that he didn't have enough rations for the men. He ordered the Legion to build huts like those at Valley Forge on a beautiful peninsula on the banks of a winding creek, surrounded by a prairie. There was enough grass to feed their cattle and horses here. The soldiers cut a deep trench around a strong stockade built to protect them during the winter. Wayne named this fort Greenville.

Gout and headaches debilitated him during the next months but just before Christmas, he was well enough to order the men twenty miles north to the spot of the St. Clair massacre.

It was a warm December day, temperatures hovering near the fifty degree mark. Two years had passed since the massacre of St. Clair's troops here. Wilkinson and his men had visited the lonely battleground in wintertime after the battle. Then, snow had mercifully covered the mangled corpses, defiled first by the Indians and later by wild animals. They had buried a few, but the hundreds killed here were beyond their attempts for burial in the frozen ground. No snow covered the ground now as General Wayne's troops walked silently in awe among the scattered skeletons.

Wayne ordered, "Men, find all the bones so that they can be given decent Christian burial." The men set to the task knowing full well that they themselves might be in a similar condition in the near future, and hoping someone would bury their bones, if they were unfortunate enough to require the service. Wayne sent for the Captain of the Scouts, William Wells. When the young man was presented to him, somewhat more subdued than usual, Wayne opened, "You were at the battle with St. Clair, were you not?"

"Yes Sir." What could the General want with him, William wondered. In his poor state of health, he'd been completely impatient and intolerant, even of his aides. Did he mean to punish him for the massacre two years ago?

General Wayne looked at him rebukingly for a moment. finally he broke the silence. "Wilkinson didn't find the cannon brought here by St. Clair when he was here two years-ago. Did the Indians drag them off?"

"No Sir."

"Well blast it, man! Where are they?"

Wells thought the General was about to strike him. "We buried them around about the area. I'll show the men where they are." He was edging away from the General when Wayne stopped him.

"Don't leave my presence until you're dismissed. What about the rest of the equipment?"

"The Indians carried away everythin' they could use. Even their clothes. You kin see the skeletons ain't wearin' any."

Wayne looked at him murderously for a moment, wanting to lay the blame for the massacre on someone, but realized he needed the help of this man who knew the Indians so well. "Go show the men where the cannon are hidden. You're dismissed for now."

Two cannon were fished from the creek and three three-pounders buried by the side of an old fallen tree, retrieved. These were cleaned and a salute of nine volleys was fired, making the forests reverberate with the racket.

In the following days a stout fort, dubbed Fort Recovery in the fervent hope that it would be true, was built on this spot. Then a wide road was cleared to Fort Greenville, twenty miles south for the transport of supplies. A Captain Gibson was named commandant of the fort and told to keep his men busy scouting the forests between the Grand Glaize river and Fort Recovery. Then Wayne and the army returned to Fort Greenville to wait out the winter.

The two forts, Greenville and Recovery, stood strong, firm protection for the men, in the heart of Indian country. Four blockhouses were each equipped with musket-proof doors and shutters and they had fittings for small howitzers. Trees were cleared for a thousand feet all the way around so that the Indians couldn't sneak up on them under cover. It was time to impress their close neighbors of their strength.

These two forts were very near the Delaware villages of Buckongahelas, chief of the Muncee Indians, a Delaware subgroup. The Delaware had moved to settle on the White River in Indiana after being pushed west by the white men.

William Wells, Robert McClellan and Henry Miller rode toward the Muncee town that lay along the White River to invite the Delaware to Fort Greenville so the Indians could see its strength. These three had become an established scout party, the one Wayne most often requested to bring in Indians for interogation.

They rode silently, single file, Indian style. As soon as they entered the forest they became Indians in speech and actions. Closer inspection would be necessary before Indians would fire on them because they wore Indian dress. An inch of slushy snow covered the ground that January day. Breaking out of the forest, the White River came into view. Here they watered the horses and then tied them back in the brush, out of sight. Lying down on the south side of the river bank, where the snow was melted, they rested, soaking up the winter sun as they ate the bread and meat in their pouches.

"We goin' ta jest ride into the Delaware village 'an' ask them ta come ta a party?" McClellan asked.

"Why not. George White Eyes is a friend of mine," Wells answered.

"Hey, that's good, ifin' you don't ketch a hatchet 'fore you see him. They's not goin' ta be too happy since ya captured some of their people for Wayne to question," Miller said as he chewed on his meat. "I say we lay low here an' wait for somebody comin' down river ta take our message in."

Wells looked up at the blue sky with a few fleecy clouds floating overhead. Scooting down the bank into a more comfortable position he said, "Not a bad idea. Wake me when one comes along."

All was quiet for a time as the men rested. After awhile McClellan asked, "Is it true ye're married to a squaw?"

"Yep." Wells answered.

"One of many an Indian flower he's favored," Miller giggled.

Wells grunted and turned on his side. McClellan couldn't deny his curiosity. "Well, how many gals ya had, Wells?"

He could see he wouldn't get any peace unless he answered. "High up braves usually have a couple squaws, if they kin afford it. But, though I've dipped in here and there, I ain't never had but one squaw at a time." Looking up at the deep blue of the sky again he lay back, thinking of the years of his youth spent with the tribes.

"When I was stole by the Indians, I was jest a youngun, full of juice, but didn't know nothin' 'bout women. I guess I was a show off, but the Indians liked that. Anyways, Gawaiahatle, the one 'at adopted me, was related to Little Turtle. We went an' stayed at Little Turtle's town on the Eel River from time to time.

The Turtle had a beautious sister. A young widow. She was so good lookin' I used to spend a lota time jest starin' at her. Her face was like a quiet meadow with two lakes for eyes that I coulda drowned in. I was only 'bout fifteen at the time and she was probably in her early twenties. Well, I got so hot for her that I took to followin' her around when nobody was lookin'. One day she was bathin' in the Eel and I stood back in the brush watchin'. Then she come out, naked, all tan, glistenin' with water. When she started up the path back ta camp, I jest couldn't help myself and I grabbed her."

"Ye're lucky you're still wearin' your hair, her bein' The Turtle's sister. What happened then?"

"As you might guess, we started meetin' in the woods on a regular basis. I was jest a kid and had no thoughts of livin' on my own then. 'Sides I was a captive. Had no freedom or rights. But after awhile, The Turtle asked me to come ta see him. He said he would give me his sister and I could be a free brave in the village."

"I'll bet his sister asked for you," McClellan said.

"I don't know," Wells mused. "She wasn't one to talk much."

"Them's the best kind," Miller said, with a smirk.

"She ain't the one ye're married to now?" AskedMcClellan.

"No. Anahquah died." He said it flatly with supressed pain.

"Well, were ya married long or had any kids or anythin'?"

"We had just got a little place of our own fixed up. I was livin' in a cloud of love when she started bleedin' one day and jest died quick." He sighed and after awhile continued. "I guess Little Turtle felt sorry for me 'cause after awhile he offered me his own daughter, a girl some 'at younger than me. Well,I told him I didn't want no other squaw. But as time went on, as young boys will, I begin ta see she had some good assets."

The others smiled. Suddenly all three became silent on hearing the quiet approach of a horse on the path. Without so much as a sign, they shrank into the brush and were invisible.

A Delaware brave silently dismounted, watered his horse and bent to drink himself. Then he felt a hand on his neck. A voice said in Delaware, "Don't move. Now get up slow."

The Delaware rose, mortally afraid for his life. Then he saw it was a man he knew. Relaxing, he said, "Why you ambush me like that, Apeconit?"

The men drew back, lowering their guns. Wells said, "Jest didn't want you to club me fer an' enemy first. You alone?"

The Indian glanced around the forest and then back at his captor. His mind worked through the possibilities of a lie being believed or whether it was necessary to lie at all.

"You're alone," Wells stated. "I don't aim ta harm you. Jest want you to take a message to George White Eyes for me. Tell him General Wayne invites him ta come ta the fort for a meal. Oh, and tell him to come in with a white flag."

The Indian smiled, visibly relieved that that was all they wanted. "It will be done. I was out scouting the fort now and am returning to the village."

"Well, don't fail to tell the chief we're watchin' you too," Wells returned.

The next day a party of Delaware, including George White Eyes, appeared silently in ceremonial costume at Fort Greenville with the white flag.

General Wayne was delighted, receiving the chief with a warm welcome. The cannon was fired and then they retired inside for a great feast, all calculated to impress the Indians with the fort's strength and provisions. Wells was constantly by his side, interpreting. After the meal, Wayne rose to give a formal speech to show the savages what a great and powerful man he was. Standing at the end of a crude split log table, he began. "The eyes and heart of the President of the United States are ever open to the voice of peace. He has instructed me, his chief warrior, to listen to that welcome voice from whatever quarter it may come."

The Delaware looked at Wayne curiously. He could see the man was a war chief, not a diplomat, and his speeches of peace were meaningless.

Wayne continued, "Don't listen to those bad white men who have neither the inclination nor the opportunity to help the Indian cause. As head of the American army, I demand that the tribes call off all raiding parties and return every white man in Indian possession within a month to Captain Gibson, who I left in charge at Fort Recovery."

The Delaware was visibly taken aback at the twist the speech took. He had come here as a guest, not as any kind of diplomat for the Indians. He wasn't empowered to return captives or make peace. Also, he had grievances of his own to air. When it was his turn to speak he rose and said with great dignity, "I have come here bringing love to you all in the hopes that you will accept it. But I must complain of the Captain Gibson, Commander of the northern fort. He has kidnapped some of our people. Three young squaws have been taken away from their people. We would have them returned to us, unharmed."

Wayne's eyes popped open and shut and his mouth bent to a firm line. Looking at Wells he asked in a pained tone, "Is this true?"

"If he says it is, it's probably right. He don't have no cause to lie about that."

Turning back to the chief he said, "I'm afraid I must apologize for the behavior of my men. The girls will be returned tomorrow, I promise. Now, I'd like you to have a tour of our fort here and meet my men. Come. I'll show you what a white man's fort is like." Aside to his aide Wayne said, "Move the men from place to place as we go so it looks like we've a couple thousand more men than we have."

The Indians were taken outside to tour the fort, doubling back and forth, while the aide moved men from place to place. George White Eyes later told the British that Greenville was guarded by 4,000 men, that its circumference was two full miles, and the cantonment was heavily guarded.

The next morning Wells' scouting party was sent to Fort Recovery to get the Indian girls and return them to the Muncee Delaware town. Arriving at the Fort, Wells was presented to Captain Gibson.

"What you want, Wells?" The Captain asked, with superiority.

"We're ordered to return those pieces you lifted from the Delaware. Where are they."

"What are you talkin' about man?"

"Don't play dumb with me, Gibson. The girls. Wayne's 'bout to spit nails. He was tryin' his best ta impress a Delaware Chief, demandin' that they return white captives, and he's showed a horse's ass all 'cause you got some of their women stashed away here."

"The hell you say."

"You'd be a fool if you cross the General, Gibson. Best turn them girls over."

Gibson looked at him angrily and then decided he had no choice but to comply. Soon the three girls were relieved of their current cooking chores and turned over to the scouts, carrying some things they'd received as "gifts" during their stay. Wells looked at them reprovingly, shaking his head. In Delaware he said, "Your folks goin' to beat you good when you get home."

The girls eyed each other nervously. Now that the lark was over, they'd have to face the music. Soon the party of six mounted horses for the ride west to the Delaware village.

Fort Recovery was only about thirty miles from the Delaware villages. The distance could easily be covered in a few hours. but they had a late start. Wells' scouts had already ridden twenty miles from Fort Greenville. By the time they convinced Gibson to give up the women and got underway, it was afternoon. At first the men and women rode separately, but as time passed, the horses walked more slowly and couples paired off. Slowly they walked through the forest, getting acquainted.

Henry Miller rode beside a short, somewhat chunky girl who had a very square face, but quick smile. Up ahead, McClellan was vigorously using sign language, to the amusement of the quiet big boned girl who looked very capable of taking care of herself. Wells found himself intrigued by a mischievious girl of seventeen who was doing her best to enchant him. As time went on, it was clear she had a quick intelligence, always ready to pounce on any error of judgement in his remarks, to show him in a foolish light. Their conversations would be a battle of wits, with Wells taking the position of older, therefore wiser personage, to protect his arguments.

"What did you girls think you was doin', goin' off with an army of white men like that?" He growled.

"It wasn't our fault we were taken captive. You act like we wanted to be at the fort, gathering firewood and cooking. We were only slaves."

"Wasn't that what you wanted? What about all them trinkets you come away with?"

"We would have been fools not to take them. We were working at the sugar camp when the soldiers came past. I guess we were a little farther away from the camp than we should have been, when the men swooped down on us. They laughed and said we were their captives, wanted for questioning."

"I'll bet you girls was tryin' to sneak off so you wouldn't have to help your folks with the work."

The girl gave him a sly sideways look. "We didn't want to be stolen." Looking at him for a moment she said, "I've seen you before, somewhere. I think it was at Anderson's town. You were an Indian then. What are you doing pretending to be a white man?"

"That's none of your business," he said gruffly.

The girl shrugged her shoulders as if uninterested but continued to look at him curiously as they rode along. Finally Wells said, "I lived with the Miami and was a messenger between the Long Knives and Indians. I came through the Delaware towns along the White River a year ago. Apeconit's my name. What's yours?"

"Call me Nancy, like the soldiers did. I live west of Anderson's town at Natico. That's why they called me Nancy." She ran the two names over her tongue several times. "I know some other words of the Long Knives. I learned a lot from the white men." She looked at Wells from under long black lashes."

"I'll bet you did." Wells shook his head. "They didn't hurt you did they?"

"No. Do you want to see the presents they gave me?"

"No! You are a very bad girl. You should not do things for men for gifts."

All innocence she asked, "Why not?"

Wells groaned and rubbed his face. She was afterall young and inexperienced. "Blast it, don't you know anything? In your village a woman who slept with a man other than her husband could have her nose cut off. Right?"

"Yes, but I was not in my village and I have no husband so where is the harm?"

"If the other braves knew what you did, they would not marry you, but would jest take advantage of you."

She grinned wickedly. "We will not tell them." Kicking her horse and laughing out loud, she rode ahead, making him hurry to keep up.

They had taken so much time in their flirtations that the sun was dropping rapidly. Though Muncee town could be reached if they hurried, they decided to make camp for the night along the Mississinewa River. Though the water was generally shallow, there were deep pools here and there. It would be better to cross in full sunlight, they agreed.

The girls gathered firewood and built stick and bark leantos to ward off some of the night time cold, while the men hunted rabbits. The meat and bread they brought along would have to do for the meal. Later, huddling around the fire for warmth, they talked of doing a few Indian dances.

McClellan said, "Always wanted to learn some of them jigs but what do ya do for music?"

Nancy said, "We sing it. Usually we have a drum and She-she-qua. (rattle)" The girl started a rhythmic chant that seemed to be all timing and no tune. The other girls joined her in the chant and began to dance. Soon Wells and Miller leaped to their feet, to join in. McClellan watched them awhile. A chill ran along his backbone when it occurred to him that he was the only one here that was truly white. The others were really savages, only taking a white coat when it suited them. Then, the chant's rhythm flowed through his body. He looked at the girls, pretty because of their youth, and jumped up to dance with them. A moon rose in the sky, casting shadows on the cold ground, but the couples didn't notice as they completed the ancient ritual.

When they had enough dancing they settled once again around the fire. "Looky here what I got." Miller brought out a flask of whisky that was passed around. The girls made faces at the strong taste, but drank it down. They piled the fire higher and after a time, the group quieted. Wells found himself with his arm around the soft flesh of the mischievious Nancy. Now she was only sleepy as she leaned against him. It had been a long time since he'd been with a woman. He thought, probably be more'n a year 'fore I see Sweet Breeze again. It was cold in the forest. Sleeping by himself would be uncomfortable and it'd be a kindness if he kept Nancy warm through the night. After smiling to himself because of his duplicity, he said, "Lets get some shuteye, Nancy."

She crawled into the leanto, fixing the robes they brought for a warm bed and crawled under them. The other couples followed suit and soon there was no sound in the forest except for the popping fire, howl of a wolf, and an occasional giggle.

The girl was like a fine Kentucky bourbon. Slow sips of her over a period of time could be most refreshing, William thought as he smoothed her black hair between his fingers. But she'd have to learn not to give herself so easily to other men. "Nancy, would you like to be my squaw?" He whispered.

"Unhun." She snuggled sleepily closer to him.

William stared into the darkness, trying to figure out how he could keep this girl. He'd have to provide meat and other supplies and he'd have to find a place for her to live that wouldn't be invaded by the army. Yet, he wanted her to be close enough that he could visit her from time to time. Considering the country that he knew like the back of his hand, he thought the safest, yet most accessible place would be on the upper

Mississinewa, near where it joined the Wabash. The white men didn't know of the few Indians who lived there, yet the place could be quickly reached by canoe on the Wabash from Kekionga, or on the Mississinewa from the forts. As a scout for the army he was completely free to come and go at will, so visiting her would be no problem.

"Nancy, I think you should move up to the Mississinewa where it is safer from the army. I would build a cabin for you there."

Nancy opened her eyes. She could hardly believe it but he was serious. There would be prestige in being the woman of Apeconit. She was the age when it was necessary to find a man, and he was certainly a fine one to have.

William continued, "I won't be able to stay with you, 'cause I'm with the army. So I'd like your folks to live near you."

"You'd have to ask my father about that. But he might agree if he thought it was a safe place. He may be going to battle against the Long Knives himself."

He hadn't though of that. If her father were gone, the women would have less protection. Maybe the problem wasn't worth the trouble. But then, Nancy pulled him to her, making all the difficulties of life go away for a little while.

The next day the three couples entered the Delaware village with the girls. They were surrounded by a crowd of villagers, George White Eyes among them. Smiling he said, "I am surprised to see Kitcho Shemangan is a man of his word. Thank you for returning the squaws."

"Think on it George White Eyes. When he says he means to beat the Indians in battle, he means that too. If I were you, I'd stay out of the big war that's coming."

The Delaware looked at him with a suddenly closed face. "I know you live as a white man now; an enemy. We heard that you left the Miami forever."

Wells could see that he was on dangerous ground so he said to placate the man, "Now, you know if I was totally a white, I'd never be standin' here, talkin' to you like this."

Later, Wells escorted his charge to the cabin of Nancy's father, Fishbait. The cabin area was messy and smelled of decaying meat. Wells began to regret, somewhat, taking Nancy as his own when her people lived like this. The door was opened by a squaw around thirty-eight, of medium height. She said, "So, you decided to come home from the white men's camp. You're lucky your father is off trapping or you'd have a good whipping."

Nancy lifted her chin haughtily. "I was captured by the enemy and you treat me like a slut. I should have stayed with the people who appreciate me." She pursed her mouth into a pout.

"Ah, Fishbait's squaw, I'd like to have a word with you." Wells said, as embarassed bystander.

"Say on."

The woman would make a difficult inlaw, Wells could see. But he had come this far..... "I would offer to take the girl as my woman. I am paid by the Long Knives to be a scout. I could give her a better life than she might have with some of the braves."

This threw new light on a bad situation, Fishbait's squaw could see. "She is not promised to any brave. After her "capture", it might be hard to find a good husband for her. What do you say about it Nancy?"

Nancy's mischievious grin was back. "I would be his woman."

Wells continued, "There's one problem though. I'd like you to move up to the Mississinewa where it is safer. I am afraid the Long Knives might raid the villages here, as they already did when they took the girls. If your brave leaves you to fight against the Long Knives it would be safer for you too, there."

The woman considered the man's words. It was possible they would all have a better life if they had a white man helping to support them. "We wouldn't move until warmer weather came, but it is a very possible thing. Since my man is gone, I give my permission for Nancy to be your squaw. You may come here whenever you wish."

Wells and Nancy left the cabin to walk by themselves in the field for a time before he left. "I won't be able to come often, but I will provide for you, and I'll be back to help build a place for us on the Mississinewa."

Nancy smiled gaily up at him. "Bring me some calico and beads next time, Apeconit, and I will show you how much I like them."

Wells laughed, lifting her into the air and swinging her around in a circle. "I'm probably a fool, but you are just like maple sugar. Hard to resist."

Chapter XIII

Kekionga (Fort Wayne, Indiana) Spring of 1794

Maconaquah and Meshinga expertly removed the contents of their cabin, packing everything in sacks of buffalo hide. Since they moved so often, they knew exactly how to pack their goods not easily replaced at the new campsite. Everything had its place in the bags. They had already made their maple sugar and there were over a hundred pounds that would have to be moved, plus the remaining corn supply.

Scouts were keeping an eye on General Wayne's army whose northern most fort was less than two days journey south. With the approach of spring, it was feared he would attack. To insure their safety, the Indians were moving from Kekionga, up the Maumee to the Auglaize River, near the Shawnee villages. This was closer to British Forts. It was thought they should not remain in villages already familiar to the Americans. They had been burned out twice and would surely be burned again. Yes, it would be safer upriver with the Shawnee.

Strong Bear came in asking, "Meshinga, are you ready for the canoe to be loaded?"

"I guess so. But I am getting too old for all this moving from place to place. also, I do not like moving onto the land of the Shawnee. The women will make fun of we Miami who come and harvest their cattails for our mats. They will say we are stealing their good poles to build our wigwams."

"Would you rather remain in the village to greet the white soldiers when they come? By the time they arrive they will look with favor on any woman, even one as old as you." Strong Bear threw back his head, laughing at his joke even as Meshinga heaved a loaded buffalo sack at him. She was nettled when the sack missed its mark, falling ineffectually a few feet in front of her. She sighed thinking that she wasn't as strong as she once was. Then she said sourly, "We don't know for sure they are coming, and even if they did, Little Turtle would be victorious, just as he was before."

"Perhaps, but Little Turtle is worried this time. The new Big Knife chief is one who never sleeps, it is said. His soldiers stand guard all the time. Then too, the new army will have many more men than the one before. Little Turtle would like to make peace with the Long Knives as he says something whispers to him that the Indians will lose the next war."

Meshinga straightened up, stretching. The last few years had been hard. More and more braves were being killed in wars and raids by the white men. That meant there were fewer hunters to suppy meat for the camps. Some braves took the wives of those who fell in battle, feeding them and their children as their own, in addition to the wives and children they already had. But, Meshinga knew no one would want her if something happened to Strong Bear. Then too, Maconaquah showed no interest in remarrying. It was a worrisome thing. Since leaving her husband, Tuck Horse, she didn't appear to have any interest in men. Meshinga and Strong Bear were no longer young. What would happen to Maconaquah at their death? She hoped she could see her only child safely married and perhaps even with children, before she died.

Maconaquah entered the cabin, her bright hair lighting it up like a ray of sunshine. She began carrying the heavy loads to the canoe. She had already saddled their horses to ride along the banks of the Maumee while Strong Bear paddled the canoe. Though she was short, she was young and strong, and as good a shot as Strong Bear. All along the river bank other squaws were filling canoes for the move up river where it was safer. How exciting it all is, she thought. A new village means meeting new friends and there might be interesting braves among the Shawnee. But she was worried about her parents. They seemed to be failing before her very eyes. This move seemed harder for her mother than any before. Shrugging off her fears, she thought, I am strong and have no children to care for. I will take care of them and do all the work to make the trip easier. When the final things were packed and her parents ready to leave, she gave the horse a swift kick in the ribs, speeding ahead on the new road, never giving the old village a backward glance.

That same day, a few miles away eastward, men watched as water flowed, gurgling softly past the Auglaize riverbanks. A soft March breeze slowly moved the tree branches while a red winged black bird sang a song that would always bring to mind an Indian cornfield. Three pairs of eyes slowly raised above the windfelled tree. Eighty yards ahead lay an Indian camp where three braves cooked a saddle of venison, completely unaware that they were being watched.

Wells motioned Henry Miller to shoot the brave on the right. He'd shoot the left hand one. Then McClellan, who was so swift, could run down the remaining Indian and they'd have the captive Wayne wanted for questioning. Steadying the rifles on the fallen tree, they carefully aimed so there'd be no chance for error and fired. The two Indians fell, writhed for a moment, and became still. McClellan jumped over the tree, running at full speed toward the remaining Indian as he ran toward the river. With a flying leap, he was on him. The two tumbled down the river bank to land finally, mired in the mud at its edge. The Indian stood off balance, and pulled a knife from its holder, ready to stab his attacker, but McClellan was too fast for him. Raising his tomahawk, he said, "Drop the knife."

The two extricated themselves from the mud, climbing to the top of the bank where Wells and Miller had just finished scalping the two Indians. They made a thorough search of the bodies, taking everything of value, before collecting their horses, on one of which they placed the sullen prisoner for the ride back to the fort.

The brave was silent, not answering when asked which Shawnee village was his home. Miller studied him for some time. He'd lived in a Shawnee village as a captive himself, so it might be he once knew this man.

"Hold up a bit. I'd like to see what this feller looks like without his paint," Henry said.

The other two looked at Miller hesitantly. Wells said, "This here Shawnee country ain't a place to waste time in. There's more where these come from, you can bet on it."

"Hell, it'll only take a minute. I need a drink of water fer me an' my horse anyways."

The men scrutinized the surrounding forest beyond the open land along the river. No one was in sight. Walking the horses down the river bank, Miller said in Shawnee, "Get in there and wash off that body paint yer' wearin'."

The Indian gave him a killing look, but did as he was told. As the mud, and reds and yellows of paint floated away, they all could see that under his tan he was a white man. To the other scout's surprise, Henry said coaxingly, "Chris, is that you? It's me, Henry. Your brother."

"Henry?" The Indian asked, still standing in the river.

"That's him!" Henry said excitedly. "It's my brother that stayed ta live with the Shawnee when I left!"

McClellan groaned. "And ta think we coulda shot him."

Wells surveyed the man in the river who was still Indian in every respect, though no longer painted. "I wouldn't trust my back ta that bugger, even if he was yer sister. He'll have ta be presented to Wayne as a hostage." In Shawnee he said to Christopher, "Keep your hands where I can see 'em. I've got my pistol aimed square at your back. If you want to keep your hair, don't make any false moves."

The man remained silent and sullen though he looked at Henry from time to time as they rode along. Henry kept up a constant chatter, sometimes talking in English and at others in Shawnee. "I went back ta farm with Pa in Kentucky after I left the Shawnee. When Wayne, Kitcho Shemangan, offered pay fer solderin', I signed up. We need the money home on the farm. Hell, its been years since I seen you. It's a wonder I knowed you at all."

The other offered silence.

"If you wanted to, I'll bet Wayne would hire you ta be a scout like us. With your two friends dead, the Shawnee won't know you're with us whites, and the Big Knife army."

Silence.

"What's the Indians' plan now? Are they gettin' ready to attack any of the forts?"

Silence.

"You ain't goin' ta get nowhere with him," Wells said. "It'll take him awhile to come back to the fact that he's a white man. I mind when I first went back to my brother's farm in Kentucky. Hell, ya shoulda seen me, a wild eyed Injun. I went around lookin' at everythin', plannin' in my mind ways to attack them." He laughed out loud. "Seems like a hunert years ago."

"Ya'll help me change his mind. If you could change yours, married to an Indian princess, he sure kin change his." Henry nodded his head to accentuate his answer. "It'll jest take a little work, thas all."

"Damn sight o' work, 'pears ta me," McClellan said as he watched the white colored Indian riding ahead of him. "Ya got ta' change the color of his brains."

During the following months Henry Miller and Wells worked with Christopher every free moment. He was kept under locks in the guard house where General Wayne would question him from time to time. At first, there was no response from the young man who'd lived so long with the Indians. But slowly, the arguments of his brother and Wells, convinced him that he could be a white man. A white man who could earn a horse and daily bread by working for the United States Army. Then Wells and Miller convinced Wayne to release Christopher, whereupon he was armed and mounted to work with Well's scouts, later becoming one of Wayne's most trusted scouts.

Wayne sat in his Fort Greenville cabin, rubbing his leg. The gout got worse all the time, though he felt better now in the warmth of the early July weather. More and more of late, he reflected on the fact that he might not live much longer. He began writing a friend in the East, his last will and testament. Thoughts of doom were uncharacteristic of the man. All his life, he'd had more energy than normal men. He tackled enormous tasks, overcoming obstacles other men would never dream of attempting. Always, he'd worked long hours to accomplish the task at hand, earning the Indian's description, the man who never sleeps. But the process aged him. Now the strong possibility of never seeing his Pennsylvania home again stared him in the face. The Indians were worthy opponents and this could be his last battle. Now he only awaited the arrival of the Kentucky Militia before making his final move to attack.

"What is it?" He asked at the knock on his door.

"We got bad news from Fort Recovery Sir."

"Come in." Wayne put the will aside, dreading news from the northern fort. So far, it seemed Gibson had brought him nothing but trouble as commander of the supply post. Thinking of previous problems his mind winced at the thought of the latest development.

The messenger burst into the room. "We was attacked by the Indians, sir!"

"Does the fort still hold?"

"Yes sir. But we lost twenty-one dead and they's almost thirty wounded. That included several officers. An' that ain't countin' the quartermaster's men.

"What in heavens name happened?"

"Well sir, the last load of flour that was jest sent up to the fort got there safe and was unloaded two days ago. Then, yesterday, the horses was started down the road with the quartermaster's men, but the army escort wasn't ready to leave jest yet.

Well sir, they wasn't fur down the road when they was attacked by two thousand Indians. Most them men wasn't even armed. Only eight struggled on their bellies back ta the fort, outen 'bout sixty. I hate ta tell you this, but the Injun scout, Jemmy Underwood, told Gibson they was Indians in the woods 'fore the pack train started out an' Gibson didn't pay no mind."

Wayne struck his palm with his fist. "How many of the horses did they get?"

"All of 'em, sir. 'Bout three hundred sixty."

"Damn!"

"Gibson sent out the Dragoons and Cavalry, outside the fort walls, but they was jest too many Indians. That's how we took our casualties. After they come back inside the fort, the Indians kept up steady fire the whole day and part of the night, but they couldn't make it into the fort. We popped shells and six pound shot at 'em and they took some losses themselves, but no more'en we did. They spent a lota time turnin' over logs lookin' for that cannon they hid after attackin' St. Clair. Sure glad Wells showed us where it was at."

"I take it they're gone now, since you're here."

"Aye. Gibson sent the Chickasaw Indian scout, Jemmy Underwood, out again when the Indians stopped firin' on the fort. Jemmy told him the Indians was all leavin' so Gibson went out an' hollared for them ta come back an' fight, but they only hollared back an' kept on goin', usin' our packhorses ta carry their dead."

Wayne mused, "Maybe it wasn't a bad thing to happen anyway. The Indians aren't known to stay grouped for more than one battle at a time. If they've satisfied themselves with this one fight, it may be that a good many will go home to their villages. That'll make it easier to defeat those that remain when we make our move."

"Sir, if I may be so bold, you got problems along that line yerself."

As Wayne looked at him questioningly, he continued. "Jemmy went out an' scalped as many of the Indians lyin' dead as he could. Now that he's got the Miami scalps he come for, he's takin' his Chickasaw brothers an' goin' back home ta Carolina."

Wayne let out his breath in a long sigh. Complications never ended. "Tell the Chickasaws that if they stay and fight with the army I'll give them each a hat with feathers in it, to show how they are respected."

When the messenger left, Wayne returned to finish the letter to his friend, telling him of his last wishes.

By July 28, 1794, Wayne's army included his American Legion with the addition of the recently arrived Kentucky Militia as it started north for the long planned battle. No untrained novices were these, but men who had a definite routine of movement and encampment so as to be protected, even at night, from surprise attack. Equipment and uniforms shone, spotless. The only ones exempt from sweating in the hot clothing were the scouts, sent ahead to see if Indians lurked in the neighborhood.

Wayne hoped to make it look like the army would attack Kekionga, rather than the Indians nearer the British forts closer to Detroit. The scouts were to take a captive to find out if the Indians believed this was the direction the army would take. Well's scouts lay well ahead of the main army on the Maumee banks, waiting for a passing canoe.

McClellan squirmed on his stomach, behind raspberry bushes, gun primed, ready to fire should a group of Indians come along. Only one was needed. The scouts usually killed any extras in an Indian party. An irritating deer fly seemed to have decided McClellan would make a good meal. It flew just above his head, seeming to know the exact distance to stay away from the man's hand for safety. Landing finally, it was just ready to take a chunk of meat. McClellan watched it with a malignant eye, his hand poised to strike, when he heard the rhythmic splash of paddles in the distance. Letting the fly suck his juices, he slowly moved the gun into position. Hesitating, he saw the canoe carried a family group; a brave, squaw, and two children.

Suddenly from the leafy growth to the left, Wells jumped out from under cover yelling, "Scouts don't ya'll shoot 'ere I give ya a ball in the the head!"

The Indians in the canoe, seeing they were almost under fire paddled in splashing disarray for the opposite shore.

"Gawaihaetle, it's me, its me! Apeconit." There was silence, except for the birds of the forest and sound of flowing water.

Looking back questioningly the brave said, "Apeconit?"

"Fellers, come on out and meet my old Indian father." Slowly the scouts came out from their cover, rifles still trained on the Indians. "Put down those guns! I wasn't joshin' when I said I'd kill anyone who shot at these people. This is the fellow who fed and clothed me when I was jest a boy. His squaw here cared for me when I was sick." The scouts shuffled their feet, looking at the brave in distrust, not wanting to come forward to shake hands. They mumbled a hello and looked at the ground.

Wells looked at them in disgust a moment, but understood. Turning back to the adopted father of his childhood he asked, "What are you doing here? This is no place for women and children."

"I wanted to fight with the others and was going to join them at the Maumee Rapids. The women and children are being sent north, to be near Detroit and the British."

"Don't do it, Gawaihaetle. Wayne's hot on our tail an' he's got almost five thousand men with him. Take my mother here and go back home to Kenapacomaqua. Tell the Indians to make peace, 'cause they got no chance against Kitcho Shemangan."

Gawiahatle was not a hot headed youth. He was over forty and could see the logic in what Wells said. He'd only come to fight to stand beside his kinsman, Little Turtle. But Apeconit meant even more to him than did The Turtle. If he said they were in severe danger, it was the truth. "I will go back home, Apeconit, and try to keep the Eel River Miami from going to the Maumee Rapids." As the two men parted, the Indian said, "May the Great Spirit watch over you, my son."

Major Samuel Wells watched his men cut through the giant Tulip Poplar, standing well back as the monster fell with a roar of cracking branches. Wayne himself had been foolish enough to be whipped by branches of a falling Beech tree. He could have been killed, but leaped aside with alacrity not expected of one with gout. Escaping with only internal injuries, he was mending as the new fort was being built.

Its walls were rising nicely, but not nearly as fast as General Wayne wanted. He said he expected Fort Defiance to be built in two days, much to the chagrin of his men. But as they anticipated, they were now working into the second week. It was being built on the old Indian village site, Grand Glaize, where the Auglaize and Maumee Rivers met.

Samuel's brother, William was away, taking yet another captive for questioning. He rested on his axe a moment, thinking about the peculiar twist of his position. Here he stood, in Indian country, his brother's chosen land. Now he was the uncertain one, a stranger in a strange land, while William, Captain Wells, was in his element. William seemed to have become a legend among the men. His adventures were told and retold. Whenever he returned from the forests with a captured Indian, they stood ready and eager to hear about the new adventure as William and the scouts embellished the tale.

Strange, he thought, considering his brother and Indian wife. Sam had grown fond of the quiet creature, Sweet Breeze, while she stayed in his Kentucky home over the winter. Thinking on it, he wondered that she, with her fragility and tranquil ways stayed with his brother, who more and more appeared to be a boisterous, murderous adventurer, whose scruples were easily bent.

When Sam arrived with the Kentucky Militia a few weeks ago, William had been curious about how Sweet Breeze was getting along. But being a man of great energy, and probably equal appetites, Samuel was surprised his brother did not pine for her more. As for himself, he'd give almost anything to back working on his farm, though now in early August, harvest was not yet upon them.

The political atmosphere among the officers was tense. Wayne and Wilkinson were constantly at each other's throats. Sam considered the crafty Wilkinson. He was a man who craved power, never ceasing in his efforts to put Wayne in a bad light, probably hoping to lead the army himself. Out of this vast number of men, some promising officers had developed. The twenty-one year old Lieutenant, William Henry Harrison, fresh from Virginia, was an intelligent man and quickly picked up by Wayne as his right hand man. Now Harrison was working on a plan of battle to present for Wayne's consideration.

Other men who appeared leaders were William Clark, George Rodgers Clark's brother, and Meriweather Lewis who had become Clark's fast friend.

Samuel wiped the sweat off his face and wondered if any good would come of this campaign. When William returned he'd ask him if he'd thought of starting a farm in these parts. The ground was fertile. After the battle, it might be a possibility afterall.

Two miles below the British Fort Miamis, far up the Maumee River near the place called Roche DeBout, Wells' scouts approached a Delaware war camp. It was dusk so they'd have to hurry to accomplish their mission and get back to the fort before dark. On the wide trail leading to the town, a brave and his squaw rode unsuspectingly toward them. The three dressed as Shawnee braves attracted no attention in these parts. As they passed each other the scouts suddenly crowded the Indians with their horses. The woman started a shrill, surprised cry. Miller threatened, "Quiet squaw, else I kill you."

They were told to dismount and walk into the woods. There the scouts tied them up away from the heavily traveled trail. "How'd the Shawnee know to leave the village, Grand Glaize before the army came?" Wells asked sternly.

The man and wife looked at each other. Wells kicked the man who replied, "There was an army deserter that told us the army was coming, so the people fled."

"Who's been picked as the Confederation chief?"

"Blue Jacket. Little Turtle didn't want to fight at all. He said something whispered to him that The Chief Who Never Sleeps would defeat the Indians. So, the tribesmen picked Blue Jacket and Buckongahelas to lead."

The capture had been too easy. Wells turned to his companions saying, "Let's leave these critters tied up and go into the camp for a little fun."

Miller agreed. "I wouldn't mind takin' a little Shawnee hair. I still owe them devils a few licks."

Only McClellan was reluctant, but said nothing as the others had already mounted. So far, they'd always known what they were doing.

Casually they rode into the Indian encampment of warriors gathering for battle. In the central area a bright fire danced, lighting the darkened circle. Over it swung a cook pot, hanging from a tripod of sticks. Several braves approached the horsemen, greeting the strangers, while others sat in the dark resting.

Wells questioned an Indian standing close by his horse. "Did you know Kitcho Shemangan is almost here?"

"We keep watch."

"When are your braves going to join the confederation for battle?"

A brave sitting in the shade said in another dialect, "These men ask too many question. They could be spies for Kitcho Shemangan for all we know." The surrounding group of warriors began closer scrutiny of the newcomers.

Wells heard and understood. Alarmed he gave a whistle, the signal to Miller and McClellan to shoot. All three fired point blank into the Indian standing nearest him. The other braves became a melee of bodies, reaching for the attackers to pull them from their horses, while the horses reared, trying to get away. Others ran for their guns. The scouts broke out of the group, laying flat on their horse's necks, prepared to flee. They weren't out of the campfire's light before the Indians fired back. Wells actually heard the crunch of broken bone as a bullet smashed his wrist. Dropping his rifle from the damaged hand, he galloped away into the night following Miller's lead.

McClellan, reluctant last member of the party, caught a shot in the back, just under the shoulder blade. The pain almost caused him to fall off the horse, but he held on, drawing on his great strength, expecting the shock of another bullet at any moment. The horsemen roared away from the camp expecting the tribesmen to follow, but none did, for fear of ambush in the dark by the men they pursued. As they rode the shrieks and war whoops of the outraged braves faded in the distance.

About a mile from the camp, they pulled up. "How bad off are you fellers?" Miller drew his horse nearer McClellan whose bare back was covered with blood. "It sure as shootin' looks real bad. Think you can ride?"

"For a little while I think." It was difficult to speak. "How far are we from the army?"

"Least thirty miles. Couple hours ride."

Wells bit his lip. The pain in his wrist was excruciating. "I dropped my gun back there. I've had that gun so long, it's like loosin' part of my body."

"It'll be easier ta get a new gun than mend your hand I recon. What we goin' ta do about them captives we got hogtied in the woods?"

"Take the dogs with us," Wells groaned. "You get them, Henry. We'll start towards the army. Maybe we can make it before we bleed to death."

Miller circled back through the black forest to fetch the Indian couple. Finding them after an exasperating search in the dark, he said, "I'll fill you full o' lead if you let out any kind of a hollar." After settling the subdued pair on their horses, they rejoined the others.

"McClellan ain't goin' to make it far," Wells said. "I think it's best if you ride on ahead and bring back the army surgeon. Bring buffalo hides and rope to make a travois. If I can get him ten miles down the trail, I'll be lucky."

Miller agreed. "Stay on the same trail we come on. I'll be back as fast as I can." He galloped away with the Indian couple while Wells and McClellan slowly followed, McClellan fighting the urge to lapse into unconsciousness with the horse's every step.

Two hours of hard riding brought Miller to the bedded down army camp. Throwing the reins to a private, Miller ordered, "Put these Injuns in the guard house. McClellan and Wells was shot. Where's Wayne?"

"In his tent."

Gaining the General's audience Miller speedily told the story.

"Are you in a shape to ride back with the surgeon?" Asked Wayne.

"Compared to Wells and McClellan I'm fit as a fiddle, sir. All I need is a fresh horse."

Wayne's swiftest dragoons and the surgeon followed Miller as quietly as possible through the black night forest. Miller thought, some nights its almost as light as day. Why couldn't it be like that now, stead of so black I might run smack into a tree. Not knowing how far the wounded men could travel, Miller anticipated spending a lot of time hunting them. He was greatly relieved when Wells hailed him from a spot just off the trail.

"You fellers is sure a sight for sore eyes! McClellan's bad off, with the shakes now."

By candle light, the army surgeon examined the semi-conscious McClellan. Deciding he could be moved, he was wrapped in blankets to be pulled by the ancient Indian method of a travois, through the forest. McClellan was gently laid on the platform of buffalo hides attached to two poles that would be strapped to either side of a horse.

"They sure made a mess of your wrist." The doctor commented. "I see you got the bleeding stopped. There's not much I can do for it, other than clean it up some. You'll have to keep it straight and stiff if you want it to heal."

"Will it mend good as new?"

"That only time will tell, but you're out of active duty for now, young man."

During the ride back to the fort, Wells felt a curious relief. Fortune had intervened and he wouldn't need to fight against his adopted people, the Miamis, after all.

William Wells is pictured in his formal uniform as a captain of the United States Army.

Chapter XIV

Battle of Fallen Timbers, August 20, 1794

Maconaquah heard the sound of muskets and shouts of men faintly in the distance. Strong Bear's family fled to the northwest corner of Ohio as advised by the chiefs in advance of General Wayne's army. But hoping to gather spoils from the battle fields, they foolishly lingered behind the other fleeing villagers.

It was about ten o'clock, only an hour after the battle was begun. A stream of fleeing warriors proved that the Americans were winning.

Strong Bear decided belatedly that perhaps they had made a mistake remaining so near a great battle. "We will travel north, nearer our Fathers at Detroit, Meshinga. I do not like the number of strange warriors who are about. In fact, we might be wise to find a hiding spot and lay under cover until there are fewer soldiers and warriors in the forest."

Meshinga agreed. "It is foolhardy for an old couple and young squaw to travel in the forest full of hostiles. We will make camp by the small stream we crossed. There are probably fewer warriors behind us than up ahead, since most seem to be running that direction from the Big Knives."

Strong Bear wearily said, "We should not have stayed behind, but with our crops burned by the army how will we survive the winter without the spoils from the army? I am getting so stiff in the joints that riding a horse while hunting is hard. The only deer I kill now are stupid ones."

Maconaquah glanced at him worridly, then smiled and said, "Father, you are so silly. Why you are not old. Only tired from all this traveling."

The old couple and young girl followed a small stream a long distance but could not seem to travel far enough to be beyond the sound of guns. Finally, worn out, they made camp without a fire and ate parched corn and dried meat.

The next day they stayed where they were rather than risking travel among unknown braves and not knowing the position of the American army. Finally, the second day after the battle, they traveled as quietly as they could due west, away from the area in which they had heard sounds of battle.

That evening Maconaquah and Meshinga wearily unloaded the horses to make camp. "I am tired of all this moving around," Maconaquah said. "One day I will have a nice cabin, croplands and animals of my own so that I don't have to go from place to place with a heavy pack on my back."

"You'll have to make some agreement with the pale faces so they stop burning your crops, my rose. And how will you manage that?" Strong Bear teased.

"I will move far away from everyone else. If there are no other Indians around me, why would they want to burn me out? I have done nothing to them."

Meshinga sighed. "I am an old woman now. Too old for this constant running from armies. I should have a wigwam with a couch of furs on which I'd lie while my grandchildren serve me."

The wind stirred in the treetops and the dark woods about them seemed inhospitable. They were very alone and vulnerable here, far from the burned villages along the Maumee, separated from the villagers who had traveled on ahead of them. The old couple in their sixties and a young woman of twenty-two would offer little resistance to any attackers. Cold rain started during the night, causing the huddled family to be in additional misery.

Maconaquah was awakened late in the night by a low moaning that seemed to come from the black woods behind them. the hair on her neck rose as she wondered at the unnatural noise. Was it a spirit? Don't be a coward, she said to herself. You are Little Bear Woman, as brave as any Miami warrior.

The moaning came again. This time, she realized it was an animal. Picking up a gun and knife, she left her sleeping parents, hoping to kill the animal for fresh meat. Quietly she walked, making no sound on fallen leaves or twigs, just as she had been taught. The sound came again from a hollow log. Raising the knife, she peered inside the end into the frightened brown eyes of a man.

"No, don't kill me," he gasped. Then, unable to help himself he moaned with pain.

Maconaquah immediately assessed the fact that the man was wounded and hiding inside the log. "Can you get out of there by yourself? Come out and I will tend your wound."

"I don't think I can move. I was stabbed by the Long Knives."

"I'll pull you out then." Roughly she dragged him from his hiding spot. He was a big Indian so the chore was difficult for the girl of less than one hundred pounds. The pain must have been severe for the man passed out as she moved him from his primitive shelter. As he lay on the wet leaves, unconscious, she looked over her find at leisure. From the markings and paint on him the man was a Miami, though she didn't know him. He was naked except for the loincloth, customary garb of a Miami male. As he said, there was a nasty looking wound in his mid right abdomen. He was not young, appearing to be past his mid thirties. Perhaps as old as forty. His luxuriant black hair was shaved, leaving a wide strip down the middle of his head, as did most Miami braves. The skin was not as light as many of the Miami, but he had a strong featured face, pleasant, not mean looking, she thought.

Touching his skin, she knew he had a fever. I'd better get that wound cleaned up and some water in him. He may have been without water for two days, she thought. Returning to the stream, she collected water and cloth to give first aid. On her return, she saw that the man was conscious again.

"I am cold." His teeth began chattering in the cool night air.

Maconaquah looked at him in surprise. She hadn't thought of that. Rather than make another trip back through the woods she stepped out of her skirt and laid it across him. Then she began cleansing the caked blood, tree bark, and dirt from the wound. Lifting his head she gave him a drink. He was beginning to feel better she thought as she saw him appraising her bare legs. Then, he closed his eyes and went to sleep. For awhile, Maconaquah sat there in the moonlight looking at him. She felt a certain power knowing that his fate was entirely in her hands. It had been some years since she had been with a man. Her experiences with her husband had not been particularly bad, it was living with his drunkenness and immaturity, and lack of caring that had been difficult. This man's face looked firm, perhaps intelligent. She ran her hand lightly over the muscles of his forearm. It could be interesting to keep him alive.

After walking back through the moonlit woods to where her parents were still sleeping, oblivious to her recent discovery, Maconaquah dug through the pack of clothing and secured another skirt and a robe of buffalo hide. Then she gently shook her mother, so as not to wake her father.

"Mother, there is a wounded Miami back in the woods."

"What? Is it morning? A man is here?"

"There is no danger. It's still night. But, I need to know what to put on the man's wound."

Meshinga had by this time raised herself from her dreams. "Where is this man, child?"

"Come, we will take more water along and this robe." The two women returned to the sleeping brave where Meshinga could view the wound to diagnose treatment.

"He has fever. You have cleaned the wound well. It doesn't look too bad so we can probably save him. Now we will have to prepare sumac leaves and root of pallaganghy for him to drink. Also, get some roots of the reeds growing in the stream to make a preparation for the wound.

Maconaquah gathered the necessary items to make the medicines. Then Meshinga took the reed roots, cleaned them and mashed them into a pulp. This was placed on the wound to draw out any foreign substances in it. Then the sumac leaves and the roots of the pallaganghy were taken in equal parts and crushed separately until they were almost a powder. Mixed together they were placed in a small kettle and two times the amount of sumac berries were added. The whole was simmered in water. This preparation would be given for several days to cleanse any internal clots from the body. Another root called Ouissoucatcki was ground to increase the patient's strength. A little was put in warm water for him to drink.

After all possible was done to increase the stranger's comfort, the mother and daughter returned to their camp to discuss the events with Strong Bear. They had quite a problem on their hands. The American army was not more than ten miles away, and the injured Indian appeared to be in no condition to travel. If they remained here they were in danger, but they agreed they must stay and care for him rather than flee to the outskirts of Detroit where they might have some protection by the British.

At first light Maconaquah rose to prepare a meal. The food situation would have to be assessed. The Indian in the woods had nothing with him. He must have been wounded in the battle with the Big Knives and simply escaped with his life. They had a small supply of corn and it was fall. The winter would be very grim indeed. Maconaquah had been taking more and more responsibility for feeding the family as her parents failed in strength, so she felt it was her duty to plan for their wants during the coming winter.

The thing to do now was to set a few lines for fish. This done, she began making the medicine preparations and cooked some corn meal in water. After getting a small kettle of water she carried this and the wood bowl of mush to the Indian. In the space next to the log she found the man sleeping fitfully.

Gazing at her as he woke, he said, "So I was right. A red haired paleface was here last night, and a good looking one at that."

Without commenting she knelt by his side and proceeded to wipe away the medicine preparation on the wound, none too gently.

"Oww, be careful woman or you'll kill me!"

"Not yet. It would be wise to be courteous as you are at my mercy."

Placing a hand on her thigh he said, "True, true. I will be as meek as a dove."

Pushing aside his hand, she commented, "Rather like a rutting buck it appears to me. I do not think you need my care so I will leave."

"No wait, squaw. I will be your humble patient. I cannot move as you can see. I would die without your help. Why are you here anyway? All the tribes were told to leave and go north because the big knives were coming."

"We should have left but my father thought the confederation would win the battle and there would be spoils to gather from the dead. My father is old and cannot trap as he once did. We needed the goods from the soldiers. What happened anyway?"

"Blue Jacket was the war chief picked to lead the Confederation as you probably know, but he is not as clever as Little Turtle. Little Turtle would not lead us because he thought we should not fight this war against The Chief Who Never Sleeps. I think the real reason The Turtle would not lead our braves was because his son-in-law, Apeconit went to fight with the Big Knives. But I would not dare speak such a thing.

We had an ambush set among a treefall caused by a tornado. But Blue Jacket had us all strung out for a space of two miles. Now, I am war chief in my village and I tell you that was a bad maneuver. The Big Knives came and the concentration of braves was so thin in the battle line that they moved right through us. It wasn't long until our braves were in total flight. Many ran to the British fort, two miles away. They pounded on the gate but the British would not let them in. Our true friends and allies, the British, did this to us. All their promises to help us were nothing but lies. Now we see they are not our friends."

"With your wound, how did you get so far from the fight?"

"I was fighting with my braves a little to the left of the main charge. A soldier rode past on a horse and drove his sword into my side. I fell. Then when the American army had passed, I rose and ran into the trees. Then, I walked on. Then I stumbled on and finally, I crawled into the tree when I could go no further. I didn't even have a gun to protect myself from wolves. So when I heard you nearing my hiding spot, I thought my last moment had come."

"Because of you we all may see our last moments soon. We aren't very far from the army. The soldiers could come on us and kill us with little trouble."

"I doubt that. White soldiers know that a stroll in the forest alone could cause a loss of their hair. Even though they defeated our braves, they will remember that. If you are camped by the stream though, you should move back here in the woods as I did. There is less chance of traffic here. Also, your father could keep watch for unexpected visitors."

"My father grows more feeble with every passing day. I am the one who keeps the watches now."

"You? You are nothing but an overgrown papoose. Why I could lift you with one hand." As he moved toward her the wound showed him he could do no such thing.

"Really? Well, this papoose could tattoo your chest with dancing squaws and you couldn't do a thing about it." She laughed a nasty little laugh as she left for the riverside camp to move it back into the woods by the wounded brave.

In the following days Strong Bear doubled back the way they had come to see what was going on in the American camps. He spoke with some Indian scouts who said the army was camped a few miles down river from the British fort but showed no sign of attacking it. They did not appear to be planning a move on Detroit either. This was good news for the little Indian family since they had a good start in that direction and planned joining the villagers there for the winter.

Maconaquah was enjoying the process of getting to know the handsome brave, entirely at her leisure since he could not move about. The wound had not gone putrid and was healing well due to Maconaquah's constant vigilance and Meshinga's excellent knowledge of herbal medicines.

After his afternoon sleep, she opened the conversation. "Your squaw will be weeping since you did not return with the others."

"Why do you say that? I have no squaw."

"Most braves have squaws. Why don't you?"

"Where is your husband, oh nosey one?"

The impish smile she had been wearing was replaced by a sullen frown.

"Ah, so you are married. That's all right. I enjoy married women."

Maconaquah sputtered at that, "I am divorced. but we were speaking of your wife."

"Since you will be so rude as to persist, I have no wife. There has never been a woman swift enough to catch me."

"Ha! You mean never one that would have you." She jumped up to run away but was not quick enough. A hand grasped her ankle causing her to fall sprawling on top of him. Her indignant brown eyes were only five inches away from his grinning ones. She sputtered, jumped up and ran from his view, his laughter in her ears as she ran.

Meshinga kept an eye on the proceedings with interest. After Maconaquah left her husband, she had steered clear of men. She was very bitter after her previous marriage. Meshinga knew that she and Strong Bear were in failing health. They probably could not survive many more winters. With the army ruining the tribe's food supply, their chances were reduced. She worried about the fate of her unmarried daughter, especially because she appeared to have no interest in men.

As the warm days of August continued, the brave grew stronger. He offered to help with such chores as he could while lying on his side. The skinning and cleaning of a rabbit or squirrel was one job that was rather tedious, but caused him to feel somewhat useful.

Maconaquah was surprised that he offered to help with jobs usually delegated to women. "If you are really a chief, why do you do such work?"

"I don't like to see a pretty young squaw worked too hard. Don't forget to speak up. Remember, my name is not Shepancanah, Deaf Man, for nothing."

"You had no business being in a battle like that when you can't hear well. It's no wonder you were almost killed."

Deaf Man laughed. "It may be surprising to you, but I can still shoot a musket or brain a white man, even though I am deaf. I'm a better shot than most, some say." Reaching for her wrist he said, "It doesn't effect my skill with young squaws either."

Disengaging his hand, Maconaquah handed him a deck of cards, one of the favorite pastimes of the Indians. "It is your turn to deal, my friend." As the cards were placed in her hands, Maconaquah said, "Why are you really unmarried? A man as lecherous as you wants a wife."

Deaf Man contemplated his cards seriously. "I have never needed to be married. The feast is everywhere spread before me and I need not pay for it." Observing Maconaquah's scowl he laughed. "Long ago, when I was a young brave, I was once tempted to marry. There was a young squaw, well built," he gestured lewdly with his hands showing how, "and I mooned like a lovesick wolf who has no pack. She was not interested in a bashful brave, such as myself. She wanted a brave who captured many scalps and brought white men's goods to the village. I did not enjoy killing others for sport. So one day, she went to the wigwam of an older brave, one who was skilled at killing white settlers coming down the Ohio.

Great was my grief. I went on raiding parties to prove what a man I was but mainly, I became disgusted when I took the lives of others. The people of my village were impressed and made me a chief. But I had learned it is more important to be proud of myself and my actions, than to please others. Since then, no squaw has touched my heart. Though they have touched other parts of my body." He smiled wickedly.

Maconaquah was touched by this candid speech. "My husband was such a one as the brave who married the young squaw. But bravery does not make a good man. Do you see the scar on my face? That is just one of the blows he gave me. I left him and now he is probably married to his only love, whisky." The two continued playing the card game silently.

Strong Bear came up to the couple playing cards. Stiffly he lowered himself beside them. "Shepancanah, if you can travel, we should move our camp to a place with more game. I would think it a great favor if you would spend the winter with us to help supply meat for the cook-pot. We have no young braves who are relatives and I am too old to hunt."

Maconaquah protested, "Father, I can do the job. We don't need charity."

Deaf Man said, "I owe you a great debt. You saved my life even though you placed your own in danger by doing so. I will stay the winter and hunt for you when I am able. In the morning we will begin moving towards Detroit, though the game will be more plentiful somewhat to the west. And it would be wise to build a log cabin before winter."

Strong Bear was surprised at how relieved he was by Deaf Man's words. Even with his wound, Deaf Man made decisions for the family that were shrewd and sound and he was a jovial man, a joy to have around. Of late, Strong bear was finding it increasingly difficult to travel, which unfortunately they had to do constantly because of the wars with the whites. He and Meshinga had to rely almost totally on Maconaquah. She was young and strong, but slightly built, lacking enough muscle to do tasks such as building their winter quarters. The problems of surviving the next winter had seemed overwhelming to him.

When a morning meal of cooked oppossum and black berries was finished, the party of four readied themselves for the trip north. One would have to walk as they had only three horses. Most of the time, that one was Maconaquah, the only able bodied person in the group. It only took two days to travel forty odd miles to the west of Detroit. They selected an area some ten miles west of the British stronghold to begin work on winter quarters. Here they found abundant game. During September and October the family built a cabin, collected black walnuts and hickory nuts, dryed blackberries and collected crab apples. The winter would be harsh without the crops from their gardens. Deaf Man proved to be a very efficient hunter keeping Maconaquah busy preparing the hides of animals he killed. These hides could be traded at Detroit for the other necessities of life. As Strong Bear said, once again the Great Spirit had smiled on them by providing this brave in their time of need.

A bright November day Strong Bear felt a surge of energy. He gathered load upon load of firewood which he stacked by the doorway of the cabin. That night, the family was awakened with the sound of his vomiting. Meshinga went to him outside the cabin to help. She brought water from the nearby creek, but it did not seem to help him. Finally, leaning on Deaf Man, Strong Bear was able to return to his pallet of furs inside. As Deaf Man arranged the blanket over him, Strong Bear grasped his hand. "Meshinga, bring Maconaquah to me, as I want to say some words of importance to her."

Maconaquah dropped to her knees beside the old man's bed. Strong Bear looked at her in a fashion that seemed queer to her. It was as if he were fixing her features in his mind one last time and then he spoke. "Deaf Man, for providing for my family, I give you my daughter, Maconaquah, for your wife."

Deaf Man's eyebrow raised only a fraction of an inch. "I will be a good husband to her, you may rest in peace. And Meshinga will be as my mother."

"You are an honorable friend, Deaf Man. Now, if Meshinga will come here to me."

The two left the room to give the dying man and his wife some privacy. Meshinga lay down on the bed beside her husband one last time, placing her arm around him and pulling the blanket over them.

Outside, Maconaquah and Deaf Man walked completely silenced by the sudden turn of their fortunes. Stars shone brightly into the clearing. In the distance an owl screeched. Deaf Man broke the silence. "He was a very good man. I hope that one day I may have as much wisdom as he."

Maconaquah looked at him sideways, touching his hand. "You will....my husband."

Deaf Man drew her to him and they walked arm in arm back to the cabin.

Signing of the Greene Ville Treaty. This painting by Howard Chandler Christy shows Little Turtle making his final address to General Anthony Wayne. Between them stands William Wells, acting as chief interpreter.

Chapter XV

Near Detroit, June, 1795

Maconaquah held her stomach with one hand while carrying the kettle of water with the other. She felt tired all the time now, it seemed. Perhaps it wouldn't be too terrible to sit down for just a moment. Easing herself down on an obliging rock, she took the unusual idle moment to appraise the view. Their tiny cabin stood on a small creek whose banks were very gentle. In the slowly flowing water minnows flashed here and there among the rocks. In the forest surrounding the clearing, a crow cawed to his fellows that it was not safe to fly down for meat scraps. Someone was there on a rock. Sunlight shown into the clearing but the forest muted it, making shadows deep into the space.

Maconaquah missed the gossip of the villagers, here so far from everyone. But as Shepancanah said, they had been safe here, away from the possibility of attack or starvation among the others. The winter had been spartan, but they survived. Others huddled together in their villages did not do as well. They'd learned that many went begging at the fort built by the Long Knives at Kekionga.

Time to get back to work. There was much to be done and pregnancy was no excuse for loafing. Beside the cabin Meshinga sat idle. She did little these days. Time seemed to have stopped for her when Strong Bear died. Now she could talk of little but what they used to do together. To get her interested in something other than her grief, Maconaquah said, "What do you think we should have to eat when Shepancanah returns from Detroit?"

The old woman collected herself, looked at her hands, and then at her daughter. "Maybe I could get a pot of hominy started. It's been a long time since I bothered to make any."

"That would be good Mother. I'd like to work hoeing in the field awhile. We are so lucky that Shepancanah traded for the seeds. Next winter we will have plenty to eat."

"He is a good man. He brings in more hides to make trade than two women can tan. Such a good man."

Maconaquah patted her stomach laughing. "Soon we'll have two good men, and if not that, more help to tan hides!"

Rubbing the center of her back she fetched the hoe leaning against the side of the cabin. Weeds grew lushly around the plants sown among the tree stumps in the clearing. This was the first year anything was planted here and the ground was stubborn in its ancient hardness. But the seeds grew eagerly in the virgin soil. As she chopped, birds whistled to each other. The clearing was a curious bright spot, surrounded by the gloom of the dense forest. They were so isolated they could have been on a ship in an ocean of trees.

Then, far in the distance came the sound of a horse, slowly coming down the path. It probably was Deaf Man, but she went to get the rifle, as a precaution. After watching from the forest, the two women ran forward with smiles at the sight of their returning brave.

As usual, his horse was loaded with food and supplies. "Where's my reward for a long and dangerous trip?" Deaf Man chuckled.

Maconaquah came forward to touch her husband nuzzling his cheek. Deaf Man put his arm around her and patted her stomach. "Hello to you too, little brave."

"Deaf Man, it might be a squaw child. She might not like being called a brave."

"Maybe we'll have one of each." He laughed as her mouth dropped in shock at the very idea. "I've got something for you here." Opening the packs he brought out a roll of blue cloth. "I brought these for you with money left over." Opening his hand he gave her a pair of silver earrings with a fine design. Maconaquah's eyes sparkled.

"Thank you, my husband. And to think I don't even have corn bread made for you to eat. I didn't think you'd be back for a day or two."

"A peace treaty council is being gathered at the Big Knife Fort, Greenville. I will be going to get any goods they may give out to the Indians, and to give my advice. But I wanted to be sure you had enough provisions and knew I was going before I went. The council may last several weeks."

"Why aren't they having the council at Kekionga? The Big Knives have a fort there and it would be where the most people are."

"I don't know. The Chief Who Never Sleeps said he didn't want to bury a bloody hatchet there where it was first raised. To bury it there would disturb the spirits of the unburied dead he said. But I think he is afraid we would attack him at Fort Wayne. That fort is not as strong as the one at Greenville and it is farther from Fort Washington where they get supplies."

"I wish the white men would go away and leave us alone. Haven't they had enough killing and burning yet?"

"Now you're forgetting your skin is white, my Rose. Why do you think I didn't ask you if you wanted to go along to the council? Your white people may look for you yet."

"But I can't remember them. How would they know me?"

"I don't know, but you must stay out of sight of the soldiers, else they steal you from me. Anyway, we wouldn't want anything to happen to our little brave on the trail."

The two went into the cabin where Meshinga was already fixing a bowl of stew for Shepancanah. He sat at the table he'd made during a blizzard last winter, to eat it. Maconaquah had many questions about what the indians were doing near Detroit. She was rather envious of them, since there was so much more to do there.

Detroit was a strange sight for anyone coming to it for the first time. The town itself was a crowded mass of wooden frame buildings of one or two stories, some well finished and furnished, and inhabited by people of many nations. The streets were so narrow that two carriages could scarcely pass each other. Ships, some large vessels of war or merchant men lay at the wharf or sailed up and down a mile wide river as if going to and from the ocean, but in fact to Lake Erie.

As Maconaquah sat watching him eat she asked, "Have the people left Detroit already for the council?"

"Many have. Some went to Kekionga first to get food and such from the fort. Many are hoping to move back there."

She sighed. "I'd like to go back too, where there's people to talk to. If the chiefs make peace, we could move back couldn't we?"

"I think they will decide on peace. So far, Little Turtle, Blue Jacket and Buckongehelas seem only interested in the whisky the land jobbers in Detroit give them. But they went to Ketcho Shemangan in the winter. They signed a treaty promising not to make war until after this treaty conference. Your friend, Bad Bird's squaw, made the string of blue wampum given to the Big Knife chief to seal the agreement. The chiefs are afraid of General Wayne. They think they will have to make peace."

"I will be glad if they do. This running away, making cabins and gardens only to have them burned up, is no way to live. I would not want my children to live this way."

"I'm not sure the treaty will be good for us though," Deaf Man said slowly. "The young men will not know what they should do if there are no more wars, and what if the Big Knives take our land? Only time will tell us if it is a good thing."

By mid June Shepancanah was on his way to the council. It was to get underway on June fifteenth, but the Indians were accustomed to gathering slowly for these meetings. At Fort Greenville Wayne gave a formal opening speech but it was a futile gesture. The major chiefs were still in Detroit, drinking with Canadian land jobbers.

It was a three day ride to Kekionga. Entering the old Miami capital Deaf Man surveyed the damage done by the Big Knife army. Most of the villager's homes had been burned, though some of the better cabins still stood. Perhaps the soldiers had used them for themselves. The stout new fort called Fort Wayne stood inside the fork made by the junction of the St. Marys and Maumee Rivers. It had two block houses and a square palisade. A separate blockhouse was raised in front of it. Five hundred acres around the site were cleared of trees. Around it was dug a shallow ditch or moat.

Near the fort stood a few new cabins of French traders. Apparently they felt it was safe to return. Over a year ago they'd fled with the Indians in the face of the advancing American army.

Dismounting beside a small wigwam with a barely smoldering fire Deaf Man said to a squaw, "Greetings. I am Deaf Man, a Piqua Miami. I am going to the council meeting, at Fort Greenville. Have other braves gone there from this place?"

The woman appraised him, judging him safe enough to talk with. "Braves go south for many days now. They still come through Kekionga every day. Most visit the fort here. The Big Knife chief gives them tobacco and corn."

This was surprising news. "By what name is the chief called?"

"Hamtramck. Many of the old people would have starved in the winter except that he gave them food. If he weren't a paleface, I would say he is a good man."

"Was the winter hard here? My family and I spent our time near Detroit and we haven't been back since before the war."

"Aye, it was a very bad time. Few Indians stayed here except old people who had no family, some widows, and their children. There were around ninety of us, and no corn to eat. My husband was killed by Kitcho Shemangan's army. With no braves to hunt and no crops, we almost starved. But, the chief, Hamtramck, shared what he had with us and we survived. It is said the white men in the fort had little themselves. Chief Hamtramck even bought food from the traders to give us."

"I have some pheasants I killed on the way. Would you cook them and then I will go on to the council meeting."

The woman was only too happy to do this. While she cleaned the birds, Deaf Man continued to learn news about the Miamis. "Do you think many will return to live here?"

"That would depend on whether a peace treaty is signed. Many Shawnee returned to their villages along the Maumee last winter, but few, other than those of us with no braves, returned here. Now the braves are traveling through Kekionga to the meeting at the Big Knife fort, Greenville. Maybe they will see it's safe to live here."

"I would like to come here, even though I am from Piqua. My squaw misses other women. We live in the forest, far away from any others."

"Aye. With the traders here, it is good to trade for things, when you have a need and the furs to pay for them. Who is your squaw?"

"Maconaquah. Her mother, Meshinga lives with us also."

"You married Maconaquah? The woman is lucky at last. Her first husband beat her, even though she was one of the most valued of squaws. Her red hair is a sign of special courage and spirit. We did not like to see her brave, who was only a Delaware, beat her."

"We're going to have a papoose before long."

The woman grinned broadly, clapping her hands. "It is a good sign. Our people are fewer all the time. I was beginning to think the white men would kill us all.....that our people would be no more in the land."

A wide plain abloom with flowers surrounded Fort Greenville. From the distance Deaf Man saw hundreds of Indians, some racing their horses up and down the meadow, trampling the flowers. From the action about the place, he concluded that the meetings had not yet started. It was surprising how many had come. It appeared that all nations east of the Mississippi were represented. Later he learned that there were more than eleven hundred warriors here, representing twelve tribes.

Riding up to a group of Miami he knew, he jumped off the horse, somewhat less agilely than he had planned, because of his weight. "Hello friends. A long winter has passed since I last saw you."

"Shepancanah, old friend! We thought you were killed in the fight with Kitcho Shemangan. Though we never found your body, we looked for it. You are like a spirit, who has come alive again!"

"I was wounded. See the scar?" They crowded around and poked and prodded the well healed wound.

A rather short, bow legged Miami said, "That was a bad one. It's a wonder you lived!"

"A beautiful red haired squaw saved my life. Every day she poured out her care for me, so how could I help recovering? I had to, to find out about all of her charms."

The braves laughed, pounding him on the back. "Deaf Man, you haven't changed. You're still a dog with the squaws."

"Where have you placed your blankets? Is there any food given out by the pale faces?"

"We have sleeping places in those buildings that the army guards used. They will give you some pork and whisky inside the fort. Tell them you just arrived so they will give you a ration. Several interpreters will speak for you. Apeconit and the Shawnee captive (Christopher Miller) are among them."

"Deaf Man enjoyed the entertaining events during the next weeks wholeheartedly. It had been such a long time since he'd seen old friends. The braves had one continuous party, singing, dancing, racing horses, and eating, all at the American Government's expense. As Wayne had said, he wanted them to live just like his own men, eating three meals a day, and to sleep in quarters just like those of his men. He'd laid down some rules opening day, saying there was to be no fighting and the braves were to be in their camps after dark.

After some time, the Indians became increasingly bored as they waited for the principal chiefs. New groups of Indians arrived almost daily, giving some entertainment with their speeches to General Wayne. One group arriving shortly after Deaf Man was a party of forty Pottawattomi from near Lake Michigan. Their principal chief, a very old white haired man named New Corn, spoke for them. He was a wrinkled, shrunken man, but had kindly eyes, soon becoming the most popular person at the assembly. He exuded wisdom and kindness, and was always interested in the problems of the others. He was the epitome of the senior statesman. In his arrival speech he said:

> "I have come here on the good work of peace; no other motive could have induced me to undertake so long a journey as I have now performed, in my advanced age and infirm state of health. I come from Lake Michigan. I hope, after our treaty, you will exchange our old medals, and supply us with George Washingtons. My young men will no longer listen to the former; they wish for the latter. They have thrown off the British and henceforth will view the Americans as their only true friends. We come with a good heart and hope you will supply us with provision.

General Wayne asssured them that they would be provided with plenty to eat, though there were complaints by a few of the Miami that they didn't have enough. Others complained about the long wait for negotiations to start, but Wayne could do nothing until all important chiefs were assembled.

June 23 Little Turtle finally came from Detroit with seventy-three braves. It was eight days after the council was to have begun, but now Wayne started private negotiations in earnest. To occupy the restless braves,

Wayne gave an entertainment during which he hoped to impress the Indians once and for all of the might of the American army.

It was July 4th, 1795. The nineteenth birthday of the Declaration of the United States. A booming cannon brought the Indians to the parade field. Wayne spoke saying, "These cannon bursts are a harbinger of peace and gladness. I want you to join in the celebration of this day that is so important."

The legion began firing blank cartridges, raising an earsplitting, though otherwise harmless, display. They raised the American flag with all pomp and ceremony, while the sub-legionary bands played martial music. Then the army was drawn into parade formation to sing a hymn of which the general gist was that peace was being made. Finally, a sermon was given on peace, justice, and freedom from slavery.

Ten days later, exactly one month after they were to have begun, the treaty council came to order. On the broad plain in front of the fort, General Wayne, backed by three aides said, "We have stirred up and replenished the council fire we have previously covered up a month ago."

The eight interpreters began interpreting his words to the twelve tribes of more than eleven hundred men. William Wells and Christopher Miller were among them. Wayne said after swearing in the interpreters. "These interpreters whom you have now seen sworn, have called the Great Spirit to witness that they will faithfully interpret all speeches made by me to you and by you to me; and the Great Spirit will punish them severely hereafter, if they do not religiously fulfill their sacred promise."

"Wayne continued, "I will read to you the treaty made on the Muskingum river, at Fort Harmar, in 1789 at which time your chiefs sold, for payment, to the United States certain lands north of the Ohio. I wish this treaty and all previous treaties to be recognized as the basis for the treaty we are to make now."

He held up a huge carved copy of the United States coat of arms, turning around so that all could see it. Pointing to the eagle he said, "Brothers, you may choose either the sheaf of arrows, held in the talon of the eagle, as a sign of war, or the olive branch that stands for peace."

After the treaty was read, the Indians met to consider their reply. Little Turtle rose to speak. The naked Miami was a striking figure, one of great authority and power. His stern face was set in an uncompromising line. He was the lion of the forest, an Indian panther, king of all present. Anthony Wayne, with all his egotism was awed by this primitive man of power. But Wayne was backed by the war machines and knowledge of the eighteenth century. Little Turtle would have to comply with his demands. Little Turtle had been defeated.

Wells interpreted for The Turtle as follows. "You have told me that the present treaty should be founded upon that of Muskingum. I beg leave to observe to you, that that treaty was effected altogether by the Six Nations (Iroquois) who seduced some of our young men to attend it, together with a few of the Chippewas, Wyandotts, Delawares, Ottawas, and Pottawattamies. I beg leave to tell you that I am entirely ignorant of what was done at that treaty."

Latter a Chippewa chief spoke for the Ottawas, Chippewas, and Pottawattamies, or The Three Fires, to the effect that they neither knew of any previous treaties, nor received any payment for the lands in question that they felt they also owned.

Where were these lands that were ceded in previous treaties," Little Turtle asked. Wayne outlined the boundaries of the lands in question. A recess was called while the Indians deliberated.

In a private council with Wayne, Blue Jacket let him know that the Shawnee would go along for peace, if he received gifts from the Americans as he had from the British.

The next day Little Turtle spoke passionately about the land that he knew was his. He knew if he gave it up, the Indian's hunting grounds would be compressed. Speaking as well as he could, knowing how much it would mean he said;

> "General Wayne, I hope you will pay attention to what I now say to you. I wish to inform you where your younger brother, the Miamis, live, and, also, the Pottawattamies of St Joseph's together with the Wabash Indians. You have pointed out to us the boundary line between the Indians and the United States, but now I take the liberty to inform you that that line cuts off from the Indians a large portion of country which has been enjoyed by my forefathers, time immemmorial, without molestation or dispute.
>
> The print of my ancestor's houses are everywhere to be seen in this portion. I was a little astonished at hearing you, and my brothers who are now present, telling each other what business you had transacted together heretofore at Muskingum, concerning this country. It is well known by all my brothers present, that my forefather kindled the first fire at Detroit; from thence to its mouth; from thence, down the Ohio, to the mouth of the Wabash; and from thence to Chicago, on Lake Michigan; at this place, I first saw my elder brothers the Shawanee. I have now informed you of the boundaries of the Miami nation, where the Great Spirit placed my forefather a long time ago, and charged him not to sell or part with his

lands, but to preserve them for his posterity. This charge had been handed down to me. I was much surprised to find that my other brothers differed so much from me on this subject. For their conduct would lead one to suppose, that the Great Spirit and their forefathers, had not given them the same charge that was given to me, but, on the contrary had directed them to sell their lands to any white man who wore a hat, as soon as he should ask it of them.

Now elder brother, your younger brothers, the Miamis, have pointed out to you their country, and also to our brothers present. When I hear your remarks and proposals on this subject, I will be ready to give you an answer. I came with an expectation of hearing you say good things, but I have not heard what I expected."

Tarke, or The Crane, chief of the Wyandotts and keeper of the peace calumet rose to speak in rebuttal to The Turtle's speech.

"Elder Brother: Now listen to us! The Great Spirit above has appointed this day for us to meet together. I shall now deliever my sentiments to you, the fifteen fires. I view you lying in a gore of blood. It is me, an Indian, who caused it. Our tomahawk yet remains in your head. The English gave it to me to place there. Elder brother, I now take the tomahawk out of your head; but, with so much care, that you shall not feel pain or injury. I will now tear a big tree up by the roots, and throw the hatchet into the cavity which they occupied, where the waters will wash it away where it can never be found. Now I have buried the hatchet, and I expect that none of my color will ever again find it out.

I now tell you that no one in particular can justly claim this ground; it belongs, in common, to us all: no earthly being has an exclusive right to it. The Great Spirit above is the true and only owner of this soil, and he has given us all an equal right to it.

Brother: you have proposed to us to build our good work on the treaty of Muskingum: that treaty I have always considered formed upon the fairest principles. You took pity on us Indians. You did not do as our fathers, the British, agreed you should. You might, by that agree-

> ment, have taken all our lands; but you pitied us, and let us hold part. I always looked upon that treaty to be binding upon the United States and us Indians."

Wayne gave the United States position to Little Turtle's speech two days later on July 24th. After his opening remarks he answered the complaints of "The Three Fires" about not getting paid for lands given up at the Muskingum treaty session as follows:

> "If you did not receive a due proportion of the goods, as original proprietors, it was not the fault of the United States. On the contrary, the United States have twice paid for those lands–first, at the treaty of Fort McIntosh, ten years ago, and next at that of Muskingum, six years since.
>
> Younger brothers: Not-withstanding, these lands have been twice paid for, by the fifteen fires, at the places I have mentioned, yet such is the justice and liberality of the United States that they will now, a third time, make compensation for them"

Having answered their claims, he turned to the Miamis, the most powerful group of Indians, to answer Little Turtle's claims.

> "Brothers, the Miamis: I have paid attention to what The Little Turtle said two days since, concerning the land which he claims. He said his fathers first kindled the fire at Detroit, and stretched his line from thence to the headwaters of Scioto; thence, down the same, to the Ohio; thence, down that river, to the mouth of the Wabash; and from thence to Chicago, on the southwest end of Lake Michigan, and observed that his forefathers had enjoyed that country undisturbed from time immemorial.
>
> Brothers, these boundaries enclose a very large space of country, indeed: they embrace, if I mistake not, all the lands on which all the nations now present live, as well as those which have been ceded to the United States. The lands which have been ceded, have within these three days been acknowledged by the Ottawas, Chippewas, Pottawattamies, Wyandotts, Delawares, and Shawnees.
>
> The Little Turtle says, the prints of his forefathers' houses are everywhere to be seen within these bound-

> aries. Younger brother, it is true, these prints are to be observed; but, at the same time, we discover the marks of French throughout this country, which were established long before we were born. These have since been in the occupancy of the British, who must, in their turn, relinquish them to the United States, when they, the French and Indians, will be all as one people." (He gave a white string of wampum)

Then naming the various locations where French and British settlements were already standing, namely Detroit, Chicago, and Vincennes, he added:

> "However, as I have already observed, you shall now receive from the United States further valuable compensation for the lands you have ceded to them by former treaties.
>
> Younger brother: I will now inform you who it was who gave us these lands, in the first place. It was your fathers the British.

Wayne read to them a section of the peace treaty made with Great Britain and the United States in 1783 which relinquished to the United States all country south of the great lakes. He continued:

> "The British on their part, did not find it convenient to relinquish those posts as soon as they should have done; however, they now find it so and a precise period is accordingly fixed for their delivery. I have now in my hand the copy of a treaty, made eight months since, between them and us, of which I will read you a little. By this solemn agreement, they promise to retire from Michilimacinac, Fort St. Clair, Detroit, Niagara, and all other places on this side of the lakes, in ten moons from this period, and leave the same to full and quiet possession of the United States.

This speech was responded to by a buzzing undertone as the Indians didn't know this. They were shocked that the British had actually given up their claims to the Americans. All their promises of support had been lies after all.

> "Brothers: All nations present, now listen to me! Having now explained those matters to you, and informed you of all things I judged necessary for your information, we have nothing to do but to bury the hatchet, and draw a veil over past misfortunes.
>
> I will, the day after tomorrow, show you the cessions you have made to the United States, and point out to you the lines which may, for the future, divide your lands from theirs."

During the following days Wayne showed them the lands previously given up by treaty and what lands he demanded now. He wanted most of Ohio, a six mile section at Kekionga, and several two mile tracts of land. Little Turtle did not want to give up some of the Miamis most important and most beloved lands. He gave a long speech of which the following is a section.

> "Elder brother: you have told us to speak our minds freely, and now we do it. This line takes in the greater and best part of your brother's hunting ground; therefore, your younger brothers are of opinion, you take too much of their lands away, and confine the hunting of our young men within limits too contracted.

The Turtle then outlined those lines he wished to be the boundaries of the United States. Answering Wayne's claims that the British and French already claimed much of their land, The Turtle continued:

> "I was much surprised to hear you say that it was my forefathers had set the example to the other Indians, in selling their lands. I will inform you in what manner the French and English occupied those places.
>
> Elder brother: these people were seen by our forefathers first at Detroit: afterward we saw them at the Miami village–that glorious gate, which your younger brothers had the happiness to own, and through which all the good words of our chiefs had to pass, from the north to the south, and from the east to the west. Brothers, these people never told us they wished to purchase our lands from us."

Little Turtle protested giving up a piece of land two miles square at the carrying place between the Maumee and Little River, a branch of the Wabash.

> "Elder brother: The next place you pointed to was the Little River, and said you wanted two miles square at that place. This is a request that our fathers, the French and British never made us; it was always ours. This carrying place heretofore proved, in a great degree, the subsistence of your younger brothers. That place has brought to us, in the course of one day, the amount of one hundred dollars. Let us both own this place, and enjoy in common the advantages it affords.
>
> You told us, at Chicago the French possessed a fort. We have never heard of it. We thank you for the trade you promised to open in our country; and permit us to remark, that we wish our former traders may be continued, and mixed with yours.
>
> Elder brother: On the subject of hostages, I have only to observe, that I trust all my brothers present are of my opinion with regard to peace and our future happiness. I expect to be with you every day when you settle on your reservations and it will be impossible for me or my people to withhold from you a single prisoner; therefore, we don't know why any of us should remain here.(As hostages until captives were returned.) These are the sentiments your younger brother presents on these particulars."

After Little Turtle's speech, various other chiefs spoke regarding lands in their territories claimed by General Wayne. One of these speakers was the old favorite, the Pottawattamie chief, Blue Corn. The old man stood up, looking out over the field covered with Indians sitting on the ground. He looked over the beloved land with sadness, for he knew it was soon to be theirs no more. Beginning his speech in his old thin voice he said:

> "My friend, when I first came here, I took you by the hand. You welcomed me and asked me for my great war chiefs. I told you they were killed and that none remained but me, who have the vanity to think myself a brave man and great warrior. The Great Spirit has made me a great chief, and endowed me with great powers. The heavens

> and earth are my heart, the rising sun my mouth, and thus favored, I propagate my species.
>
> I know the people who have made and violated former treaties. I am too honorable and brave a man to be guilty of such unworthy conduct. I love and fear the Great Spirit. He now hears what I say, I dare not tell a lie.
>
> Now my friend, The Great Wind, do not deceive us as in the name of the French, British and Spaniards have heretofore done. The English have abused us much; they have made us promises which they never fulfilled; they have proved to us how little they ever had our happiness at heart. We have severly suffered for placing our happiness on so faithless a people. Be you strong and preserve your word inviolate and reward those Frenchmen who have come so great a distance to assist us.
>
> My friend, I am old, but I shall never die. I shall always live in my children and children's children." (A string of wampum).

When the old man sat down, a soft breeze touched their faces. They were silenced for a moment. It was as if the Great Spirit indeed had seen and heard.

Wayne hadn't really listened to the speech. Blue Corn was not an important chief afterall. While the old man was speaking the general was thinking out his rebuttal to Little Turtle's speech. Little Turtle was the man who counted here. In essence he spoke for three quarters of the Indians in these parts. Now it was Wayne's turn to speak.

After his opening statements he got to the meat of the message, outlining why the United States should have the lands he claimed. First, he reassured them that they would build a fort on Lake Sandusky to protect both Indians and whites from mutual enemies, meaning the British.

To Little Turtle's claim that giving Ohio to the Americans would restrict their hunting, Wayne had this to say:

> "Nor will this line prevent your hunters or young men, in the smallest degree, from pursuing all the advantages which the chase affords; because, by the seventh article, the United States of America grant liberty to all the Indian tribes to hunt within the territory ceded to the United States, without hindrance or molestation, so long as they demean themselves peaceably, and offer no injury to the people of the United States."

About the two mile piece of land on the Little River, that the Indians called the carrying place, he explained that it shouldn't cost them more to lose the income from it. "After all," he said, "the fees are added to the cost of trade goods, so it is the Indians who actually pay for these fees."

> He continued, "Those people who have lived at that glorious gate, the Miami villages, may now rekindle their fires at that favorite spot; and henceforth as in their happiest days, be at full liberty to receive from and send to all quarters, the speechs of their chiefs as usual; and here is that road the Miamis will remember." (A road belt was given)

"Now all ye chiefs and warriors, of every nation present, open your ears that you may clearly hear the articles of the treaty, now in my hand, again read, and a second time explained to you that we may proceed to have them engrossed on parchment, which may preserve them forever."

After the articles were read, a role call of the Indians showed the treaty acceptance to be unanimous. Many years of work had gone into the achievement of this moment. Wayne could hardly believe he had done it. Smiling he said to the group, "It will take several days to make copies of the treaty for each tribe. In the interim, we will eat, drink, and rejoice, and thank the Great Spirit for the happy stage this good work has arrived."

The 3rd of August, 1795, the treaty was signed by the sachems, chiefs, and principal men, a total of eighty people. Twenty thousand dollars worth of small ornaments were distributed. Nine thousand five hundred dollars were to be paid to the tribes annually of which the Miamis received one thousand dollars. Less than one sixth of one cent per acre.

Little Turtle and Blue Jacket were given land grants near Fort Wayne on which a house would be built by a government paid carpenter. All chiefs received large George Washington Medals. Little Turtle asked that William Wells be made the Indian Agent at Fort Wayne.

When word of this treaty reached the East, a flood of settlers started west to buy and settle on the newly ceded lands.

Chapter XVI

Fall 1795

The brown spotted mare didn't like the constant gallop to which she was being pushed. It was too hot for such work, especially carrying the two hundred ten pound Deaf Man. Finally, she flatly refused to keep up the pace, falling to a fast walk. In disgust, Deaf Man climbed off, walking awhile to give the pony a rest. She was loaded also with a few items he had received at the treaty session. It had all gone very satisfactorily. Some of the chiefs were unhappy to give up their lands, but he personally couldn't see as how it made any difference to him. And, he'd gotten these presents. Maconaquah would be thrilled to have them.

Thinking of her and the stage of her pregnancy, he jumped back on the horse, who gave a corresponding snort of protest, but it was only a few more miles until they reached their cabin.

Reaching the small clearing they called home, he gave the Miami shout of arrival, but heard no answer. Alarmed, he swiftly moved toward the cabin to see if something was wrong. Before he could burst through the closed door, Meshinga opened it, stepping outside with a finger to her lips.

"What is it? What's the matter?" Whispered Deaf Man.

"Shhhh. Maconaquah's sleeping. She had the baby just this morning after a very hard day and night of it."

"Is she all right? What of the papoose?"

"She'll be all right. It just took longer than for some squaws. Maybe it is because she is a white woman." Meshinga sighed wearily. "Anyway, your squaw child was a very big baby."

"My papoose," he said in wonder. "Where is she?"

Meshinga quietly opened the door, taking him inside where Maconaquah lay, very pale, on the couch of furs. Beside her lying on a pad of milkweed down was the child, the smallest, frailest human Deaf Man had ever seen. Kneeling beside the bed a great protective feeling for his wife and child overcame him. Sticking out a rough finger, he touched the baby's hand that was almost smaller than the finger. The hand opened, grasping his finger with a fiercely strong hold of total trust and dependence. He realized that for this infant he was one of the most important things in life. Deaf Man smiled at his newfound importance.

"Deaf Man?" Maconaquah opened her eyes groggily. "When did you get back?"

"Just now. I see you have been busy getting me another hide scrapper."

"Aye, but she will have to grow up a little bit first." She summoned up a weak smile. Strong Bear sat beside them, taking her hand in his while he grinned somewhat foolishly at this amazing gift that was all the more astonishing because he had in some part made her. "What would you like to name her, Deaf Man?"

He looked at Maconaquah in surprise, then down at her hand he still held. Holding it up and pointing at her little finger he said, "Kekesequa. Cut Finger, because she is the daughter of the one with a cut finger."

"Deaf Man, can't you think of some name with a nicer sound to it? My brother cut that finger off with an axe when I was just a little girl, and it's not something I like to remember." Maconaquah was regaining some of her old spirit.

"It reminds me of you, Rose. Kekesequa it will be."

Maconaquah held up her hand looking at it. The little finger without its tip reminded her of her white family that she hadn't seen for so many years. "Some day I will tell Kekesequa about her white grandma and grandpa. It might be important to her that she is half white, who can tell," she said slowly. Then remembering the reason Deaf Man had been gone she asked, "Do the people live at Kekionga again?"

"Some few have set up their camps there. The Big Knives have built a fort, but Kitcho Shemangan said we could move back if we want to."

Maconaquah thought of the women she knew and missed. Looking at the sleeping child she said, "When the baby is a little older it will be good to live near the others again."

"They gave us some things after the treaty was made." He brought out the pack of goods to show her the beads, needles, thread and a new hatchet. "We are to get some money every year also."

"For what did we get these things?"

"Kitcho Shemangan wanted some of our land. But he said we could still hunt on it, so we will still get to use it. We are supposed to give up all of our white captives. Do you want to go back to your people?" He looked at her in apprehension as the thought struck him that she could now leave the Indians.

Maconaquah smiled in amusement. "Not today, I am too tired." Then relenting because of his look of uncertainty she continued, "I have forgotten all about my white relatives. Now, we could use some pheasants or rabbits. Nursing mothers have big appetites. And I need a little rest yet. Go on with you, Kekesequa's father. Bring us some meat."

Reassured and smiling, Deaf Man went out to the forest for a pleasant hour of hunting.

The August heat was oppressive for others returning to their wigwams after the treaty session that had lasted nearly two months. William Wells returned to the house he'd built for Nancy on the banks of the gently moving Mississinewa. This part of the country had always been particularly pleasing for him, mainly because it was so private. Just off the Wabash River, it was settled by few Indians, most preferring to live nearer the traders at Kekionga or Ouiatenon. Since few lived here, the soldiers had never invaded this land, and at this point in time, weren't even aware of it.

The cabin he'd built for his squaw was near that of her parents. Most of the time, Wells was away, and she needed them nearby. She was after all, very young. Chuckling water of the Mississinewa flowed below the cabin built under a giant old pine tree whose branches sighed softly in the breeze. The sun was hanging low in the sky as Wells rode up. It was that special time of day when work was done, but not yet time to prepare the evening meal.

Nancy sat on a log beside the cabin walls, working colored beads into a pair of deerskin moccasins. Her black hair hung down freely, not dressed tightly in the usual Miami style. The white muslin blouse was left out, not tucked into the skirt waistband, it was too hot for that.

Wells tied the horse in the woods, quietly so as not to attract her attention. Sneaking up behind the cabin, he carefully edged his way around the side, then pounced on her, pulling her onto the grassy ground.

"Eeeee," she shrieked. Then seeing it was Apeconit, she slapped him on the arm. "Apeconit, you're lucky I didn't have a tomahawk by my side. I would have given you such a chop."

He laughed, giving her a great bear hug. "As you can see, my eyes are ever on you. You can never tell when I might come creeping up, so you'd better keep any other braves hidden."

She tried to hit him again, but he held her arm so she couldn't. The two rolled over and over on the ground wrestling until her energy was gone. "I quit. I won't hit you any more Apeconit."

"Promise?"

"I promise." He let her get up to brush off her skirt. Then, when he was least expecting it, she gave him a great slap, and turning ran into the woods. Wells gave chase. Catching her he picked her up, carrying her into the forest to a grassy bed.

"I missed you, Nancy, and not because of your cooking!" Resting on his elbow, he smoothed her smiling face with his hand. "It's time I spent some time jest huntin' and layin' in bed with my squaw."

"What did you bring me Apeconit? I would like more silver broaches to sew on my blouses."

"Well now, I brought you some pretties but more than that, I brought lots of things you need to run this place." Patting her stomach he said, "Hey, you're gettin' kinda fat."

She jumped up, shaking the hair out of her face, turning away from him.

"What's the matter Nancy? You aren't really mad at me 'cause I wrastled you, are you?"

Nancy didn't say anything but pensively picked at a tree branch. "Would you still come to see me if I was an old squaw? A fat old squaw?"

"Well now, I'm not likely to see that. You're some younger than me. 'Sides, one of these days, my luck will run out and some old Shawnee or maybe one of your relatives will thunk a knife into my back."

Nancy turned back, frightened at the thought. Then seeing his lecherous face, she said huffily, "I'm going to get a whole lot fatter. I'm going to have a papoose."

Wells was dumbstruck. For some reason, he'd never considered the possibility. "When?"

"Oh," she said airily, "sometime this winter. But it shouldn't concern you. You'll be off riding with the scouts, whooping it up, never giving us a second thought."

"If that's what's botherin' you, you don't need to worry. My job as army scout is over. The army done went home, all except about fifty soldiers at Fort Wayne. Little Turtle wants me to be the Federal Agent for him, but there won't be much doin' this winter. The Indians all signed a peace treaty and Kitcho Shemangan went back to his cabin in the East. So, little darlin', I'll be all yours this winter."

A dimple appeared in Nancy's cheek, as she smiled at the prospect. Jumping on him she said, "Apeconit, it will be such fun with you here. We'll make traps, ice fish, and then go to the trading post and get lots of good things."

"I'll have to go to Kekionga ever so often to report to the fort. But I've been with the army so long that it will be good to stay at home, smokin' and watchin' the sunset. After awhile, when the papoose comes, I'll tell her stories, like I told my daughter Ann."

"You have children? You didn't tell me, Apeconit," she pouted.

"You knew I was married to Little Turtle's daughter. She's with my brother many days ride south of here. It wasn't safe for her and the girl here with a war goin' on, and me fightin' on the side of the white men. The Indians could have taken revenge on her if I'd left her here, so I took her to my white kin, where it's safe. Later I'll bring them back and live at Kekionga."

"Well, what will happen to me?" wailed Nancy.

"Mischievously Wells said, "We could all live together like some braves do with their squaws. Little Turtle himself always has at least two wives."

"That would be alright," Nancy said.

Staring up at the trees, Wells said, "It's true, it would be alright if I were Indian, but I'm a white man. I'll be paid to do a white man's job. White men never have more than one wife. In fact, they frown on it as bad medicine. What I'll do is take care of you while you live here and keep another house at Kekionga for Sweet Breeze. But I promise you, Nancy, you will never want for anything. I will give you everything you need.

Fort Wayne had held its ground stoutly on the banks of the Maumee river for just less than two years. These years had been hard ones for John Hamtramck, its commandant. The first winter Indians begged food constantly, pitiful beggers because their crops were all burned by Wayne's army. Supply trains from Cincinnati were unpredictable so the few troops stationed here were in constant want themselves, but what food they had, they divided with the Indians.

Now, in the summer of 1796 things were running more smoothly. The Indians lived again on the river's opposite shore. Once again, corn grew in the wide fields of Kekionga. But Hamtramck wouldn't be sad leaving this place. Ever since he'd come here, hardship and want were all he'd seen for everyone, white or red.

The waving cornfields seemed to beckon him. He began walking toward them to see how well it was growing when the man he'd been waiting for rounded the curving road up to the fort. The tanned, broad shouldered shirtless visitor was a person he always enjoyed seeing, though they couldn't have been said to be friends. "Ah, Wells. Back to livin' with your Indians again, I see. Heard you had a papoose last winter. That right?"

Wells tied up the horse at the fort's hitching post, eyeing the man warily who seemed to take great personal joy from teasing him. "The messenger said I was wanted for government work. What you got in mind?"

Distracted from his teasing, Hamtramck said, "Wayne wants you to go to Detroit to interpret for him. By the Jay treaty made with the British last year the United States is to receive all lands below the Great Lakes, so Wayne's goin' there personally to receive the town." Hamtramck looked out across the river again at the beautiful land filled with corn, thinking that he'd miss this land after all, and the enjoyment of farming it. "He wants me to move to Detroit to be the commandant there."

Wells studied him, not knowing what was wanted of him. Hamtramck continued. "I believe Little Turtle will get you appointed as Indian Agent here, so you'll be living in Kekionga in future years. Whereas I won't."

This was no new information for Wells. Hamtramck continued. "You know what I think of squaw men. Other whites will think the same. If you want to be respected, you'll have to learn to be content with just one squaw."

"What the hell business is that of yours?" Well's face flushed with anger, the hands at his sides forming fists.

"I'd like you to be my partner. You'll be here in Kekionga and you could run the farm I've laid out across the river." Pointing to the land opposite, he said, "The land I staked out lays there, right under the fort cannons so it will have good protection. You could run it and also do the Indian Agent business. It would make a right good living."

Well's face, a study of anger, slowly relaxed as he looked at the land, considering the possibilities. "I always thought I might farm. My brother Sam, said he'd give me slaves to help if I decided to. It might work."

"If you agree on it, we'll draw up the papers. You'll have complete control of it, as I mean to take my family to Detroit but I will want accounts done right. I'll expect my share of the crop money. This year will be lost for farming. Too late to do more than clear land. And Wayne wants you to go along to Detroit. He said some of the Indians might go to Philadelphia too. You'll be wanted to interpret for them there. That'll be your chance to get Little Turtle to ask that you be appointed Indian Agent. If you play your cards right, you could become a very wealthy man in that position. You'll be the one that gives out the Indian annuity payments and controls all the goods the government gives to the Indians."

With sudden insight Hamtramck said, "Yessair, in that capacity, man, the highest and the mightiest in the land will have to consult you because of your influence with the Indians." Smiling his old malicious smile he said, "Best hide them two or three extra squaws you got way out in the woods, so no one will know, or reflect on your reputation. You'll have to think of that, after all, if you're to be considered a serious man of influence."

Wells scowled. The man could be so aggravating. But he could see the farmland was a very favorable piece. It would have access to the river for shipping crops, and next to the fort it would be protected. Hamtramck would soon be gone to Detroit and he would be his own boss. Yes, the deal had very good possibilities. Without taking his eyes off the land he said, "Let's draw up the papers John. You have a bargain.

The trip back to Philadelphia had been very satisfactory. When Wayne arrived there in February, they'd rung church bells for an entire day, saluting him by firing guns for the returning war hero. It made the four years he'd spent on the western campaign all worthwhile. Then there was the charming Mary Vining. Smiling at the thought of how he, at 51, had turned her head, he considered again the possibility of marrying her if he returned to Philadelphia. Gossip had it that they were engaged, but Wayne hadn't wanted to commit himself. He knew he would have to return to the West to accept Detroit from the British. With his gout acting up again, he hated to make that kind of plans. Life was uncertain enough with the best of health here on the frontier, and he was fond enough of Mary not to want her to tie herself to a promise...one he in all likelihood couldn't keep.

Strange, the changes that had occurred east in Pennsylvania during the few years he'd been gone. He'd felt a stranger, even on his own farm. People weren't the same. But, he'd gotten right to work, defending sections of the Greenville Treaty to the Congress and trying to preserve a regular army in the face of those who wanted it dismantled to a mere skeleton. He'd made them see that an army was important.

But, pleasant though it was back in civilization, he had to return to the frontier to accept Detroit from the British. Afterall, there were no wars to be fought in the East, and he was first, last, and always, an army man.

In August General Wayne and his entourage arrived at Detroit after it was received from the British for him in July by a Captain Moses Porter. He was surprised as he approached the town. Twelve hundred Indians swarmed about him, shaking his hand, shrieking with ear splitting yells, and firing their guns into the air. Apparently, they looked at the Americans as liberators from the British, placing him in the position of their personal "Father".

He was impressed with Detroit. It was an amazing jewel of civilization, stuck here in the midst of the wilderness. Built something like a fort, it was well defended by staunch blockhouses with sturdy gun platforms to show strength to would be attackers, white or red. At either end of the main street were solid gates, closed at sunset. The town rule being that no Indian was allowed in town after the gates were closed.

Making his headquarters in the old British Indian agent, Alexander McKee's house, Wayne began receiving Indians, learning more about the chiefs; deciding for himself which ones would have to be coddled and watched. Sitting by his fireside, slowly drinking from the barrel of good wine, he reflected on the personalities of the different chiefs. First there was Blue Jacket, a man who, if paid and shown deference, would be loyal to the Americans. Then there was Blue Jacket's rival, Little Turtle. This man was more complex. He could be very dangerous, Wayne thought. He always was ready with well thought out complaints and arguments. It would be a good idea to build both of these men houses, close to Fort Wayne where they could be watched. General Wayne decided he'd have a carpenter sent out to do the job. It would be worth the expense.

Wayne stroked his face, pondering the position of the scout and translater, William Wells. For some reason, Little Turtle had a great preference for him. He'd already made a request that Wells be made Indian agent at Fort Wayne. The United States would benefit if Wells, who knew their language and ways so well, was placed in that position, and kept happy, so that he would in turn keep Little Turtle happy.

He considered his muslin swathed outstretched legs, propped up on a footstool. The pain at times now was almost more than he could stand. He winced wryly at the clear possibility he wouldn't live much longer. Shaking his head he thought of the work he still needed to do. If I don't provide properly for the Indians now, making them happy with what they get from the United States, that rascally Wilkinson might ruin everything when I'm gone. He grimaced at the dark corners about the ceiling, appearing to look for the dark spirit of the man he hated.

Wilkinson had been working against him from the very beginning of this wilderness campaign. He'd done everything possible to make him look bad to those in power in Philadelphia. And it was entirely possible he'd replace him as army commander if he died. Grinding his teeth he whispered vehemently, "Damn the man!" Then, shifting in the chair, he groaned slightly, at the pain this brought. Yes, there was little time to wrap up the accomplishments of these past years; to make the Indians happy enough to abide by the peace treaty they'd signed at Greenville.

He'd already arranged to send several chiefs to Philadelphia. Now, if he could influence the new Secretary of War, McHenry, to take care of Mr. Wells, it was probably the most he could do to guarantee peace. Mustn't delay, he thought. Since no-one was about to hear, he groaned out loud as he got up to get paper, ink, and quill to write to the Secretary.

Headquarters, Detroit
3rd, October, 1796

The Honble. James McHenry Esqr, Secretary of War

Sir: Enclosed is a list of the Names of the Chiefs & Nations they represent–& who this day embark for the city of Philadelphia, under the charge & conduct of capt John Heth of the 3d Sub Legion in order to see & converse with their great Father the President of the United States of America agreeably to the Unanimous request of all the Chiefs who signed the treaty of Greene Ville.

Among whom is the famous Shawanoe chief Blue Jacket, who, it is said had the chief Command of the Indian army on the 4th of November 1791 against Genl St. clair, The Little Turtle a Miamia Chief who also claims that honor, & who is his rival for fame & power–& said to be daily gaining ground with the Wabash Indians–refuses or declines to proceed in Company with Blue Jacket: he possesses the spirit of litigation to a high degree, possibly he may have been tamper'd with by some of the speculating land jobbers,–the enclosed Original may serve as an instance.

Mashi-pi-nash-i-wish, the principal Chief of the powerful Chipewa Nation, & a firm friend of the United States, has taken suddenly & Dangerously ill, so as to prevent him from proceeding to Philadelphia, The other Chiefs are accompanied by three good interpreters, Viz Capt Wm Wells for the Miamis & Wabash Indians, Chrisr. Miller for the Shawanoes, & Whitmore Naggs for the Chewas Ottawas & Putawati(mes).

The Wyandotts–purpose to proceed by Land from Sandusky by the way of Pittsburgh, under the Conduct of Mr. Isaac Williams, to whom & to Mr. Wells, we are much obliged for bringing about the late treaty.

Mr. Wells has render'd very essential services to the United States from early in 1793 until this hour by carrying messages–taking prisoners, & gaining intelligence,–it was he who first brought me an account of the failure of the proposed treaty under the conduct of General Lincoln, Mr. B. Randolph, & Colo Pickering.

In the Campaign of 1794 I appointed him captain of a small Corps of confidential Spies–a few days before the Action of the 20th of August, he captured two Indians, from whom we obtained interesting information, but in attempting the same evening to take another small Camp of Delawares near Roche DeBout he received a severe Wound from a rifle ball, so near, as to shatter the bone of his right arm to pieces (after killing two of the Indians) & which continued to exfoliate, for upwards of Eighteen Months, by which his arm is so much disabled as in my opinion will entitle him to a pension, this in the end may be found as Economical, as it will be just & political-for unless the public reward those kind of people, with some degree of liberality–they can not expect to be served with fidelity in future.

With those impressions, I have the Honor to be with perfect Esteem & respect, Sir your Most Obt & Very Huml Sert.

Anty. Wayne

Chapter XVII

Wells' Farm, Kekionga, Summer 1797

The sound of the great hammer pounding the wedges echoed far into the distance. They were set every few feet, to split the long hickory log into rails. This one trunk would make enough rails for maybe thirty feet of fence, Wells thought, sweat running down his face in rivulets, though the weather was cool. Pounding away on the wedges, he thought with disgust how disappointingly things were going on the farm.

Jest like I always figgered, them bucks ain't worth a plugged nickel when it comes ta farmin', he thought angrily. Nope. Them fellers could never be bothered doin' an honest day's worth of sweat, even when I offered ta pay a king's ransom. Maybe I should hire the squaws. He grinned at the thought, never missing a stroke with the hammer. The only trouble with that idea was that the squaws were already overburdened doing their own farming.

Continuing in his self pitying thoughts, he reflected on the fact that even with all the money they'd given him in Philadelphia last winter, here he was, breaking his back, and he couldn't even use the money to get the Indians to do his work. Occasionally, he'd hired soldiers on their off duty hours to help, but it wasn't enough with all the work needed to start up the farm.

Putting down the hammer to take a breather, he went to get the tin cup, dipping water from the wooden bucket he'd brought along. There had to be an easier way to handle this farmwork, he thought. His other plans hadn't worked out well either. There'd been a strange silence from Philadelphia. He hadn't heard anything from the government about his appointment as Indian Agent.

Gazing over the vast fields that had yet to be harvested, he considered how he'd had to work so hard that summer that he had little time to visit Nancy and their baby, Jane, still living on the Mississinewa. His self appointed responsibilities seemed almost more than he could bear. If only there were someone he could talk to, to discuss his problems with who would in some way understand. Taking a moment, he went through the list of people who were friends, cataloging them in his brain, as to what help he could expect of them.

Hamtramck. Wells grimaced at the name. If the man hadn't acted so superior to him, they might have been friends. Yet, Hamtramck had always felt intimidated by Wells' physical attractiveness and his aura of savage strength. And so, Hamtramck never failed to speak degradingly to him, by so doing, trying to reduce his awe of Wells' physical superiority. No, he could never speak to Hamtramck of his problems or fears.

General Wayne had always been aloof and not interested in the problems of his officers. Besides, he was dead now. He'd been in his grave since last December, while Wells and the chiefs were in Philadelphia.

His squaw, Nancy, was too young. And even with age she'd never be capable of any meaningful discussion or problem solving except on the most superficial basis. Thinking about her, Wells decided he was glad she was far away in the Wea village. Now he only saw her when he wanted to and didn't have to put up with daily demands for presents or constant worthless chatter.

No, the only person who would listen to his problems and understand was Little Turtle. Thinking of him he decided it was time to make a visit to his town on the Eel River. His nerves were shot because of his overwhelming problems, but Little Turtle's cold logic would put everything in a better perspective. With that thought, he went up to the house to throw some food and clothing together for the brief trip.

Riding to Little Turtle's town was in itself refreshing. The much traveled road was wide and had many landmarks and memories. Passing the spot where Little Turtle had ambushed Harmar's army he looked at the trees trying to see if bullet holes could still be seen in them. But it had been seven years since the fight. There was little to be seen now in the summer of 1797. Finally, he came to the shallow Eel or Kenapacomoco River. The river here was very narrow compared to downriver at the village Kenapacomaqua. The horse splashed easily across to Little Turtle's cabin.

The chief sat in the shade of a giant maple tree, carving a new pipe for himself. As Apeconit approached, he rose to greet his old friend that he looked on as a son. "How good to see you. But it surprises me that you come in this season. Is something wrong?"

Wells grasped the older man's hand, feeling secure in his presence as in the days of his youth. But remembering he was grown now and had to shoulder his own responsibilities he said, "I came to see you, Father, for advice. I work hard but nothing goes like I'd planned. It's discouraging."

The Turtle noted the sad downturn of Wells' lips. It always amazed him that this courageous, strong man could get so depressed. Seriously contemplating the design he was carving into the long pipestem, he began, "Spring time comes after the cold winds of winter. Girls run about, picking violets, praising the Great Spirit for his goodness in returning the warm weather. For awhile they think of their good fortune everyday. Then, slowly, they begin to take the hot days for granted. And soon, they have forgotten all about winter. Then, the Great Spirit sees they don't remember the good thing he gives. The Great Spirit growls, blowing out his cheeks to blow coldly with the ice of winter on the young girls who dared forget the gift he gave. If life always ran smooth, we would not remember the good things we have or appreciate them."

The Turtle glanced sideways to see the effect of the story on the red-haired man. Wells lay on his back watching clouds passing high above. The Turtle continued, "It has been too long since I saw my daughter. It is time to bring her back from Kentucky."

Wells stirred guiltily. "You're right. But, I didn't have a cabin built for her before. And now, crop time ain't the best time to get her. But, I need some darkies to help me with the farm. I could get some from Sam. The farm's jest more'n I kin handle by myself. I shouldn't be here today, but I needed to get away a little. Besides, I haven't heard anything about my position as Indian agent. What do you think I should do about it?"

Little Turtle put the pipestem to his lips, testing its shape. "It may be that a different man is the chief of the Fifteen Fires. It may be that the one we talked to last winter is gone now, and the new man doesn't know of what we spoke."

"So you think we should go to Philadelphia and remind them?"

"It seems a good idea."

Wells set his mind to planning the trip. "We should go in the fall, after I get the crops harveted. Then on our return, instead of comin' across Lake Erie, we could boat down the Ohio River, stopping at Sam's to get Sweet Breeze, Ann and some slaves. Aye, that would work perfect."

He sat silent, thinking ahead. It had been three years since he'd seen his brother or Sweet Breeze. Though it was not unusual for Indians to be absent from their squaws for long periods of time, because of the great distances and slowness of travel, three years was a definite stretch of any wife's patience. Guiltily, he wondered what she thought of him. Since he'd had Nancy to entertain him, he hadn't retrieved Sweet Breeze as quickly as he otherwise might have done.

He should have gone after her last year after the trip to Philadelphia with the Indians, but the Indians had needed an interpreter to accompany them back home. He'd come with them across Lake Erie, rather than going down the Ohio past all the white settlements. After all, so soon after the many Indian attacks on white settlements along the river, it would have been dangerous to take them down it.

Then he'd been busy getting the farm started, and any leisure time was spent with Nancy and their daughter, Jane. But, he couldn't expect Sweet Breeze to continue to be patient. Besides, Little Turtle wanted his daughter back home.

"It always helps me to plan things in my mind, talkin' with you Mishikinokwa. We will plan to leave for Philadelphia when the leaves fall."

It was December when they finally started to Philadelphia. They left as late as possible before Lake Erie began freezing to a solid block of ice. There had been one delay after another, getting the crops harvested and sold.

Once in Philadelphia, as usual Little Turtle was the toast of the town. The year before, he'd received much publicity when he was inoculated for smallpox. Once again he and his handsome interpreter were in demand for all the fashionable parties. Little Turtle's picture was painted, in an army uniform, by a celebrated artist of the day.

Wells talked with the secretary of War, James McHenry, about his possible position as Indian Agent at Fort Wayne. He was paid his salary of $480 for interpreter, but nothing as Indian agent, though Wells came away believing he would have the job when it was created.

After the pleasant months in Philadelphia, the two men rode over the mountain roads to the rough and ready town of Pittsburgh at the Ohio River's headwaters. From there, they took a perogue down river toward Louisville, Kentucky. The wet and windy weather was tiring for the men during the month of travel over high mountain paths and the Ohio River at high water time. This country was not strange to Little Turtle. In the days of his young manhood, he'd led many raids on settlers here. But now that was all a thing of the past. He enjoyed the trading posts and the river town taverns, being always the center of attention, a celebrity.

When Samuel Wells plantation finally came into view, William was struck by the beauty of the new brick house. It was built in the colonial style with two stories, tall windows flanking the center doorway. Across the front was a wide porch, complete with rocking chairs. To one side of the rear part of the house was another small brick building, used as a summer kitchen. Cooking would be done here in hot months to keep the heat out of the main house.

Behind the original cabin some distance from the new home were a row of cabins used for the slaves Samuel owned to farm the place. Wide fertile fields were neatly fenced by zigzag split rail fences. This was the way he wanted his farm to look, William thought to himself as he knocked on the big wooden door.

Mary opened it looking with disbelief at the red haired man before her. He wore a well tailored traveling cloak over the army uniform he'd been given in Philadelphia. "William? William, I can't believe you come back to us!" she said joyfully. She looked curiously, somewhat taken aback, at the Indian accompanying him, also dressed in an army uniform, though wearing mocassins. "Your friend is...."

"Little Turtle, Sweet Breeze's father." In Miami he said, "Meet my sister-in-law."

The two gravely shook hands, Mary momentarily at a loss for words. Regaining her composure, she said, "I'll go get Sweet Breeze." The curving staircase ending in the wide central hall seemed to come from the upper floor without any support. She called up, "Sweet Breeze, we have company."

A moment later a fine boned woman, dressed in a wide skirted white dress with a small pink print, silently decended the stairs. Lace edged the collar and cuffs of the long sleeves. She had a lace shawl drawn around her, to ward off the chill of the fireplace heated house.

Her black hair was wound on top of her head in a chignon, softly draped about the high cheekboned face. Almond eyes now gazed at William in shock. He stood there, transfixed. He had forgotten just how haunting her beauty was, like that of a deer, peering from a thicket, mystery and innocence in its eyes.

"Apeconit?" She came forward, taking his hand. "Father." Suddenly losing her reserve, tears slowly coursed their way down the walnut tinted cheeks. "I have missed you so much."

Little Turtle's face cracked into a small smile. "We came to get you Wangopath. Our camps are sad with your absence."

William came out of his trance, realizing this exotic beauty was really his wife. He said, "I missed you too, Sweet Breeze." Taking her hand shyly, he led her into the parlor where they sat down.

Sweet Breeze wiped her eyes with a handkerchief. "Why didn't you come for me? I can't understand. I have waited so long to go home to Kekionga. After Sam came back from the war with General Wayne, I was sure you would come right away for me, but I have waited and it has been three summers since you sent me here." A look of mixed sorrow and anger came into her face.

William looked down at his hands, and then back at her, trying to mask the guilt he felt. Finally he said, "There was no home for me to take you to after the soldiers came. Then, they built a fort at Kekionga and the Indians didn't return there until a year ago. I felt they might take out revenge on you for their dead killed in the war with General Wayne.

I had to make two trips east to the Fifteen Fires. Then, I had to get my farm started. Sweet Breeze, had it been a good thing, I would have come to get you before this, but I felt you were better off here with Sam." He looked at her sadly, seeing the pain in her eyes the years of separation from her people had caused. He could see in that moment, that he had been shallow and uncaring. "I promise to make it up to you Sweet Breeze. You will have a good house to live in when you go home with me."

Mary had been watching the proceedings with interest. Trying to ease the situation she said, "Ann and my children are all in school at Hoglands Station. But they'll be along soon and you can see how big your daughter's grown. She's getting to be quite the young lady and knows her first reader."

"Can she keep up with Rebecca?" Smiled William.

"She certainly tries. But being some younger, she hasn't been in fist fights with the boys, like your niece. I swear, William, if I didn't know better, I'd say Rebecca was your daughter. She's certainly got a devilish streak from somewheres."

"Now, Mary, that musta been from the Uncle Haden branch. I 'spose you heard how he almost killed a man in a fight once."

"Oh, I've heard all the family stories, especially how your father, Samuel, saved the life of Colonial Floyd when he gave him his horse in the battle near Shelbyville with the Indians in 1781." Then aghast at what she'd said in Little Turtle's presence, she covered her mouth. But seeing no change in the Indian's face, she decided he didn't understand her. She continued, "Actually William, we've heard more tales about your adventures than of any of your kin. I swan, you're a local hero."

Pleased, William said, "Life don't seem to have many dull moments, that's a fact. Where's Sam?"

"He's been over in Shelby county lookin' at some land. With him goin' to Lexington so often he thought it might be a good idea to get a place near there to live, least part of the time. You knew he was Louisville's State Representative in 1795 and '96? He thinks land values Lexington way will go sky high."

William said, "I'd hoped to see him and ask him some questions about my own farm I'm startin' 'crost from Fort Wayne. I could use his advice."

"He'll be home tomorrow, or leastways this week. You'll stay awhile won't you?"

"Cain't stay too long, maam. It's well nigh onto plantin' time, but I will stay out the week. It's been too long since I seen my brothers and sister. Travel bein' what it is, it'll be awhile 'til I'm in these parts again."

Just then the kitchen door banged open and a noisy flock of children came into the room, stringing coats and hats behind them. Nine year old Rebecca with long red hair bounced across the room, flinging herself on her mother. She was followed more slowly by the seven year old, Ann, who went to stand quietly by Sweet Breeze, staring at the newcomers.

"It's Uncle William," Shrieked Rebecca with abandon. Then, halting in her forward plunge, at the sight of the severe Little Turtle, she moved back, somewhat cowed, against her Mother.

"Ann, don't you remember your Daddy?" asked William. The girl looked him over with her brown eyes, smiling a little. He did look familiar, but she remained by her mother, hugging tight against her. It would be a long while before she felt easy with him. She had been away from her father for more than half her life.

"Who's that?" asked Rebecca, pointing at Little Turtle.

William grinned, taking her on his lap. "This is the great chief Little Turtle, Ann's Grandpa."

Rebecca peered at the Indian who was watching her. "How, Indian," she said.

Little Turtle picked up a strand of her red hair, and said to Wells in Miami, "The squaw child looks like a little Wild Carrot(Apeconit). Ask her if she wants to come live with me."

Wells grinned. "He wants you to be his little girl. What you say to that Rebecca?"

Rebecca looked at him closer, to see if he was fooling. Deciding he wasn't so fierce after all, she said, "Maybe, some time."

The adults laughed at the brash young girl. Losing interest, the youngsters flounced out of the room to get their toys.

Later, a fine fried chicken dinner was served by a slave in the long formal dining room. During the meal, William could hardly take his eyes off Sweet Breeze. She was a lady in every respect, using the silverware better than he did. Little Turtle and Mary carried on an amusing discussion, combining pidgin English and sign language. Rebecca had insisted on sitting next to Little Turtle and she plied him constantly with requests for Indian words. He was amazingly patient, thought Mary, but he said he had many children of his own, and now many grandchildren.

After the meal, William said, "Sweet Breeze can take me out to the barn. I'd like to see what horseflesh you're ridin' these days."

"Take a look at the black stallion," Mary answered. "Sam just bought him this winter. He's only two years old, but Sam says he holds real promise as a race horse."

The couple walked out into the spring evening's moist air. Neither saying anything as they walked toward the barn, a strange shyness between them. Inside the barn, the young horse was in its own stable, and snorted nervously at the sight of the stranger. "Ain't he a beauty?" exclaimed William. Opening the door to the stall, he placed a hand on the horses neck to gentle him, then ran his hands over the muscled body and down the legs.

"Be careful, Apeconit. He is a wild thing. He bites and kicks."

William laughed. "I'm used to wild things, remember? You ain't such a wild thing as you used to be, though, are you?"

"What would you expect? I've lived here a long time now. I'm not the same."

It was true, she wasn't. No longer was she the docile young wife, who took every word he said as the law. He'd disappointed her and now would have to make amends.

Closing the stall door, he moved toward her. Putting his arms around her he looked down into her eyes. "Sweet Breeze, I said I was sorry I left you here so long. As I see it, it was for the best. You were safe here and you learnt some of the white men's ways."

She frowned, trying to shrug away from him, but he held her tight. William continued, "I ain't an Indian any more. The highest ranked white men look at me as bein' important. And I want them to respect you too. If you're my wife, it's important you know how to run a house like a white woman."

Her eyes flashed in anger. "How could you make me stay here all that time, never coming even to see if we were still alive."

He let her go, turning away. Then he said, "Maybe I was wrong. I've made some mistakes, I admit. But, if you will still be my squaw, I promise I will never leave you alone so long again. We will start over as if it never happened."

She was silent a moment, then touched his hand. "I will still be your squaw, Apeconit. But, I am no child now. I stand on my own feet. If you leave me again, I will move to my father's house. There are others who would want me. Even white men have asked me if I have a husband. I could have another man."

Wells looked warningly at her. He wasn't used to being treated in this fashion. Yet, her father was here with him. She could reject him totally if she wanted and still return to her people, with Little Turtle. It was a hard moment, but he looked at the beauty she was, and swallowed his pride.

"Maybe we should seal the bargain," he said mischieviously, kissing her on the neck. She struggled a moment, then relaxed against him. As they clung to each other it seemed amazing to both that they had ever been angry or thought of anyone else.

Two days later, Sam returned from the lands he was developing into a farm near Lexington. As always he was delighted to see his younger brother. "Come ta take away my sister here, did ya," he said, hugging

Sweet Breeze. "Don't know if I'll allow it, you son-of-a-gun. You'd best prove to me as how it's safe up north or I'll set y'all down ta plowin' on my new acreage."

William stuck out his hand to wring his brothers. "You been right kind to take care of my wife and daughter. But as you mighta guessed, she pines ta go home. Bein' an Indian, she jest might scalp you if ya don't let her go now."

Samuel laughed saying, "William, William How I wish you'd pick a piece of land nearby so I could look on your scalawag face from time to time. And I'm goin' to sorely miss your wife. She's quite a lady. Half the bachelors in Louisville been hopin' you'd bite the dust in one scrape or another, so they could pick up where you left off."

"I can see that. I shoulda come and got her sooner but I've had to make a couple trips out East with the Indians and then I'm startin' a farm of my own. Didn't even have a cabin built until last summer. I need your advice on what to raise and such."

Sam winked at William. "Bet you come to get the darkies I promised to let you have too. Well, I won't go back on my word. I'll give you enough slaves to help you work your farm. That will be your part of Pa's inheritance."

"I'll be much obliged. I've tried to get Indians to work, but they ain't used to farmin', leastways the men aren't. There's about fifty soldiers at Fort Wayne, but the commander only allows them to hire out in their off hours, and most don't want to work two jobs. I got three hundred twenty acres as my army pay with Wayne, and then I'm overseein' a farm that I'm in partnership with Hamtramck. To tell you the truth, I bit off more than I could chew, by myself. I really need them darkies."

"You're gettin' paid wages by the government too, aren't you?" asked Sam.

"Aye. I'm the official interpreter. They keep promisin' me that I'll be the Indian Agent at Fort Wayne and get more money, but I guess they haven't decided what they want an agent to do."

"If nothing materializes in a year or so, go to the capital again. A new president is elected every four years and there's a big change-over of men in power. You want to keep them reminded you're there. They get so wrapped up in politics they forget about the people way off in the corners of the country. I know quite a bit 'bout that, jest being a representative for two years. And I'll help you any way I can. My Kentucky friends and I have a little bit of power, so let me know when you have trouble with the Philadelphians."

William stuck out his hand. "Appreciate it, Sam. And I 'specially thank you for keepin' my family safe these years."

"Speaking of that, I want your children to make somethin' of themselves and they can't, 'less they get their schoolin'."

"I'll send her back for that later. Now, let's have a look at the new plow you bought. I've a mind to buy a couple ta take north with me."

Several days later, William and his family started north with four pairs of slaves, seed, plows, and pigs for his farm at Kekionga.

Chapter XVIII

Louisville, Kentucky, January 1809, Eleven Years Later

Rain dripped from barren tree branches while a leaden January sky represented the fact that it was several months until spring. The winter was mild so far, and the Ohio luckily unfrozen. Wells' return trip from Washington had been hellishly hard. Marpock, the Pottawattomi chief, had been the very devil to handle all the way to the capital and all the way back. The chief, drunk most of the time, had taken up the idea of eating one of the other chief's wife. He perversely dwelt on the plan to the point that Wells took him seriously. He knew just how dangerous Marpock was and that he might actually follow through on the plan, so he had to watch him every second. By the time he'd left the Indians at Cincinnati he'd been ready and willing to place a bullet in the Indian's retreating back. It'd probably save everyone a lot of trouble, he thought.

The whole idea of taking the Indian delegation to see the President was to show Marpock, an influential Illinois chief, the population and strength of the United States so that the British could not influence him to make war against the settlers or the Osage Indians. With the maniac, called the Prophet, and his brother Tecumseh trying to raise the Indians to some sort of holy revival, the firebrand, Marpock, was dangerous indeed. The difference between him and the other two was that he could be reached and influenced while the Prophet would not listen to any white man. In fact, the Prophet accused Wells of keeping the Indians away from their religous meetings with the Great Spirit, suggesting Wells be hanged. The Prophet insisted the Indians should go back to the old ways and morality before they were contaminated by white men.

It had been Wells' suggestion that the War Department pay for the trip East for all influential chiefs in the area, to counteract the unrest caused by the Prophet. Nine had made the trip. His aging father-in-law, Little Turtle, the Turtle's heir, Richardville, Captain Beaver, a Delaware, Captain Hendrick, the Delaware's agent, as well as several Pottawattomie and their wives made the long trip. But they were plagued by poor health and of course the drunken Marpock. On the return trip, one of the Pottawattomie remained behind in Baltimore because of illness.

He had finally rid himself of the whole unwieldy bunch, sending them north over the road from Cincinnati while he continued downriver to Louisville. It was a long time since he'd seen his brother, Sam, or his four children being educated in schools there. Now he'd take his eighteen year old daughter home to run his household.

Sweet Breeze died in the small pox epidemic. Strange how both Sweet Breeze and Nancy were gone now, within such a short time of one another. For years he'd kept up the facade of being a perfect husband while he kept his squaw, Nancy, and their child, Jane, at the village on the Mississinewa. He was fairly sure Sweet Breeze knew of his other family, but she never spoke of it. After all, Sweet Breeze's father, Little Turtle kept two wives in the same house. It worked out well for them. The young girl did most of the household work the older woman no longer found easy to do.

But Wells, a white man, never spoke of Nancy or any of his other casual encounters with squaws. It would not have been seemly behavior for the Fort Wayne Indian Agent. William Henry Harrison, Governor of the Indiana Territory, looked for any excuse to have him fired from the post. Already he'd demanded to see the record books of government funds and goods Wells disbursed to the Indians.

William was totally unprepared for his bereavement after the loss of Sweet Breeze and Nancy. He'd taken them for granted. Even though the land was filled with violence and sudden death, he'd never considered that it might happen to his own family or even to him. Now he faced the idea of his own ageing and death. He was thirty-eight. His body though still muscular, was heavily built, showing the years of prosperity he'd had as Indian Agent, and because of his large farm at Fort Wayne.

He felt lucky that his children had been away from Fort Wayne during the terrible epidemic. Little Turtle was innoculated for smallpox as a novelty on one of his trips to Philadelphia. But it was no joke. The disease that raged among the Indians left him unscathed, enjoying life, plagued only by gout, while hundreds of others suffered and many died.

Following the good road to his brother's farm south of Louisville, he thought it would be pleasant to stay in the South for several months. Winters in Fort Wayne were cold, often including deep snows while here an inch or so of snow seldom fell and if it did, quickly disappeared. It was time to get reacquainted with his children. They were growing up too fast, far away from him.

Drawing up before the large brick house, once again he marveled at the structure that belonged to his brother. A negro slave came to care for his horse as he stepped onto the wooden porch steps. He carefully wiped his feet on the wooden strip expressly for the purpose.

Mary opened the door in surprise. "William, how wonderful to see you. We got your letter about Sweet Breeze's death, and we're sorry to hear of it. Come in and Cornelia will fix you a bite to eat."

William kissed Mary on the cheek then threw off his cloak to a waiting negro. "I swan, Mary, everytime I come back to this place I feel jest like a savage."

"Go on with you now. We all know you're a savage. You're Rebecca's favorite one. Speaking of the girl, where is she?" Mary called up the open stairs, "Becca, come see what company we've got."

Down the stairs tripped a vision of beauty, long red hair falling in soft waves, curls bunched about her shoulders. Her white skin was slightly freckled and the slender figure wore a wide skirted dress of cotton muslin, with a gathered border. "Uncle William?" she screeched in tones quite unlady like. She ran forward with abandon to give him a warm hug. "How long can you stay?"

"Oh, maybe a couple years," he said laughingly. "I swan, you remind me of an Indian girl I used to be half in love with."

Mary said, "How you do run on. An Indian with red hair? Becca, you know how your Uncle spins yarns."

"Fact be known, there is one like that. Course, she was a white person, captured as a child jest like me, and now she's an old married woman with cares and children. Jest like me." William smiled remembering the story he often told of his capture by Indians. He was somewhat of a legend among the white population because of it.

"Did she ever go back to her kin like you did?" asked Rebecca

"No, she's been married to a chief for years and years and doesn't want anything to do with white folk. Then too, her relatives never come lookin' for her like your father did for me. Her name is Maconaquah, but she is famous among the Miami as The White Rose."

Rebecca was entranced by the story. "I'd like to meet her Uncle William. Mama, I want to go live at Fort Wayne for awhile. You always said I could go for a visit one day. Oh, please, can I?"

Mary smiled at her daughter's predictable response to her Uncle. She always wanted to run off into the wild forest, like he had. "We'll see."

William teased, "Your daughter could find an army man for a husband at Fort Wayne. I got several in mind that would fill the bill jest right. At twenty she ain't got so many years to go afore she's a spinster."

"Now, William, you scalawag. I'm not in a hurry to lose this girl of mine. Get away with you."

"Mama, he's only teasing." Rebecca always jumped to her Uncle's defense. They were so similar in nature that she protected him if she could. "Ann is ready to go home to care for the house since her mother died anyway. She says she's had enough of schools and wants to go home. I'll just go with her."

At the mention of one of his children, Wells said, "I'd like to bring all of the children here, from their school for a few weeks. I may take all of the girls home with me." Pensively he added, "It's been lonely there without them."

"You wouldn't take William Wayne out of school would you? At only eight the boy has hardly begun his education. Samuel wants him to go east eventually to West Point Military Academy, like what our boys did."

Willliam answered defensively, "It ain't a fancy school that makes a good soldier out of a boy. Survivin' in Indian country cain't be taught out east."

Mary soothed, "We aren't sayin' he wouldn't turn out well at Fort Wayne. It's just that times are changing and we think he'd have an advantage in his career if he had a good education. You know yourself, that you'd not have your appointments as Indian Agent without your being able to read and write well. Why, if you'd gone to some good school in the East you'd probably be governing the Indiana Territorys 'stead of William Henry Harrison."

William sat down on the couch, then said, "Harrison would never be able to handle the Indian problems like I do. He'd jest kill all of 'em off or move 'em out west. Say, where's Sam?"

"I sent our man, Thomas after him. How's your farm doing?"

"Pretty fair. My slaves got a good crop for me last year. The Miami got all hung up with their religious meetin's with a crackpot called the Prophet, last summer and didn't get their crops in. Course then my crops brought a right good price. Game gets scarcer all the time so the Indians would starve if they weren't gettin' money from the government. I figure I might as well have that money for food as some whisky trader."

"This man, The Prophet, is he one who could cause war?"

"I thought so in 1807 but its kinda died down now. The Indians enjoyed his revival meetin's for a year or two, but now he's talkin' about real war, they're not that interested. The Shawnee always was a hotheaded nation. Young bucks are always interested in war, but the tribes as a whole are more sensible than that. No, the whole shebang left Greenville, south of Fort Wayne where they had a big camp and moved to a place above Ouiatenon, called Prophet's Town. Most of 'em are half starved and I don't expect trouble from the eighty to one hundred warriors he could raise."

Mary arched her eyebrow at him. "I wouldn't want to send my daughter up where there's an Indian war going on."

"Why with her redheaded temperment, she'd fit right in." Wells laughed, slapping his leg, while Rebecca grimaced.

Just then a gust of cold wind swept into the room as Samuel came in from the wintery outside. "I mighta known my little brother was here, bringin' all this cold down from the north." He heartily shook William's hand. Samuel was very distinguished looking. White hair at his temples accentuated the effect of wisdom, with a touch of aggressiveness in his eyes. He looked to be a man of power and experience. A Colonel in the Kentucky Militia, he had position and prestige in the community.

William replied, "Actually, I come here by way of Washington. It was a mighty cold trip down the Ohio this time of year. I'd be happy ta stay a few months ta warm up my bones 'fore I go back on the trail."

"My house is yours, as always. I sent Thomas to get the children at the academy. We'll jest enjoy ourselves for awhile. I got plenty of rail splittin' all saved up for you."

"Jest like the first time I come here, a lazy savage, huh Sam. You sure as hell worked my butt off so's I wouldn't want to stay here and farm."

They all laughed remembering the day seventeen years ago when William first was brought back to this farm after being a captive of the Miamis. William continued, "Aye, they's been a lot happened in the last few years. Maybe a lot goin' to happen yet. We got a crazy Shawnee to contend with these days. He's got religion and thinks he's the savior of the Indians. Goin' to turn them all away from liquor, and all white men's vices he claims. He may have a point too. Harrison is tryin' to buy up all the land. The Turtle and I fight it as much as we can, but the lands are still sold to the government a little at a time. With the game disappearin', the Indians need that government money to live on, so they sell more land. It's a vicious circle. As more land is settled, more game disappears."

Sam said, "Why don't they take up farmin'?"

"Hell, it ain't as if it hasn't been tried. Those Quakers that come out to teach farmin' to the Indians two years ago, give up right quick. They shoulda been teachin' the squaws, 'stead of the bucks. Then they mighta' got somewhere."

The cheerful sound of children's voices came from the outer room. William's four children bounded in asking, "Papa, when'd you get here?"

William smiled, so very glad to see them after their long separation. "Just got here. How y'all be?"

Ann at eighteen was quite the young lady while Rebecca, eleven, Mary Polly, ten and William Wayne eight, were still rambunctious youngsters. As half-breed Indians none had red hair like William nor the coal black color like their mother's, but rather a dark brown. William Wayne had blue eyes like his father, while the girls all had brown eyes like their mother.

Mary Polly said, "There's new kitties in the barn. Would you go with me to see them?"

William Wayne elbowed his sister out of the way. "Uncle Sam bought me a penknife." Reaching into his pocket he began withdrawing such a collection of sticks, stones, and nails that the adults all laughed.

Wells put an arm around the boy and girl. "I'll be stayin' for quite awhile. We'll get around to all those things beginin' right after dinner."

Ann came forward to sit beside her father. "Where was Mama buried?" she asked.

"Right out in the orchard, next to the Maumee. We had a beautiful burial ceremony and the white flag is kept up so the Great Spirit can find her."

"I wish I had been there." Ann looked down at her fingers smoothing the velvet fabric on the couch. A tear slipped out from under her lowered eyes.

"Honey, I'm real glad you wasn't. The pox took a lot of the people. It was bad enough losin' Sweet Breeze without losin' some of you too. You got a few years ta live yet. Those people that had it and didn't die got terrible scars. You bein' an unmarried gal, don't need that."

"I want to go back to Kekionga. You'll need a woman in the house now with Mama dead."

"Well, that's why I come ta get you. I plan to take you back with me. If you kin convince your Aunt Mary to let her go, we'll take Becca along for company."

Rebecca said, "The Frazees in Louisville are havin' a party Saturday night. We're invited and I'm sure they'd want you to come too, bein' an eligible bachelor an' all. They're havin' dancing and some other entertainment. There's sure to be men from the fort there too."

"Sounds real entertainin'. Course, jest comin' from Washington, it won't be near as fancy as what I'm used to."

"Now, Uncle William, don't you get on a high horse with us. Maybe you could be the entertainment showing off Miami yells and dances."

"Girl, you're gettin' too big for your britches. I don't allow as how I kin put up with you for months on end at Kekionga."

"Oh, I was only teasin'. Anyone can see you're a perfect gentleman." Rebecca leered at him after this remark.

Mary interrupted, "That's enough bickering you two. I swan, anyone would think you was brothers and sisters." William and Rebecca looked at her in surprise, and then laughed, because it was true, they were like brother and sister.

Saturday afternoon the house was a flurry of activity as Ann, Rebecca and Mary tried on various dresses, picking the ones that were most becoming. Sam and William worked on the harness, and dusted off the carriage in which they would ride. Finally all was in readiness for the dance. Great buffalo robes were used to keep them warm against the January weather on the ride into town. As the four horse team clipped along, a fine snow started down, dusting them with frost. The women rearranged their bonnets so their hair would not be ruined by the wetting.

Finally, the carriage drew up in front of a large new two story brick house built in the colonial style. A slave took the carriage at the door, driving it to a nearby field where a row of carriages were parked.

Sam said to William, "The influential men of Louisville will be here tonight. It's a good time to make your mark as a man of influence yourself. Mayhap they can be of value to help you from time to time."

William answered, "I may need their help. I wouldn't be at all surprised if Harrison don't try to get me relieved of my job as Indian Agent. He's been workin' at it for years. As governor of the Indiana Territory, he pulls a lot of weight in Washington."

Inside the house in the wide central hall Mr. and Mrs. Frazee received the Wells, greeting William with warmth after his introduction. The rooms were softly lit by many candles. Fireplaces were piled high with logs and a four piece string quartet played a minuet at one end of the long, wide room used now for dancing. On the other side of the entrance hall was a large formal dining room. A punch bowl brimming with cider graced the center of the table laden with plates of chicken, sliced bread, cakes, butter and jam.

Sam and William joined a cluster of men, all dressed in formal long-tailed coats in a corner as far from the music as they could get. A distinguished gentleman was saying, "Real estate is the quickest way to make money. I believe that we'll be able to solve the water problem here in Louisville and then land will shoot sky high. With all the river traffic stoppin' here on the way west, I don't see how the town can help but grow. I only regret I didn't fight in any of the wars to get some free land grants from the government."

Another man slapped Sam on the shoulder. "Sam here ain't got that problem. Tell me Sam, has there been any fights anywhere that you missed?"

"If there was, I'll get the clock turned back so I can go back and do 'em. But, my little brother here, Captain William Wells, is the man you want to talk to about fightin' Indians. He's the Indian Agent up at Fort Wayne."

The men in the circle all shook William's hand. A younger man, George, asked, "Is it safe to settle in those parts, or are ya riskin' your life if you buy government land up in Indiana?"

William thought about it a moment. "Only the southern Indiana acreage has been bought from the Indians, and that's fairly safe to settle in. But, the British haven't give up yet. They're tryin' ta get the Indians stirred up agin' the Americans yet. A Shawnee name of The Prophet is givin' me plenty of worry. He's tryin' to get the Indians to go back to their old ways and have nothin' to do with white men."

George said, "I been thinking about gettin' married and movin' into Indiana territory to start up a farm. Where would you think the best ground is for such?"

William stroked his face, eyebrows raised. "Truth be known, the best ground is still in Indian hands, 'bout a three, four day hard ride due north. If I was you, I'd buy a piece of land about a day or two's ride north, improve it, and then, if the land is sold by the Indians up north, sell your farm for a nice profit, go north and start over. Course, you'd better be good at choppin' wood. In the good lands in Indian country the trees grow so thick you kin hardly squeeze twinxt 'em."

Just then Rebecca came grabbing William by the hand. "I want you to meet a friend of mine, and dance her around the floor." As they approached a group of ladies, William was struck by one in particular. She was a young girl, about the same age as Rebecca with coal black hair, piled in curls on top of her head. Her intelligent black eyes were mature for her age, and hinted at mystery and banked passion. They looked up at him curiously as Rebecca said, "William, this is Mary Geiger, Frederick Geiger's daughter."

The two were silent as William glanced down past her haunting eyes to the bare shoulders and breasts pushed high, as was the fashion, showing so much of the rounded bosom that little was left to the imagination. "I like your....dress," he said. "Would you care to dance?"

"I don't know if it is the safe thing to do sir. I've heard that you are really an Indian, only wearing a suit when it's to your advantage."

"I kin assure you madam, Indians don't dance like this." He grabbed her hand, pulling her onto the dance floor, where they joined the others. As they rose and swayed to the music, their eyes never left each others, and when the steps brought them to each other William held her indecently close. On one such encounter she said, "Sir, I'm getting a pattern on my chest from the buttons on your coat."

"Would ya like me ta take it off?" Without waiting for her answer, he removed the coat and now danced in the linen full sleeved shirt he wore under it. On their next pass holding her close he said, "Is that better?"

Smiling only slightly she answered, "Much."

The dance ended and William took her arm, folding it firmly under his as he directed her into the dining room. There he filled a plate full of food for her, and they sat on the ladderbacked chairs lining the walls.

"That's enough food to feed a horse," Mary said.

"Got to fatten you up some. 'Sides I'll help you eat it. Are you married?"

"You don't waste any time do you? Though as an Indian I suppose you don't know the finer points of etiquette."

"Maam, I don't have time to waste, else, I'd beat around the bush fer an hour or so 'fore I asked."

Mary smiled slightly. "In that case, no, I'm not married."

"Why not? You're sure as hell one good lookin' woman. With the army men posted at the Fort here, its a miracle there's any unmarried women in all of Louisville."

"I was engaged to a sergeant, but he drowned in the river. Since that happened, I just haven't gotten around to wanting another beau."

William looked at her dark eyes and then out across the room filling with people. "The people and smells of 'em here can crush a man. Up in the Indian country, its still wild and free. There's no one lookin' over your shoulder judgin' your actions, the clothes ya wear or the way you act."

"It must be awful lonesome," she observed.

Instantly brought back to the present he smiled saying, "Actually I lied. What with the fort and the traders and Indians there's plenty of people at Kekionga. But if a day comes when ya feel 'em all pressin' in, if they should want too much of yer private self, it's only a short ride to a lake or river in the forest where there's not a soul for miles."

She touched his arm. "You must love that country very much."

He looked at her strangely for a moment, then said, "It's always been hard for me to decide where I belonged...with the white people in Kentucky or Indians at Kekionga. But I jest realized, I don't need to belong with either ones. I'm me, and where I'm happiest is up in the Lake Country. I don't intend to have any more doubts in my life as to who I really am. You know," he said, flushing, "I never talked to anybody like this before."

Mary looked at the powerfully built man. His eyes that had always had a restless quality were now calm. He had self assurance, wealth, and prestige both from his prominent Louisville family and his service with the army. He was a very desirable man. "I'd like to see this...Kekionga," she said.

William took her hand, feeling a shock, the spark of life, jump between them. "I got a fair sized farm there. Good house. Ain't brick like this'en, but it's a good one. Got enough slaves that life runs easier than for suttler women. Now, if you want trade goods, we have quite a few tradin' posts at Kekionga. And if you want to go for a trip to other trade houses, we jest take a couple days ride on the boats up ta Detroit. Our

French women like to go there from time to time. They claim there's more ta pick from."

"The Indians, are they safe to be around?"

William laughed. "You're askin' the wrong person 'bout that. I was raised by them from the age of thirteen. Been married to two of them. Hell, they's jest people."

"We hear that they get drunk and kill each other, that's why I ask, partly."

"That they do. You have to understand. The Indian uses liquor as an excuse. Let's say he's real mad at somebody for somethin' but he cain't jest walk up ta him and knife him, or her, if it's his wife. Well, he gets drunk and then anythin' he does is blamed on the liquor. Everybody will say, it weren't old White Corn that kilt his wife. It were jest the liquor he drank. The Shawnee have a custom whereas they are to hollar out as they come home drunk so's everybody will have a chance ta run hide. It's tough luck if he finds them, who he's mad at. And he will hunt for 'em."

"You really, really know them don't you." As she watched his face something of the old restless look came and then went away.

"Like I said, I never was real sure whether I was white or Indian, but that's gone now. Will you marry me?"

Embarrassed, she tried to pull her hand away, but he would not release it. "I don't know you. We only just danced a dance. How can you....."

"You know me." William's eyes were peering into her's with a heat that she recognized, and was embarrassed to realize she was returning with almost equal strength. He bent his head, placing his lips on her's, giving her a kiss that she had always thought was the kind only married people exchanged.

Pulling away she said, "People will see."

William threw back his head and laughed. "You know me. You're like me, only civilized."

With quiet fervency she said, "If I said I might marry you, I'd expect you to court me, like is proper."

"Anything that don't take too long I'll do. I got to be back up North for plantin' time, late March."

"That doesn't give us much time. Will you come to our house for supper tomorrow night?"

"I'd be honored Ma'am." He kissed her hand, and then turned it over and licked the palm. "Yes Ma'am, I'll do any courtin' you want, long as it don't take too much time."

Chapter XIX

Fort Wayne, March 1809

Captain William Wells and Mary Geiger were married March 3, 1809. Mary's father spent most of the four weeks between the dance and the wedding trying to dissuade his daughter from marrying the stranger and going to an unsettled country, all to no avail. The two were wildly in love and spent almost every waking hour together. After seeing them in a distant field in a position entirely immoral, he gave up.

The newly weds spent two days at Samuel's plantation after which William, Mary, his children, and Rebecca all started the long trip north. William agreed to send the younger children back to Sam's for schooling when Rebecca returned home to Louisville at summer's end.

Mary watched Rebecca setting the fire for their meal. They still had plenty of provisions brought from Louisville, but they wanted a fire to warm up while they ate dinner. Removing the little book from the saddle bag, she sat on a fallen moss-covered log to write about the previous day's trip.

Monday. We crossed the Ohio River, at Cincinnati, on flatboats without misshap, even though the river is swollen from spring rains. It's been a dry year and we are lucky. There's no flooding. We have so many packhorses that it takes William and William Wayne much effort to keep them going at a reasonable speed. William says there's not much town ahead here in Ohio, 'til we reach Fort Wayne. Hope we don't have to sleep in the rain. Rebecca and Ann make the trip very jolly. The little girls, Becca, and Mary Polly, are always playing one game or another, and the weather, so far, has been pleasant for travel, though I doubt very much it can remain. Rain clouds are scudding in this very minute.

Putting the book back into the saddle bag, she hurried to pack up the food. William came to speak with her before settling the horses into their line. "I know of a suttler not far from here. I think we'd best get to his place where we can stay the night. Looks like a rainstorm comin' up."

The group rode faster as the wind began whipping the trees above them. Gusts of rain raked over them, soaking their clothes thoroughly as they made their way toward the cabin. Reaching it in a downpour, they jumped off their horses into the muddy yard, and ran to pound on the door of the place. It was opened by a woman who said, "Land of Goshen! Come in outa the wet." Inside they almost filled the room of the tiny cabin. "Where you folk headed?" asked the woman.

"Fort Wayne," answered William. "Could you put us up for the night?"

"Sure can. We can put up jest as many as we got floor space. I guess I'm kinda in the business of puttin' up travelers, here on the Wayne road. I'll have some fried taters and bacon fixed 'fore you can say Jack Robinson."

"We'll be much abliged Maam," Mary said. I and my girls will help get it ready."

The children had warmed up a bit from their soaking and began to look at their surroundings. From a bed on the far side of the room, four young children, all under six, silently stared back at them. Their garments were something like sacks, with almost no sewing except for the sleeves. Their hair was untended, dishwater blond in color, and large blue eyes peered from the round little faces.

Rebecca questioned the woman, "How long you lived here?"

"Good while now, since 1803. Though there's more people movin' in all the time, we still don't get so much company as what we'd like. My chillun don't know how ta act 'round strangers. Guess you kin see that."

Bacon was sizzling in the skillet set on the iron rack above hot coals. The cabin was very dark, even in broad daylight, the only light coming from the fireplace. "Be glad when warm weather comes. Then, we kin open the door and see what we're doin'. Though it's been right nice weather off an' on through February. But I'll bet the ice ain't out of the lakes up north where you're goin'."

William hearing this remark laughed. "We ain't goin' ta the frozen North after all, though spring comes later than here. I got ta get back for spring plowin'."

"Thought those lands was still held by Indians up 'round Fort Wayne."

"They are, but I'm the Indian agent. Got certain advantages." He winked at the woman, who was flattered at the handsome man's attention.

She said, "Well, jest the same, ifen I was you, I'd keep one hand on my hair. Heard tell some of the suttlers is movin' away from Vincennes. They think Tecumseh is about ready ta land on 'em like a duck on a June bug."

"It's hard to say what The Prophet and his brother Tecumseh will do. If Governor Harrison presses for more land to be sold by the Indians, this whole territory could go up in flames."

The woman looked alarmed now. "D'you think he's likely to do that?"

"Yep. I've worked with the government and Harrison long enough to know that they mean to buy up all the land from the Indians. And it ain't been so long since the Indians began sellin' it but what they still think it belongs ta them. They don't want to sell but if they refuse, they'll have to go to war. The young braves would like that. If I was you, I'd keep my gun in sight when you're workin' in the fields."

That night the little cabin's floor was covered with sleeping people. Returning to the old road first built by General Wayne, they continued northward, staying in comparative comfort at the forts along the road. Ten days after they set out they arrived at the settlement of Kekionga, or Fort Wayne as the Americans now called it. They approached the town past a marshy lake that in late March was more lake than marsh. The town sat at the confluence of the three rivers, the St. Joseph and St. Marys forming the Maumee. Mary gazed at the rude fort, built on a rise of ground on the right bank of the Maumee. It was quite an imposing structure, built of tree logs set upright with sharpened tips. The trees used to build the fort came from the immediate area so that the ground was cleared for quite a distance around the fort, some four or five hundred acres being cleared. A cluster of cabins stood near the fort, and William explained that these were trader's houses.

"What's that bigger building, almost next to the fort?" asked Mary.

"The factory. I'll have ta go see the factor, John Johnston, ta see how things been goin' these months I've been away," answered Wells.

"Factory? What's that," asked Rebecca.

"It's jest a government run tradin' post for the Indians. Kinda used ta counteract the British givin' goods to them. When the Indians get in debt too far at the factory, they're a lot happier ta sell land to the government. Harrison offers ta wipe out all their debts for a chunk of land. All in all, though, the prices are as fair as what they can get from the other traders here." Wells shook his head as another thought occurred. "The Factor, Johnston's been a burr in my hide for a long time now. He's been tryin' ta get me relieved of my job as Indian Agent for years. Always writin' ta Harrison or the secretary of War with accusations of one kind or another. I have ta keep my eye on him, so I know what he's up to."

On the way to Wells' farm, Indians, French men, and soldiers raised their hands in greeting, then continued to stare after the woman riding beside Wells and the flaming haired Rebecca. Mary and Rebecca tried not to stare in their turn at the Indian women walking or riding with a child or other pack strapped to their backs, but it was hard not to. Very few Indians ever came to Louisville. Louisville was not a town that was tolerant of them. Mary was well acquainted with Wells' half breed children, but they did not seem Indian in either appearance or actions, having lived so much of their lives with Sam. The Indian women were very clean and appeared to prefer cotton skirts and blouses to buckskin garments. Their hair was done up neatly in the Miami club style.

Crossing the Maumee River they arrived at Wells' house on the banks of the little stream named Spy Run because of William's days as head of General Wayne's spies. The house was a rambling affair, having apparently started out as a rough cabin and then being added on by someone who actually knew how to build. There were two stories with windows and a side porch. Back of the house were a number of other cabins housing Wells' slaves. A young orchard near the river looked ready to burst into bloom, buds swelling with the milder weather.

Well's children raced their horses for the barn, then, giving them over to a young black boy, streaked off to the orchard.

Rebecca asked, "Where are they goin' in such an all-fired hurry?"

William replied, "To see Sweet Breeze's grave."

Rebecca looked at Mary to see what effect this remark would have. Mary was studying her husband's face, but seeing no sorrow there, she turned to the business of carrying their goods into her new home.

Just inside the door of the original cabin was the main room of the house. A wide fireplace took up the center wall. Here cooking, eating, and sleeping were all done originally. Now, it was a sitting room and office. William's desk, obviously bought in the east, rested beside a window at one end of the room. Most of the chairs were ladder back style with woven split hickory seats, but mixed with the homemade furniture were a sprinkling of fine pieces, either brought up from Cincinnati or shipped over Lake Erie and down the Maumee from the East. "It looks very comfortable," Mary commented.

William watched her closely as she appraised her new surroundings. He said, "We have money to buy some good things now an' then. Ain't exactly savages here ya know. Becca, bring your grip upstairs and I'll show you your room." The two carefully ascended the very narrow, steep stairs of rough wood to the upstairs bedrooms used by the children and guests. Here two large rooms held a number of beds, that were made of straw ticks, some topped by feather beds, all on rope springs.

Returning to the main floor, William directed Mary to their bedroom that was in a leanto, added as an after thought to the house. Mary was very surprised to see a Hepplewhite Field Bed, with its delicate frame and canopy top sitting in the center of the room. A fine matching chest of drawers stood against one wall with a round mirror holding two candles in its framework hung on the wall above it. A blanket chest and rocking chair completed the room while on the floor was a handsome braided rug. Mary said, "Oh, William, I was expecting to find a simple cabin in the woods. You have a regular plantation here. It is all quite lovely."

William flushed with pride. all his life he'd worked for this and now, he had a wife of civilization who appreciated it. "If there's other things you want, we'll go to Detroit, or maybe even to the capital, Washington."

Mary sat down on the bed, smoothing the quilted bedspread with her hands. "I would like to go back to Louisville from time to time, to visit my folks."

"That we will. When its time for the children to go back to school after the crops are in, we'll go for a visit."

The next morning after William had set the field hands to plowing, he rode to the Indian factory next to the fort. Inside the poorly lighted building the smell of furs, rope and foodstuffs met his nose. From it's depths came the store clerk to greet him. "Johnston ain't here," he said in an unfriendly tone. Johnston's hatred of Wells had rubbed off on this man who worked with him. He continued, "Gone to Kirk's settlement in Ohio to settle up affairs. Seem's you was successful in gettin' William Kirk fired from his civilization agent job teachin' the Indians ta farm, while you was in Washington."

"I don't know what you're talkin' about, though I always thought what Kirk was doin' was a waste of time and money."

The man continued, "It certainly looks suspicious with Kirk gettin' his letter of bein' fired right after you go ta Washington. And you always doin' you're damndest ta give the man trouble."

"Well, the whole truth is, I had nothin' ta do with it."

Little Turtle had requested that the Quakers or the American Government send teachers of farming to the Miamis. People had come for this purpose several times and William Kirk was the most recent example. Other Indians were opposed to taking up white man's ways. Wells himself was somewhat jealous of any others who worked with or influenced the Miamis. He had given both William Kirk and John Johnston a great deal of trouble in their efforts to civilize the Indians. Hoping to change the subject from the irritating Kirk he asked, "Are the Indians turnin' in many furs from winter hunt?"

"Nope. We only got about one third as many as last year. The Prophet's been tellin' the Indians not ta deal with white men, but ta go back ta the old ways. Guess they think that means they won't need furs for trade goods, since they won't be buyin' anythin' from us. Fact's are, they jest turn around and steal what they want. We ain't gettin' the quality furs they want back east neither. They want more beaver 'stead of so many coon skins. Ain't been gettin' much beaver brought in atall."

"A hungry Indian's a dangerous one, but they'll still have their government annuities. Tell Johnston I stopped by when he gets back." William returned to his farmwork as April was the farmer's busiest time of year. He now owned 320 acres of his own land. His position as Indian Agent added to his chores. It was his job to give out the government money and goods to the Indians each fall and to keep the Secretary of War and Governor of the Indiana Territory advised of Indian activity. Wells was also the Kekionga Justice of Peace and was called upon occasionally to perform marriages or other duties. All his work had made him a very wealthy man; the envy of even Governor Harrison who reported to his superiors that he didn't understand how Wells could make so much money, honestly.

In the past few years, John Johnston, the factor, had accused Wells of cheating the Indians out of their government money. Wells did a poor job of keeping his accounts and in 1806, the Secretary of War, Dearborn, had ordered him to turn over his accounts for inspection. He was warned that he would not get any more money unless he sent proper vouchers for it. The inspectors of his accounts had been John Johnston and the commandant of Fort Wayne, Whipple. They found a number of charges they felt were not in keeping with the intent of the Indian agency. Thereupon, Dearborn warned Wells to use government money correctly and economically.

Wells was careful then to keep better records, but decided to submit a few expenses and grievances of his own. He claimed that other Indian agents lived in houses built by the government whereas he had built his own which was now a cabin of twelve years old, "rotting down over my head." Also, he had supplied his own firewood for which the government usually paid.

Dearborn wrote Governor Harrison that he thought Wells was too attentive to pecuniary considerations. Also, he wrote factor Johnson telling him to inform him of the state of the Indians, though this was Wells' job. Dearborn continued,

> I fear that he calculates on making money by supplying the Indians...I have no doubt of his improper interference with the intentions of the Government to aide the Indians through Mr. Kirk.... and I am satisfied that for several years past, Wells has been very intent on making money, and is at the same time very jealous of any interference with his concerns with the Indians in his Agency. In short I have lost much of my confidence in his integrity.

Though Governor Harrison and Secretary Dearborn distrusted Wells, they felt he was too valuable to dismiss because of his knowledge of and intimacy with the Indians. If he were made an enemy, he could cause a great deal of harm, perhaps raising the Indians to a new war. But over the years, John Johnston sent communications of growing Indian distrust and dissatisfactin with Wells. Little Turtle was declining in importance because of his age and poor health, having contracted gout.

Several weeks later a cold April drizzle dripped off the trees as John Johnston rode toward the Wells' farm to deliver the message for which he'd worked these last six years. Now he could take his revenge for all the times the egotistical Wells had taken him for a fool, talking to the Indians in their language in front of him, and then giving him his own personal rendition of their answers. For Johnston, everything was either black or white. If an Indian was to be given so much money, that would be how much he received. Should his crops fail, his house burn, or other misfortune befall him, that was his problem. He, John Johnston, was charged with certain duties as storekeeper of the government trading post, and he would uphold his duties to the letter of the law.

In Johnston's mind, Wells was a character who bent with the wind, holding no principles inviolate. Johnston, could never tell what Wells would do in a given situation. Wells did the basic work of giving out the Indian annuity money correctly, but was very.....creative, in the way he allowed government property, such as the plows, to be used by the Indians. Usually, the man kept such items stored on his own farm, and so of course used them himself.

In contrast to the ease with which Wells gained wealth, life had been one of constant struggle for Johnston. He was an Irish immigrant who as a young boy took a job as wagoner for Anthony Wayne during Wayne's Indian campaigns. Even then he disliked the flamboyant Wells who had become a legend during the Wayne campaign with his constant tales of adventure while capturing Indians for interrogation. After Wells was shot by Indians in a spy venture, he'd been a hero among the army men. Johnston was an intelligent man and had not been impressed with Wells' braggadocio.

Following Wayne's war, Johnston returned to Pennsylvania to open a store with his brother. This failed and he became a law clerk. After marrying a Quaker girl, the job of Indian Factory factor for Fort Wayne, featuring $1,000 a year and three rations a day was an appealing one. After all, he was already familiar with the country, having served with General Wayne. So he took the job,and traveled with his bride 850 bone wearying miles to take up his new life.

Once in Fort Wayne, he had become ill with the fevers and pain of malaria. The goods for the trading post didn't arrive until the following spring, and then, they appeared short of the number of items said to have been sent. Someone, or ones, had stolen some of the goods. This new evidence of human failure gave him great pain. He was a stickler for honesty and detail. When the humans he dealt with failed to measure up to his standards it gave him further evidence of how depressing life was. But now, one of those imperfect people was to get his due. He was to deliver Dearborn's January letter to Wells, relieving him of the job of Fort Wayne Indian Agent, and take it himself.

Johnston's knock was answered by a dark haired beauty he never had seen before. "Yes?" Mary Wells said.

Johnston asked, somewhat flustered by the sophisticated white woman, "Wells 'bout the place? I'm here on government business."

Mary looked at him doubtfully and then went to call William from the barn. When Wells came in he said, "Johnston, I been lookin' for you ta get back. We got a lot to ketch up on since I been ta Washington."

"That's what I came to see you about," Johnston answered hesitantly, somewhat cowed as always by Wells' masculine vitality. "I received this letter from secretary Dearborn some time ago, but you weren't here to receive it." He handed over the missive for Wells to read.

Wells carried the letter over to the window and then swore softly, "I'll be damned! You finally did it!" His face was filled with such fury upon reading that he was fired from his job that Johnston, his enemy, took a step backwards.

Defensively Johnston said, "It's long overdue that you left the job Wells. You ought to be horsewhipped for your part in Kirk being fired as civilization agent in Ohio."

"Kirk couldn't handle money. That's why he was fired. I had nothin' to do with that."

"I think you're lyin," Johnston replied. "You've been against the Indians being civilized and taught to farm ever since the first Quakers came out to teach them. Why Little Turtle himself asked the Quakers to come teach farming. Why you don't help in it, I never could figure."

Wells crumpled the letter in his hand and said through clenched teeth, "I'll fight this Johnston. The Indians will be told how you connived to get me fired. I've got friends in Kentucky that will go to the President for me. You'll not win in this yet."

Johnston said not another word, but turned and left the house. Mary came in shortly after this, and was alarmed at the murderous look on her husband's face. "What did the man want?"

Wells sat down beside the fire and gazed into its depths. "I've been fired as Indian agent. Johnstons been give the job. Johnstons been workin' agin me for years and now he got me fired."

Mary was unsure of what this would mean for them. "Do we need the money? You have the farm and you are Justice of Peace."

William looked up at her and realized she didn't understand the importance of the power he had with the job. He not only controlled the Indian's money, but had a great part in influencing history, by seeing that they did not go to war against the white men. So far, he'd convinced many Indians not to throw in their lot with the Prophet and Tecumseh. But after being relieved of his position by the government, he thirsted for revenge. If he wanted to, he could help cause the Miamis to go to war against the settlers.

"It ain't jest the money. Without the job I won't be nothin'. Not here, not in Louisville, not in Washington. I jest have ta get it back."

Mary was inexperienced in such matters but she wanted to help. "Maybe we could get people to send letters of recommendation to Washington. The new commander of the fort here, he's a friend of yours isn't he? Wouldn't he have some influence on what they thought in Washington?"

Wells answered slowly, "Yes. Captain Heald would send a good word for me. 'Sides, I been meanin' ta introduce Becca ta him. He'd make her a good match. I'll invite him over for supper an' see what he has ta say."

Handsome thirty-four year old Nathon Heald was only too glad to partake of the good southern cooking offered at the home of William Wells. Heald had been stationed as commander of Fort Wayne for two years, since 1807. He was a reserved, very correct, easterner of good family, coming from a long line of army men. His father, Colonel Thomas Heald, was the commander of the company who marched to avenge the attack on Lexington and Concord during the Revolutionary War. His blond, blue-eyed good looks would have attracted the ladies, but his cool aloofness and army career had so far rendered him wifeless.

As the tall man, dressed in army uniform was introduced to Wells' daughters, wife, and Rebecca, the young girls all began to sparkle. A dimple appeared in Rebecca's cheek upon seeing such a gorgeous available male in these remote parts. When she was introduced to the man, she held out her hand taking his a trifle longer than necessary saying, "Such a pleasure to meet a refined man in this wilderness after havin' only my old savage uncle here as company, day after day."

Nathon, warmed by the lovely girl's hand in his, noted at first glance the strong resemblence to her uncle. "Maam". His eyes were held by hers for a moment. Then without any further word, he followed his hostess, Mary, to the long trestle dinner table.

Rebecca was not accustomed to so little attention or to being passed off as unimportant. Pushing aside her cousin, Ann, she manuvered herself to the place beside the Captain, and then observed his long fingered hands from under lowered lashs as grace was said. All were seated and the meal of pork roast, buttered potatoes, dandelion greens, new baked bread and apple pie was begun.

"How do you like Fort Wayne?" Captain Heald asked his hostess, Mary.

"It's a lot colder than Louisville," she answered. "It'll take a bit of gettin' used to, after livin' in such a big town. Take's a mite of plannin' ta get those things you need. I've already got a list of things to buy when we go south this winter."

Rebecca took center stage saying, "I think Fort Wayne's the most excitin' place I've ever been. I've been wantin' ta come visit Uncle William for years but Mama would never let me before. I jest love to watch the Indians. They're so exotic....so savage. My favorite one is Little Turtle and he's to come stay with us for awhile."

"How do you happen to know Little Turtle?" asked Heald.

"Oh, he stopped at our place in Louisville with Uncle William when I was jest a little girl. I guess he's not feelin' too well these days. He's got gout. What do you think of Fort Wayne?"

Captain Heald took another helping of potatoes and answered, "It seems pretty much like any other post. I've got the same supply problems, same discipline problems. I think most men are in the army because of some female problems back East, rather than any burnin' interest ta serve the country."

"Is that true of yourself?" asked Rebecca with a wicked smirk.

Heald allowed himself a small smile. "My family's always been in the army. Never occurred to me to do anything else."

Rebecca persisted, "Surely, a man handsome as yourself is hounded by dozens of women."

Heald withdrew, embarrassed, saying nothing. This man would be a tough quarry to trap Rebecca could see, because of his innate shyness, but well worth pursuing for the enjoyment of the hunt, and to test her skill.....

William who had been engrossed in thoughts of his own now said, "'Spose you heard I was relieved of my job as Indian agent."

"Yes. I was very surprised to hear that. How did it come about?"

"That bastard Johnston, pardon ladies, has been tryin' to get my job for years. He sent a bunch of tales ta Washington that I cheated the Indians out of their government money. Now you know I did no such a thing. You was there yourself last fall when I give them their money."

"Yes and I saw no improprieties. I can't think how he would perceive himself a better man for the job. He can't even speak their language."

Wells asked, "Would you write a letter to that effect to the Secretary of War? The only way I can think of ta get the job back is ta have letters of recommendation sent by men of character, such as yourself."

Heald smiled. "I thank you kindly sir, and I don't forget the advice and help you've given me since I've been Commander of the fort. I will write telling them that you have done a good job as Indian agent. Perhaps you should write a letter to the Secretary yourself arguing your case."

Wells mused, "That might be a good idea. Governor Harrison might send a letter for me too. We ain't always seen eye to eye, but generally, we've worked together."

Rebecca broke in to say, "Daddy always said William would have been made Governor himself if he'd had a better education."

Mary looked at eight year old William Wayne who was edging slowly off his chair, trying to leave the table without notice. "Samuel Wells has plans to send William Wayne to West Point, so he'll have the chance his father never had."

All eyes turned to the young Wells boy, son of Sweet Breeze, Grandson of Little Turtle. After a pause, Mary said, "You children may be excused from the table." Chairs scraped on the floor as the three youngest children made a hurried exit. The adults returned to the sitting room to continue their talks. After a polite interval, Captain Heald made his departure.

In Rebecca and Ann's shared bedroom later that night, they discussed the reserved man. "Ann, what do you think of him?" asked Rebecca.

Ann took down her braided hair laughing, "It's plain ta see how he got ta be so old and still a bachelor."

"Don't you think he's attractive?" asked Rebecca.

"He's handsome enough, but doesn't have much money. He's just a Captain. I'd rather marry somebody with money."

"Well, you're your father's daughter. I....I'd fancy living at some army post far out in the wilderness where life was never dull. If I needed money, I could always ask Daddy for that."

"Well, if you want to marry that one, it's goin' ta take work. Hard work!" Ann smiled as she dipped her head to blow out the candle. Rebecca eased herself back onto the narrow bed, and looked at the moon floating above the trees outside the window. I'm not afraid of work, she said to herself before closing her eyes.

May passed into June and the Captain had not come to call. Rebecca waited patiently at first, but now doubted that Captain Heald had any interest in her. If he had, he would certainly have shown it by this time. Disinterest was a new experience for her. In Louisville the fort's soldiers fell over themselves to get her attention at every party or dance. She began to think that Heald had missed the ancient signal in her eyes. She decided she'd have to be more aggressive if she were to have him.

William's wife, Mary was having a hard time adjusting to frontier life. A very young woman, she had the difficult task of learning how to run a large household that included supervision of several slaves. Little time remained to entertain her house guest, Rebecca. At times Rebecca helped in the kitchen, but the house was not hers or her primary responsibility. And so Rebecca took rides in the afternoon, hoping by chance to cross the path of the elusive Captain Heald. Usually her cousin Ann accompanied her, but on this particular June Day, Ann was busy sewing a dress and had not wanted to go with her. Rebecca paced restlessly then left the others and rushed out into the bright sunlight.

The barn boy saddled the gray mare with its intriguing spots that were like little stars on its back flanks. She wore a somber brown riding dress so as not to show soil and a forest green bonnet that subdued the red locks bound in a coil on the back of her head. Here and there a few red strands blew in the breeze as she rode.

Crossing the river, she slowly rode up the road past the fort. Rebecca hoped the Captain would be out somewhere to notice her riding past.

The huge timbered doors of the fort stood wide open. Inside, soldiers could be seen working on harness equipment. Others were chopping wood. She tried to appear as if she were not searching the faces for the one man she sought. Farther down the road in the field outside the fort, other men worked in the garden plots that supplied the fort's vegetables and hay. One of these men watched, shading his eyes, as Rebecca slowly passed. Then from the distance she heard him call, "Miss Wells, wait up a minute."

Rebecca pulled up the Apallusa, who contentedly began eating grass while she waited for the Captain's approach.

"Miss Wells, it is somewhat imprudent for you to ride about alone this way. An Indian who's had too much to drink might take a fancy to your horse, or you, and then where would you be?"

Rebecca looked down at the tall blond Heald, dressed in a blue workshirt and trousers. Saucily she said, "Probably better entertained than if I was sittin' at home. Why don't you ride with me so I'll be protected?"

Heald looked up at the grinning Rebecca, then back at his men. He really should stay and continue work here. Still, the lady should be escorted. "Let me get a horse and I'll take you back to Wells' place."

"Actuallly, I had in mind ridin' up the trail to Little Turtle's town. He's been poorly and I thought I'd go cheer him up."

"Miss Wells! I simply can't allow you to ride about the forest that way, unescorted."

"Then go with me. I'm not about to sit home on a nice day like this, and the name's Rebecca." She smiled engagingly melting his initial pique. Walking to the hitching post, he picked a horse at random and fetched a rifle that he placed in its holder on the saddle.

Rebecca watching asked brightly, "Are we expectin' trouble?"

Heald answered frowning as they rode away from the village, "Main problem this summer is Indian horse thefts. Johnston's been kept busy tryin' ta settle Indian claims for 'em. Since they don't trap like they used to, they're stealin' almost everything off each other."

Rebecca rode along silently for a moment then said, "Uncle William still writes reports to the new Secretary of War and Governor Harrison jest as if he was still Indian Agent."

Heald wasn't too concerned about Wells' problems and said vaguely, "If he keeps after them, Washington'll probably give him some job. Frankly, I don't see why he wants to keep one with all the trouble it brings. He seems to have plenty of money now."

Rebecca thought about it and tryed to explain it in her uncle's terms. "I think Uncle William wants to be the one who determines what happens to the Miamis. He feels personally responsible, since they are his relatives. He feels he's part Indian. And too, there's a lot of power in the job. He always got a real bang out of goin' ta Washington or Philadelphia makin' deals with the politcians. Men he felt were important. Bein' the man to deal with for the Miamis made him important in the white man's world. But now, the Indians don't pay as much attention to Little Turtle since he's a sick old man. Uncle William's power over the Miamis came from Little Turtle. He needs a government job to be important in Indian's eyes."

Heald slowed his horse on the shaded trail. "You really like all the intrigue surrounding the Indians here don't you."

Rebecca was somewhat surprised. It had never occurred to her there were people who weren't interested in Indians, the frontier, and what was happening there. "Don't you love it here? The freedom to do or be whatever you feel like without all the old society biddies breathin' down yer neck? I wouldn't care if I never went back to Louisville."

Heald looked at the thick forest along the dirt trails. The heat, the bugs, the uncomfortableness of the times. "Facts are, I'd give a lot to be sitting on my folks' wide front porch back East, drinking a tall glass of apple cider, with the closest Indian two hundred miles away."

Rebecca said without thinking, "I didn't realize we were so different."

Heald and Rebecca allowed the horses to come to a stop while they silently appraised one another. Their deep basic differences stood between them. Rebecca loved adventure and being away from the criticism of society while Heald preferred an ordered tranquil life filled with well kept houses and lawns, obedient children, and women who were well corseted. Even so, the physical attraction between the two could be seen, and most certainly felt. Cardinals sang their noisy songs and robins fought for their territories as the two sat silent in the forest, trying in their minds to come to some conclusion.

Heald finally said, "People will talk, us riding off into the forest that way. Your reputation will be ruined if you continue in such escapades, Miss Wells. It's time for you to go home."

Silently they rode back to the Wells' farm; Rebecca unusually subdued. The man was not one that she could twist around her finger with casual flirting. It appeared he did not want her. Her lower lip firmed with anger at the thought that he had told her what to do, and now was enforcing his orders. She would not allow it. In the future, if she wanted to ride out alone, she would, no matter what he said.

On arriving in front of the Wells house, she waited for him to lift her down. After he lowered her to the ground, she stood next to him looking deep into his eves as his hands lingered on her waist. Heald's resolve to forget her weakened, but Rebecca couldn't hold the facade of fragile maiden long. Into her eyes returned her accustomed look of independence as she turned away to go into the house. The Captain stood watching her, confused by the extreme attraction he felt for her, even though he knew they were unsuited in temperment. Rebecca stopped at the door, turned and said with a dazzling smile, "Come callin' another time, Nathon."

Nathon Heald rode back to the fort lost in thought. Rebecca was not the woman for him, though she appeared to want him. She would not fit in with his relatives and probably would always be restless back east. It was best just to stay away from her because her beauty was enough to make him lose the best of his intentions. If they were alone too often...it was hard to say what might happen. Since she appeared to be attracted to him, it was up to him, the older wiser person, to protect them both from an unhappy future. He would simply lose himself in work and forget about Rebecca Wells.

As days passed, Ann and Rebecca picked up more and more of Mary's work. In the mornings, Mary stayed in bed late, the queasiness not passing until ten or later. The three young women giggled among themselves as they counted on their fingers the months before the baby would arrive. They determined they couldn't return to Louisville until well after November when they expected its arrival.

William Wells was engrossed in efforts to regain a government post. He wrote his brother Sam in Louisville, asking that letters be written to Washington in his behalf. Perhaps the old family friend, Senator John Pope, could put in a word for him in Washington.

During this time, Governor Harrison was planning a Grand Council for all Indian tribes to take place in September when the Indians gathered to receive their government annuities. Harrison wanted to buy more land even though his discussions with Tecumseh at Vincennes in July warned of Indian uprisings if more land was sold. Neither the new Secretary of War, Eustis, nor President Madison realized what the effect of pressing for more land would be. And they gave Harrison permission to purchase more land, stipulating no more money be paid for it than in the past.

Wells wrote Secretary Eustis complaining that he had borrowed money to purchase supplies while he was Indian agent, and this left him in debt. The government owed him $3,000 he said. Also, he declared his firing was cruel and unjust, and contrary to the United States' interest. The Indians suffered from want of his services, he claimed, and he would be happy with the job of Indian Agent or as "Head of Civilization."

Later, Wells wrote Harrison that he would help negotiate the 1809 Treaty to be held in September at Fort Wayne. Harrison decided it was best to let Wells help, even though he suspected him of intrigue with the Indians. After all, Wells and Little Turtle could ruin the negotiations if they were angered sufficiently. It was better to play along with them, and act as if they were being of help. Harrison wrote Eustis that Wells should not be placed in a position to handle government money.

Rebecca and Ann Wells spent the summer plotting how they'd capture a husband. Rebecca had given up somewhat on the handsome but illusive Captain Heald. Whenever she crossed his path, he said hello, but nothing more. The French families of the town enjoyed giving parties and the two lovely unmarried girls added a cosmopolitan touch and so were in much demand.

When not planning what to wear to a party or helping the pregnant Mary, Rebecca listened in on her Uncle's conferences with the Indians. Once at the end of May, she had seen the mysterious Shawnee religious leader, The Prophet, in deep discussion with her Uncle. She watched the tall Indian awhile speaking intensely eloquent Shawnee, but then not knowing the language, she left, returning to household chores. Later she'd asked her Uncle what the Prophet said, and he replied vaguely that the man wanted to know what Harrison's intentions were.

"What did you tell him?" she asked, curious.

"Jest the plain truth. That Harrison wanted the Indians' land. But, I told him not ta mention my name, or that he talked to me. Harrison would use whatever I said ta any of the Indians against me." Wells sat down with an expression suggesting great fatigue. "Maybe I ought ta jest go back ta Louisville. Get myself a farm there. Mary'd like that."

Rebecca was dismayed at this possibility. "Uncle William, you know you couldn't stand it there, so far from your own kind. Mary made up her own mind ta marry you and live here. She'll get used to it. And once the baby comes, she'll have interests of her own. After the baby comes, she can go to Louisville for a visit with her folks and you can talk to politicians there who'll help you get your government job back."

William looked up at his niece, who was so like a sister. "Course you're right. I ain't never been happy in the south more than a couple months during winter. But, I'll have to work at it to keep the peace here. Otherwise, it won't be safe for any white man at Kekionga."

The hot July weather was perfect for washing clothes, the women of the Wells household decided. Loading all the months accumulated wash on the wagon, they drove down to the river. The old slave man, Josiah, drove the wagon filled with chattering children and young women. It creaked and groaned on its way to the shady river bank, where he lifted down the heavy wash tubs to the ground. Rebecca and Ann removed their shoes and walked down the river banks, wood buckets in hand to begin bringing the water up to fill the wooden tubs. They would scrub the clothes on scrub boards and it would take all day. This wasn't done more than once a month and less often in winter.

Rebecca was wearing her worst old work dress. It wasn't seemly to swim with little clothing on, but if she should happen to slip while getting water for the wash tubs, nothing would be lost wetting this old dress. She planned to slip often as perspiration dripped off her face from the heat of the day. Rebecca said to Ann, "If it were me, I'd just wash 'em in the river, like I seen the Indians do. Seems a sight easier than haulin' all this water up the hill."

Ann was very slowly filling her bucket, in order to spend more time in the cool river. "Mary don't want to be thought of as an Indian. She wouldn't be caught doin' anything so uncivilized."

Rebecca raised her eyebrows at her half breed cousin's remark. "You don't like her much do you Ann?" Ann said nothing and Rebecca continued, "You got to think of it this way. Your Ma's dead now. You know your father ain't one to do without a wife. So, you might as well accept her."

Ann set down the bucket and "slipped" sitting down in the cool water fully dressed. Sighing at the comfort she answered, "He could have married an Indian. He always had Indian wives. I don't know why now, all of a sudden, he picks a white woman. And Mama hardly cold in her grave."

Rebecca looked up on the bank where Mary was arranging the food for their lunch. Then she slipped too. "Are you goin' ta marry a Miami brave and live in a wigwam, Ann?"

Ann looked at her startled. "Course not."

Rebecca continued, "Well like it or not, your daddy's got more white blood than you. He's all white and he's jest now gettin' ta enjoy the benefits. He likes ta have a wife he can take around in society in Louisville. I hope you'll look at it like that, rather than to think he doesn't want an Indian woman."

Ann lay on her back, floating, gazing up at the deep blue sky, her dress spread out around her on top of the water. After awhile she said, "Maybe I'll be married 'fore long anyway, and not live here with them."

Beyond the trees on the far side of the river, thick black smoke was billowing up, apparently near the fort. Ann saw it first saying excitedly, "Looks like Fort Wayne caught fire!"

As Rebecca watched the smoke a picture of the blond Captain Heald came to her mind. Jumping up she called to Josiah, who was fishing downriver. "Get the horses. We're goin' to help fight that fire." They loaded the wooden buckets and tubs back onto the wagon. The horse pulled the wagon into the river where they filled the tubs with water before continuing to the fort. Rebecca hollared, "Faster, faster," all the way to the cluster of buildings that surrounded the fort. But as they came into view, they could see it was not the fort, but the blacksmith shop and Indian factory that was on fire.

The place was swarming with Indians, soldiers, and French traders, all dashing ineffectually about, some even bringing water. Josiah drove the horses near the buildings and Rebecca jumped down, ordering Ann to fill the buckets from the tub as she and Josiah ran to the building, throwing water on the fire. It had a good start and by this time, nothing could be done to save the building. Some of the trade goods had been drug out and mysteriously disappeared, but the place was going to be a total loss. Rebecca was running with another bucket when she was grabbed from behind and swung around.

A man said, "What are you doin' here? This is no place for a lady. You could get hurt."

Rebecca was angry at being stopped, then embarrassed when she saw it was Captain Heald who held her arm. Her hair was a sodden wreck from the river and her soaked clothes stuck to her body. Never the less, she raised her freckled nose in the air and said, "What do you care?"

Heald's teeth clamped together and a stern scowl filled his face. He would take no backtalk with all the danger here. "You get the children together and get the hell out of here. Right now!"

Rebecca looked at him, an argument on her lips, then changed her mind. A triumphant thought came to her. He did care what happened to her after all. "At least get your men to use the rest of the water we brought. Then we'll go," she said.

Heald had no time to think about them further. The water was quickly used and Rebecca urged Josiah to drive them away, seeing that Heald was correct. It wasn't a safe place to be.

Later that night, William Wells arrived home with the news that the Indian factory and blacksmith shop were total losses. He reported this with a smile on his face. His enemy, Johnston, would have his hands full now, trying to rebuild the factory as well as carrying out the job of Indian Agent. At this same time Johnston was supposed to be contacting all the Indian tribes to come to the treaty session being held in September.

During August Nathon Heald's face appeared in Rebecca's mind over and over, twisted in concern for her safety. Why was it that he kept himself far away from her? He obviously felt something for her and yet completely ignored her. She finally decided he must be holding out for a woman that was more lady-like. Raised in the East, he probably was unused to frontier women who could work as hard or shoot as well as a man. If she were to get his attention, she'd have to polish her manners, she decided.

In mid September a new face appeared in Wells' large living room office. Governor William Henry Harrison arrived in Fort Wayne September 15th for new treaty talks. Rebecca appraised the man who was by turns friend or foe of her Uncle. When introduced to the tall, rangy man, she saw he was handsome, though his face was rugged with an overlong nose. The overall impression was that of a man with an enormous ego, and vast self importance that was fulfilled by his great intelligence and good family connections back East. Rebecca saw her Uncle had no chance in the struggle for power against this man. Harrison was sophisticated in ways Wells could never be. But the two were equally aggressive. Harrison still needed Wells to help deal with the Indians and keep them in line, so they would not join Tecumseh against white settlers. But Rebecca could see that Harrison would be happy to rid himself of Wells, the troublesome rival for power, should it be convenient.

She listened to part of their conversation before leaving the room. Wells said somewhat warily to the man who'd shown deep distrust of him, "Did you come from Vincennes over the new road?"

"Yes. Cut the trip down quite a few days, when we took it from Vincennes to West Bend, Ohio. Course we came the old Wayne Trace north from there." Harrison was not interested in wasting time on pleasantries. "What's your opinion of the local Indians' feelings toward selling more land to the government at this treaty?"

Wells shrugged. "They never want to sell land. You know that by now. With The Prophet tellin' them it's a sin ta sell it, they're less likely than ever to be willin' ta sell." Harrison said nothing as he stroked his face thinking. Then he said, "I saw Tecumseh in Vincennes in July. Can't seem to make out what he's goin' to do. One minute he implies he'll make war and then the next he'll say he doesn't plan to attack white men. I've had a French trader spy in his camp up above Ouiatenon, but haven't got much information, as to his intent."

Wells said, "I doubt Tecumseh could raise over a hundred warriors to fight, and he will want to fight if you buy more land now."

Harrison scowled at Wells, who had opposed his land purchases from the Indians so many times in the past. "I thought you were past the days of being a squaw man, an Indian lover, now that you're married to a white woman."

Wells half rose from his chair. What a joy it would be to tear this man limb from limb. But, they had to work together. Nothing would be gained with an angry scene. If he alienated Harrison now, he'd never get another government post. He sat back down. "As Indian agent, its always been my job to help Indians with all their problems, as well as to inform the government what they're up to. That way of thinkin' ain't easy to forget, even if I don't have the job now."

Harrison thought of the accusations made by the Delaware that Wells cheated them out of their government money. Perhaps they had merit and perhaps not. In any event, he needed Wells now to help persuade the Indians to sell their land. "If you help me get the treaty for land sales passed, I'll send Washington word to get you reinstated in a government job."

It was a tempting offer. Wells knew full well that any future position he might hold was under Harrison's control. Though he loved the Miamis and felt one of them, as he grew older he thought more and more of doing what was best for himself, unemotionally, and often unethically. "I'll do whatever I can," he said.

During the last two weeks of September, 1809, Indians of various tribes around Fort Wayne assembled for the treaty session. This was the time of year they received their government money for land sold in the past. Now, Johnston circulated the word that Harrison wanted to buy more land and all tribes who claimed ownership should come to the Grand Council. In the past, some tribes had not attended such treaty sessions, and later didn't honor the treaty because they were not consulted. Harrison wanted no doubt that the Indians knew what land was being sold and that they had agreed to sell it.

Little Turtle had declined in influence, now that he was almost sixty and had such bad gout that he didn't get around much. Harrison sent his secretary, interpreter to Little Turtle's town to talk with Little Turtle's nephew, and heir apparent, Jean B. Richardville, or Pe-che-wa. This was the man who would honor any new treaty. But Jean Richardville was no fool, and knew selling the land was a mistake. He would later amass a fortune because of his business acuity. Jean Richardville would not come to the treaty session. He was sick, he said.

Delaware, Pottawattomie, and Eel River Miami camps sprang up at Fort Wayne, growing larger day by day. Harrison visited chiefs individually, outlining the lands he wished to buy. He gave them strong inducements to sell. While the negotiations went on, beef, bread, flour,and salt were given to the Indians. They were promised whisky and money when the treaty was signed.

Rebecca enjoyed the excitement of the gathered tribes. Nearly 1400 had come for the entertainment of the council meetings. She rode among the wigwams with Josiah in tow as body guard, stopping to watch dances or games. Once she took a meal with an Eel River Indian family after she was recognized as "Apeconyare", relative of Apeconit, her Uncle. The Indian women and she tried to talk with one another through sign language and random words, laughing at their ludicrous efforts.

Finally the tribes were all called together to begin deliberations. Ann and Rebecca sat on a blanket near William Wells who interpreted for some of the Indians. At these gatherings a number of interpreters were needed in different parts of the crowd to change English into the individual tribe's language. Out of the corner of her eye, Rebecca saw Nathon Heald standing somewhat near by, looking very much the guard, arms folded and mouth stern. She smiled a small smile to herself, then concentrated on the proceedings.

It appeared that the Delaware and Pottawattomie Indians were willing to sell the land, but the Miami, who claimed to be sole owners, refused. One branch of the Miamis, the Mississinewa Indians, wanted to know why anyone else was being consulted, as they were the owners. The day ended in impasse with nothing agreed.

Rebecca smiled at Captain Heald as she left the proceedings, being careful to appear very lady-like. Heald nodded, but made no other acknowledgement. William Wells returned home hours after the girls, having spent long hours talking with the Miamis about the land sale.

It was two days later that the Miami finally agreed to cede a strip twelve miles wide west of the Greenville treaty line and a strip west of Vincennes. They still were not happy with the agreement and would flock to The Prophet with their complaints. Harrison passed out their money and then left Fort Wayne to travel down the Wabash where the Wea and Kickapoo Indians would have to agree to the treaty. They would be told that it was to their benefit to leave their camp sites on the land sold on the lower Wabash to move higher up, near other branches of their tribes.

In Harrison's report to Secretary of War, Eustis, he said he had bought 2,600,000 acres of the finest land for less than a half cent per acre.

After Mary's delivery of a baby boy they named Samuel Geiger Wells, the Wells family returned to Louisville in December, 1809. The trip south was one of misery and regret for Rebecca. It was hard to believe that she'd had nine months to attract Captain Heald and failed completely. Her ego was shattered. The man may have had many faults, but the escaped quarry was always most prized. Louisville bachelors would never measure up to Captain Heald.

True to his word, Governor Harrison sent a neutral letter recommending Wells to a government position at Fort Wayne. In January Secretary Eustis appointed him the job of interpreter, a job that wouldn't involve the exchange or handling of government money.

April 1811

Cool fingers of April wind stroked Captain Heald's face as he rocked in the chair on his parent's wide porch in New Ipswich, New Hampshire. He watched sheep grazing in the open field, rocking, rocking, hoping that each cycle rocked might bring him peace of mind or an answer. He spent more and more of his time, alone, away from his parents, trying to sort out the meaning of his life and what he should do with the rest of it.

In October he'd left Fort Dearborn, the lonely outpost the Indians called Checagou, where he'd been transferred as the new commandant in 1810. Soon after that he'd demanded a leave to return home, East, for a visit. Otherwise he'd resign from the army, he'd said. The furlough had been granted and he'd returned with great joy to his childhood home. It had been wonderful, being back among the old familiar surroundings and relatives. Years had passed, since his last visit. Years of forests, savages, and hardship in which he'd pictured these people living a more desirable, more civilized life. But after being here a time, he'd become restless. He didn't belong here. His job was in the West, the commandant of a remote fort, day by day struggling with Indian problems and those of his soldiers. He'd learned a new truth. He might get discouraged and want to run away from the weight of his problems, but without them, he soon became bored.

Then there was Rebecca. He'd tried to forget the freckled face, red hair flying about in an untamed mass that he'd always wanted to smooth back. She was a wild thing. Spoiled by her father's wealth, she would think nothing of doing whatever she wanted, going ahead with her words or plans, embarrassing him without a second thought, if he gave her the chance. But as he rocked, the answers slowly came to him. He was no longer an Easterner. His home was out west, on the great frontier, with Rebecca.

Bridal wreath forsythia was in full bloom when Nathon Heald dismounted in front of the imposing brick house of Samuel Wells. A slave boy took his horse and he climbed the steps to the porch, to knock on the fine front door. "I came to see Miss Rebecca Wells," Heald said to the maid who gave him a full appraisal before leaving to fetch her mistress.

In Rebecca's upstairs bedroom she reported, "They's a 'stinguished genmun askin' for Miss Becca."

Rebecca was busy repairing a torn hem and asked curiously, "Didn't you know who it was Cicely?"

"No Maam. But he surely is a good lookin' one. All dressed up in travelin' clothes. Got blond hair, he do."

Rebecca started. Dropping the mending, she jumped to her feet, to run, sweeping halfway down the curving open stairway where her hopes were fulfilled. It was Captain Heald who stood below in the wide hall looking up at her. In his eyes was the queston she'd waited so long for him to ask. She flew down the stairs to circle him with her arms.

Chapter XX

Fort Dearborn, (Chicago) August 14, 1812

Ocean blue sky reflected the color of Lake Michigan showing the small group of Miamis that their wild gallop across the plains of northern Indiana was almost at an end. Soon the lake itself rose on the horizon, preceded by sand dunes topped with tufts of beach grasses and oak trees. Their horses passed over the trail through marsh leading to Fort Dearborn, the place Indians called Checagou. So far they'd seen no smoke in that direction. Perhaps they were in time before the Indian attacks Wells knew were imminent.

Only a month before, the American fort at Mackinac was defeated by a group of 140 warriors led by a British officer. News of its defeat flew on winged Indian moccasins to all parts of the Indian Nations. It seemed the Prophet and his brother, Tecumseh, had been right. The time was at hand for the Indians to take back their lands from the white men, and they were being led by the British standard.

Fort Dearborn's situation was tense after the murder of two men at a farm three miles south of it in April. Then settlers in the surrounding houses had flown to the fort. During the summer several hundred Pottawattomie warriors and their families had been congregating nearby. America declared war against England in July after Mackinac's fall. Now, in early August, General Hull, head of the Northwest's defense stationed at Detroit, sent word to Captain Heald at Fort Dearborn that he was to evacuate the fort before Indian attack.

Hull then sent a message to Fort Wayne for an escort to go to Fort Dearborn to help protect the families of the soldiers there, as they evacuated the fort. There were only a small number of able bodied soldiers at Dearborn, far fewer than the Indians that seemed poised for attack. Wells offered to take a party of Miami warriors to Checagou. He had a very important personal reason for going. His favorite niece, Rebecca was there.

After marrying Captain Heald in May of 1811, the couple was stationed at Fort Dearborn. Knowing that the Prophet and Tecumseh had inflamed the Indians to all out war, Wells knew the only possibility of getting Rebecca out alive was for him and his friends to go to her rescue.

As the fort hove into view Wells leaned forward in the saddle surveying the possible approaches the Indians could make in attack. He could see the fort was built in such a way that it was protected. To the south and west, the ground was cleared for gardens and hay fields. The East was protected by the river and lake, while a prickly forest west and north were cleared for a quarter of a mile for defense.

Built in 1803 it was said to be the neatest and best built fort in the country. Set in a bend of the Illinois River, it was surrounded on two and a half sides by it. Built on a slight elevation two blockhouses stood at the northwestern and southeastern corners of a quadrangle, the whole enclosed within a double line of palisades. A covered passageway led the eighty feet to the river so that the fort might have water in a state of seige.

A considerable number of houses and outbuildings dotted the plain adjoining the fort. These housed an Indian interpreter, government storekeeper, and several civilians, notably half breeds and traders. As the horses rode up to the unmolested fort, Wells decided that if he could prevent the army from evacuating as they'd been ordered, the structure could survive an Indian attack.

Captain Heald hurried to greet the group that included thirty Miami warriors and a Corporal Jordan of Fort Wayne. "William, you are a savior in our time of need! I certainly didn't expect to see anyone come to escort us back to Fort Wayne."

"I thought it best. You know the United States declared war on the British?"

"Yes, a runner brought the news and then the word from Hull that we are to evacuate the fort. Since we got the letter we've been getting things ready to leave. Hull said to give all the extra goods to the Indians and destroy our extra ammunition and arms."

Wells reflected on it a few minutes. "Course he don't want it ta fall into Indian hands. But, if I was you, I wouldn't leave this place now. With the Indians gettin' ready for war all through the country, you'll never make it back to Fort Wayne, even with my friends and me here ta help. What are the actions of the Indians here?"

Heald said somewhat defensively, "I can't tell that they're any different than usual, though there were some threats after we dumped the extra liquor in the river last night. Our interpreter was killed and I've done without since then. Course the trader Kinzie understands them and he says we shouldn't leave. But, he just doesn't want to lose his trade. And being French, he doesn't fear for his neck. He's lived in these parts so long that he's got plenty of Indian friends."

"When are ya plannin' ta leave?"

"In the morning."

"Damn it man. It's suicide! You'd best stay here where you got a good fort between you and the Indians. Now that they took Fort Mackinac their blood lust is up. The whole frontier is ready to go up in flames."

Heald reflected, "Things aren't getting any better. All summer more and more warriors have been gathering here. The longer we stay on the more there'll be. No, we might as well leave now. Besides, I gave out the goods to the Indians already. I asked them to accompany us to Fort Wayne and I'd give them a reward for it."

"Heald, you can't trust these Indians. They been waitin' for years to take back their lands. If you wait in the fort, there may be soldiers from Detroit come to support you."

Heald's jaw hardened into a firm line. "We can't. The extra arms were destroyed last night."

Wells looked at his relative for a few moments knowing there was nothing to do now but take their chances leaving the fort. Turning away from his fears he changed the subject. "Say, where you hidin' my favorite niece? You been takin' good care of her ain't you? If you ain't I'd have ta take off your skin piece by piece like my Indian inlaws taught me."

Heald smiled. "I always knew you would, so I tend her real careful. Come on and I'll get her." The two tall men, one in buckskins and the other in army uniform, walked toward the section of the fort in which the Healds lived. Their cabin was in total disarray. Cicely, Rebecca's slave girl, held her baby in one hand while she stirred a pot of stew hanging in the fireplace. Rebecca's back was to the door as she bent over an open trunk, packing their things for tomorrow's trip. Her face lit when she heard the two at the door. Just as in the days of her childhood when not an old married woman of twenty-four she squealed, "Uncle William." Jumping forward she gave her uncle, who was so like herself, a hug. The two stood apart looking with great affection and satisfaction at each other. Their red hair and fair skin, deeply freckled in the summer season could have marked them father and daughter.

"Let's see if bein' an old married woman's give you any wrinkles." Wells, at forty-two,could get away with a bit of foolery and he carefully inspected her face. "Don't see none. Guess your husband won't have ta be skinned after all."

"Oh, Uncle William, you're always so.....savage. Ya'll come sit down here and tell me the news. Cicely, get him a bowl of that stew and some cornbread. Now, Uncle William, how many new babies have you got?"

William with a straight face pretended to consider the matter seriously. "The three girls are back home on the farm at Fort Wayne with Mary. I sent William Wayne, back down ta Sam ta go ta school. He's twelve now and quite a handful for Mary. He never did take ta me marryin' a white woman after his maw died. Sam says he's done real well in school and if he keeps up, he'll soon be ready for West Point Military Academy."

"I meant the babies. Mary's babies."

"Oh. Well, let's see." William held up his hand to count them off. "There's little Sam. Gettin' ta be a real cute bugger and he's startin' to talk now. Then our little girl, Julianna, never made it through her first winter." Wells thought about the past year and it's many illnesses suffered by all of those at Fort Wayne. "Mayhap the next one will be a girl."

"You don't mean Mary's expectin' again? Uncle William, you rascal! You only been married three years. I swan. Saints preserve us poor innocent women." Rebecca rolled her eyes to the ceiling.

Wells laughed at her protestations and then said, "We got another one in the oven and that's a fact. How come you ain't got a youngun? Bein' married for a year with no baby is downright scandalous for a member of the Wells family."

Rebecca quieted, looking toward the fire. "I had one in April. My baby boy died 'cause there was no good midwives ta help."

William frowned in concern. "Why, you'll have lots more yet, enough ta keep you in a continuous torment." Remembering where they were he added, "If we can get away from here alive, that is."

Earlier in the day, Heald had held another council with the Indians. His soldiers refused to join it and instead trained a cannon on the participating Indians who complained loudly that the whiskey and ammunition had been wasted in the river. Now Black Partridge, a friendly chief of the Illinois River Pottawattomie, came to Heald wishing a private talk.

Black Partridge was a tall, handsome Indian, intelligent and older than most of the braves. He had long been a friend of the white men, but the daily runners bringing messages of Indian victories against the Americans had outweighed his arguments for peace and friendship with the white men. Now they had voted to attack the troops as they left the fort and nothing he said could stop them.

"Long have we been friends Heald," He opened, "But now, linden birds have been singing in my ears. The whites must be careful on the march. Perhaps it would be wise not to go."

"I thank you for the information," Answered Heald. "But we have prepared to leave the fort. I would be honored if your tribe would provide a safe escort for the caravan as we go."

"I cannot promise anything, but perhaps the people will escort you." Black Partridge lifted his arms to his neck removing the necklace given to him long ago by the Americans. It was a medal with the picture of the President of the United States embossed on it, strung on a leather thong. "Because the young warriors are bent on mischief and I can no longer stop them, I give you back this token." Sadly the Indian looked into Heald's eyes, hoping he really understood. Then, he turned to leave.

Heald raised his hand to say hesitantly to the Indian's back, "Go in peace." Black Partridge, not looking back, continued down the path.

August 15, 1812 was to be a hot and cloudless day. Ninety-six people rose early to ready themselves for the trip. Blankets were hurridly folded into saddle bags. Babies and children were dressed and fed, fires doused, and horses saddled so that all could be in the procession line by nine o'clock. Perhaps they would pass several miles before the day became unbearably hot. Two baggage wagons were provided and into one all children not of walking age were loaded. A number of women rode in the other.

Scouting ahead of the group rode William Wells and fifteen or so of his Miamis. They were expecting a fight. Wells had taken black gunpowder, smearing his face with it until it was black, the traditional Miami garb for a battle that might include death. The rest of his dress was that of a white man, even to the hair tied by a ribbon trailing down his back.

Behind the scouts rode fifty-five regular troops, and then the twelve militia that protected the wagons of baggage, women and children. After these rode the remainder of the Miamis. Rebecca and her friend, the young Mrs. Helm, rode on horses beside their husbands. As the little procession started ahead a drummer beat time for the picollo player who played the somber music, The Dead March. This was done to irritate Captain Heald. The soldiers still didn't think they should leave the fort.

As they made their way south along the river until it met the lake a small number of Pottawattomi joined them on the landward side, but the large number of Indians that were promised for safe escort were nowhere to be seen. A row of sandhills or ridges ran parallel to the beach about a hundred yards from the waters edge. Silently the Pottawattomi escort disappeared behind the ridges.

The main procession was about a mile and a half from the fort. Wells and his Miamis were well ahead when they saw the feathered head-dresses of many Indians all in a row behind the sandridge, ready for attack. Wells brought the horse to a halt and it reared in surprise. Gazing ahead he saw a group of ridges that might be successfully defended if the soldiers could make it to the spot. Wheeling his horse, he kicked it in the side, galloping back toward the soliders, twirling his hat, the sign meaning "we are surrounded." Now all along the line of sand ridges the heads of the waiting Indians could be seen. War whoops filled the air as they began firing on the men with their muskets. "Charge!" Captain Heald commanded. The Militia galloped ahead toward the low hills, firing as they went. Indians in front gave way, letting them pass. Several soldiers were shot from their horses as the group made its way to the hills. As they gained a place they could defend the Indian horde surrounded them a force of nearly five hundred, pouring in a constant fire upon the trapped men.

Left behind were the stranded wagons, abandoned to the attacking Indians. The twelve men of the militia guarding them, fired their guns at the crowd of Indians surrounding them, desperately slashing with bayonets and musket-butt, but they were quickly cut down. A young brave cutting past them gained the wagon filled with children. With his tomahawk he slashed left and right at the screaming children until all but one were killed. Cicely, Rebecca's slave, and her infant lay covered with the mingled blood of the children, silent in death below the grimacing Indian.

In the other wagon Indians were trying to take the women captive. One woman who had always said she'd never be taken captive fought desperately. Finally the Indians decided she wasn't worth the effort. Her skull was split by a tomahawk.

Wells who had been fighting with the soldiers looked back and saw the desperate battle taking place at the wagons. Racing his horse in their direction in a last hope of saving them, he spied the youth in the children's wagon, killing them all single handedly. "So that's your game," Wells shrieked in Pottawattomie. "I can kill squaws too." He turned the horse galloping toward the Pottawattomie camps along the lake. A fusillade of Indian bullets ripped into the horse. Wells took a bullet in the lungs. The horse went down, pinning Wells' leg beneath it. As the Indians leaped toward him he shot several before the pistol ran out of bullets. Rebecca rode dazedly toward him blood running down her arms from several wounds. She looked in shock at her uncle and he gasped, "Tell my wife I fell defending my people."

Just then an Indian approached, aiming his gun at Wells who lay in agony on the ground pinned by the horse. He motioned for the Indian to go ahead and shoot. The sound of the gun and Rebecca shrieking wildly were insignificant noises amidst the din of the battle. The Pottawattomie knelt beside Wells, slitting the cloth and skin covering the still pumping heart. Ripping the organ from the body, he ate the dripping heart of William Wells. In so doing he paid him his highest tribute. He meant to gain the courage of William Wells by this act.

Rebecca's friend, Mrs. Helm, daughter of the trader Kinzie, was in the rear of the procession preparing her mind for death. The "protecting" Miamis had disappeared at the first sounds of battle. Now she was alone, a watcher of the terrible fight. A Pottawattomi approached her, knife uprised to take her scalp. Grabbing his arm, she wrestled for her life, staving him off, but her strength was swiftly ebbing away. Just as she thought the end was at hand, a larger Indian swooped her off her horse, carrying her kicking and thrashing to the lake. Wading in up to his waist, he pushed her down, holding her so that only her nose was above water. Calming a little, she raised her eyes and saw the face of chief Black Partridge above her, smiling slightly to himself. This was his way of saving her life. When the battle around the wagons was finished, he took her to the fort.

Rebecca Wells Heald, still sitting in shock on her horse, was wounded in six places. An Indian chief claimed her as his and conducted her back to the camps. As they rode in, a squaw saw the saddle blanket on Rebecca's horse. She wanted it. Running up she tugged away, trying to get it out from under the saddle, while Rebecca was still in it. Coming to herself, Rebecca's red hair flashed as she lashed savagely with her horsewhip at the woman, gritting her teeth at the pain from her wounds. The woman shieked an oath and retreated.

Her captor laughed, delighted. "Apeconyare, brave woman," he said, recognizing she was like her uncle, Apeconit

The two dismounted, whereupon a French Indian halfbreed trader, named Chandonnai saw the niece of William Wells and decided he would rescue her. Sidling up to the chief he said, "What do you want to trade for this yere squaw?"

"I keep her. No trade."

"Hell, she'll probably die on ya. Look there and there." He poked at her wounds. "I'll give ya a mule for her, and he ain't got no holes in 'im like this one." The trader snorted.

The chief frowned. "You got whisky?"

"Yes, I'll throw in a bottle of that with the mule." The exchange was made and Rebecca followed her new owner away to his cabin where she was temporarily safe.

The soldiers that still lived had reached an elevation in the dunes where they were out of range of Indian muskets. There was a lull, as the Indians weren't eager to risk their lives by rushing them. Captain Heald looked around the little group to see what their losses had been. In the distance he saw that all the militia around the wagons were dead, including his wife's uncle, Wells. The remaining women and children were being led away by Indians to the Pottawattomie village farther down the beach.

After taking a head count of his men he said to Captian Helm, "There's only twenty-nine of us left, out of fifty-five."

Helm answered, "Five are wounded so bad they won't be fit for fightin', and they're just the worst ones."

"How many do you expect is out there?"

The silence after the battle was almost audible with the only sound being the waves breaking on the beach in the distance. "Oh, I recon 'bout five hundred or so. You know we ain't got ammunition to take out that many. They'll jest pick us off one by one or wait until dark to rush us."

Heald reflected while looking at the innocent blue sky, "We never had a chance."

There was some action now below their perch. Heald asked, "Who is that?" A man was advancing toward them, unarmed calling out, "Hello, come down and parley."

Helm said, "It's the half-breed Pottawattomie that worked for the trader Kinzie."

"What do you think of it? 'Spose it's a trap?"

"Well sir, I don't see as how it makes a difference. Might as well go down and see what they have ta say."

Heald slowly rose from behind cover to walk haltingly because of his wounds, down the hot sand toward the French, Indian breed. The Pottawattomie chief, Black Bird, came forward to speak for the Indians. The three stood in a slight valley of sand between the forces as they talked.

Black Bird opened, "You surrender and we give you your lives."

"How can I be sure you won't kill us soon as we're out of cover?"

The hostile chief's eyes glinted and he said, "You cannot be sure. But we will keep the men for trade and as slaves. At least you will live. If you do not, we will kill all." He made a slashing movement with his hand.

Heald hated being at the mercy of this dirty stinking heathen before him. "I'll have to talk to the others; see what they say." He returned up the dune to the men.

"What are the terms?" Asked Helm.

"He says we can live if we surrender." Speaking louder to the others he said, "Men, they say if we surrender they'll let us live."

"That's a damn lie!" Spat out one of the men. "I say we stay here and kill 'em as they come at us. Then at least we'll have gone down as men 'stead of under some squaws scalpin' knife."

One of the others said, "I'm for surrender."

Heald said, "How many are for surrender and how many against it?" Most of the men were in favor of surrender as it offered some chance of life, whereas if they remained where they were, they'd certainly die.

Heald returned to the waiting Black Bird with his answer. "We will surrender on your promise that the men will live. Also, I will pay a hundred dollars for every living captive."

Black Bird smiled evilly. "It is agreed." Turning, he gave an ear shattering whoop, signaling his men. The heads of hundreds of warriors appeared, noisily whooping, ready to take their captives.

Wounded soldiers slowly came down off the sandhill to be immediately surrounded by the Indians. Those in serious condition leaned on their fellows as the processession passed down the beach. Indians grabbed their horses. All their clothing except for a shirt and breeches was stripped away. The hot beach seemed unsuitable for the horrors that had taken place. They passed the wagons, so recently filled with their families, guarded by friends. Now the white sands were red with blood. Men looked in mute horror at the naked bodies of men, women and children, almost all of whom were headless. A cry escaped Captain Helm's throat as he saw the headless body of a woman that he thought was his wife. Tears started down his cheeks. At that moment he wished to God he hadn't given in to these terrible savages, but had killed them, as many as he could, until he was killed himself.

The Indians motioned the soldiers to get in a circle. Sweat formed in little beads on Helm's forehead in fear of what this could mean. But the Indians only argued among themselves deciding who should have which men for captives. Finally, all were taken by one or another and led off to their camps. As Helm's group approached the fort, he was amazed to see his wife sitting among several squaws, crying. When she saw him, she tryed to get up to go to him, but the squaws yanked her down where she sat. He could see she was in a state of shock, but he could do nothing. Several yards away was the body of one of the militia. Mrs. Helm nodded toward the dead man saying dully, "An old squaw ran him through with a pitchfork."

Helm stared dumbstruck at the man, so brutally murdered after being terribly wounded in the battle, and had a premonition that few, if any, of the survivers would live. He was wounded slightly himself. Would he share the fate of that soldier? Then his owner, Mittatass, jerked him back to the present, leading him toward a village on the Illinois River.

Meanwhile, Black Partridge took Mrs. Helm, the daughter of Kinzie the trader, to Kinzie's cabin for safety. A few days later she was taken to St. Joseph and ultimately onward to Detroit with the Kinzie family. Mrs. Kinzie also interceded for Mr. Helm, convincing Mittatass to trade him to a trader for two mares and a keg of liquor "when practicable." Helm and his wife would be reunited in the Spring after both threaded their way back east.

Rebecca in the quiet of Chandonnai's cabin listened to the screams of soldiers as they were tortured by the Indians. She asked, "Did you see my husband, or was he killed?"

"Don't worry little missy. I seen him. The squaws is jest killin' those fellers who is wounded too bad ta travel."

Now she knew he was alive, she became feverously nervous that the Indians would torture and kill him too. "I'll give you anything if you'll find him and bring him here. My family is rich and would pay money for our return."

The trader looked at her thinking of all the possibilities her offer could mean. His eyes worked their way over her body, then turned away. She was wounded too severely for any of that, he decided. Saying nothing he turned away.

"Please, think of the money you could have if you returned us to our people. I'd give you more than you'd make in a whole year of trappin'."

The man turned back, considering it. "When they've cooled down some I'll go and see what I can find out."

Later, true to his word he went among the several Indian camps to seek out the captive, Heald. Finally he found him lying unattended. He had two rather serious wounds and wasn't a threat to the Indians. Chardonnai said quietly, "Mr. Heald, sir, jest get up quiet like and follow me."

Heald looked around and seeing no-one was watching got up to follow Chandonnai. A squaw ran up saying, "No go. You no take!"

Chandonnai answered, "Fool. This man is a relative of Apeconit. Ain't it enough that you done kilt one of our own kind? Now this man is his kin, and I'm takin' him." He turned and walked determinedly away. The squaw watched in indecision and then let them go.

The next morning Chandonnai loaded a canoe with the wounded couple setting out for St. Joseph, some ninety miles around the bottom edge of the lake. A number of Indians escorted him, as they intended to attack Fort Wayne to the South. The Fort Wayne trail met the Chicago trail at St. Joseph, so it was convenient for them to go along with the group.

When they were out some distance on the lake, Rebecca looked back and saw smoke rising from the fort. In the distance Indians could be seen leaving with their horses, their families, and their captives, to return to their villages. The mutilated bodies remained on the beach for the gulls and wolves. In a few years white men would return, and be awed by the number of bones left, testimony of the slaughter.

Hour after hour the canoe passed through the water. Gulls wheeled overhead calling their mournful cry, matching the moaning Rebecca and her husband did occasionally. Their wounds were severe. To take her mind off her pain Rebecca looked at the scenery. The beach along which they traveled was a desolate beauty of unspoiled sand, flanked by high dunes. Today the water was relatively still, only small waves constantly, timelessly, lapping the shores.

Later Rebecca began to think she wouldn't be able to stand it any longer in the canoe. If only she could stand up, just for a moment. She spent fifteen minutes contemplating the luxury of moving about. Then, miraculously, on shore a young doe stopped to drink Lake Michigan's water. A shot from one of the other canoes felled the animal, and all the canoes turned toward the beach. The Indians pitched a camp for the night while others dressed the deer. Then, they signed for Rebecca to come make some bread. She poured a mixture of flour and water onto the deer skin, and began kneeding the dough. Finally, she wound it around sticks that would be placed over the fire to cook. At length she took some of the bread and deer meat to her husband who lay somewhat away from the others.

"Try some of this mess I made. It's 'sposed to be bread."

Captain Heald was very weak but also very hungry. Crunching into the hard brown exterior he said, "Honey, that's the best bread I ever ate. I was beginin' to think I'd never eat again."

"You've still got your underwear on, don't you?"

"Yes. I think we'll be needing what's sewn into it before long. It's lucky for us you sewed the money in them, because the Indians took my other clothes I was wearing. We'd be left without a cent."

"You're not plannin' on hirin' the Indians to take us to Fort Wayne are you? I've been listenin' to them on the sly and it looks like they're goin' to do Fort Wayne the same as they did Dearborn."

"No, I think if we went North, we'd be safe with the British. Eventually they'd trade us back to the States, like they do most captives. We'd be a lot safer there than with the Indians in the mood they're in." The couple looked over toward their captors who did not seem hostile in the least, now that they were away from the others. But the Indians looked forward to another battle and its plunder at Fort Wayne. For the time being they were almost cordial to their captives.

The next day they arrived at St. Joseph where they stayed with William Burnett, the local trader. An Indian doctor was called to treat their wounds. Here they were surprised to find Sergeant Griffith, another survivor from Fort Dearborn, brought for trade to St. Joseph.

After the Indians bought supplies they left on foot down the trail south to Fort Wayne. They would join others in the attack there. This gave the Healds a chance to escape. In the village a half-breed Pottawattomie named Alexander Robinson, had a good bark canoe. He agreed to paddle the three to Mackinac for one hundred dollars. His strong squaw would help. The deal was closed, and the Healds, Sergeant Griffith and the Indian couple continued up the side of Lake Michigan on a trip that took sixteen days.

Fort Mackinac lay far north at the junction of the great lakes, Michigan and Huron. it had returned to British hands in July, when taken by Indians led by a British Captain. Now, British Captain Roberts found he did not enjoy this lonely outpost of which he was newly in charge. He could scarcely believe his luck when a beautiful young redhead and her husband appeared at his door.

"Captain Heald, United States Army, delivering myself to your hands." Heald saluted tiredly. "I'd give you my sword but the Indians got that when they took my post, Fort Dearborn."

Roberts rushed forward with chairs for the pair. "That's not at all necessary, I'm sure." Somehow the sight of the young couple, so worn and with such grievous wounds, made him feel personally guilty, responsible for their condition. "Please, let me put you folks up in my quarters here until you can recover yourselves." He looked apologetically around. "You can see it's not much, but whatever I can do for you, I will. Are you all that's left of the Dearborn Fort?"

Rebecca said dejectedly, "We and Sergeant Griffith were all that come away together. But there were about forty that survived the attack. The others are captives. Probably dead now."

"Forty? Well, how many was there to begin with?"

"Roun' ninety-five. We hadn't left the fort more than twenty minutes when half the people was kilt. It was such a terrible bloody fight. The Indians hackin' everyone up." Rebecca's face crumpled and she began crying with great heaving sobs. Heald was startled. He'd never seen Rebecca cry before and now her sobs continued on and on. Nothing either man could say or do would stop her. The two men left the room, leaving her to herself while she cried about her uncle's death, her scarring wounds, and her friend Mrs. Helm, who she didn't know was still alive. She cried for an hour before she finally was able to stop. All their hardships poured out in a flood of tears.

The men miserably passed their time in small talk as Rebecca sobbed on the other side of the door. "I could parole you and send you down to Detroit. You knew we British recaptured it, same day as Fort Dearborn was attacked?"

"We heard that at St. Joseph." Heald said wryly. "It's amazing the speed at which the Indians carry news. The Indians that captured us went to attack Fort Wayne, but once they get back ta St. Joseph and see we left, they may light out after us. Won't be hard for them ta guess where we went. Fact is, I was surprised we made it up here without gettin' our hair lifted. Would you protect us if they came to take us back as their captives?"

"I'm not sure I could do that. The garrison we have here is so small. But I would try. Probably the best thing to do if you expect them to follow is to go down to Detroit. There is a man here who owns a sailboat.

You wouldn't be out in the elements like you were on the long trip up Lake Michigan. Matter of fact, I'll lend you folks the money to hire the boat."

"Thanks all the same, but we got away with a little money. We'll leave for Detroit just as soon as we can get rested. We appreciate all that you've done too and I'll certainly tell my superiors what kindness you've shown us."

A few days later the couple began the long trip down the west side of Lake Huron reaching Detroit September 22. The British officer in charge, General Procter, arranged passage to Buffalo, New York across Lake Erie on a sea going ship, Old Brigg Adams. This ship had been American held until Detroit fell to the British August 15. From Buffalo the travelers went to Erie, Pennsylvania and finally south to Pittsburgh where they remained at Fort Pitt for two weeks recuperating. During this time Heald wrote a report of the capture of Fort Dearborn. Finally, on November 8 they started down the Ohio to return to Louisville, Kentucky, Samuel Wells' house. They reached Rebecca's childhood home eleven days later, three months and two thousand miles after leaving Checagou.

Louisville, Kentucky, November 20, 1812

Rebecca's grin stretched from ear to ear as the carriage pulled up in front of Samuel Well s'brick house south of Louisville. The fact that her feet actually stood on this ground once again was almost beyond belief. She had traveled such a long way, and endured so much. Not even waiting for her husband, she jumped down from the carriage and ran up the steps into the house. "Mama! Where are you Mama?"

Mary came hesitantly to the front hall, then surprise and shock filled her face. The thin girl before her, dressed in a ragged torn dress and cape was her daughter. Mary rushed forward, enfolding her Rebecca in her arms, holding on with all her strength because she'd thought she was dead. "Oh Becca, when we got your things, and were told you and William were dead, we thought we'd never see you again. How did you happen to be so mercifully delivered?"

"I'll tell you the whole story after a bit. We've traveled thousands of miles to get here since we couldn't get through Indian country to the north. But we have to help Nathon inside." Heald, with the help of his cane, was managing to bring himself in. His wounds still gave him much trouble, as they would for the rest of his life. Sam was called in from his chores and told the joyful news. They were still alive! When all had settled down on living room chairs the family continued to catch up on all that had happened since the Fort Dearborn massacre.

Rebecca asked, "You said you got some of our things from Fort Dearborn. How'd you do that?"

Mary went to the sideboard and brought out a packet of items. "Our old friend, Colonel O'Fallon, recognized these things as yours. They were brought down the Illinois River by the Indians and sold to a trader out at St. Louis. He took the things to the fort there and Colonel O'Fallon saw them. He was so good to send them to us, as remembrances of you and William. They said you were all dead." Mary heaved a sigh at the pain and tears this news had brought.

Rebecca picked up the comb, ring and brooch and the sword belonging to her husband. "I still can't believe we're actually here, safe. I had six different wounds, mostly on my arms." She showed her parents her arms that were almost healed. "And then we were so lucky that a man named Chardonnai helped us get away. So many others died or stayed as Indian captives. And to think I really loved it there along the lake. So peaceful it seemed. Now I could never go back, even if there was peace. The sight of it would make me remember Uncle William....and the terrible way he died." They were all silent thinking about it.

After a few moments Mary said, "You must go to William's wife, dear, and tell her of his last moments."

Nathon Heald asked, "Is she safe here in Louisville? We heard at Cincinnati that Fort Wayne had been attacked by Indians and how Governor Harrison rescued the fort with his army, but there was no word of Mary Wells, or the girls."

Sam Wells took up the story. "Mary and William's daughters just arrived in Louisville recently themselves. After the Indians attacked Fort Dearborn, they congregated around Fort Wayne, layin' plans as ta how they'd take it. Took 'em a week to finally work themselves up to lay attack. That was September 5. Well, they laid seige ta the place for over a week. Then they heard that Harrison and us was comin' with a massive army and they all skeedadled. By the time we got there, we took the fort back without a fight. Course we burned up a number of Indian towns 'round about the place after that. Now the Indians are still killin' settlers here an' there, ever' chance they get."

Rebecca's eyes were sparkling with the tale of danger. "Was Mary in the fort when they were attacked?"

"Yes, she went to the fort, but then a friendly Shawnee Indian, name of Logan, took a bunch of civilians over to Piqua, Ohio, to John Johnston's farm. Mary and the girls was along. You remember Johnston, the fellow that William always was at odds with? The one who took his place as Indian agent. Anyhow, Mary come on down ta Cincinnati, and over to Louisville. I don't expect she'll go back, now that William is dead and their place burned. Then too, she has a new baby...a boy she named Yelverton, after my brother."

Rebecca looked down at the floor, at the mention of her uncle's death. She had loved him so much. He'd always been her hero, and now it seemed impossible that he was gone. But she'd seen his death with her own eyes. He had died as he'd lived, in vigorous, exciting action. "When peace comes the girls will go back to Fort Wayne to live with their Grandpa, Little Turtle, I expect."

Sam rubbed his face thinking on it. "No, Little Turtle died there on William's farm in the orchard. July it was. He had a bad case of gout Mary said, and had been poorly for some years. The Indians didn't pay him much attention toward the end. I suppose that weighed hard on him too. Mary said the military give him a hero's funeral."

Rebecca continued, "But think of William's farms. I'm sure the girls will go back to claim them when the Indian's settle down. After all, they're half Indian themselves. They belong at Kekionga."

"True enough," answered Sam. "But I'm keepin' William Wayne for myself. Never did a creditable job of raisin' William when he was a boy. Now, I've got the chance to redeem myself by doin' a good job with his son. After West Point, he'll be a military man and maybe have the honors denied his father."

Rebecca looked at her father's set face and said nothing.

Sam then asked, "Heald, what you plannin' ta do, now that your command was burned up, so ta speak?"

Heald was not amused. He was well aware that his career in the militry was over after the terrible slaughter at Fort Dearborn that many said was his fault. Then too, his wounds were such that he could no longer be an able bodied soldier. "I had thought of startin' a little farm here near Louisville. But if Rebecca gets the wanderlust, as she's been known to do, we may move out near St. Louis. Heard there's good land to be had there."

"You'll want to get in better shape afore you start out for the wilderness again. Stay this winter with us and look over the possibilities around here." Sam continued, "I wouldn't mind seein' what its like out west for myself." He looked around the room at the other members of the Wells family. He'd fought in many battles against the Indians. His father and brother had fallen in battles against them. Now his daughter and her husband wore fearful scars from a brush with the savages. Sam had nine children. Would his family continue to be in violent conflict with the red men? It was their way of life. If life got boring, there had always been a battle to liven it up. The excitement of conflict was in his blood, and he would seek it for the rest of his life. The only thing that could change this would be if the Indians died out, gave up, or moved away, out west.

Sam mused, "I'll be gettin' a chance to take revenge for what the Indians done to you. The Kentucky Militia will join Harrison in the spring to take back what's ours from the British. An' believe me, when I see Indians I'll be shootin' ta kill." His eyes glittered as he thought of what the Indians had done to his daughter and brother.

Rebecca studied her father and thought of herself as an extension of her slaughtered uncle. Slowly she formed the words. "I'm not sayin' you shouldn't fight the British. They've been behind Indian attacks for years. But to say you're goin' ta kill Indians, is like sayin' you'd kill Uncle William. I truly believe he was Indian in his heart. When you and the Kentucky Militia joined Harrison against Tecumseh at Tippecanoe, you were partly to blame for what happened at Fort Dearborn. The Indians talked of nothing else the whole summer before we were attacked."

Sam stared into the burning embers in the fireplace. She was right of course, but there was nothing he could do about what had taken place. Though he'd always spoken for peace with the Indians, he'd always joined or led fighting against them. Now with William and Little Turtle dead, there was no alternative other than military force to bring peace. They'd have to clear the British from the American forts so the Indians would have no backing to fight for the land again.

Chapter XXI

Battle of the Mississinewa, December 17-18, 1812

The recent deep snow was a welcome thing. It covered the clustered wigwams and cabins of the Ottawa village in a mantle of safety. Maconaquah smiled thinking that she could relax a little now. Perhaps her work of packing up food and goods would not be needed after all.

Outside the rude cabin, Maconaquah's two sons played Fox and Geese with other children in the snow. They were still adolescents. Maconaquah's fervent prayer was that Shepancanah would not allow them to fight the Americans. Shepancanah was deaf as a stone post now. An old man of sixty-two, he had not joined in any battles during this war of 1812. At the Council on the Mississinewa in May, the Indians at Mississineway had decided not to join Tecumseh. It had been a wise choice. Harrison's troops had put them to flight when he attacked Tecumseh's encampment near Ouiatenon. Then, when other Indians beseiged Fort Wayne, the Mississinewa Indians had stayed away. They kept a low profile and so far the tactic had protected them.

Maconaquah and Shepancanah settled in the Ottawa village on the Mississinewa River in 1810. There were too many white men coming to Fort Wayne. Maconaquah, as always, feared her identity as a white woman might be detected. Also, more and more Indians there drank too much whisky. It was a dangerous place to live. With their three young children they had moved to a quieter place, an Ottawa village near the town Mississinewa, where the Mississinewa River joined the Wabash. So far, it had been the ideal spot to live. White men did not appear to know much about this land and did not come to distroy these towns.

All this fall of 1812 the Americans had made forays against Indian villages. Many towns north of Fort Wayne had been leveled by Harrison's troops. But the Indians expected this. They knew the laws of revenge.

After the Indians had surrounded Fort Wayne in September, Harrison's thousands came from Cincinnati to reclaim it. The Indians fled. Harrison's troops were too many to fight. Knowing their towns would be put to the torch, they deserted their villages near Kekionga. Many warriors had gone to Detroit to join Tecumseh to fight the Americans. As expected Harrison's men, under the leadership of Samuel Wells, had burned many Indian towns including Little Turtle's town on the Eel, leaving the house built especially for Little Turtle by the government, standing; a monument to his cooperation with the United States Government.

The tribes settled along the Mississinewa River watched the carnage of northern Indian towns in dred. Finally they decided peace overtures might save them. Shepancanah, Deaf Man, was among the chiefs that went to Fort Wayne, September 23, offering good will. But the white soldiers still feared the Indians. In mid October the Americans made a foray against Eel River Indian towns. So far, towns along the Mississinewa had been spared. Indians from other places came in droves as it appeared to be a haven of safety.

In November an army advanced in western Indiana from Fort Harrison up the Wabash River burning Tecumseh's rebuilt town and two other villages. Now, December 17,1812, the large American army had left Fort Wayne. They had gone to fight the British in the forts at Detroit. The Indians at Mississinewa felt that they were in a haven of quiet, like the eye of the hurricane, as desolation of Indian villages took place all around them.

Now the snows of winter had come. Americans were surely not so foolish as to come against them now, when no grass for their horses or food for their stomachs would be available. Maconaquah set Cut Finger to work on the pile of furs Shepancanah and the boys had trapped during fall hunt. Every day they scrapped the inner surfaces, getting them ready to trade, when the frontier had quieted enough for the return of traders seeking their furs.

Shepancanah lay on the couch near the fire smoking as the women worked. He smiled to himself as he looked at the furs, satisfied. He might be growing older, but he could still gather more furs than the young men. His squaw had a bag hidden under the dirt floor, filled with coins and silver showing the success he had been over the years. Their home had more goods than most other Indians, but they were careful not to show their wealth in an extreme way. It would be unwise to make other Indians jealous.

Maconaquah sat back on her heals, resting a minute from her exertions. She said loudly to her husband, so he could hear, "Now that it is winter, white men will stay by their fires and we will be safe."

Shepancanah took his time before answering. "Don't think they will not come again. When the white man buries the hatchet, he always leaves the handle sticking out."

Maconaquah shook her head. "If they come, you are too old to meet them in battle. And the boys are too young."

Shepancanah gave her a reproving look, calmly tamping down a new load of Kinnikinnic in his pipe. His wife, at thirty-nine very much younger than he, could be exasperating when she threw his age up at him. Except for his deafness, he was in good physical condition, but as always, he gave a mild mannered reply. "I am still a war chief. If I am needed, I will fight."

The day wore on calmly until toward noon. Then a brave rode into the village on a lathered horse with news that shattered the village peace. Braves surrounded his horse as he gasped out the words that his village south east on the Mississinewa was attacked.

Young Frances Godfroy, or Palonzwa, newly elected war chief, led the brave to the council house where the story was hurridly related. The brave said, "They attacked us without warning at dawn. I don't know how they did it. They must have marched all night to give such complete surprise."

Godfroy asked, "From which direction did they come? How many are there?"

"It seemed like about 600 soldiers. They came up along the Mississinewa from the East. They didn't come from Fort Wayne. Must have come from somewhere in Ohio. Our people were still asleep when they attacked. They killed nine and took forty-two squaws and children captive. Then they burned the village except for the largest cabin where they keep the captives."

While the young man paused to catch his breath Godfroy asked, "Did you kill any of the white dogs?"

"One. We all fled across the river. When they thought we were gone the Big Knives sent a few men into the woods and we killed one. Then, we went to the next village west on the river. We had barely gotten everyone away from there when the army came and burned it. They took all the horses. We didn't have time to catch them, but at least our people got away. If we don't attack them, they will surely come up the river, and burn this town too."

This comment started loud buzzing among the crowd. Godfroy shouted, "We will do the same to them!" A war shriek was the crowd's response, the din itself seeming enough to cow the fiercest enemy.

When they had quieted Godfroy said, "Shepancanah, old war chief, will help plan the attack." They decided it was to be before sunrise when the soldiers were still asleep.

Camped on the grounds of the most eastern village, the soldiers suffered from frostbite and lack of food. They had come away from Dayton, Ohio with but three days rations. The territory into which they ventured was unknown to them, and they didn't realize it would take three days just to get there. The guide had been here only once before himself. He bent shrubs and twigs on his return to Dayton, but had become somewhat lost himself on this march. The army marched three days and all night in deep snow and frigid December cold before they came upon the Mississinewa villages. They had been lucky in their surprise of the first village. Now they expected counter attack by the Indians. Two hours before sunrise the gaurds gave a false alarm. At this everyone got up and began preparing a scanty breakfast of captured Indian corn and beef.

Silently the Indians formed their lines, going single file as was their custom. A twig snapped, alerting the two American guards already nervous as cats. Immediately they fired, warning the others. Then they jumped to their feet, running back to camp, followed by screeching Indians. The Indians formed a line about sixty yards from the camp behind a thick growth of trees. The army quickly saw their disadvantage, being stationed in the open at the edge of the Indian town, while the Indians were under cover.

Americans fell back behind their horses, tied some twenty paces away. Though it appeared they were pinned down, the army did not falter. Up and down the line, even as comrades fell to stinging bullets, men called out in encouragement, "Fight on!" Horses tied and unable to get away were falling like flies as they served cover for the men. The wounded men were led to places of relative safety in the rear behind trees. But some were shot again as they tried to watch the battle. The winter sun rose weakly above the winter horizon, half an hour high, and still the battle raged. Now the smoke from gunfire was so thick it looked like river fog. The Indians could only be seen by the flash of their guns. "Fight on!" was the frequent cheer. Then suddenly from the Indian's side a hoarse voice bawled out, "Fight on and be damn to you!"

In a number of the white men's minds a question mark formed at these words in their own tongue. Who were they fighting after all? Now it appeared that the Indians were in retreat. A mounted group on the American side decided to give chase. As they were forming their line, the Indians that remained behind covering the retreat fired on them, cutting them down in their tracks.

All during the battle, the Indian captives jailed in the cabin kept up a continuous hollaring and gibbering, as if they were a cheering squad.

The battle had been brief, but so mutilating to both sides that the Americans were not in a position to follow, nor the Indians to make any more ambushes. As the smoke cleared from the square depression along the Mississinewa, where the army had been encamped, forty Indians and twelve Americans were dead. Sixty-four soldiers were wounded. The Miamis carried away their injured men, leaving none behind for mutilation.

Nervously they peered through the forest toward the trail leading eastward. The horses were packed with food, hides, and everything that could be carried, and hidden back in the woods. They had been told to leave the village and head north, but Maconaquah stayed behind waiting for her men.

Maconaquah chewed a fingernail as she worried. Both she and Cut Finger stamped their feet in the cold. Once again Maconaquah thought, Shepancanah is a fool to go to battle with the braves. An old fool! At his age and totally deaf! But he had promised her he would stay in the rear with their young boys. She had demanded and then begged him not to go. But he'd said the boys needed this chance to see battle. He would stay in the back, just watching. Maconaquah could not change his mind so she'd busied herself packing, to flee north. Where they'd go, she wasn't sure. Most villages of the Miamis had been razed. They'd probably have to go, beggers, to the Pottawattomi, north and west.

She watched the cold water of the Mississinewa in its timeless journey toward the Wabash. Once again she vowed to herself, "One day I will have a cabin of my own, far away from the other Indians. Then the white soldiers will not burn my house. They would have no need. Why would they burn one lone house, away from the Indian villages?"

Sooner than she expected, braves began returning, many bearing wounded men. Maconaquah and others trickled from their forest hiding to meet them. The men were quiet. There were alarming gaps in their numbers. Here and there among the women the hair raising sound of the death wail rose like a ghost into the air. Among the braves, true to his word, was Shepancanah and the boys, without a scratch on them. Relief flooded over her as she ran to embrace her family.

Wearily Shepancanah dismounted from his pony, strangely quiet, though the boys excitedly told a tale meant to impress her and Cut finger of their bravery. With an expression of disbelief she asked Shepancanah, "Is it true? That you beat them?"

With a gesture of disgust he shook his head. "We kill them, they kill us. No one wins. It is only a fool who goes into such a fight. It was very hard, but I kept the boys back, out of the fight. One day, I will not be with them. I won't be able to sit a horse in battle. Then, woman, who will win when they go to battle?"

Maconaquah thought of the consequences of future fights with the white men, when her family would not be so lucky, as they had been today. The only thing to do, was to learn to survive, not to win. Without another word, she went to get the horses for the trip into the forest, far away from invading armies of the Big Knives.

Chapter XXII

Deaf Man's Village on the Mississinewa, January 1835

The sky to the northwest was developing an ominous blue-grey tinge that heralded a snowstorm. Tree tops of the great black forest began a slow swaying, raising the hair on the man's neck in fear of what might come, for he was miles from any kind of shelter. The approaching clouds were full of snow. Maybe it would pass over, but then again it was better not to tempt fate. Ewing slowed the string of pack horses to a slow trot while he considered his options. Nervously he spoke to his companion. "Not goin' to make it to Logansport tonight, Netti. Might wind up frozen if we try it." He patted the horse on its shaggy rump. "Think you could get us to Peru?" The horse blew through its nostrils negatively. She was used to being talked to by George. Here in the Indiana wilderness there was seldom anyone else.

The wind blew a sudden downdraft and great flakes of snow began a steady descent. George said, "Hell, its ten miles yet to Peru. We'd best find a friendly cabin double quick." In January it was wise to hole up in a warm cabin at the first sight of snow, for a full fledged blizzard could swiftly bear down behind the first innocent flakes.

He looked over the edge of the cliff along which he traveled the familiar Indian trail. Below, the Mississinewa River flowed sluggishly, ice formed along it's edges. Enormous trees rose on both sides. The ground here was not as rich as in other parts of Indiana. Sycamores, lovers of river banks, were in abundance, but other trees grew not quite as thickly as in the rich ground south of this place. "Course the surveyors noted that fact," George thought out loud, "Leave the poor ground to the Indians, bet they said. It is that beautiful though." He took a moment away from his continual thoughts of business to admire the primeval forest with the backdrop of a purple snowstorm advancing toward him, all framing the river making its constant journey toward the Wabash.

A slight breeze moved through the tall grass, now hollow reeds, along the rock-solid frozen trail. George was well familiar with this country that was the Miami reservation and knew the location of the Indian cabins scattered throughout it. "I could go to Chief Godfroy's trading post," he mused. "On the other hand, Deaf Man's Village is closer. The family that owns that farm is well-to-do and would take me in with a good meal included in the bargain." Knowing he'd be welcome anywhere he chose, he kicked the horse in the side, speeding it down the trail.

The biting cold did not penetrate the wool great coat he wore over the buckskins. A coonskin hat was pulled down well over his ears. Inside the well-made boots he wore two pairs of hand-knitted wool socks. Ewing was a tall,well-proportioned man with excellent manners, as much at home in a ballroom as among the Indians trading furs. He had a catlike elastic step, much admired by the Indians. His mind was extremely quick, especially when a business deal was under consideration, and then no one could equal him. The major flaw in his character was that he was extremely nervous. When pressed, the princely manners evaporated and a knife or gun would appear, ready to serve, in his hand.

He was well known and liked by the Miamis and they often enjoyed a few drinks together. The thought of whiskey warming his throat made George smile as stinging wind began its work on his face. Addressing the long suffering Netti he said, "A few drinks don't hurt no one, 'spite what those Presbyterians say." Then grimacing, he remembered the serious brawl he'd had recently with a French trader following an evening at the tavern. Downright embarrassing coming to with your face in the filth of the road. Frowning he thought, better watch yourself George. Wouldn't do to kill somebody now with all the land deals hanging fire. As Ma says, think straight, upright, and pure. He straightened his back. Otherwise, who'll trust you in a deal? Can't have the Indian agent suspicious either because those Frenchies are all just itching to get my fur trade so they can buy land on the side from the Indians.

Raised in the frontier towns of Ohio and then Fort Wayne, Indiana, he'd cut his teeth to the trading of furs in his father's Fort Wayne trading post. As whites enlarged and filled the town, the Indians moved west. That meant a new trading post was needed there to buy their furs and sell them goods. Logansport was the town built strictly for this purpose, and the Ewing brothers owned the post. With his fluent knowledge of the Miami language, his keen intelligence, and a brother who was a lawyer, George was well on his way to being one of Indiana's first millionaires.

His visit to his family's Fort Wayne and Lagro trading posts had been successful. The piles of furs he left there would bring a good price in the East. New supplies were on order to be ready for the Indians when they received their government annuity money. These trade goods, when sold to the Indians, at a considerable mark-up of course, were guaranteed to be paid for, direct from the United States Government. The money first passed through the hands of the Indian agent at Logansport. The Indians bought on credit. Then when the government paid their annuity once a year, the traders were on hand to get their money. So far, no questions had been asked concerning the bills. The illiterate Indians were not likely to question the listing of their purchases, and often not even the prices of the goods.

As Ewing neared Deaf Man's Village that was really just a number of farm buildings, trees became sparce giving way to snow covered fields. The ground showed clearly that a plow was used...unusual on the Miami reservation. Schools were arranged now and then to teach the Indians to farm, but they'd been failures. Mainly Indians relied on government money to live.

Log buildings set in the open field loomed into view through the descending large snowflakes. Snow covered the ground around them, making them look as neat and clean as in a painting. The main building was a large double cabin. That and several outbuildings gave the place a very prosperous look as compared to other farms of the day. After riding into the yard, a large bubbling spring drew Netti's attention while George called out, "Hellooo." People white or red, in the sparsely settled forest liked to know when someone was about.

"Who's yere?"

"Ewing, the trader."

The door of the cabin opened and a French-Indian half-breed looked out, gun in plain view in one hand. Seeing a familiar face, the man placed the gun inside and came out to greet the visitor. Ewing now knew why this was a wealthy farm. Indians with French blood often prospered while their full-blooded brothers declined into poverty. Full-blooded Indians just don't understand white men's business deals, he thought.

Loudly in Miami, the trader said, "This here blizzard's going to cut into my trip. Do you have room in your barn for a frozen fur trader tonight?"

"Eh, Ewing! We put ze horse in the barn. You come in by the fire. Warm ze toes. Backside too." The tall Indian smiled broadly in welcome. The bleak day had turned festive with an unexpected guest. Winter days were long and lonely. He continued, "Looks like a real blizzard for sure. What's a smart feller like you doin' out yere in this weather?"

"Been Fort Wayne way. Go there purty often." The men grunted as they unpacked the heavy burdens from the horses in the barn and then fed them good sweet hay. "This is some place you got here. Good set of buildings. Not too close to neighbors, and yet close on to trading so you can get your goods easy. I saw you several times at my post. Brouillette's your name isn't it?"

"Jean Baptiste Brouillette. Aye, my wife, her sister and children and I live with Deaf Man's Squaw, my mother-in-law. As to the neighbors, since they opened that land north of us to sell to whites last year, we had many ponies stolen."

"If Chief Deaf Man were here they wouldn't dare I bet," George said sociably. "How long's he been dead now?"

"Over four year. But he was in his eighties. We think. He was a good man when young they say. But in the years I knew him, he was deaf as a stone post. Used to go out huntin'. Come back with no game and wonder why. In the old days no others was better'n him, they say, as hunters. I'd come out to meet him, heard his horse's bells from way off. No game in the woods he'd say. Hell, the deer heard them bells, same as me." The two men laughed as they walked through the whirling snow toward the cabin.

George continued, "Yes, the land north of you sold quick, what with the canal goin' through Peru now. Soon all the forests will be one big field and we fur traders out of business."

Entering by the heavy timbered door to the cabin, the men made a bee-line for the fireplace. There sitting on a ladder-backed chair beside the fire was a very old wrinkled Indian squaw, in long calico skirts. Dangling from her pierced ears were several pairs of silver earrings. A black silk shawl, richly embroidered, was draped around her shoulders, while on her legs she wore red leggings and moccasins. It was obvious that she did not feel well for after introducing herself as Deaf Man's squaw, she said little and generally acted as if she felt poorly.

Looking away from her to the surroundings, George was relieved to see that everything was neat and clean. Quite a contrast to many of the Indian cabins with which he was familiar. A table stood in the center of the room. Several beds or couches of furs and clothing were along the wall. Pegs in the wall were piled with hanging clothes, further testimony to the family's wealth. Apparently the cooking was done in the other room. Jean Baptist's wife, Kekesequa, or Cut Finger, began setting plates on the table from the shelf on the wall.

Cut Finger held herself with the proud bearing of a Miami, though heavy set. She looked about forty. The black hair was pulled back in the Miami clubbed hair style which accentuated her high cheekbones. She smiled a Mona Lisa smile often and spoke little. Light skin with a touch of olive marked her as Miami. She was the elder of the two daughters. "Join us in our evening meal," she smiled.

A younger, more vivacious woman entered the room, bringing her baby and a youngster of about two. The few chairs and three-legged stools were pulled up and the gathering seated themselves.

"This venison and hominy really hits the spot, Maam."

"Thank you," Cut Finger smiled. "Do you pass this way much?"

"Often enough. Course I trade furs with most of the Indians at the post in Logansport, but occasionally I bring a load of goods down to Chief Godfroy's trading post or go to Fort Wayne. Our family has trading posts in Missouri, Iowa, Michigan, Kansas, Wisconsin, and Minnesota. Keeps me busy. Don't have much time to socialize."

Jean Baptiste commented, "You married a French gal, didn't you?" Slyly he continued, "Daughter of the trader that wanted some of the fur trade in these parts, weren't she?"

George grinned, "You got me there. Smoothed things out real nice. Marry the girl and you marry the family." The old woman gave him a glare with this comment while the sisters looked at him in surprise. Jean Baptiste laughed.

"That is for true. But I take good care of my family. It can be said my old Mother here wants for nothing and does no work."

Time to change the subject, George could see. Pointing at the baby the younger sister was feeding he said, "That's a mighty purty baby you've got there."

The girl of around nineteen smiled engagingly. "This is Blue Corn." The baby slobbered a little and then broke into a toothless smile. Its dark brown eyes set in a round face.

"Here, let me take her for awhile. I promise not to drop her." The baby was passed over and all watched as George bounced her on his knee. "Where's your daddy young lady?"

There was a pregnant moment of silence. Then the old woman spoke, "He was a nephew of Chief Godfroy but a drunkard and worthless Indian. He beat my daughter and threatened to kill her. So now, she lives with us."

George raised his eyebrows, embarrassed by his casual question. He demurred, "It was none of my business."

The old woman continued, "Do not feel embarrassed. I was married to such a worthless Indian myself, as a young girl. A squaw who stays with a man who beats her is a fool." The others around the table nodded their heads. It was becoming increasingly clear that the old woman was the strong head of the household and the others showed great deference to her.

After a lengthy silence while the wind whirled around the cabin, George changed the subject again. "Have you been Fort Wayne way recently?"

Jean Baptiste answered, "There's no need to go there with the trading post at Logansport now. Fort Wayne, or Kekionga, was once the home of the Miamis, but who of us would know it now? Not even our ghosts, I recon."

"You're right for certain. The place booms. You can almost hear it. There's hardly a trace of the old Miami Indian capital although the French still live together on one street."

The group leaned forward to hear about their old home. "Flat boats come down the Maumee with materials for the Wabash and Erie canal. Course the river's froze up now. But all them builders working on the canal got to have supplies. There are over a thousand men working on it. Course you know that, with the canal going right through Peru. Guess the Irish and Germans have had some terrible fights in the camps. Wish I was around to see it but I've always got business to do. No time for much fun."

Baptiste commented, "We have been told to stay away from the camps. Much sickness and dying there."

"Yep. They say you can smell the camps from away off. But it'll all be worth it in the end. You should get more for your crops and pelts now since they can be shipped out of Peru, and on up the Wabash River to the Fort Wayne market."

Jean Baptiste answered slowly, "That's true, but with the riffraff buying the land around here and stealing us blind, we may have nothing to sell. The reservation gits smaller every year. We are afraid the government will take our land away too. Treaties are signed that say we can keep the land forever, but forever don't last long. Soon the government's back wantin' more land, the chiefs sell it, and the Indians got to move on. The chiefs git the money and everyone else gits to move."

George agreed. "Aye. The land North of you was taken by the government just last year in 1834 wasn't it. Now you're seeing what its like to have white neighbors. Wish I could be encouraging but if William Henry Harrison gets elected president, Indian affairs will go downhill. In Fort Wayne all the talk is about the election. He's relying totally on his defeat of The Prophet in 1811 to get him elected. So he's a big enemy of the Indians for sure, and it looks like he has a real chance of getting elected."

The old woman stated emphatically, "That fight with The Prophet wasn't such a feather for his bonnet. His army didn't kill The Prophet, or Tecumseh, and he didn't win the battle. We always heard The Prophet came out ahead. The Miamis weren't in that fight either. Harrison's always been a land grabber and won't be satisfied until every Indian is forced from Indiana."

George had heard this argument from Indians before and wanted them to know how the white men looked at it. "Surely you don't overlook the fact that the Indians are paid for the lands with the yearly government annuity money. I wouldn't have a business if it weren't for that. The furs brought in are no longer enough to pay for all the goods I sell your people. It's the government payment that pays for 'em."

Jean Baptist said, "That is true, and on what will you make your livin' when zee last Indian is pushed off this land?"

"I'll probably have to move west, the same as you." The fire crackled in the fireplace as they silently contemplated what appeared to be a dismal future. Then family members began leaving the room to prepare for the night's rest. The old woman pointed to a pile of furs and blankets near the fireplace to be used as Ewing's bed. Then she continued to sit by the fire after the others left the room. George removed his boots and lay down under the furs. Then all was quiet except for the crackling fire. The old woman continued to sit there, fidgeting, as if wanting to say something, yet she held back, not sure that she should.

Looking at her more closely George could see that she looked like any other Indian grandma. Brown eyes, weathered, wrinkled skin, fine boned face, greying reddish brown hair. She started when he said, "Does rhuematism keep you awake at night?"

"Yes, I have been ill for a long time now. I can't eat as well as I should and always have aches and pains. I feel I won't live much longer. There's something I want to tell someone, but I fear to tell it. It's been on my mind a long while. A spirit whispers to me that I should tell this before I die."

This statement raised George to a sitting position. Dramatically she said, "I am by birth a white woman." Pulling up a sleeve of her bodice she showed him her upper arm. Indeed, her skin was white!

In great excitement George exclaimed, "Good God! But now that I see it, it doesn't surprise me. Your hair is not the same as that of Indians. What was your white name?"

The woman struggled to compose the story, as the firelight threw shadows on the walls of the log cabin. "It was so many years ago. It is hard for me to remember as I was so small when captured. The main thing I remember was that my father's name was Slocum and he wore a black hat."

"He was a Quaker," stated Ewing. "Where did you live?"

"I don't know except that it was on the Susquehanna River. I never told this story to another white man because I didn't want to leave my Indian family and I was afraid the whites would take me away. Now that I am about to die, I felt I could tell it. I have always been treated well by the Miamis and loved my Miami parents."

"Have you lived here then all your life?"

"No. For many years I and my husband lived at Kekionga, now known as Fort Wayne. When I was a child my Indian parents went there from Niagara. Then there were the wars with the whites. We lived away from there until the treaty was made with the chief who never sleeps, General Wayne. Then we moved back to Kekionga. As more and more white people came to that place we moved to the Ottawa village on the Mississinewa. My husband, The Deaf Man, was war chief for a time. My two sons who died young are buried with him, but I wanted some white person to know my story. Now that I have told it, I can die in peace. Do not tell my family I have told you this. They would be afraid someone would come to take me away."

George couldn't let her go just yet. He wanted to hear more about the old days. "Before my trading post was moved to Logansport in 1828, I lived at Fort Wayne, or Kekionga, as you say. I heard many tales about the Indian agent, William Wells, who was captured as a young boy by the Miamis. Did you know him?"

A smile lit her face, crinkling it into unused lines. "Apeconit, The Carrot, or Man of the Earth as some called him.

Aye, I knew him. Laughing she said, "He was a scalawag, with all his squaws. Some say he cheated the Indians when he was agent, but I never believed it. He was so handsome, and so rich he could afford the squaws. Helped me more than once, aye, he did." Now the old woman seemed to be talking almost to herself. "He was probably the bravest man, white or red in all the country then. When he died, killed by those dogs, the Pottawattomies, they ate his heart to get his courage. When he was young, and lived as Indian, he was Little Turtle's finest warrior. Then after his brother came and took him back to Kentucky, he came back to the Miami." She looked at George, as if he were challenging her words. "He decided to live and work for the Miamis," she smiled, "when he wasn't working for himself."

The old woman was silent a moment, thinking back to the days of her youth. "Wells was with General Wayne against the Indians in the last war-the head spy. But when it came to the actual fight, he wasn't in it. He got shot in the arm just before it and wasn't fit to fight, they said. But I'll wager he got himself shot just so he wouldn't have to fight against his adopted father, Little Turtle." The cabin was silent as the old woman sat staring into the fire. finally she rose saying, "Now I go to my rest."

The tale was such an unusual one it kept George from doing his usual monetary mathematical exercises before closing his eyes. Fort Wayne was becoming a major trade center, yet only forty years ago it was exclusively Indian territory. White men that were not French or British lost their scalps in horrible ways when attempting to carry messages there. This woman had seen all the Indian wars and changes of the place from Miami Indian capitol to white man's boom town. His fertile imagination raced through the possible adventures she must have had. Why she lived right in the middle of the Indian wars with the Americans before the Miami Confederation was defeated and Indiana opened for settlement.

A touch of envy nibbled his adventurous soul. His life seemed boring in comparison. Oh sure, there was plenty of drunken brawling, but no out and out wars, where a man could see he'd won a fight. Life seemed to be just one complex business operation. No adventure. Then it occurred to him, he could make adventure happen. He could finish a story. He would locate the white family of this old woman and be a hero in the process.

He smiled into the dark at the challenge this presented. What had happened to the old squaw's family in Pennsylvania who all these years must have thought her dead? How could he contact them to tell them their sister was still living? She had come from a large family, she said. Some must still be alive. They would want to know about the old woman's daughters living in Indiana. With his knowledge of the country and his eastern connections, there must be some way he could get in touch with them. With thoughts of interesting things to do tomorrow, he closed his eyes, a smile lingering on his lips.

The next morning Ewing brought out a half dollar to pay for the night's lodging, but the family would not take the money and asked him to stop again soon. Free hospitality was a tradition with the Indians. He returned to the trail along the Mississinewa until he reached Peru and the Wabash River. Then he continued along it the sixteen miles west to Logansport.

The land on the Mississinewa was all that remained in Miami hands of the entire state of Indiana. The once mighty Miami nation was decimated by disease, wars and whisky to a fragment of their original numbers. No longer a proud race, they now relied on the government dole for the majority of their support. Soon there would be no more lands to trade for goods and they would be moved west of the Mississippi. There was no place in the growing agricultural based society for Indians, even though the government money they received supported businesses like Ewing's.

The final low hills along the Wabash were passed and he entered the fledgling bustling trade center, Logansport. Named for a friendly Indian named Logan, it was one of the northernmost settlements in the state. There was nothing much north of it along the Michigan road that ran north and south the whole length of the state, except trees, swamps and Indians until one reached South Bend. The town was built largely because of the Indian agency moved here from Fort Wayne in 1828. Traders such as Ewing moved their operations here right along with the agency since their livelihood depended on it. As Fort Wayne was settled by white men, the Indians moved away from what had once been their major town, Kekionga, to the Mississinewa River.

Logansport nestled between two rivers, the Eel and the Wabash, the waterway through which whites and Indians traveled for more than a hundred years. Six miles up the Eel River, the Eel River Miamis once had a village called Kenapacomaqua until it was destroyed by Wilkinson's raiders just previous to St. Clair's battle with the Indians in 1791. Now most of those Indians lived on the reservation near Peru. Tract by tract, treaty by treaty, their lands were purchased and then sold to pioneers. Traders like George prospered nicely through government land sales, as one had only to be at the auction of these lands to pick up some nice bargains. The government usually sold land for $l.25 per acre if not bid higher. If the buyer was smart, like George, he'd buy land ceded to a chief for even less. Some immigrant farmer needing land would buy it, and the trader turned a quick fat profit.

The road slowly descending to the rivers was wide and deeply rutted because of use by heavy wagons when thawed. Now it was frozen into humps, difficult for horses to walk over. As George looked down toward the town clustered on the low ground next to the rivers he thought, hope she don't flood when the ice breaks. What a job it was to move everything in the post to the upper floor. He grimaced as he passed the place in the road where an enormous chunk of ice was left after such a flood the previous year.

Raising his hand he said, "Clyde," as he passed a townsman outside his cabin chopping wood. Others were outside tanning hides and tending animals. Near his post, building materials were strewn about for the canal that was going straight through the center of town. What a mess, he thought, but sure as shootin' it'll make me rich. He rubbed the soreness in his hips as he thought, soon as the canal is in I can just lean back and rest when I go to Fort Wayne, 'stead of gettin' saddle sores on my butt.

Lazy smoke rose from chimneys of snow covered cabins, filling the air with the homey smell. Dismounting before his post he looked out over the peaceful scene, lit by bright sunlight. The deep blue sky had just a few small clouds, far above in the atmosphere. The snow storm was gone. Maybe I'll keep some of the ground on the flatlands around here 'stead of sellin' it all off, he thought. Ground's so rich the corn jumps right out of it, the suttlers say. And then life would be peaceful. No more sleepless nights wonderin' if I'll be wiped out in a fire. Coming back to reality he thought, hell, I'd be bored to death. I guess I'd rather be awake at night than dead to the world from cuttin' all them trees. Aye, a trader I am and a trader I'll always be.

Thinking about his business brought him to his current sticky problem. When the government money came for the Indian's annuity payment, his bills for their credit buying would be for more than the payment. He mused, I could just take a loss, but I'm not about to do it. But what if the Indian agent decides to look at my books? George broke out into a sweat though the day was cold. There were things on the books that wouldn't bear the light of day. Guess I'll just have to look like the very pillar of the town. If I could find that old squaw's relatives, I'd be such a hero the agent wouldn't dare raise a question against me, the Miami protector. This thought brought a chortle. George Ewing in such a role was hilarious. But how can I find them, he worried. Sighing he reflected, probably be like lookin' for a damn needle in a haystack. But the thought of the challenge of the search excited him. The old woman said her family lived on the Susquehanna, in Pennsylvania. But the river traveled the entire length of the state. He knew the largest town on the Susquehanna was Lancaster, Pennsylvania. But what if the old woman's relatives were dead or didn't remember her? The possibility of their being found was very slim but he decided he would send a letter to Lancaster in the off chance that someone would know of them. With the challenge of the day solved, he returned to the duties at hand required by a thriving trading post in 1835.

It had been a taxing day for Mary Dickson, Postmaster of the Lancaster post office. The mail had to be taken care of and then there was the garden that needed planting. Spring brought a host of chores. Crops had to be planted along with the usual household work. There was little time to spend reading a letter that wasn't addressed to anyone in particular, just to the Lancaster, Pa. Postmaster. Nevertheless, she would do her duty and take a few minutes to read it.

Logansport, Indiana, Jan.20, 1835

"Where in God's creation is Logansport?" she wondered. Somewhere out in the wild west, seemingly. She continued reading.

> Dear Sir: In the hope that some good may result from it, I have taken this means of giving to your fellow citizens-say the descendants of the early settlers of the Susquehanna-the following information; and if there be any now living whose name is Slocum, to them, I hope, the following may be communicated through the public prints of your place:
>
> There is now living near this place an aged white woman, who a few days ago told me, while I lodged in the camp one night, that she was taken away from her father's house, on or near the Susquehanna River, when she was very young-say from five to eight years old, as she thinks-by the Delaware Indians, who were then hostile toward the whites. She says her father's name was Slocum; that he was a Quaker, rather small in stature, and

> wore a large brimmed hat; was of sandy hair and light complexion and much freckled; that he lived about half a mile from a town where there was a fort; that they lived in a wooden house of two stories hight, and had a spring near the house. She says three Delawares came to the house in the daytime, when all were absent but herself, and perhaps two other children; her father and brothers were absent working in the field. The Indians carried her off, and she was adopted into a family of Delawares, who raised her and treated her as their own child. They died about forty years ago, somewhere in Ohio. She was then married to a Miami, by whom she had four children; two of them are now living-they are both daughters-and she lives with them. Her husband is dead; she is old and feeble, and thinks she will not live long.

Mary looked at the remaining pages to be read. The letter just went on and on and she had to get home. She skimmed the remainder of the letter, picking out key phrases.

> She thinks she was taken prisoner before the two last wars, which must mean the Revolutionary war as Wayne's war and the late war have been since that one.

What wars was this man talking about? Mary wondered. There had been the Revolutionary war, she knew.

> She has lived long and happy as an Indian, and, but for her color, would not be suspected of being anything else than such. She is very respectable and wealthy, sober and honest. Her name is without reproach. She says her father had a large family, say eight children in all-six older than herself, one younger, as well as she can recollect; and she doubts not there are yet living many of their descendants, but seems to think that all her brothers and sisters must be dead, as she is very old herself, not far from the age of eighty.
>
> I have been much affected with the disclosure, and hope the surviving friends may obtain, through your goodness, the information I desire for them. If I can be of any service to them, they may command me. In the mean-

time, I hope you will excuse me for the freedom I have taken with you, a total stranger, and believe me to be, sir, with much respect,

Your obedient servant,
George W. Ewing.

Very interesting, Mary mused. She decided that if she heard of any missing relatives, she would tell of the letter. Folding it into its envelope, she laid it aside and hurried off to her other work that urgently commanded her attention. The letter remained unread again for two years.

Picture of Maconaquah, or Frances Slocum painted by George Winter in 1839. Copied from the book, The Journals and Indian Paintings of George Winter 1837-1839. Cut Finger, or Ke-ke-se-qua, is on the right and O-zah-shin-quah, or Yellow Leaf, is standing with her back to the artist.

Chapter XXIII

Lancaster, Pennsylvania, March 1837

What a rat's nest this is, Mary Dickson said to herself as she began sorting through a huge basket of accumulated dead letters. It was the first time in years she had a few free hours to do such work. Having sold her interest in the local newspaper, The Lancaster Intelligencer, she had only the post office to handle now. She'd meant to go through the old mail no one had claimed for years, but just never had the time. Now she examined each letter to see if there was any hope of finding it's owner.

Down in the stack was one from a George Ewing addressed to the Lancaster Postmaster. This time she thought more about its possibilities than the first time she'd read it, two years ago. A section that seemed to stand out was as follows.

> There is now living near this place an aged white woman, who a few days ago told me, while I lodged in the camp one night, that she was taken away from her father's house, on or near the Susquehanna River, when she was very young, say from five to eight years old, as she thinks-by the Delaware Indians.

Further down it continued:

> I can form no idea whereabout upon the Susquehanna River this family could have lived at that early period, namely, about the time of the Revolutionary war, but perhaps you can ascertain more about it. If so, I hope you will interest yourself, and if possible, let her brothers and sisters, if any be alive–if not, their children–know where they may once more see a relative whose fate has

> been wrapped in mystery for seventy years, and for whom her bereaved and afflicted parents doubtless shed many a bitter tear.

Mary sat back on her chair, lost in imagination concerning the story. Why hadn't she seen its possibility as a news article before? She'd give the letter to the young man, John Forney, who had just bought her newspaper. He'd seemed somewhat at a loss as to how to fill the paper each week. This letter would help, and would even make a good story.

Forney was a gifted writer who immediately recognized a good readible tale. He published the story in an extra large edition that included among the columns a number of temperance documents. As a service the paper was automatically sent to all ministers in the area, because of these bulletins.

A few days later the Reverend Samuel Bowman sat down on his porch rocker to enjoy his mail. It was a rare occasion to receive a newspaper. He would read it from cover to cover. He read with interest the Washington news concerning the economic panic of 1837. Apparently it was being followed by a depression. President Harrison, though newly elected, was trying to set things right.

Further down the page was a letter from someone out West, in Indiana. Skimming it, his eyes lit on the phrase,

> 'say, the descendants of the early settlers of the Susquehanna the following information; and if there be any now living whose name is Slocum, to them I hope the following may be communicated.

"Slocum, Slocum," he mused. The name was very familiar. Slowly he remembered them. As a young man he was the Episcopal minister in Wilkes-Barre and knew several members of the large Slocum family. Thinking on it further he dredged from distant memory local stores of Indian raids on Wilkes-Barre and how the youngest Slocum girl had been carried off. Out loud he spoke in wonder, "God works in mysterious ways!" With that he rose to collect the sissors. He would send this artical immediately to Joseph Slocum of Slocum Township, Luzerne County, Pennsylvania.

Fifty-nine years had passed since the attack on the Slocum house in Wilkes-Barre. Of the ten brothers and sisters, only Mary, Isaac, Joseph, Jonathan, and of course Frances, were still living. The eastern brothers and sisters had done well in life. They had many children and gained wealth, making a good life for themselves. They had scattered, helping to settle Ohio, New York, and Pennsylvania. Upon receiving the letter of France's discovery, a flurry of correspondence began between the relatives. Finally a letter was sent to Logansport, Indiana to George Ewing, fur trader, by Joseph Slocum's son, as follows.

Wilkes Barre, Pa., Aug.8, 1837

Geor. W. Ewing, Esq.,

Dear Sir: At the suggestion of my father and other relations I have taken the liberty to write to you, although an entire stranger.

We have received, but a few days since, a letter written by you to a gentleman in Lancaster, of this State, upon a subject of deep and intense interest to our family. How the matter should have lain so long wrapped in obscurity, we cannot conceive. An aunt of mine–sister of my father-was taken away when five years old, by the Indians, and since then we have only had vague and indistinct rumors upon the subject. Your letter we deem to have entirely revealed the whole matter and set everything at rest. The description is so perfect, and the incidents (with the exception of her age) so correct, that we feel confident.

Steps will be taken immediately to investigate the matter, and we will endeavor to do all in our power to restore a lost relative who has been sixty years in Indian bondage.

Your friend and obedient servent,
Jon. J. Slocum

"Well I'll be damned!" said George Ewing upon receipt of the letter. "I knew the mail was slow, but two years for delivery is beyond belief." He shook his head then frowned as he thought of the Indian's current plight. "The old Miami squaw's going to need all the help she can get so she won't get moved off her land by the government. I'd best get a letter out right away that will bring her kin out here double quick."

The Pottawattomi Indians to the north were soon to be moved west. So far the principle Miami chief, who lived at Fort Wayne, had resisted removal efforts, but George knew it wouldn't be long until all Indians would be removed from Indiana. The financial panic had made the squatters less tolerant of the Indians, perhaps because they competed for the valuable furs.

Prompt attention to detail was one of George's traits that helped make him the business success he was. He immediately sent out a long winded reply as follows.

Logansport, Ind., Aug. 26, 1837

Jon. J. Slocum, Esq, Wilkes-Barre,

Dear Sir: I have the pleasure of acknowledging the receipt of your letter of the 8th instant, and in answer can add, that female I spoke of in January, 1835, is still alive; nor can I for a moment doubt that she is the identical relative that has been so long lost to your family.

I feel much gratified to think that I have been thus instrumental in disclosing to yourself and friends such facts in relation to her as will enable you to visit her and satisfy yourselves more fully. She recovered from the temporary illness by which she was afflicted about the time I spent the night with her in January, 1835, and which was, no doubt, the cause that induced her to speak so freely of her early captivity.

Although she is now, by long habit, an Indian, and her manners and customs precisely theirs, yet she will doubtless be happy to see any of you, and I myself will take great pleasure in accompanying you to the house. Should you come out for that purpose, I advise you to repair directly to this place; and should it so happen that I should be absent at the time, you will find others who can take you to her. Bring with you this letter; show it to James T. Miller, of Peru, Ind., a small town not far from this place. He knows her well. He is a young man whom we have raised. He speaks the Miami tongue and will accompany you if I should not be at home.

Inquire for the old white woman, mother-in-law to Brouillette, living on the Mississinewa River, about ten miles above its mouth. There you will find the long lost sister of your father, and, as I before stated you will not have to blush on her account. She is highly respectable, and her name as an Indian is without reproach. Her daughter, too, and her son-in-law, Brouillette, who is also a half-blood, being part French, are both very respectable and interesting people-none in the nation are more so. As Indians they live well, and will be pleased to see you. Should you visit here this fall, I may be absent, as I purpose starting for New York in a few days, and shall not be back till some time in October. But this need not stop you for, although I should be gratified to see you, yet it will be sufficient to learn that I have furthered your wishes in this truly interesting matter.

The very kind manner in which you have been pleased to speak of me shall be fully appreciated.

There are perhaps men who could have heard her story unmoved; but for me, I could not; and when I reflected that there was, perhaps, still lingering on this side of the grave some brother or sister of that ill-fated woman, to whom such information would be deeply interesting, I resolved on the course which I adopted, and entertained the fond hope that my letter, if ever it should go before the public, would attract the attention of some one interested. In this it seems at last, I have not been disappointed, although I have long since supposed it had failed to effect the object for which I wrote it. Like you, I regret that it should have been delayed so long, nor can I conceive how any one should neglect to publish such a letter.

As to the age of this female, I think she herself is mistaken, and that she is not so old as she imagines herself to be. Indeed, I entertain no doubt but that she is the same person that your family have mourned after, for more than half a century past.

Your obedient humble servant,
Geo. W. Ewing

Isaac Slocum was impatient to reach Peru, Indiana, though he knew he would arrive more quickly than the others. He was an old man. Perhaps he would miss his chance to see Frances if he didn't go now, he reasoned. He'd always been curious about the sister he'd lost so long ago. He was two years younger than Frances and she was his favorite playmate before her capture. It had been a great personal loss when she was stolen. Now, amazingly, she was found, after all these years.

Joseph Slocum, of Wilkes Barre, Pa., would travel by stage over the new National Road, picking up their sister, Mary, who lived south of Columbus, Ohio, and then continue to Indianapolis. From there they'd come north to Peru where they'd meet Isaac.

Isaac left his Belleview, Ohio home in the early fall weather, traveling twenty miles to Sandusky, Ohio by train. Sandusky was a Lake Erie port town with little in the way of entertainment. Isaac was very glad when the Star, a steam boat complete with paddles, rounded the lake bend to dock at the wharf. Since the Star was notorious for its bad food, he'd already eaten at a tavern. Then too, there might be rough weather, you could never tell on Lake Erie. It might be his last chance to eat without an upset stomach.

The boat finally got underway at four p.m. Isaac went below deck to find his berth but after one look at the narrow bed with it's greasy sheets and pillow without a case, he decided he'd spend as little time as possible in it.

Returning to the seats on deck, he sat down by a little family grouping that looked friendly. A thin black bearded young man and his wife introduced themselves as the Joel Thompson s, moving to take up residence in Indiana. A young child dressed fussily in a long dress of about six months smiled up at Isaac. Isaac stuck out a thick finger, touching a blond curl. He asked, "Where you folks headed?"

"We're from Jaunieta County, in Pennsylvania," the man said, speaking in a thick German accent.

"Sakes alive! I'm from the Wyoming Valley, 'fore I settled in Ohio. We were almost neighbors."

"You had better land in the Wyoming Valley than we in the mountain country of Juanietta County. We hear Indiana has flat, rich black soil. I'm a blacksmith by trade. We'll buy a bit of land and be beholden to none." The young man looked out across the water of the great lake at the September sun-set, seeing his hopes of a better life instead of the waves.

Isaac offered, "I moved to Belleview, Ohio, back in 1823. There was still Shawnee thereabouts then. The land was that untamed. Now there's a railroad at my door. If I was a young man, I'd go west again. Its gettin' too crowded when you can hear the sound of another man's ax."

The young German said, "We would have moved to southern Indiana'ceptin' that land is sold already. We heard of an auction of new land, got from the last Miami treaty, so we're headed for Fort Wayne."

The young wife at his side leaned forward to say somewhat timidly, "I just hope the Indians don't go on the warpath."

Isaac laughed, "They haven't had any real trouble with Indians in Indiana since 1814. Why there ain't even any soldiers at old Fort Wayne. They disbanded it near on twenty year ago. No, the Indians live on reservations now and are pretty much like poor white folk, I guess. Speaking of Indians, my sister is one. I'm on my way west to see her."

They stared at him wide eyed wondering if he were joking. Then Isaac launched into the story of how his sister was captured by Indians all those years ago, and now she'd been found. He was going to see her for the first time in sixty years. The calm lake and pleasant company had made the day enjoyable they all agreed. Wishing each other luck they retired to their berths.

The Star reached Toledo and the Maumee bay by afternoon the next day. Travelers going to Fort Wayne boarded a fast moving, comfortable packet boat that traveled at the speed of eight miles an hour. The captain said it would take only fifty-six hours to travel the 242 miles. Isaac found the food good and enjoyed viewing the relatively new towns they passed. Toledo stretched along the Maumee river for four miles, and was quite a prosperous city. As the town, Maumee, swung into view, they watched the widely scattered houses strung for a distance of two miles and laughed, saying either the town wanted to be able to say it was two miles long, or they had high hopes of more population. Later when the river narrowed, the passengers left the comfortable boat to travel the remaining distance to Fort Wayne by stage coach.

Fort Wayne was a thriving frontier town of 1500 people and growing. Though the rest of the country was in financial difficulty because of the panic of 1837, Fort Wayne merchants supplied only local farmers and trappers and was little effected by the crunch. They had the Miamis' government payments and the fur trade that was currently doing well because of fashion's demand for mink, deer, and above all raccoon for fur trimmed dresses.

Isaac stayed overnight in Fort Wayne and embarked on a canal boat down the Wabash River the next day. The Wabash canal was in its final stages of construction, having reached Logansport this year of 1837. Isaac was to learn that riding a canal boat was one of the most pleasant ways to travel. The travelers sat on top of the low cabin and the boat, pulled by horses on a parallel path, traveled at such a gentle pace that one could get off and run alongside upon occasion. Most spent their time playing cards or exchanging recent news.

As the country passed slowly by, Isaac was impressed by the fertility of the ground. The country was beautiful. Flat lands, the Wabash flood plains, extended for a mile on either side of the river forming a valley that would be unexcelled for growing corn. Gently rising hills on either side finished a perfect landscape. The Miamis owned the land along the river and their white corn was entering the harvest stage.

It was only a day's restful trip to Peru by canal boat. Disembarking at the quiet village, Isaac carried his bag up the log steps to the porch of the hotel. Setting the heavy bag on the floor, he shouted, "Is anyone here?" A rustling came from the upper level and then a rather thin man descended the stairs.

"I kin tell ye're not from these parts 'cause ya didn't yell, who's yere. What can I do fer ya?"

"I'm Isaac Slocum of Belleview, Ohio. Are there any people here lookin' for me?"

"You thinkin' 'bout a bounty hunter?" the man asked smiling mischievously. Noting Isaac's raised eyebrows, he hastened to add, "No one by that name's been wanted as I kin recollect."

"Well then, can you tell me where I can find a James T. Miller?"

"Now there I kin help. Bet you'sa fixin' ta visit the Miami and need an interpreter. He'll be at the general store, 'crost the street."

Crossing the rutted road to the store built of sawn wood Isaac reflected that this river town was enriched by a saw mill, a rare thing in the forests of Indiana. Entering the store he was struck by the unusual nature of the goods. Wildly colored bolts of cloth were stacked temptingly on the counter where they could be handled by women shoppers. Barrels of flour, tobacco, and coffee were among the food staples. From the ceiling hung smoked hams and bacon. Mixed at random were harness, forged nails in barrels, a shiny plow, hoes, spades, saws, mallats, axes and anything else to please the heart or need of a pioneer.

"What kin I do fer ya?" The approaching youth was little more than a teenager, but apparently capable of doing a man's job, tending the store.

"I'm Isaac Slocum and I need an interpreter. Are you James Miller?"

"None other. I'll be glad to hep ya. George Ewing said you'd be along one of these days. Goin' to see Deaf Man's squaw ain't you?"

"I had hoped to see her soon as possible. Could we leave tomorrow at first light?"

The sun was just rising as the two set out on horseback crossing the Wabash river at the ford and following the worn path along the Mississinewa river to the old Osage village, now combined with the Miami. Here and there were small cabins surrounded by tall blue grass and corn fields scatterd at random. Some Indians could be seen lounging about their cabins and others were at work in the fields, this being harvest season. Those in the fields had taken their horses as they seemed not to like walking anywhere if possible to avoid it. The ponies were tethered beside their tents that they pitched in the fields where they dried corn and cooked food. James explained, "At night they return to their cabins to sleep but they always take their wigwams with them when they go to work. Seems a waste of effort don't it?"

The path turned left to pass the settlement of the last war chief of the Miamis, Francis Godfroy. Here were clustered five or six two story log houses on a raised piece of ground not far from the Wabash River. The grouping was called Mount Pleasant. His trading post was within a square log enclosure of about a half acre. "Want to stop and meet the old chief?" asked James.

"Not today. Perhaps when my brother and sister arrive." As they came closer to the home of his sister, Isaac became all the more eager and anxious to finally see her after all these years. The country through which they passed was mostly continuous forest. Bird calls filled the air and the horses started up rabbits and pheasant. Finally Deaf Man's Village, really just a collection of farm buildings, appeared on the path ahead. They pulled up their horses in front of the large single story log house that was two houses joined together by a shed.

Cut Finger opened the door. She knew Miller and bid them to enter. Just inside the door sat the object of the Slocum family's years of search. Deaf Man's Squaw was the very picture of aged Indian woman. She put down her sewing and rose with great indifference and was introduced to the stranger by the interpreter.

Isaac couldn't help the tears that slid down his cheeks when he saw her. He said through Miller, "After all these years of wondering what happened to you, I can scarcely believe I have seen you with my own eyes."

Maconaquah did not show any surprise at his arrival and with typical Indian stoicism said, "You are welcome to this house. Could we offer you a drink of water?"

"Yes, thank you," Isaac said, disconcerted. "My family searched for you for years. they made long trips into Ohio and once even went to Detroit. Mother's been dead many years. She went to her grave wonderin' where you were."

The old woman's face completely lacked emotion. "Two years ago I told Mr. Ewing that I was long ago captured by Indians because I thought I was ready to die. But there were many captives who lived among the Indians. Perhaps I am not your sister."

Isaac took her left hand in his. The end of her forefinger was without a nail and disfigured. "How came this finger to be injured?"

Maconaquah wrinkled her forehead thinking, then said, "Long ago my brother struck it with a hammer in the shop, before I was carried away."

With great elation Isaac said, "Sister, I was that brother."

Maconaquah looked at him suspiciously. "I am not sure I can believe you. I don't remember you." Her years as an Indian, constantly under attack by white men and later pushed off tribal lands had left their mark. She could not trust white men and apparently did not believe that he was her brother.

After they stood around for a time, with little said by either party, he said, "My sister, Mary, and brother, Joseph, are coming from far away Pennsylvania and mid Ohio. They want to meet you also. I will return with them when they arrive. Sadly he left the place. It had been a great letdown. The meeting had not been the joyous occasion he had looked forward to.

During the next few days as he waited for his relatives he spent much time thinking about what it was that was important in life. Blood ties could be replaced it seemed. Others, no matter how savage, could take their place.

Friday came, a lovely September day. Mary and Joseph finally arrived in Peru, coming by stagecoach from Indianapolis. Isaac was very glad to see them as it was several years since they'd been together. Mary lived at Circleville, Ohio, twenty-five miles south of Columbus. Isaac embraced them and then asked, "How did you survive the trip?"

Mary answered, "The stagecoach vibrated so going over the planks of the National Road, it's a wonder I have a tooth left in my head. And those men with us, always sticking their heads out the window afirin' at passenger pigeons. I declare, I'm more dead than alive."

Joseph wanted to get in a few words, though it was difficult with Mary around. "I came four times as far as you, Mary, all by stage from Wilkes Barre. It sure is a wilderness in this northern part of this state. Indianapolis has a good many farms but the farther north you come, the wilder it gets. I expected to be attacked by Indians any minute! The last twenty-five miles was through their reservation and there wasn't a white man to be seen!"

Isaac answered, "If its Indians you want, your sister Frances is a perfect example. I already went out to see her and she didn't even admit to being my sister." He paused, "It was very disappointing."

Mary piped up, "Well I for one need to wash up sir. Direct me straight away to a hotel and a bed. These sixty-nine year old bones want a rest."

The three retired to the hotel where Joseph and Isaac shared a room. Soon they were engaged in talk of politics. "How are the banks doing out in Pennsylvania? We've heard a lot of talk about some of them closing," Isaac queried.

"There have been several that closed. There's no new building these days, I can tell you that. Everyone is just tryin' ta ride out the hard times as best they can. A number of people are packin' up and movin' out west, which is to say, I guess they're movin' to Indiana or farther. There's plenty of room here for those who want to endure the hardships of the frontier. A man could buy his necessaries jest by trappin' fur in these parts. Though he'd still have ta have the price of his land, say a dollar and a quarter an acre."

"Many of the immigrants we're seein' in Pennsylvania don't have that," Joseph said.

"Well here in Indiana, they've hired on lots of poor, expecially the Irish, ta build these canals and the roads. There don't seem to be the hard times that they're havin' out East. But at your age, Joseph, I doubt you'd be interested in movin'. Sixty-two, ain't you?"

"Yep. After this trip I feel like a real old man. Pioneering is for the young. My son is thinking about comin' out to be a missionary for the Indians though. Havin' an Aunt who's an Indian has turned his thoughts that way real strong. What'd you say about Frances not recognizing you?"

Isaac looked sadly across the room and then said," You know, it's amazin' how she's a perfect Indian. You wouldn't know her ta be a white person by lookin' at her. But I hit her finger with a hammer when we was little. And sure enough, the old woman has a deformed finger. The very one I hit. I can still remember the licking Ma gave me for doing it. Yes, she's Frances all right. But it's damn disappointin' to get no recognition from her. We'll try again tomorrow and see if she remembers any of us."

The next morning a party of five traveled in a wagon to the Indian settlements. This time a half breed Indian, educated in Kentucky, a Mr. Hunt, accompanied them as well as John Miller. When they had traveled half the distance they stopped at Chief Godfroy's post to meet the famed man. Entering the main building the interpreter introduced them to the chief with great gravity. The chief was very dignified and polite, a noble looking man of fifty, and weighing 300 pounds. He had a majestic and solemn countenance. A blue calico shirt fell to his knees that was covered with ruffles and Indian leggins were worn on his legs. He was over six feet tall and wore his hair tied in a queue down his back. They told him of their mission and he in turn said he would do anything in his power to help.

The party returned to their journey to Deaf Man's village. Not far from the farm, the latest husband of Maconaquah's youngest daughter joined them on horseback. He hollared, "Hieeee!", kicking his horse to follow along side. He was one hundred percent Indian, in dress and actions and his boisterous presence lent a festive air as they approached the cabin.

When the party alighted at the cabin door and was ushered into the presence of the old woman, their high spirits quickly evaporated. She wore the stone cold reserve of the Indian when introduced to a stranger.

Isaac said, "These are your sister Mary, and brother Joseph."

Joseph immediately said, "Yes, she is our sister. She has a certain family resemblance." The old woman made no response. The brothers and sisters felt ill at ease as the Indians made no reply and felt dejected. Mary began crying quietly, and the old woman acted as if she were worried they might try to rob her or carry her away. The two brothers walked about nervously wondering how she could be a relative and treat them this way. They had come this great distance to see her, traveling many days at great expense. It was a great disappointment.

Joseph tryed to melt the woman's icy reserve saying, "Tell me again about your capture." She began, "My father's name was Slocum and he wore a broad-brimmed hat. He lived by a great river and I had seven brothers and two sisters." She held up the number of fingers to show them. "We lived near a fort. Three Indians carried me away a great many winters ago from under a stairway."

There was no doubt that she was their sister. Maconaquah continued with information about her family. "My oldest daughter's husband is half French. He does all the outdoor chores. Kekesequa had two children but both are dead now. My youngest daughter has three children and this is her third husband."

"Do you remember your name?" asked Mary.

"No. Maconaquah is my Indian name. It means Little Bear Woman."

"Was it Frances?"

A strange occurance then happened. A fleeting emotion crossed her face and then it cracked into a smile. "Yes, Franca, Franca!" Now she recognized that they were telling the truth and the painful situation changed somewhat, but very slowly. As the conversation ended, she sat down on the floor and began scraping a deer hide. The others could see they were dismissed. Jean Baptist took them outside to show them his plow of which he was very proud. He was the only Indian on the reservation that raised corn the white man's way, with a plow. In the surrounding fields fenced with split rail fences were upward of a hundred horses and many cattle and hogs. Jean Baptist took them to see the oxen he used for plowing. After the farm tour the party returned to the cabin where Frances continued scrapping the hide, seemingly uninterested in their presence.

Isaac said, "We would like you and your family to come to town to have dinner with us."

When this was interpreted she looked at them in distrust. Her lifelong fears of being carried away from the Indians by white men might be coming true and she said as much to the interpreter.

"They don't want to take you anyplace, only to take a meal with them as white relatives do," the half breed interpreter said.

She wasn't convinced. "I must ask Chief Godfroy his advice. If he says it is alright, I will come tomorrow." On this promise, the party returned to town. The meeting had been strange to say the very least, but perhaps in time some of her reserve would melt and shę would recognize them in a more satisfying way as her brothers and sister.

The Slocums were devoutly religious people and the Sabbath was a sacred day on which people did not entertain. The fact that Frances was thinking of visiting them tomorrow, on the Sabbath, came as quite a shock. It hadn't occured to them that she remembered nothing of their religion.

Mary said, "Do you suppose she doesn't know tomorrow is Sunday? Don't you suppose the Indians know the days of the week?"

"Maybe she doesn't care," said Joseph.

Isaac had more experience with Indians, living nearer the frontier. "She probably doesn't belong to a church as we do. This would be a good place to send a missionary."

"I suppose you're right." Mary looked down at her primly folded hands. "It just seems so strange, her not knowing. She is living testimony of the Psalms scripture,`I am become a stranger unto my brethern and an alien unto my mother's children.' I would never have believed it was possible if I hadn't seen it with my own eyes."

The next day the sun's position marked ten o'clock when Deaf Man's family rode Miami style, single file, into Peru. The four were dressed in their most colorful outfits, the sun glancing off many silver broaches decorating their garments. This signified an important occasion so the town folk followed them as they rode ceremoniously to the hotel where they tied up their horses.

Isaac and Joseph met them at the door, smiles wreathing their faces. They were surprised and delighted that they made good their promise. They wanted them to come inside immediately, but Jean Baptiste held up his hand, saying, "Go get John Miller." This meeting was going to be conducted according to Miami etiquette and before they did anything, a formal pledge of friendship must be exchanged. All waited for the interpreter to come.

After Miller arrived Cut Finger, or Kekesequa, the oldest daughter, brought in a package rolled in a clean white cloth. She placed it on the table and said, "We give this gift to pledge our friendship for you."

Miller said, "Mary, you must be the receiving person." Mary removed the cloth on the hind quarter of deer. She and her brothers each gave a little thank you speech. This being done, the Indians seemed at ease and from that time gave total confidence and trust to their white relatives. All this time the room was filling with townfolk, even the windows crowded with faces of the curious, eager to see the unusual events.

Issac took the floor to relate the Slocum family history. "After the Indians carried you away, Mother was distraught with grief. Only six weeks after that Indians came back and kilt father and grandpa. Mother was heartbroken over that but never gave up the hope of finding you. Our oldest brothers, Giles and William went to Niagara looking for you when the Revolutionary War was over, but heard nothing. Then in 1797 four of us drove a herd of cattle up through Canada to Detroit in the hope of finding you among the Western Indians. We searched diligently among the tribes there, and even told five traders we'd give a $300 reward for information. They told us they couldn't tell us, even if they knew of your whereabouts because the Indians would take revenge on them. We begged and pleaded with them, but they would not change their minds, so we had to return home empty handed."

Frances spoke up, "We heard through the traders that white men were looking for me, so I remained out of sight of any white people. I was newly married and also afraid of white men."

Joseph took up the story, "About that time a female captive learning that our family was looking for Frances came to our Mother saying she was captured as a child on the Susquehanna. She didn't know who her father was and wanted to see if Ma was her Mother. Well, she wasn't anything like our Frances. Ma told her, you aren't Frances but stay with me as long as you please and maybe some-one else may give the like kindness to my own girl. She stayed a few months but then left and we never heard of her again. Ma died in 1807 at seventy-one years of age."

Mary said, "I was the one who carried Joseph to the fort the day they took you away." She saw that Frances was getting very tired so she said, "I believe we should take a rest now until after dinner. Then we would like someone to write down Frances' story."

The group left off their discussion until after the meal cooked by the hotel. As the townfolk looked on they enjoyed a meal of fried rabbit, mashed potatoes, tomatoes and mellon served at the long table. Frances didn't like white man's cooking and when the others finished eating, they discovered she had disappeared. She was found out on the porch, rolled in her blanket on the floor, sleeping. Everyone returned to the hotel lobbey to wait a respectful time for the old woman to complete a nap. When she returned her story was copied down.

Isaac asked, "Did you ever grow tired of living with the Indians?"

"No. I was always treated well and kindly and never thought about my white relatives except for a little while after I was stolen. My family moved about the countryside often but we lived at Kekionga as many as twenty-six or thirty years. I was there at the time of Harmar's defeat. At the time this battle was fought the women and children were all made to run north. I cannot remember whether the Indians took any prisoners, or brought home any scalps at this time. After the battle they all scattered again to their various homes, as was their custom, til gathered again for some particular object.

I was married to a Delaware. He afterwards left me and the country, and went west of the Mississippi. The Delaware and Miami were then all living together. I was afterwards married to a Miami, a chief and a deaf man. His name was She-pan-can-ah. After being married to him I had four children, two boys and two girls. Both the boys died while young.

I cannot recollect much about the Indian wars with the whites, which were so common and so bloody. I well remember a battle and a defeat of the Americans near Fort Washington which is now Cincinnati. I remember how Wayne, or "Mad Anthony", drove the Indians away and built a fort. The Indians then scattered all over the country, and lived upon game which was very abundant in those days. After this they encamped all along the Eel River. After peace was made we all returned to Fort Wayne and received provisions from the Americans, and there I lived a long time.

I had removed with my family to the Mississinewa river some time before the battle of Tippecanoe. The Indians who fought in that battle were the Kickapoos, Pottawattomie and Shawnee. The Miamis were not there. I heard of the battle on the Mississinewa, but my husband was a deaf man, and never went to the wars, and I did not know much about them."

She stopped speaking and there were a few minutes of profound silence. The curtain of time had parted for just a moment as the listeners lived through those years of wars through her words. Now the curtain fell and they were back in the dusty hotel, farmers eeking out a frugal living from a land filled with trees.

Joseph said, "We live where our father and mother used to live, on the banks of the Susquehanna, and we want you to return with us. We will give you of our property, and you will be one of us and share all we have. You will have a good house and everything you want. Oh, please come back with us Frances."

Frances answered very firmly, "No, I can't. I have always lived with the Indians. They have always used me very kindly. I am used to them. The Great Spirit has always allowed me to live with them, and I wish to live and die with them. Your wah-puh-mone (looking glass) may be longer than mine, but this is my home. I don't wish to live any better, or anywhere else, and I think the great Spirit has permitted me to live so long because I have always lived with the Indians. I should have died sooner if I had left them. My husband and my boys are buried here, and I cannot leave them. On his dying day my husband charged me not to leave the Indians. I have a house and large lands, two daughters, a son-in-law, three grandchildren, and everything to make me comfortable. Why should I go and be like a fish out of water?"

Then Jean Baptist, her son-in-law spoke. "I was born at Fort Harrison, two miles from Terre Haute. When I was ten years old I went to Detroit. I married Cut Finger about thirteen years ago. The people at Logansport and Peru have known me ever since the country was settled by the whites. They know I am hard working, manage well, and maintain my family respectably. My mother-in-law's sons are dead, and I stand in their place to her. I mean to maintain her well as long as she lives, for the truth of which you may depend on the word of Brouillette."

Frances interjected, "What he says is true. He has always treated me kindly, and I hope my connections will not feel any uneasiness about me. The Indians are my people. I do no work. I sit in the house with these, my two daughters, who do the work, and I sit with them."

Joseph had not given up for he knew Frances' nieces and nephews and old neighbors back East would want to see her. "Won't you at least go and make a visit to your early home, and when you have seen us, return to your children?"

Frances shook her head. "I cannot, I cannot. I am an old tree. I cannot move about. I was a sapling when they took me away. It is all gone past. I am afraid I should die and never come back. I am happy here. I shall die here and lie in that graveyard, and they will raise the pole at my grave with the white flag on it, and the Great Spirit will know where to find me. I should not be happy with my white relatives. I am glad enough to see them, but I cannot go. I cannot go. I have done." She made a sign with her hand to show that it was her final word.

Brouillette was animated, delighted by the old woman's speech. She had given him a rare pat on the back and shown how much faith she had in him. He said, "When the whites take a squaw, they make her work like a slave. It was never so with this woman. If I had been a drunken, worthless fellow this woman could not have lived to this age. But I have always treated her well. The village is Deaf Man's Village, after her husband. I have done."

Cut Finger said, "The deer cannot live out of the forest."

Yellow Leaf agreed, "The fish dies quickly out of the water."

Frances said, "I am tired and go to my home." The four left the hotel with much jingling of the broached clothing, to mount horses for the ride home. The three brothers and sister would not dare embrace Frances to say goodby, but felt sad upon her leaving. Because of their advanced ages and the great distances separating them they might never see her again. Standing outside the hotel, they watched the horses ford the Wabash single file and then break into a trot down the trail to the last bastion of the Miamis in Indiana on the Mississinewa River.

Epilogue

November 6, 1838, a treaty was made disposing of the balance of the Miami reservation in exchange for money and goods. Certain lands were ceded to individual Indians, those of special rank or privilege. Of special interest the treaty specified the following:

To O-zah-shin-quah, and the wife of Brouillette, daughters of the "Deaf Man", as tenants in common, one section of land on the Mississinewa River, to include the improvements where they now live.

September 28,1839 Joseph's two daughters came from Pennsylvania to Peru to visit their Aunt. Much of our story information comes from letters of these girls.

In 1840 a final treaty was made stating that all Miamis not specifically given land should abandon their homes on the Wabash in five years from the time of its ratification. The Miamis had by several treaties ceded 6,853,020 acres of land to the government in return for $1,261,707 and 44,040 acres. The remainder of the tribe had to leave Indiana and go to Kansas.

Frances wrote her brothers, Isaac and Joseph, Mary being dead, asking for help. She had not been named specifically in the grant given to her daughters so theoretically she had to move with the other Indians. The Slocum s decided to make an appeal to Congress asking that she and her descendants be allowed to remain on the land given to her daughters.

Twenty-one other Indians, all friends and relatives of Maconaquah, were included in this appeal. Benjamin Bidlack, representative for the Wyoming District of Pennsylvania, made an impassioned appeal to the Congress on her behalf. The resolution was passed with no dissent. Accordingly, Frances Slocum and her relatives stayed in Indiana when the Miamis were moved west in 1846.

George Slocum, son of Isaac, was a minister. He visited his Aunt Frances at Deaf Man's village in 1845. Then in 1846 Frances asked Isaac to give George to her. George brought his family west in November, 1846 to begin farming, missionary work, and to help Frances' family.

Frances died March 9, 1847 and her daughter, Cut Finger, four days later. Today a monument and graveyard for the family of Maconaquah, Frances Slocum, stands on a hill overlooking the picturesque Mississinewa reservour near Peru, Indiana.

William Wells descendants by Sweet Breeze were Ann, Rebecca, Mary Polly, and William Wayne. An illegitimate child, Jane Griggs of Peru, Indiana was later claimed by the children of Sweet Breeze as a sister. Mary Geiger Wells' children were Samuel Geiger, Peyton, and Julianna, who died an infant.

Ann married Dr. Turner of Fort Wayne. Rebecca married a Captain Hackley who hung himself in 1835. Mary Polly died in 1843, and William Wayne, a graduate of West Point, 1817, drowned when a steamboat sank in Lake Erie in 1832. He was not married.

Mary Geiger Wells' sons died leaving no heirs. Today letters in Louisville's Filson Club file indicate relatives of the Wells family are in Florida, Oklahoma, Utah, Kansas, and Texas.

Jane Griggs, Wells' illegitimate daughter, apparently lived with her Indian relatives near Peru, Indiana. Her descendants lived in Peru as late as the 1940's and perhaps still do.

Rebecca and Nathon Heald farmed for a few years in Louisville, Kentucky but in 1817 moved to Stockland, now O'fallon, Missouri to farm. Heald died in 1832 and Rebecca twenty-five years later. The farm was still in the family fifty years ago. Just before Heald died, Chandonnai came with Indian friends for a visit. Nathon killed a beef to celebrate the occasion. Rebecca and Nathon had many children.

Just because you have a lot of something does not mean you won't run out. This was a homily not recognized by the Indians and it came as a great surprise to them when all the land was sold. In the early 1930's a suit was filed against the United States Government and again in 1951 that the Miamis were underpaid for lands ceded in the treaty of 1826. An article in The Louisville Times April 17, 1979 states that the Miamis claims were settled in their favor and the additional money would be paid to proven decendants, based on the 1826 true value of the land.

Bibliography of Principal Sources

American Heritage Pictorial Atlas of United States History, The American Heritage Publishing Co. 1966

American Pioneer Magazine No. 9- September 1843, Letters of Colonial Hamtramk.

American State Papers. Indian Affairs, 2 vols., 1832-34, Washington, D.C.: Gales & Seaton.

Anson, Bert, *The Miami Indians,* University of Oklahoma Press, 1970

Banta, R.E., *The Ohio,* Rinehart & Co., Inc. 1949

Barnhart, John & Riker, Dorothy, *Indiana to 1816, The Colonial Period,* Indiana Historical Bureau & Historical Society, Indianapolis, Indiana, 1971

Boden, Temple, *History of Kentucky, Vol. I* S.J. Publishing Co., Chicago & Louisville, 1928

Brice, Wallace A., *History of Fort Wayne,* Fort Wayne: D.W. Jones & Son, 1868

Brown, Lloyd Arnold, *Early Maps of the Ohio River Valley,* University of Pittsburgh Press, 1959

Buell, Rowena, *Memoirs of Rufus Putnam,* Boston: Houghton, Mifflin & Co., 1903

Burnet, Jacob, *Notes on the Settlement of the Northwest Territory.* Cincinnati: Derby, Bradley & Co., 1847

Clark, Thomas, *A History of Kentucky,* The John Bradford Press Lexington, Ky., 1954

Carmer, Carl, *The Susquehanna,* Rhinehart & Co., Inc. New York, Toronto 1955

Cleaves, Freeman, *Old Tippecanoe: William Henry Harrison and his Time,* New York: Scribner's, 1939

Cockrum, William M., *Pioneer History of Indiana,* Oakland City, Indiana Press of Oakland City Journal 1907

Collins, Lewis and Richard, *History of Kentucky,* Louisville, 1874

Denny, William H., 'Military Journal of Major Ebenezer Denny... with an Introductory Memoir,' Historical Society of Pennsylvania Memoirs, VII(1860), 205-409

Dillon, John, *History of Indiana* Binghan & Doughty, Indianapolis, 1859

Draper Collection, *American Monthly Magazine* Vol. 19 pg.431

Dunn, Jacob P., *True Indian Stories,* The Sentinel Printing Company, Indianapolis, Indiana 1909

Eckert, Allan W., *Gateway to Empire,* Little Brown & Comp. 1983

Edmunds, David, 'The Vincennes Treaty of 1792' Indiana Magazine of History 1978

Esarey, Logan, *History of Indiana 3 Vol.,* The Hoosier Press, Fort Wayne, Ind. 1924

— *Messages and Letters of William Henry Harrison. 2 Vols.,* Indianapolis: Indiana Historical Commission, 1922.

Ethnological Researches, Respecting The Red Man of America, J.P. Lippencott & Co. 1856

Filson Club Files-William Wells and William Graves materials. 1943

Filson Club History Quarterly, Vol 27

Finley, Rev. James. B, *Autobiography of or Pioneer Life in the West,* Edited by W.P. Strickland, Cincinnati, 1854

Fort Wayne & Allen County Staff of the Public Library, 'The French and British at Three Rivers-St. Mary, St. Joseph & Maumee Rivers,' 1952

Funk, Orville,'Tales of Our Hoosier Heritage', Outdoor Indiana Magazine, 1965

Graham, Lloyd, *Niagara Country,* Duell, Silvan & Pearce, N.Y. 1949

Griswald, Bert J., *The Pictorial History of Fort Wayne Indiana. A review of Two centuries of Occupation of the Region about the Head of the Maumee,* 2 Vol, Chicago: Robert O. Law Co., 1917

Havinghurst, Walter, *Wilderness for sale: The Story of the First Western Land Rush,* New York: Hastings House, 1956

Heckewelder, John, *History, Manners, & Customs of Indian Nations Who Once Inhabited Pa. and the Neighboring States,* Historical Society of Pa., No 820 Spruce St. Philadelphia 1876

Hill, Herbert R., 'Redskin Napoleon and Richest Indian Both Were Hoosiers', Outdoor Indiana, July 1979

—'The Frontier Tragedy of William Wells', Outdoor Indiana, Feb., 1980

—'Clark's Final Frustrating Years', Outdoor Indiana, Feb. 1979

King, Gail, 'Frontier, Louisville', The Courier-Journal Magazine, Louisville, Ky., Sunday Oct.15, 1978

Hofmann, Charles, *American Indians Sing,* The John Day Co. New York 1967

Holliday, Murray, *The Battle of the Mississinewa 1812,* Grant Co. Historical Society

Hundley, Will, *Squawtown, My Boyhood Among the Last Miami Indians,* The Caxton Printers Ltd. Caldwell, Idaho 1939

Hutton, Paul A., 'William Wells: Frontier Scout and Indian Agent,' In *Indiana Magazine of History,* LXXIV, No. 3 Sept. 1978

Jefferson County Inventory and Settlements-Book 3, March 1812, Louisville, Kentucky Courthouse

Kentucky State Historical Society, Register Vol 24, No 72

Kinietz, Vernon, *Delaware Culture Chronology,* Indiana Historical Society Indianapolis 1946

Kinzie, Mrs. John, *Wabun,* Rand McNalley, 1901

Kirkham, Kay, *A Genealogical and Historical Atlas of the United States of America,* The Everton Publishers, Inc. 1976

Knollenberg, Bernhard, *Pioneer Sketches of the Upper Whitewater Valley,* Indianapolis Indiana Historical Society, 1945

Knopf, Richard C., Letters to the Secretary of War, 1812, Relating to the War of 1812 in the Northwest Vol. IV in Document Transcription of the War of 1812 in the Northwest. Historical Society, Columbus, Ohio 1959

—Anthony Wayne,University of Pittsburgh Press 1960

—Two Journals of the Kentucky Volunteers 1793-94, Filson Club

—Waynes letter Pa. Magazine Vol 78, No 4, Oct. 1954

The Indiana Gazetter, or Topographical Dictionary of the state of Indiana, Indianapolis 1849

Indiana Historical Society, *Walam Olum,* Lakeside Press, R.R. Donnelly & Sons Company, 1954

Lindly, Harlow, *Indiana as seen by Early Travels,* Indiana Historical Commission, Indianapolis 1916

Littells Political Transactions, pg. 118

Logansport Telegraph, Oct. 15-18, 1836

The Louisville Times, Indiana,'Debt Owed Tribe trickles through Federal Channels' by Charlie Green, Tuesday, April 17, 1979

McAfee, Robert B., *History of the Late War in the Western Country,* Lexington, Ky.: Worsley & Smith, 1816

McClury, Martha, *Miami Indian Stories, by Clarence Godfroy,* Light & Life Press Winona Lake, Indiana 1961
McCord, Shirley S., *Travel Accounts of Indiana 1679-1961,* Indiana Historical Bureau 1970
McDonough, Robert, 'The Miami Defeat at L'Anguille', Outdoor Indiana, Sept., 1981
McDonald, John, *Biographical Sketches of Captain Wells and Simon Kenton,* E. Morgan & Son 1838
MacFarlan, Allan A., *Book of American Indian Games,* Association Press New York 1958
Mckee, Irving, *The Trail of Death,* Indianapolis Indiana Historical Society 1941
Meginness, John, *Frances Slocum's Story,* Heller Brothers Printing House, Williamsport, Pa. Reprint, Arno Press, A New York Times Company, N.Y. 1974
Mooney, James & Cyrus Thomas,'The Miami Indians, Pamplet- Logansport
Moore, C.H. Louisville News Sentenial
Morrison, Olin D., *Indiana Hoosier State: Volumne of Historical Atlas,* O.D.Morrison, 152 N. Congress St. Athens, Ohio
Niethammer, Carol, *Daughters of the Earth, The Lives & Legends of American Indian Women,* Collier Books, New York 1977
Parsons, John, *A Tour Through Indiana in 1840,* Edited by Kate Milner Rabb, New York, Robert M. McBride & Co. 1920
Pennsylvania Magazine of History and Biography-XII No 1, 1888
Poinsatte, Charles, *Outpost in the Wilderness: Fort Wayne, 1706-1828,* Allen County-Fort Wayne Historical Society 1976
—— *Fort Wayne During the Canal Era 1828-1855,* Indiana Historical Bureau 1969
Roberts, Mrs. Frank, and Dwight Smith,'William Wells and the Indian Council of 1793', Indiana Magazine of History, Sept. 1960
Quaife, Milo Milton. *Checagou: From Indian Wigwam to Modern City, 1673-1835,* Chicago: University of Chicago Press, 1933
Quaife, Milo Milton, *Chicago and the Old Northwest, 1673-1835,* Chicago: University of Chicago Press, 1913
Saugrain, *Dr. Saugrains Notebook,* Louisville, 1788
Scully, Virginia, *A Treasury of American Indian Herbs Their Lore & Their Use for Food, Drugs, & Medicine,* Crown Publishers, Inc. 1970
Somes, Joseph, *Old Vincennes,* Graphic Books, N.Y. 1962
Spencer, Oliver, *Indian Captivity 1835,* Ann Arbor University Microfilms, Inc. 1966

Thornbrough, Gayle, *Letter Book of the Indian Agency at Fort Wayne, 1809-1815,* Indianapolis: Indiana Historical Society, 1961

– *Outpost on the Wabash, 1787-1791,* Indiana Historical Society Publications No. 19, Indianapolis, 1957

Wallace, Paul,'Thirty Thousand Miles with John Heckwelder', Indiana Magazine of History, 1978

Wayne Papers, The Historical Society of Pennsylvania, Philadelphia, Pa.

Wildes, Harrison, *Anthony Wayne,* Greenwood Press Publishers, Westport, Connecticut 1941

Winger, Otho, *The Frances Slocum Trail & Little Turtle,* The News Journal, North Manchester, Indiana 1933

—— *The Last of The Miamis, Little Turtle,* North Manchester, Indiana

—— *The Lost Sister Among the Miamis,* The Elgin Press, 1936

—— *The Potawatomi Indians,* Elgin Press, Elgin, Ill. 1939

Wilson, William, *The Wabash,* J. J. Little and Ives Co., New York, 1940

Winter, George, *The Journals and Indian Paintings of George Winter 1837-1839,* Indiana Historical Society, Indianapolis, 1948

Woehrmann, Paul, *At the Headwaters of the Maumee,* Indianapolis Indiana Historical Society 1971

Young, Calvin M., *Little Turtle,* 1917

Voegelin, Blasingham & Libbey, *Miami, Wea, & Eel River Indians of Southern Indiana,* Garland Publishing, Inc., New York 1974

Order Form

Jewel Publishing
165 Congress Run Road
Cincinnati, Ohio 45215 USA
Telephone: 513-521-1149

Please send me a copy of William Wells and Maconaquah, White Rose of the Miamis.

______ copies of Maconaquah, White Rose of the Miamis @ **$16.95** each

Ohio Residents add 5% sales tax.

Shipping: $3.00 for first book and $1.00 each additional book

Name ____

Address____

____________________________________ Zip ________

Order Form

Jewel Publishing
165 Congress Run Road
Cincinnati, Ohio 45215 USA
Telephone: 513-521-1149

Please send me a copy of William Wells and Maconaquah, White Rose of the Miamis.

______ copies of Maconaquah, White Rose of the Miamis @ $16.95 each

Ohio Residents add 5% sales tax.

Shipping: $3.00 for first book and $1.00 each additional book

Name ____

Address____

__________________________________ Zip ________